DID THEY STEAL A MILLION YET?

DO THEY KNOW IT'S CHRISTMAS YET?
BOOK 2

JAMES CROOKES

Hobson House

ALSO BY JAMES CROOKES

Do They Know It's Christmas Yet? (Book 1)

Wish You Were Here Yet? (Book 3)

All titles also available on Audible, read by the author.

For Mum and Dad

CHAPTER ONE

"A dinner lady from Hillsborough stole fifteen horses?" Tash was incredulous.

"There's a big window of opportunity if you've got the balls for it," said Dot, being helped into her coat by Ernest, always the gentleman.

"How would that even work, Grandma?" asked Tash, still unable to avert her gaze from her resurrected grandfather. She'd had an unusual twenty-four hours. When she went to bed last night, her grandmother was very much a widow of twenty-one years, and when she awoke, Grandad was alive and well.

Tash pulled a woolly hat over baby Lucan's ears, happily strapped against his grandfather George's chest in a carefully fastened carrier, which George distrusted so profoundly that he opted to grip his grandson with his gloved hands as backup.

"It's not like hiring a car, Natasha," said Dot. "You just turn up at a riding school, pay for an hour, and set off. Then you just keep walking!"

"She stole fifteen horses?" said Tash. "Didn't they suspect something when she came back for her second?"

"You never go back to the same place. You need to move around a bit."

"Don't squeeze Lucan, George," said Andrea, adjusting her scarf in the hall mirror.

"Can we stop calling him that?" said Tash, giving her mum a stubborn look.

"Not until you come up with a name, no, actually," said Andrea.

"I came up with a name," said Tash, half-heartedly.

"You don't call a baby Raymond, Tash. That's a man's name," explained Andrea with her unique brand of reasoning.

"I knew a Raymond," said Ernest, his long-forgotten voice making Tash's tummy flutter with joy.

The family waited to see if there was more from the old man. There was.

"He once cycled across the Atlantic for charity."

His family considered this.

"He crossed the Atlantic on a bike?" asked George. He was astonished.

"I know. I thought it was odd," said his dad, straightening his hairpiece in the few inches of mirror that Andrea wasn't blocking. "He just came out with it. I asked what he'd done over the summer, and he said, 'I rode the Atlantic for charity'. I felt a bit daft. We'd only taken the trailer tent to Cleethorpes."

George stared at his dad, then the penny dropped. "Maybe he rowed it in a boat?"

"Oh," said Ernest, absorbing the revelation.

"Probably makes more sense, Grandad," said Tash.

Ernest looked deflated. "Well, any bugger can do that."

"I know if I were starting out in business today, I would consider it," said Dot.

"Rowing the Atlantic?" said Tash.

"An equestrian centre," replied Dot. "Jamie should give it a go."

"Don't encourage Jamie to steal, Dot," said Andrea in protest. "Where would he keep fifteen horses? And who's gonna let them out to do their toilet? He's at work all day."

"They're not like dogs, Mum. You don't 'let them out on your lunch break'," said Tash.

"Where is Jamie?" asked Dot.

"I gave him twenty quid!" said Ernest, still coming around to his shocking realisation.

"Jamie?" replied Dot.

"Raymond McNally. The guy that rode the Atlantic. Not rode, rowed. I mean rowed."

"Is that sounding different in your head?" asked Tash.

Dot turned to Tash in the hope of a reply to her main question. "Where's your brother?"

"Jamie's running, isn't he!" said Tash, hoping this would put an end to this questioning.

She knew this lie couldn't last much longer. She hoped to form some kind of feasible story for her family after they returned from their Christmas morning walk. Tash had surprised them all by insisting she lay the table for Christmas lunch, so the family could all take some air with her five-month-old son. It was a generous gesture from Tash and particularly surprising as she'd never offered to do it before, probably because she had no idea where Grandma kept her best cutlery. Or any cutlery. Grandma had even said this, and Tash was so offended she had proclaimed adamantly to the whole family that she was thirty-six years old and she bloody knew where bloody Grandma kept her bloody cutlery. What was it with her family? Always assuming the worst of her?

Tash had also suggested they all walk to the 'horse field', as known in the family. A magnificent horse could often be

3

seen taking exercise in a farmer's land that bordered the main road out to Derbyshire. The Summers family all agreed that today would be a perfect occasion to introduce the newest family member to this beautiful Shire. It wasn't long after assembling by the coat hooks in the hall that Dot started her anecdote about Peggy Marlow, an old school friend who emigrated to America and set up a riding school. Apparently, through secreting other people's horses somewhere amongst the 50 states. America really is a land of opportunity for English migrants lacking any moral fibre or scruples.

"Make sure his gloves don't fall off, Mum," said Tash.

"Stop fretting. I brought you up OK, didn't I?" replied Andrea.

"Let's not have that chat now," said Tash.

Andrea smirked sarcastically and opened the front door. Tash stood to one side to let the family past and waved her son, parents and grandparents off down the snowy path. She'd attempted to clear a walkable route to the street, and beyond that, they would be yards away from the newly ploughed main road.

"Have fun!" said Tash, maintaining eye contact with her son until he was out of sight. She needed him to know he was always more important than any distraction. She shuddered at the memory of last night when they'd been bizarrely separated by over 300 miles and 36 years.

"The Christmas crackers are in the microwave!" shouted Dot as an after-thought.

"Course they are," said Tash to herself.

"And don't ring Nathan!" shouted Andrea. "You don't have time."

That wasn't her real reason. Andrea hated Nathan. The whole family hated Nathan. Since Tash's marriage broke down, the only thing he'd contributed to her life was a baby boy. A bit of a regrettable reconciliation that lasted one night and two bottles of Prosecco.

"Can't," said Dot. "I've got the phone." Dot held up the home cordless phone that she'd pocketed on her way out. Blimey, they really did hate Nathan.

"She'd use her mobile anyway, Mum," said George helping his mum along the white pavement.

"Rowed does sound like rode, though, doesn't it?" said Ernest to nobody in particular.

Tash glanced over at the home phone base, bereft of its handset.

"Shit," she muttered to herself as she closed the front door.

Tash had no intention of calling her ex-husband. She had someone more important to speak with. But her dad was wrong; she couldn't use her mobile phone, not after last night.

She pulled her brother's Christmas card from behind the potted plastic Poinsettia on the hall table. She'd secreted the card there less than an hour ago and couldn't erase it from her mind. On the rear of the snowy Tower Bridge charity card was a mobile phone number in green ink. A phone number for her brother. Her newly old brother. When they'd set off overnight, he was 33. They'd only gone in the garage loft for a nostalgia trip but accidentally ended up in 1984 – a place it seems Jamie preferred to stay. So, this morning Tash had received a Christmas card from her 69-year-old brother. Maybe her mobile phone was worth a closer look after all.

Tash made slow progress across the back garden. The snow was deep, and each step was an almighty effort to clear the white carpet that levelled the undulating land to one perfect flat surface. Her new Ted Baker overcoat covered her spare PJs, and her Hunter wellies were slowly filling with snow. As she neared the back of the garage, she saw the vehicle that had caused her such distress yesterday. The yellowing edges of the white plastic Sinclair C5 were just visible through the snow that had settled on it overnight since her return from October 1984. She used her cuffs to clear the computer screen attached to the front. Shit, she hadn't considered water damage when she abandoned the time machine in the darkness of night. She also hadn't considered how the hell she would get the C5 back into the garage attic where she'd discovered it last night with her brother. Tash looked up to see the massive hole in the garage attic wall that they'd created on their exit when they stupidly started playing with this bizarre contraption. Pieces of split, rotten oak cladding hung pathetically in the air. The electrical extension flex hung from the opening, with the disconnected plug still inserted in one of the sockets. The machine had ripped itself free from this as they'd hideously left 2020 behind, and now it stood there, oblivious to the hell it had unleashed on them both.

Tash glanced back at the C5 and cleared more snow from the base of the computer screen to reveal her iPhone XR, impossibly bonded to the C5 chassis in two parts. There was surely no way that was going to work again. She used her Tower Bridge Christmas card as a scraper to clear all remnants of snow and ice from the phone and attempted to press the side buttons before grimacing at the glass screen, hoping it would recognise her face. It didn't.

"Siri. Siri. Wake the fuck up, Siri," Tash said, alternating the position of her mouth between the glass screen and the rear of the phone – which were bonded to the C5 about two inches apart, with tiny, coloured cables protruding from them and disappearing into a drilled hole in the chassis. These were inspired fixes to the defective machine constructed with one fatal flaw: a Sinclair ZX Spectrum personal computer unprepared for the Millennium Bug. This rendered the device stuck in the 20th century until a contrived meeting with her grandad had seen her beloved phone split into two and soldered into the Spectrum's motherboard. Now its calendar knew no bounds. Except, of course, her phone was well and truly knackered.

Then she had a thought.

Tash walked to the rear of the C5 and fumbled in the snow before she was able to extract the single power cable attached to the machine. She let out a squeal of satisfaction to see that the newly fitted plug remained attached. After some considerable grunting and swearing and pulling, the C5 was now a few feet closer to the rear wall of the garage. She took the plug and raised it in the air before inserting it into a vacant socket on the extension bank hanging from the attic. Immediately she heard a familiar beep. She glanced over at the iPhone and watched the screen flicker briefly. She smiled in disbelief and walked over one more time before frantically tapping the phone screen. It remained black.

But then something happened.

The mini Pye TV screen attached to the front of the C5 lit up as it had done when she and Jamie first discovered Grandad's mysterious contraption. But this time, it didn't display the usual 'Sinclair Industries 1982'. It was the same font and the same layout, but the screen read:

Missed calls (9) 0770 0900892
    Exit screen?

Tash stared at the screen. She slowly turned over the Christmas card in her hand and read the green ink.

. . .

0770 0900392

So close. Or maybe the 3 was an 8? No, it was definitely a 3. Or was it? She squinted her eyes and held the card closer. No, that's an 8. Yes! An 8! Old Jamie. The pensioner who sent her the card this morning. The 33-year-old brother she travelled with last night. The one who asked to remain in 1984. Old Jamie. He'd been trying to ring her. Good, cos that was precisely the person she was hoping to speak to. She needed some kind of idea of how she was going to explain his disappearance from the family. He'd not thought that through, had he? Silly prick.

She allowed herself a smile, followed by severe anxiety and trepidation about talking to her brother as a 69-year-old man. He'd lived his whole life whilst she'd slept for a few hours. She revisited that thought a few times before failing to comprehend it, and so moved on.

She leant to her phone and thought she'd give Siri another try. Maybe it might work now the whole assembly was connected to the mains power? It was worth a punt.

"Siri," said Tash. She stopped as her voice was quiet and hoarse; she was clearly more anxious than she'd realised. She flicked snow from the long seat of the adapted C5 and sat down, then swallowed to moisten her mouth and tried again.

"Siri, call 0770 0900892."

And then she waited.

What the hell would she say to him? And more importantly, what the hell would she tell her family when they returned from their Christmas Day walk? Hi guys, Jamie hasn't actually gone for a run. We got up in the night and sat on Grandad's pretend time machine for a laugh, but it turned out he'd built an actual time machine and accidentally went back to 1984, and I came home, but Jamie didn't 'cos he fell in love.

No. That didn't adequately convey the absolute hysteria of her time in October 1984. Or the horror.

Her thoughts came to a grinding halt when she heard a ringtone coming from the rear of the C5. Then her grandad answered. Except it wasn't her grandad, just someone with his voice.

It was Jamie. Old Jamie.

"Tash! I've missed you so much!" said Jamie. "How are you? How is Lucan?"

"You sound like Grandad," stammered Tash. Her brain was accepting the voice of her brother, but synapses were firing like crazy in her head, and they made her dizzy: *He's twice as old as last night when I left him behind.*

"I am a grandad!" laughed Jamie.

"This is so fucking weird, Jamie."

"I've missed you so much," said Jamie. His voice was faltering a little. "And Mum. And Dad. And Grandma." He paused for a moment. "Well, a bit. I missed Grandma a bit."

"Grandad's alive. The Oxo you gave me... You saved his life," said Tash, who now realised she was crying. In the past few hours, her emotions had ridden pretty much every roller-coaster in every Disney theme park and then zip-wired through the Grand Canyon. Naked.

"I know he is," said Jamie. Then he added, "I've kind of been spying on you all."

"What?"

"I missed you. I couldn't bump into any of you, that was too risky, but I've kept my eye on you through the years."

"Bit creepy," said Tash.

"Not really. I went from having a family to having no family. Except for Martha."

"How is Martha? Is she the lady I saw in the car this morning?"

"Hi Tash!" came Martha's older voice from the speaker at the back of the C5. "It's Martha!"

"Hi Martha," said Tash.

"That's Martha," explained Jamie.

"Yes, I kind of figured," said Tash. "Jamie, we have so much to say to one another, but they've all gone for a walk, and I said I'd set the dining table."

"You? You don't know where the cutlery is," said Jamie.

"Can you not fucking start?"

"Sorry. I didn't think you knew," said Jamie.

"It's in the drawers next to the dishwasher," said Tash.

The phone went silent for a moment.

"It's in the sideboard, isn't it?" said Jamie.

"That's what I mean," said Tash.

"Grandma didn't have a dishwasher."

"Didn't she? Doesn't she?" Tash was incredulous. "Who does all the washing up?"

"Not you," said Jamie.

"Jamie. What the fuck am I going to tell everyone? They think you've gone for a run!"

"I've got loads of ideas," said Old Jamie.

"Have you? Really? 'Cos, I have none," said Tash.

There was silence. It was a louder silence at Tash's end of the call as the white landscape around the crystallised garden amplified the sound of pure frozen nothing.

"I'm going to miss you, Jamie," said Tash. "You do realise you've abandoned me."

Her attempt at humour betrayed her genuine emotions. She did feel suddenly lonely, and the lump in her throat was brutally painful.

"Tell her, Jamie. Just tell her." Martha's voice sounded a little serious.

"Tell me what?" asked Tash.

"Tash?" Jamie sounded serious now.

"What? What is it?"

"You know the C5?" asked Jamie.

"Course I know the fucking C5. I'm sat in the bastard. I'm going to torch it once I've figured a way to get my fucking phone back off it."

"Don't do that," said Jamie.

"Get my phone back?"

"Torch it."

"And why would I not do that?" asked Tash.

"Because you need to use it one more time," said Jamie.

"I fucking don't, actually!" Tash snorted at the suggestion.

"The family don't need to know," said Jamie.

"Course they'll know. They'll be back from their walk in no time! Where the hell will they think I've gone?" asked Tash.

"It's a time machine, Tash. You won't have gone anywhere. You'll be back there. You go, then you come back to now. No time passes."

"Back here from where?" snapped Tash.

More silence filled Tash's ears.

"From where Jamie?" asked Tash again.

"December 1984," said her brother.

"You can fuck off!" said Tash. She pulled her collar up and leant into the phone. "What the hell did you break in December, Jamie? You'd only been there two months!"

"I didn't break anything," said Jamie. "It wasn't me."

"What wasn't you?" asked Tash. She was getting irritated by her elderly younger brother. She'd missed more than half of his life, he was now officially classed as 'vulnerable' by the

NHS, yet she was already pissed off with him. How could that be possible?

"Luke left a bag by the bins," said Jamie.

"Who-left-a-fuck-by-the-what-now?"

"My son," explained Jamie. "He's called Luke."

"That's MY son's name, Jamie! You stole my son's name?"

"Your son hasn't got a name yet. We called him Lucan, and you hated it."

Tash thought for a moment, then softened.

"Congratulations on your son," said Tash begrudgingly. "Can't believe I just said that. What a fucked-up Christmas."

"He's the guy that posted the card this morning."

"I figured that," replied Tash. "He's quite hot."

"Bit weird that, Tash. He's your nephew."

"Just saying. It was meant to be a compliment!"

"No, well, it is a bit weird, actually. You're his auntie."

"Trying to be nice! Move on, Jamie! Sake!"

"He left a bag by Grandma's wheelie bin," said Jamie.

"Really? I didn't know we were doing gifts. I have one wrapped for the younger you, but I'm guessing you don't want Super Mario Lego?"

"Can you get the bag?" Jamie was staying on point.

Tash sighed and did her fascist goose-step stomp back through the snow to the driveway. The hideous blue of the first bin was refusing to be hidden by the drifts of snow. Tash could see fresh footsteps and a Waitrose supermarket bag for life peeking out between that and the brown bin.

"Waitrose. Someone's doing well for themselves," muttered Tash as she grabbed the bag and marched back to the C5.

"You still there?" Tash asked the dissembled iPhone at the front of the C5.

"Still here," came the reply of Old Jamie from the speaker by the rear of the seat.

Tash delved into the bag and extracted a newspaper. She opened it up and perused the front page.

The Observer. Sunday 23 December 1984

Beneath the date was a black and white photograph of a laughing Margaret Thatcher sitting alongside a smiling President Reagan on a golf buggy. The headline read: *Thatcher deal to cool row on Star Wars.*

The Americans had scared the shit out of the world by developing a space-age style nuclear deterrent whereby one warhead would detect another in space. It would neutralise the bomb head-on amongst the increasing number of satellites circumnavigating the warming globe. Reagan had bizarrely named the development after a trilogy of kids' movies that had rounded off the previous year with *Return Of The Jedi*. The cold war between the USA and USSR was racing to a seemingly unstoppable crescendo in 1984, and its ripples had touched the creative zeitgeist. The BBC TV drama, *Threads*, had seen Sheffield annihilated under a mushroom cloud, and countless anti-Armageddon songs had captured the public's growing hysteria. Nena, Nik Kershaw, Ultravox and Culture Club were just some artists that capitalised on the potential horror and futility of the world's superpowers blowing up the planet. Commercially, though, the Liverpool boys from Frankie Goes To Hollywood cleaned up. Their ZTT record label released six remixes of the same song over the summer, keeping 'Two Tribes' at number one for nine consecutive weeks. The fact that Trevor Horn had also made it sound like nothing on earth helped too, sampling the intro to the British Government commissioned information film, *Protect & Survive*. Originally broadcast on *Panorama*, its haunting lines still resonated with an increasingly anxious public. "When you hear the air-attack warning, you and your family must take cover." The same man also advertised Barratt Homes from a helicopter – the man whose voice was later parodied every

Saturday night on *The X-Factor*. An actor called Patrick Allen. Him. That stark and impersonal spoken line had inadvertently caused sleepless nights amongst thousands of children. At least Midge Ure was crying in 'Dancing With Tears In My Eyes'. At least Midge knew he was spooking the shit out of kids.

"What have you done now, Jamie? What have you broken?" asked Tash as she scanned the small print that covered the massive paper.

"Turn to page two," said Jamie, and Tash did.

"*The Kodak Disc 4000 camera with automatic flash*," read Tash. "Didn't think Argos would be advertising in the broadsheets." She was surprised.

"Look further down," said Jamie.

"*Gays not to blame for AIDS...*" read Tash. "Christ!"

"I know," said Jamie, sharing his sister's repulsion. "Come on, Tash, the family will be back soon. Beneath that. It's circled in green!"

"*Gangland-style killing ignites London mafia fears*," read Tash.

There was silence.

"Tell me you didn't get involved with the mafia, Jamie?"

There was more silence.

"Jamie? Are you still there?"

"I'm still here," replied Jamie.

"What is this? What does this have to do with us?"

"We can stop that murder," said Jamie.

"We can?"

"Well, OK, you can."

"I can? On my own? What?"

"Not on your own, Tash. You just need to post that newspaper through my door, in 1984. I'll read it, see it's from the future, and I'll take it from there!"

"No way, Jamie. I'm home now. You're not, well you are in a way – and that's all I need to worry about: how the fuck I explain your absence to everyone else!"

"Tash, it's a perfect time. The family are out. No one will see you go. You can come back one minute from now. Thirty seconds from now!"

"Forget it, Jamie. I'm never going back there. I'm not using this machine again. And especially not for some random bloke who got the wrong side of the bloody mafia!"

There was a silence.

"It's Raymond," said Jamie.

"What about him?" replied Tash, seriously uninterested in this development from the past.

Jamie spoke again.

"They killed Raymond."

Tash felt physically sick at this information. The man who saved her life had now lost his.

"You need to save him," said Jamie.

CHAPTER TWO

The silence was broken by a strange ringing tone that sounded more like a vintage Atari tennis game than anything she'd heard from her iPhone. Tash glanced at the Pye TV screen again.

0770 0900892 (ENT. To answer)

Tash struck the ENTER key on the ZX Spectrum keyboard attached to the C5 beneath the TV.

"Are you there, Tash? How's it going?"

Jamie's voice still emanated from the C5, which now faced a cleared path towards the house. A kamikaze route for most vehicles. But not this time machine that Grandad had built. The single main cable at the rear was attached to an extension drum plugged into the wire that hung from the hole in the garage attic side. Extending her power supply had meant she needed to unplug the C5, which had disconnected the call.

"I'm here," said Tash, as she re-read the story in the antique newspaper.

'*Police are yet to identify the body of the man found in Bay 3, Butler's Wharf in Bermondsey.*'

Tash felt utterly crestfallen. What her brother was asking of her seemed so unreasonable. Together they had accidentally changed history by incapacitating Bob Geldof the moment he was due to watch the BBC news report on Ethiopia that moved him to form Band Aid and fight the famine.

"I'm not going back, Jamie," announced Tash. "But the C5 is set. Send Luke."

There was a pause as Jamie contemplated this bizarre turn of events.

"What? You want me to explain everything to my son? Explain the whole thing? He won't believe we went back in time! He won't believe I was born three years after I met his mother!"

"You never told him?" asked Tash.

"What? Why would I tell him? He could risk coming to see the younger me. And I couldn't risk changing stuff that happened in my other life."

Tash felt strangely winded by the expression 'other life'. Jamie was still very much part of hers. She'd only just started to consider how he must feel, having lived the last thirty-six years without her.

"The young me needed to find that C5 last night. With you. What we did together wasn't great, Tash, I know that. But it led to my new life. So, I couldn't tell him about any of it! What if he wanted to get involved in some way? If we changed anything at all, me and you might not have gone back to 1984, and I wouldn't have met Martha! His mum!"

The silence was broken by the strange Atari sound again. Tash looked up to the Pye TV screen – in the old-fashioned font were the words:

iMessage

Mum

5 minutes x

Oh, Christ, they're on their way back already, thought Tash.

"Shitting hell," she whispered.

"Say again?" said Jamie.

"They're coming back, they're coming back already," said Tash, with a sudden urgency in her voice. She straddled over the extended Sinclair C5 laden with alterations and accessories spewing cables across the garden. Ahead of her was the Sheffield equivalent of a bobsleigh track right up to the kitchen window.

"Tash, I've written the address on the back page, the time, the date and the address."

Tash started to growl with fury, she couldn't let out a scream, and this was the closest her body could allow.

"Fuck sake Jamie, you fucking fuck! What the fuck are you doing to me? You fuck!"

"Tash, please, trust me. You just need to post the newspaper through the front door of the address. It will take you sixty seconds, and you come right back. The time now is eleven minutes past eleven. Just programme the machine to come back at twelve minutes past eleven. You'll have time to cover it in snow and get in the house."

Tash flicked over the newspaper and saw Jamie's green ink scrawled over the bottom of the sports news. She looked up at the small TV screen and pressed the ENTER button on the Spectrum. The screen reverted to the horrible welcome screen that would haunt Tash for the rest of her life.

Destination Date: was displayed innocently on the screen.

Tash started to type her cold fingers on the rubber keys, despite the tears that were now beginning to warm her cheeks.

"Are you typing?" said Jamie.

Tash ignored him as she glanced at the paper and continued inputting the information. After entering the required arrival time and then the location, a familiar sight greeted her:

ENTER TO TRAVEL

"What if I see anyone?" asked Tash.

"It's half-eleven at night, Tash. You won't see anyone," replied Jamie.

"And I just post the newspaper and come right back?" said Tash.

"You know it's the right thing to do, sis."

Tash took a deep breath and rubbed her head with both her hands. She couldn't believe this was happening again.

She pressed ENTER.

The usual whirring noises started up, and soon the shell-shaped casting at the front turned the snow to steam in front of her eyes. The wheels started to spin but were going nowhere, impossibly slipping on the compacted snow.

"The wheels are spinning on the snow!" shouted Tash over the disorientating noise of the C5 attempting to travel through time. But Jamie had gone. Hitting ENTER had disconnected the call, focussing the Spectrum on its primary task.

Tash glanced over the side of the C5 again and saw both rear wheels spinning frantically to no effect. She scanned the garden for a sign of inspiration, but there was nothing to serve as any kind of frictional surface she could jam in front of the wheels. She stopped suddenly and glanced at her Christmas gift to herself. Her magnificent coat. She let out more fucks than her previous personal best as she dragged the coat from her arms and leant over to peer under the C5. She was able to pass the Ted Baker fabric from one side to the other over the freezing snow that sat beneath the C5. She then sat back up in the seat, her brushed cotton pyjamas now the only protection from the wintry December weather. Her arms hung over each side of the C5, each holding one side of her precious coat. She counted to three and then forced her arms backwards to jam the coat under the spinning rear wheels. If she hadn't been so distraught at the willing destruction of the chevron wool three-quarter length coat that she'd had in her online basket since October, she might have allowed herself a smug smile as it was a superb surface that gave the C5 instant traction.

Within seconds she was hurtling towards certain death at the inevitable impact with the stone walls of her grandparents' home. Except she knew better. The moment the nose of the C5 touched the limestone mortar, everything went black, just like she knew it would.

Why the hell has she agreed to this again? Sake.

CHAPTER THREE

G aywood Close wasn't really a close. It had off-shots in all directions as far as Tash could see. Not that she could see much, it was all a blur. Her hands were so cold that she struggled to squeeze the brakes on the C5 as it continued down the tarmac. That was after removing her hands from her face – a habit she'd developed when arriving anywhere on this clunky piece of junk. She spotted an army training centre sail past to her right just before realising she'd mounted the kerb. The C5 struck the tall black-painted fencing that surrounded the exercise yard used by the Air Cadets in all weathers. Not now, of course; it was 11.30pm. Tash slowly climbed off the machine, straightened her pyjama bottoms, and then tucked them into her wellies. She stopped to look around and saw countless, compact red brick dwellings sprawled around. She lifted the *Observer* newspaper from the C5 seat and walked underneath a streetlight to allow the amber glow to illuminate her brother's handwriting.

She squinted to read his instructions and then glanced up to see the numbers on a block of flats. She needed to walk down the hill a little further, and as she passed a row of garages, sure enough, she could see a row of homes nestled in the shadow of some taller maisonettes. Happily, all were in darkness, blissfully in slumber and unaware of the visitor from the future.

She was struck by how few cars were parked on the roads and wondered how Jamie would have felt about living here with so few objects of desire outside his windows.

Which got her on to thinking – why was he living here? Why had he and Martha opted to settle in this particular region of South London? Was he working now? Were they engaged? Was Martha pregnant? What was the humming noise? Was that a three or an eight that Jamie had written?

"That's a three," said Tash to herself as she tiptoed to the corresponding door. She could read the first two numbers of his handwriting perfectly, and now her eyes were growing accustomed to the darkness; she was able to make out the final number was indeed a three.

She opened the letterbox with one hand and gently slid the *Observer* newspaper through the slot with the other until she heard it fall onto the mat on the other side of the door.

That humming noise was getting louder now, and inquisitively Tash turned to watch the C5 roll past her down the gentle incline of the hill.

"Fuck!" she shouted.

An unpleasant crack combined with a dull thump as the C5 struck an ugly saloon car parked midway on the block.

As Tash started to extract the plastic go-kart from the larger vehicle's bumper, a handful of lights came on in the house next to her. Some curtains opened, and Tash quickly lay flat on the road to avoid detection. She waited until the curtains closed and the lights were extinguished before sitting up to get her breath.

She was going to be home in no time! She simply needed to resolve this minor blip.

The C5 was jammed tightly beneath the red car, and she could see that a simple tug wouldn't free it. Happily, the front chassis of the Sinclair had protected the Pye TV from damage during impact, but it was very much a case of the two vehicles now being one.

"Sake," she muttered again.

Tash had once been out with Jamie at a house party in Barnet, and they'd returned to her car to see they had been perfectly blocked into a parking space by a selfish bastard in a Clio. And so, Jamie had taught her the art of bouncing a parked car. Together, they got some momentum by bouncing the front of the Clio like it was performing in a Snoop Dogg video. From there, they simply exerted pressure to one side of the vehicle as they continued bouncing, and sure enough, it started to edge across the tarmac. Soon they were able to get Tash's car out.

And so, it came to pass that Tash found herself in pyjamas attempting to bounce a parked car away from her trapped Sinclair C5. She had to be careful not to squash the Sinclair on each bounce and soon realised that her brushed cotton pyjamas were making her extremely hot – even for late December. Her efforts caused the tyres to create a bizarre squeaking noise as they bounced and slid slowly across the cold road, so it was no surprise she didn't hear the upper window creak open on the house at her rear.

"Tash?" came a voice. "Tash?"

Tash froze. She turned her face away from the familiar voice.

"Tash? Is that you? Are you stealing Raymond's car?" asked young Jamie.

Tash slowly turned around to see her brother staring out of the bedroom window at her.

"What are you doing here?" she asked.

"I've been living here," replied Jamie with a perplexed expression on his tired face.

Tash instinctively shushed her brother. His whispering was one of his lesser skills. He was wearing those pyjamas you saw in sitcoms like *Terry and June,* or kitsch *Carry On* films. Silky pale blue with lapels and buttons up the front.

"Tash?" he asked again, still unable to comprehend what he was seeing.

Tash glanced at the house number on the door. It was three digits long and ended with an eight.

Not a three. Yep, the house that Jamie stood in definitely ended with an eight. She'd posted the newspaper through the wrong letterbox.

"Sake," said Tash to herself. She looked up at Jamie and stage whispered: "Do you know who lives at 533?"

"Tash?" That seemed to be all Jamie could say. "Tash?"

———

"Pull it, Tash. Pull now!" said Jamie, just before being shushed by Tash one more time. She did as she was told and pulled the C5 free of Raymond's Austin Princess. Or Leyland Princess, if you were forward thinking. The British car industry was hard to keep track of. Jamie's rocking on the bonnet had done the trick. Once he'd stopped hugging his sister. His cuddles weren't the best, always a little awkward with his head in the wrong position and his body too far away, but he still felt the need to squeeze his sister after almost two months alone.

Tash pointed the front wheel of the C5 into the kerbstone to prevent it from moving again, which was some achievement given every part of her brain was committed to carefully rehearsing her following words. She mustn't change a single aspect of Jamie's new life.

"We did it, Tash! They recorded Band Aid!"

"Yes, I know," she replied.

"Course you do; you've been home," said Jamie to himself. "How's Lucan?"

"Jamie, I posted something through the letterbox of 533 that I should have put through 538. You need to get it."

"What is it?" asked Jamie.

"It's a newspaper."

"We get a newspaper. Maureen has one delivered. Well, sort of. The lady next door posts it through when she's finished it."

"You need to read that one. The one I posted."

Jamie looked confused.

"I didn't think I'd see you again," said Jamie.

What the hell was Tash going to do now? Older Jamie had visited her in 2020, explicitly saying, 'don't come back for me in 1984'.

Last night they'd accidentally visited October 1984, accidentally knocked down pop star Bob Geldof and accidentally rewritten history. It was a long story, but having recovered their stolen time machine, Tash couldn't be away from her baby son any longer. She had opted to return to 2020 on the understanding she would return just one day later to collect Jamie after he'd told Bob Geldof he'd missed a news report on the Ethiopian famine.

How much simpler could a plan be?

Except for the moment she returned to 2020, an old version of Jamie appeared saying – don't go back. He'd fallen in love and made a happy life for himself.

But the young man now looking back at her assumed she'd abandoned him. She hadn't appeared at the arranged date and time, so as far as Jamie was concerned, Tash had messed up, and somehow, she had tracked him down and was here now to take him back to his life. In 2020.

Or so she thought.

"I'm sorry I didn't show up at Tower Bridge," said Jamie.

"What?" asked Tash.

"I said I'm sorry I didn't show up when you came back for me."

"You didn't show up?" said Tash, the irritation rising in her voice.

"I took Martha to Heathrow, and her flight was delayed. We had a few drinks, and I kind of lost track of time."

"You didn't show up?" said Tash. Again. She was livid at being abandoned. Not that she had been, as she'd never actually gone back for him. She was confusing herself now.

"I'm sorry. But you've found me now!" said Jamie.

Tash was very confused. She'd assumed Jamie had gone to their planned meeting place, but she hadn't turned up (because he asked her not to, as an older man). So, he'd stayed in 1984 and fallen for Martha. After all, the two older versions of them had waved at her this morning from that Range Rover. That had to be what had happened.

"What if I'd turned up like we planned and couldn't find you, Jamie! How fucking irresponsible!"

"I know, I'm sorry," replied Jamie. Then the penny slowly descended.

"What do you mean 'if'?" asked Jamie. "Didn't you come back for me? Why didn't you come back for me? You abandoned me?"

Oh, bollocks, thought Tash. She was aware that anything she said or did might impact Jamie's life in some way, and she'd seen him with his son and his granddaughter in 2020. She knew his map ahead was one that blessed him with love and with a family.

"Do you know who lives at 533?" she asked again.

"We are going home, right, sis?" said Jamie. "That's why you're here, right?"

Tash felt her head nod a little. Oh man, she was in danger of ruining Jamie's perfect life, and it was his fault.

The sound of a car interrupted their chat, and headlights lit the street behind them. They both looked over to see a Ford Fiesta police car gliding towards them. The car slowed down and then stopped across the road.

"I can't get arrested again, Jamie. What's happening?" said Tash.

A policeman climbed from the car and walked towards the two of them.

"Bit late for go-karting, isn't it?" asked the constable examining the C5.

Jamie and Tash nodded.

"Do you live in the area?" asked the PC.

"We live here," said Jamie pointing at the house behind them, the front door ajar.

"Oh, I see. Goodnight then," said the constable, and he folded his arms and stared at them, challenging them to prove their claim.

Jamie and Tash reluctantly walked up to the house, through the door and into the hall. As they closed the door, the PC examined the C5 one final time and returned to his car.

Jamie and Tash stood in silence on the shag pile carpet. Jamie looked troubled.

"I'd like to say goodbye to Raymond and Maureen before we go. They've been very good to me."

Tash felt her head nodding. She hadn't come back for her brother. This was going spectacularly badly.

"And Martha?" said Tash.

"What about her?"

"Do you want to say goodbye to her?" Tash couldn't believe she was testing his commitment to the plan to go back to 2020.

"She's in America," said Jamie. He was just plain confused.

Tash found herself shushing him again with one eye on the stairs up to Raymond and Maureen.

"Is she?" replied Tash. Now she was confused.

"Never heard from her again. Or that money."

"Really?" said Tash. Then again, just in case. "Really?"

"She tried calling that law firm, and no one answered, so she used her return ticket."

Tash was silent, but inside, her head was turned up to ten. How had they got together, then?

"Can we go in the morning?" asked Jamie.

"Go where?"

"Home," said Jamie.

Tash thought for a moment, and then she couldn't hold things in anymore.

"Someone's going to kill Raymond," whispered Tash.

"Someone's going to kill Raymond?" repeated Jamie, at his highest volume of the night so far.

"What?" came a voice from the top of the stairs, immediately followed by a slump. The voice belonged to Maureen, as did the slump as she fainted onto their purple-swirled Axminster landing carpet. It had been down for twelve years, but this was the first time she'd placed her tongue on it. She'd only got up for a wee.

Chapter Four

For the second time in two months, Jamie found himself staring at Raymond's bum cleavage peeking from the top of his thrifty C&A pyjamas as he delved deep into the wall cabinet near the TV. Thanks to a reluctant Tash who sat alongside her on the Draylon sofa, Maureen was trying some seven-eleven breathing exercises. Raymond finally stood up and examined the remnants of a bottle he clutched in his shaking hands.

"How about a nip of Advocaat?" he asked his wife.

"Really?" asked Maureen, recoiling at the idea.

"It's just for her nerves," explained Raymond as he turned to extract one of their crystal glasses that were dispensed free with three-star petrol over the summer.

He poured half an inch for his wife, which took a good minute or two. Watching Advocaat exit its vessel was a sport not dissimilar to waiting for ketchup to free itself from a glass bottle. The wait wasn't lost on the audience.

"This reminds me of the time we waited for Robbie Williams' new album, and then he dropped *Rudebox*," said Tash to a confused Maureen. "Big disappointment," she explained. The British ex-boyband's solo career had stalled commercially for this release, but he'd survived it. Not that Maureen would have known. Right now he was ten and riding a BMX in Stoke.

Maureen smelled the drink and rejected it. Tash and Jamie watched in wonder as Raymond upended the glass into his own mouth and waited for the gloop to drop. No one was more surprised than Raymond himself to see the tip of his tongue probing the glass to help the yellow custard on its way. Until now, Raymond had met the news of his inevitable demise with quiet contemplation. He perched himself on the footstool next to their four-foot-tall Christmas tree made up of silver tinsel branches and multi-coloured baubles, not unlike the ones Jamie had used to decorate Grandma's tree.

"Raymond!" said Maureen. She'd never witnessed such excess.

"I'm sorry, Maureen. I couldn't think of a way to get it back in the bottle," explained Raymond. "And I could use a little stiffener... given the current situation."

They all absorbed this news.

"It's a thick beverage, isn't it?" said Raymond, coughing a little. "It's not gone all the way down yet."

"It's better if you mix it with lemonade, I think," said Jamie.

"This isn't a discotheque!" said Maureen, disgusted at the suggestion.

Tash stifled a giggle at the word. She'd never heard it used in a sentence before.

Maureen leant back to straighten the paper chains she'd blu-tacked to the wood-chipped ceiling and walls. She took a deep breath and spoke: "So, you're taking Jamie home, are you?"

Tash wasn't expecting that.

"Well, yes," she lied. "But we'll make sure you are both safe, first," she lied again.

She looked over at the wall unit and spotted two copies of the Band Aid 7 inch single leaning up against an old Chianti bottle with a wickerwork sheath around the bottom, that had been fashioned as a candle holder. 'Do They Know It's Christmas?' sat above the Peter Blake artwork of two emaciated Ethiopians surrounded by a collage of colourful vintage Christmas images. It struck Tash as brutally effective.

"Two copies of Band Aid? Someone's fucked up there!" She laughed.

"Maureen sent them instead of Christmas cards this year," said Jamie.

"Right, yes. Charity. I'm not gonna lie, that's brilliant," said Tash.

Maureen looked over.

"Why would you lie?"

"What?" replied Tash.

"You said you're not going to lie," said Maureen.

"I see. It's an expression. Just a thing we say, you know, in the future," said Tash.

"So, you were telling the truth?" asked Raymond.

"Hundred per cent," said Tash, to two frowning faces, before adding, "yes."

Her eyes scanned the other end of the room and she spotted the dining table already set for Christmas Day. Round wicker place mats were placed at three settings, each with a limp, white crepe paper Christmas cracker, adorned with red, green and golden stickers of robins or lanterns. A cotton wool snowman had been fashioned from an old boiled sweet jar with a round ball for a head. Three gift tags hung from his scarf, clearly attached to secrets held within his hollow body.

"If what you *say* happens *does* happen ... *when* does it happen?" asked Maureen, glaring at Jamie.

"I don't know! It's Tash that found out," said Jamie.

Tash was up to her bloody neck now. She didn't know what to think, what to do, or what to say.

"Do you know who lives at number 533?" was all she could muster.

"What?" replied Maureen. She was trying extra hard to make this conversation as normal as possible, so she straightened the edges of the Christmas *TV Times* over the Christmas *Radio Times* stacked beneath. Russ Abbot dressed as a fairy added to the pathetic mood, so she switched the ITV guide to the BBC version. A painting of an ominous-looking human festive wreath was now winking at her beneath the italicised *Radio Times* logo. "Win a trip to paradise!" looked tempting at the bottom of the page. Maureen wasn't a fan of commercial television, but as they now owned a video recorder she could finally record the Queen's Christmas Day speech on ITV whilst she watched the BBC one. She'd always wondered what her hero said on the other side.

"Up the road," said Tash. "Who lives at 533?"

"It's Mrs Kaminski, isn't it?" replied Raymond.

"Stop telling her people's personal information, Raymond!" said Maureen. "And no, she's 535."

Jamie sat himself down on the armchair by the window, and Tash immediately gestured at his groin. He looked down and placed himself back inside the curious, open fly on the pyjamas he'd borrowed from Raymond. Great. Now everyone had seen his knob.

"Why do you keep asking about 533?" asked Raymond, now reaching behind their silver tinsel tree.

"There's a newspaper," Tash started to say. "There's a newspaper you need to read."

"We've got a newspaper," said Maureen. "We have it delivered."

"I've heard. Things are looking up," said Tash, glancing at

the dog-eared *Daily Mirror* that sat on Maureen's G-Plan coffee table. "*The Pill: Doctors MUST tell parents*".

Suddenly twenty Pifco Cinderella fairy lights lit up the corner of the room as Raymond straightened up after plugging them in.

"What on earth do you think you're doing, Raymond?" asked Maureen.

"We always put the tree lights on?" replied Raymond.

"At the start of the night, yes. Not in the middle of it."

"I thought Tash might like to see them. Jamie bought those for us!"

It wasn't lost on Tash that Jamie had purchased the very same ones that he'd strung on Grandma's tree when he was last in 2020.

"They're the same as..." Jamie started to say, but Tash nodded and muttered, "I know," before pointing at his groin again. Jamie tucked himself in one more time. Bloody pyjamas.

Tash turned to Maureen. "The newspaper you need to read is *The Observer*. But I kind of put it through the wrong letterbox."

"What did it say?" said Raymond leaning behind the tree to switch off the lights.

Tash looked over and then averted her eyes from his brilliant white bum cleavage.

"I can't remember exactly, but it says there's a mafia killing," replied Tash as matter of factly as she could.

"Oh my God!" exclaimed Maureen.

Jamie was intent on listening for more. "What else did it say?"

"I don't remember."

"What date was the paper?" asked Jamie.

"I don't remember," said Tash.

"Well, we need to read it, then," said Raymond.

"But it's on the doormat at 533," explained Tash.

"Why did you post it there?" asked Maureen.

"Because Jamie's *threes* look like *eights*!"

"What's this got to do with me? I've been stuck here for two months!" said Jamie.

Maureen looked a little hurt.

"I don't mean stuck. Maureen and Raymond have been lovely, actually."

"So, we need to get the newspaper then," said Raymond.

"Absolutely," said Tash. "I'm sure they won't mind you waking them. It's an emergency, after all."

Then Raymond's face registered a thought.

"It's the empty house! The tenants left last week. There's no one home."

"Even better," said Tash with a smile. "Just break in and grab it."

"We'll do no such thing!" said Maureen, straightening her dressing gown as if a judge was already appraising her.

"Well, take your chances with the whole Raymond mafia death thing, then," said Tash. "Can I use your loo?"

"Top of the stairs, the door is in front of you," said Jamie.

Tash climbed off the sofa and left the room. She re-entered momentarily to walk over and squeeze Jamie very tightly before leaving again.

"Probably a bit tired," said Jamie.

"Odd, that one. I've always said it," said Maureen.

CHAPTER FIVE

Tash noisily climbed the stairs in the hallway before tiptoeing back down them and inquisitively pulling open the door to the cupboard beneath them. She couldn't risk turning on a light, so fumbled around amongst the ironing board, washing baskets and a mountain of cleaning fluids and cloths. She soon found some batteries and power cables. To her delight, her fingers felt the drum of an extension mains cable. She lifted this slowly into the hallway and perused the walls for a plug socket. There were none.

Really?

She looked again, rubbing her hands across the wood-chipped wallpaper, knocking a suspended Father Christmas advent calendar pinned through his nose. Nope. No sockets.

WTF?

Then she looked down. Of course, this is like Grandma's place. Wired in the 1960s and all the sockets would be on the skirting boards. She was used to life where sockets had to be reachable without bending, and light switches need to be reached by wheelchair users.

Her search was successful alongside the telephone table

inside the front door. She slowly slid the plug into the socket and held her breath as she silently opened the Yale lock on the front door. She stepped outside into the cold night air with the cable unreeling slowly from the drum and gently pulled the front door as close as possible to closed without trapping the wire. She continued out into the road and down to the C5, which was exactly as she'd left it.

Tash looked up at the house one final time and whispered out loud:

"I love you, Jamie."

She was crying.

She placed the cable reel on the pavement, felt around the rear of the C5, and found the main power cable. As she lifted it to her face to use the dim glow of the orange streetlamp, she saw the all-too-familiar sight of three coloured power cables, recently ripped free from their plug. Why did she never learn? The fucking plug always fucking comes off when she uses this fucking machine.

"Sake!" she shouted.

Jamie's baffled face appeared through the lounge curtains.

"Oh shit," whispered Tash to the 1984 sky.

CHAPTER SIX

The irony wasn't lost on Tash that once again, her face was only a matter of inches away from Raymond's arse, just like in hospital in October.

"Is she still on lookout?" asked Raymond as he strained to hold open the letterbox of 533 and peer through it with the aid of his Duracell flip torch and Maureen's faux silver vanity mirror.

"*She* has a name!" whispered Maureen, who was standing at the foot of the path with her arms folded, casting furtive glances up and down the hill.

"Yes," answered Tash needlessly as she squatted on the path behind Raymond with his toolbox, as she pointed a larger torch through the obscure glass panel in the lower half of the door.

A familiar humming noise rose in her ears, and she looked over her shoulder to see Jamie wheeling the C5 up the hill past Maureen.

"Jamie!" said Tash. "What are you doing?"

"It's raining!" replied Jamie. "I'm going to put it in the garage."

"Garage? What garage?" replied Tash. "What?"

"Can you point the torch through the glass, please?" asked Raymond, still struggling to look through the letterbox.

"What does he mean 'garage'?" Tash asked Raymond.

"We've got a garage on Abbot's Park," he replied.

"Where's that?"

"Can you keep the torch pointed through the glass, please?" said Raymond, probing again to see if he could read the date on the paper in the reflection of Maureen's mirror. "It's just the next road up."

"Can you hurry, Raymond?" said Maureen, looking slightly pathetic as the rain started to soak into her burgundy velour dressing gown.

"What, you mean do the job I'm currently doing faster than I'm doing it, darling?" said Raymond.

"Yes," replied his wife.

"Righto, Maureen," said Raymond, right before he said, "Blazes!"

"Blazes? What the fuck does 'blazes' mean?" asked Tash.

"I've dropped the mirror," whispered Raymond.

"You better not have! That's seven year's bad luck if it's broken!" said Maureen.

Tash let out a long sigh and then stood up straight before announcing,

"I've got an idea. Stand back."

Raymond did as he was told and watched as Tash examined his large metal toolbox. It was one of those with a top that concertinas out into storage areas with a deeper tool compartment area beneath. A streetlamp across the road was doing a pretty lousy job of illuminating the options.

"I think my adjustable wrench might help us to...." But as Raymond spoke, Tash leant down, picked up the whole toolbox and hurled it through the upper panel of glass in the door.

"We're in," said Tash, as shards of glass fell onto the floor on either side of the door.

A dog started barking somewhere in the street.

"Well, that's another idea, I suppose," said Raymond.

Tash reached her hand carefully around the broken glass and opened the night latch. The door glided slowly open, audibly crunching broken glass as it went. It became stuck, so Tash started to force it further.

"No, that will be Maureen's..." said Raymond, but there was another loud clink of glass as the door snapped the mirror into pieces before he could say "mirror". The door stopped one final time as it met Raymond's upturned toolbox.

"Car!" alerted Maureen as she impulsively started to walk back to her house, but she was spotted by another car coming up the hill, so did an about-turn and re-joined Tash and Raymond.

The two cars met alongside the three characters dressed in pyjamas. Both vehicles were Ford Fiestas, and both had *Police* written on their side. The same PC exited his car as earlier, and Tash stepped into the darkness of the empty house as quickly as she could.

"Is everything alright, sir? Madam?" asked the constable.

Raymond stammered that it was as he placed a protective arm around his wife. The police officer glanced at the broken glass in the frame.

"Yes, we, er, we accidentally broke the glass closing the door," said Raymond.

The PC looked curious. "You live here, do you?"

They replied simultaneously:

"Yes," lied Maureen. "No," said Raymond.

The constable looked past them at the smashed panel of glass.

———

"You know what 'being a lookout' means, don't you, Maureen?" whispered Raymond as they sat together on the back seat of the Ford Fiesta. The police car was at red traffic lights.

"Don't blame me. It's her. That woman. Every time she's been in our lives, we've got arrested," said Maureen.

"It's only twice; twice doesn't mean 'every time', does it?" said Raymond.

"It's one hundred per cent, Raymond. One hundred per cent jail every time we've met that woman."

"We're not going to jail, Maureen. We're simply helping the police with their enquiries."

As the lights changed, their moods didn't, so they sat and listened to Tears For Fears singing 'Shout' on the radio, which was precisely what Maureen wanted to do.

"At least you'll be safe in prison," said Maureen.

Raymond wasn't sure this was his preferred outcome. He squirmed on the vinyl seat as heartburn from the Advocaat added insult to injury. He wondered if reporting the officer for listening to a portable radio whilst on his shift might be an excellent negotiating tool in the High Court. If things got that far.

CHAPTER SEVEN

"I'm so glad you're here, Tash. I would have no idea what to do with this kind of news," said Jamie as he read *The Observer* article.

That was singularly the most unhelpful thing Jamie could have said, thought Tash as she stood up from Raymond and Maureen's avocado-coloured loo and flushed it. She'd left the door ajar so they could chat, which was probably a good thing as she had no option to lock it. A badly drilled collection of holes sat where the lock once was.

"What's with the hole in the door?" asked Tash, as she turned on the hot tap in a vain attempt to wash her hands in warm water. The hot water tank was long since empty and wouldn't warm again until tomorrow, but she wasn't to know about their hot water rota.

"Maureen got locked in there on her birthday," replied Jamie. "We don't talk about it."

Tash resigned herself to the cold water and attempted to get some kind of lather from the pink soap bar. It still had the word 'Camay' impressed into it and the shape of a lady's head.

"Water's cold and the soap's shit," she said with contempt.

"Don't use the pink stuff – that's for show," said Jamie. "Use the other one."

Tash paused to see a crusty piece of green soap with a magnet pressed into it, hanging from a tarnished metal arm by the taps.

"That makes perfect sense," replied Tash. "Just in case Charles or Diana should stop by for a piss."

She carefully replaced the Camay back onto the shell-shaped soap dish and attempted to use the standard stuff, but it was just too tiny to be effective.

She dried her cold fingers on an impeccably folded peach hand towel and walked across the compact landing to Jamie's box room, stopping to look at a biro mark on his door frame. 'Jamie Nov '84' was written alongside a line.

"Did you measure yourself?" asked Tash, a little freaked out by the line. Did he think he was still growing at 33 years of age?

"Maureen did," said Jamie, momentarily looking up from the broadsheet newspaper. The box room was freshly painted blue, and Jamie's bedding looked new and recently ironed. It also had BMX riders printed on it. "She was kidding," he added, a little defensively. "They never had kids."

"They're really looking after you," said Tash, only slightly goading him to agree with her opinion that this was a little bit freaky. "Still wiping your own arse?"

Jamie blanked this and looked at the top of the newspaper.

"December 23rd," read Jamie. "Today's the 21st."

"Twenty-second," said Tash gesturing at Jamie's red digital alarm clock that displayed 01:09.

"So that means Raymond gets killed today," said Jamie.

Tash felt a shiver down her spine when Jamie candidly

summed up the brutal and inevitable twenty-four hours that lay ahead.

"Hope it's late on. He wanted to watch *Sports Personality of the Year.*"

Tash glared at him.

"I taped it for him yesterday when they repeated it. It was on Sunday, but we went out for Maureen's birthday. Raymond tried to set the video but got confused by the timer and recorded *Tenko* instead. That's really bleak."

Tash glared at him again.

"They actually call it *Sports Review of the Year* at the moment. Not sure when they changed it to 'Personality'. Sebastian Coe won. He was from Sheffield. I bet Grandma and Grandad were happy. Maureen wanted Torvill and Dean to win, but they came second."

Tash nodded slowly.

"We went to the Berni Steak Bar at Putney. Say what you like about a prawn cocktail, but they're totally smashing it in '84. Raymond's sister works there, she gets discount. Did you know they sacked her back in the summer for being fat? Anyone who couldn't fit into a size fourteen got sacked by Berni Inn! They even binned off a waitress for having massive tits! Forty inches! It made the papers! They backed down though and re-employed a lot of them."

"Great, tits one, pricks nil," said Tash, shivering. "Is it always so cold in here?"

"It's not been a good week for Raymond, to be fair," said Jamie, handing over a brown towelling dressing gown. She climbed into it as Jamie removed something that looked like a Twix from under his pillows. The wrapper was blue and had *Banjo* printed across the front. He ripped it open and extracted one finger of chocolate, bit into it and offered a bite to Tash, who declined.

"First the whole *Tenko* thing, then on Wednesday they got

a new Miss Ellie in *Dallas*, and on Thursday night the *Crimewatch* photofit of a sex offender looked just like him."

Tash looked horrified.

"It's not him, Tash. It's some evil bastard in the Midlands," reassured Jamie. "Then he gets arrested, and now this. You know, death... This has got hazelnuts in it. You sure you don't want some?"

"Have you heard yourself, Jamie?"

"What do you mean?" Jamie was ramming more Banjo into his mouth.

"You're going native."

"I'm just filling you in, Tash. I've been abandoned in 1984, and it's been a lot to take in. Paul McCartney was on *Top Of The Pops* this week singing with a frog; they keep showing this fucked up cartoon, *Willo The Wisp*, before dinner, and at bedtime – they show these horrific public information films. Kids drowning or being electrocuted, and some freak dressed as Death just watches it all happen. He looks like the *Scottish Widows* woman, but you can't see his face!"

"Jamie, Jamie," said Tash, clicking her fingers. "Back in the room."

Jamie stopped babbling and looked a little self-conscious. He'd just unleashed two months of abandonment anxiety on his sister, but he had so much to tell her.

"It's not all bad, I suppose," he said, calming down. "Like, TV shows just start."

"What?" asked Tash.

"TV shows," said Jamie. "They just start. They don't spend the first ten minutes telling you what's coming up. It's weird. They just get straight to it. It's far better."

"Did Raymond find a new job?" asked Tash, dropping down onto Jamie's bed before leaping up again to extract a hand-held electronic Frogger game that was suddenly bleeping very loudly as the LED frog attempted to cross a busy stream.

"Still working at the warehouse. Dudley left him the business."

"What a guy!" replied Tash, successfully finding the off switch on Frogger.

"Not really. It's just the Sinclair contract and shitloads of debt." Jamie finished off the remainder of the chocolate and placed the other finger back under his pillows.

"What a knob. The more I hear about this guy," said Tash, before spotting a TV/radio/cassette combi with the Sharp logo on it. An impressive selection of cassettes was stacked alongside it: *Now That's What I Call Music 4*, *Songs From The Big Chair*, *Alf*, *Make It Big*, and *Parade*. Hanging from its telescopic aerial on a knotted piece of string was the BBC security pass that Martha had stolen back in October. Maybe Jamie was carrying a torch for her after all. She certainly hoped so; it was only a matter of hours since she'd seen an elderly Martha sitting alongside Old Jamie in a Range Rover. Somehow they ended up together. Tash just needed to make sure she didn't impact any part of Jamie's new life in 1984, which was going to be tricky because right now, he seemed to be very keen to return to 2020 with her.

"And what do you do for a living?" asked Tash, eyeing the electronic equipment, stash of music and another hand-held machine: A *Game-and-Watch Donkey Kong*. This room looked like it belonged to a spoiled teenager.

"For a living? What?" Jamie was genuinely baffled. "I've just been hoping you'd find me one day!" He pressed the PLAY button on the cassette deck and 'Careless Whisper' started to play. The long version with the synth intro.

"Yeah – bad phrasing. But what have you been doing for the past two months?"

"Helping Raymond at work. Most of the C5 stock has

gone to the Hoover warehouses, so we've been trying to find other business."

"Hoover?"

"I know. They're the ones that got the C5 service contract."

"Hoover as in Hoover?" Tash gestured, hoovering the floor. "What's the connection with the C5?"

Jamie shrugged. "They both suck?"

"How's business going, then?"

"It's not. Sab says Raymond's gonna have to sort something soon. No money's coming in."

"She's working for him? The girl from Woolworths?"

"She's helping out when she can. She left Woollies. She's working somewhere up west now."

"So, Dad's SMART PAUSE button didn't work out, then?"

"Raymond took the plans to the bank to get a loan, then spent the whole meeting explaining to them why he didn't think it would work. They agreed."

Tash looked over at *The Observer*. "What are you going to do with that, then?"

"What am *I* gonna do? Don't you mean *we*?" said Jamie, ripping the page free from the rest of the newspaper.

"Yes, that's what I said. What are we going to do about it?"

Jamie thought for a moment.

"Well, let's just make sure we give this to Raymond so he can read it and then he can decide what to do. His murder was obviously mistaken identity. They killed the wrong guy, right? He's not connected with the mafia. He should just stay away from the warehouse until next week or something."

"Okay, cool," replied Tash, not entirely convinced it would be that simple. "We just need to wait for him to come home then?"

"Then we can go home," said Jamie. He sounded like this

was a massive weight off his mind. Tash looked away but realised she should be saying something. She didn't.

"Shall we get some rest then? Top and tail?" asked her brother.

Jamie offered Tash one of his pillows. She accepted it, and together they lifted the single quilt, stretched out alongside one another, and covered themselves up. Tash knocked Jamie's slippered feet from her face.

"Then we can go home," said Jamie. Again. It seemed to reassure him as he descended into his slumber.

Tash closed her eyes for about one second, and then a thought dropped in her head.

"Is Raymond's garage far from here?" she mumbled.

"No," said Jamie, with a yawn. He leant over and flicked off the bedside spot lamp that illuminated the room. "Literally the next road up."

Tash considered this.

"I guess the police will just bring them home when they realise they made a mistake," said Jamie. "They might be safer with them, actually."

"Does it have power?" asked Tash in the darkness.

"Does what have power?"

"The garage. Just thinking for when we need to, you know, when we need to leave."

"Yes."

"Okay," said Tash as casually as she could. "Okay."

Jamie's slippers fell from his feet and flipped back onto Tash's face.

She was unsure if Jamie heard her follow this with an involuntary whisper.

"Sake."

CHAPTER EIGHT

T ash hadn't meant to fall asleep. Even the *Wham! Make It Big* cassette clunking to a stop hadn't woken her. She'd done pretty much what Old Jamie had asked her, so she planned to tiptoe from the house and find the garage that held the C5 so she could head back to 2020. But she'd underestimated how knackered her body remained after her last journey to 1984. Her nose awoke her. It was filled with the most spectacular scent of fried bacon, and her mouth wanted a piece of the action. As she slid Jamie's size nines from her face yet again, she saw Maureen ruffle Jamie's hair and place a steaming mug of tea next to his Sharp TV combo.

"Radio One?" she asked, in a tone that implied, "like usual".

Jamie yawned and nodded, "Thanks, Maureen."

Maureen leaned over and flicked a rocker switch on top of the machine. Dave Lee Travis was just finishing a dedication to Kim and Rich in Sheffield. They'd asked for 'Invisible' by Alison Moyet. Tash wondered for a moment if they knew her grandparents. As the synth bells chimed from the mono speaker, Maureen turned to Tash.

"Cup of tea on the floor for you," she gestured at a cup and saucer resting on a coaster on the brown swirled polyester carpet.

Jamie noticed that Maureen had used the Bilton's Bounty Brown set that Raymond had bought her from Argos for her birthday, so she must be trying to impress her new house guest. Their creamy white base gave way to an unappetising thick brown rim, a design feature replicated in the wide saucer.

"I wasn't sure if you took sugar," Maureen started to say.

"I don't," said Tash.

"So I put two in like Jamie," said Maureen with no indication that this was repairable.

"That's fine, thank you," said Tash.

"Sit up both of you," said Maureen as she picked up a tray from the floor and placed it between them. Fresh from Maureen's Breville toasted sandwich maker, four scalloped and sealed-edged bacon and tomato sandwiches sat on a large dinner plate from the same range as the cups.

Tash did as she was told whilst simultaneously trying to catch Jamie's eye so they could share a moment of hilarity, but he seemed happily compliant with his new foster mum.

Maureen handed side plates to each of them, plus a piece of quilted kitchen towel that she'd folded into triangles.

"Thanks, Maureen," said Jamie, who then glared at his bewildered sister to do the same.

"Yes, thank you," said Tash.

"I've left some clothes on the other side of the door for you," said Maureen in a matter-of-fact way.

"You pick his clothes?" asked Tash, her jaw almost on her chest now.

49

"Not for him. For you. You can't wear those all day," said Maureen, pointing at Tash's PJs.

"Why do I need clothes?" asked Tash. "I'm not staying. We're not staying."

"We've decided we're all going to the police station – with your newspaper. It's the only thing to do," said Maureen.

Tash glared at Jamie. She didn't like the sound of this. What did they need her for?

Jamie started to speak. "Did they keep you long at the police…" but before he could say "station", Maureen shushed him.

"Don't want to talk about last night, thank you very much. But we will need your help later boarding up that window," was all she said as she exited the room.

"Shouldn't you be at work?" shouted Jamie.

Maureen peered her head around the door: "I'm not going to work if someone's going to kill my husband."

"No. Okay," said Jamie, nodding.

Maureen peered around the door one more time. "No crumbs in that bed; I only changed the sheets yesterday. We'll talk once you're dressed."

"Okay," replied Jamie before glaring at Tash again.

"Okay," copied Tash, trying to comprehend what the fuck had happened to her brother. She took a big bite of her sandwich. What followed next was her loudest "fuck" of the past twelve months, but happily, it sounded more like a "huck" as she had nowhere to spit the molten lava in her mouth. There are few things hotter than a Breville toasted tomato. In fact, scientists are only aware of two things with a higher temperature: the surface of the sun and the first mouthful of an oven-baked lasagne.

"Careful on the tomato, sis," said Jamie as he cleverly neutralised his grenade by nibbling the crust, then macerating tiny pieces like a reciprocating saw. Not a pretty sight. Once a safe portion was in his mouth, he held his head back and exhaled the hot air noisily whilst trying to say, "they get hot."

Tash sat with her mouth open as tears streamed down her cheeks. Saliva and tomato juice seeped slowly out of each side of her burnt mouth.

"You okay?" asked Jamie.

Tash nodded slowly. Her breath made clouds in the freezing room.

"Oh, shit! It's Saturday!" said Jamie, reaching over to the rocker switch on his Sharp and flicking it forward from radio to TV.

The ten-inch black and white screen slowly came to life, and before a picture formed, 'Lay Your Hands On Me' by The Thompson Twins played out from the speaker. The song ended as the image became clear, and the pop video made way for BBC 1's *Saturday Superstore* main desk, swathed in tinsel, balloons and baubles. Host Mike Read was sitting next to a little girl dressed as a fairy, looking suspiciously like a very young Natalie Casey. Next to Mike was a youthful-looking Bob Geldof under his familiar ruffled hair and sporting the same shirt he wore for most of the '80s. Bizarrely he was smiling and generally looked pleased to be in this brightly lit kids' studio beneath fake snow that continued to fall over them.

"We're taking your calls in a sec, the number as ever is 01 811 8055 – make sure you get permission. But first, Bob, we named the winner of our 'design a Band Aid Christmas card competition' earlier, hang on it's here somewhere..." said Read.

"Oh my God, it's Geldof!" shouted Tash. "He looks so young!"

"Shhh!" said Jamie, turning up the volume.

"It's Bob Geldof!" replied Tash. "Was he always fit?"

"Shhh!" repeated Jamie.

"Here we are, what do you think of that?" said Read, handing Geldof a three-dimensional felt-tipped interpretation of the Band Aid choral ensemble on scissor-cut paper. Evidently a child's attempt to recreate the scene on a Christmas card. Jamie squinted at the screen.

"Let's see it, let's see it," he muttered, glaring at the screen.

"That was done by..." Read examined the back of the Christmas card, "Diana Allerton from..." but before he could say "West Midlands," Jamie erupted.

"Oh, bollocks!" he was still glaring at the ten-inch screen. "That's crap! That looks nothing like them!"

"Tell me you didn't enter the competition to design a Band Aid Christmas card, Jamie?" said Tash.

Jamie glanced briefly at his sister and back at the TV. "You're not telling me that's a good card?"

Tash refused to answer. Surely he was kidding. He wasn't.

"Tell me you didn't enter the competition to design a Band Aid Christmas card, Jamie?" repeated Tash.

"It's the same with The Gallery on *Hartbeat* – they just pick out the shit stuff. Such a fix." Tony Hart welcomed artwork from his young viewers, and gave up one minute each episode to pan along a selection of them to music. Kids at home would rate them out loud, good, ace, shit, good, shit...

"Jamie, you're a grown man. You're entering competitions on kids' TV!"

Read and Geldof were on the phones now taking listener questions, and Jamie had one ear on them.

"Shh. Listen to this, listen," said Jamie. "It's about the song."

"Anita Kelleher has a Band Aid question for you, Bob," said Read.

There was the usual Saturday morning pause where the kid wasn't sure what to do next, so she was hurried along by Read. "What do you want to ask Bob, Anita?"

"Bob, what gave you the idea for Band Aid – and did all the pop stars agree to it straight away or did you have to persuade them?" said the young caller.

"He's gonna mention us, or Vicky," Jamie was giddy. "And the video!"

"Who's Vicky?" asked Tash.

"She's from his record label. We took her to his house, and she gave him the video. He's going to mention it! Shh!"

Their earlier return to 1984 had accidentally put Geldof in hospital, and he'd missed the iconic Ethiopian news report. They'd spent the following harrowing 24 hours trying to find him and show him a VHS recording of the news.

Bob held the grey BT In-Phone to his ear and answered in earnest in his usual slow Irish tone. "The idea came from watching the telly like everyone else, and I was ashamed and horrified by what was going on...."

"Watching a video on the telly!" said Jamie, hoping his correction would land with Geldof. "You watched it on video!"

"Still telly though, Jamie," said Tash.

"So many people were part of this, ya know?" continued Bob to the caller.

"He's gonna mention it!" Jamie was amazed and delighted.

"So many gave up time and concerts, and they flew in from all over the world," continued Geldof.

And that was that. He was done.

"Thanks for your call," said Read.

"What a prick!" said Jamie. "What a prick!"

"He's not a prick, Jamie. Why would he mention he watched it on video? The result was the same. That's all that mattered."

"Tash! We made Band Aid happen!"

"No. We made Band Aid *not* happen. Then made it happen again."

The next caller pointed out that the graphics department had spelt her name wrong on the screen, which Tash was particularly impressed with. Far more important than any question to a reluctant saint. Then Read lost his temper with little Natalie for wafting a knife in the air throughout the interview – in her defence, it was plastic. And she was only trying to catch snow – which was paper. Jamie continued eating his sandwich, which had cooled a little now.

"I just think he could have mentioned our part in it," said Jamie as he slurped some tea through his food.

"Is that Keith Chegwin? He looks so young," said Tash, now increasingly spellbound by 1984 Saturday morning entertainment. Legendary "Cheggers" judging kids Christmas-wrapping traffic cones in Warrington was far better than anything TV chef James Martin was up to these days. This whole set-up had notably less hair gel and posturing than Saturday mornings' *Live & Kicking* or *SM:TV Live* from her childhood.

The doorbell suddenly announced itself in a shrill tone that made Tash spill her drink.

"Killers! Could that be the killers?" she heard herself saying involuntarily. She was evidently more invested in things than she realised.

"Doubt it," said Jamie calmly. "The article says he was found in the warehouse. Most likely the milkman. He comes for his money every Saturday. They don't want to see him until new year actually. Things are a bit tight."

Jamie leant back to see out of the single glazed window behind his headboard. He rubbed condensation from the glass and watched the accumulation of water slide down the pane onto the painted cracked putty which held it in the frame. Unhappy with the result, he went for a double rub causing his other hand to spill tea onto the remnants of his toasted sandwich.

"Tea!" said Tash instinctively, and Jamie tweaked the cup accordingly whilst still straining to look outside.

"Yep, milkman," said Jamie as his eye caught the flat roof of the milk float parked behind Raymond's Princess. He slid back down onto the quilt.

Tash swung her legs out of bed onto the floor and stretched before taking another bite of her breakfast. *Saturday Superstore* was ending with a different version of the Band Aid video than the one the two of them had grown up watching. Instead of Bob, it was Midge Ure doing the finger countdown to the supergroup choir before an unknown musician's hand played the fake church bells on a blue synth. Suddenly Neil from *The Young Ones* was sort of singing along as they cut back to the studio. His was the first sitcom ever to appeal to a new generation of teenage comedy lovers. He was clutching his new album. Alongside him, a very young Karen Barber and Nicky Slater (known to Tash from ITV's *Dancing on Ice*) joined in, as did Roy Wood from Wizzard, The Thompson Twins and Basil Brush. This was one weird but unforgettable spectacle, thought Tash as she tried to swallow a mouthful of exceptionally sweet tea. The celebrity ensemble segued into a half-hearted Christmas carol, so Tash and Jamie initially struggled to hear the shouting outside the house.

Luckily it got louder, and a muffled cry of "Jamie! Jamie!" filled the box room.

Tash dashed to the window and looked out to see the milk float slowly reverse away from the Princess. Raymond and Maureen were crammed between empty milk crates, strapped together badly with sellotape, their arms bound by their sides.

It was Maureen's voice they'd heard. Raymond was gagged by a Longley Farm yoghurt pot sellotaped into his mouth. Maureen had sort of managed to spit hers out, and raspberry yoghurt was dripping down her peach-coloured cardigan. She was a human Melba.

"Jamie, get up! They're being abducted!" shouted Tash.

"Who are?" replied Jamie.

"Your fucking foster parents, Jamie! Who do you think?"

Jamie leapt up to see a solitary figure dressed in a dark overcoat tapping on the moving milk float to stop it from reversing. He reached over to a pile of empty milk crates that had been dumped on the pavement and set about stacking them back into the float to box in the prisoners from prying eyes. Once finished, he ran to the passenger side of the float, slid onto the bench seat, and it set off down the hill. The low hum of its engine was obliterated by Keith Chegwin singing 'Good King Wenceslas' in the Golden Square Shopping Centre.

"They can't get far," said Jamie, pulling off his pyjama trousers.

"Why is nothing straightforward anymore?" said Tash pressing her face against the cold, wet windowpane to watch the milk float disappear from view.

Jamie started to pull on some Brutus jeans with Y-fronts already inside them and realised he had an audience.

"It's quicker to get dressed like this. I always leave my pants inside my jeans," he explained as he wrong-footed himself and dropped to the floor, pulling a half-drunk cup of tea onto himself.

"Yes, that's really working out for you," said Tash. "Hurry up!"

"They won't get away," said Jamie, now squirming into his jeans on the floor.

"How do you work that out?"

"Dead end," explained Jamie. "They need to turn around and come back up the hill."

He reached over for another bite of his sandwich.

"Are you still fucking eating, Jamie? Stop eating. Stop it. Stop fucking eating eighties sandwiches, Jamie."

"Sorry," he replied and reached under the pillow to put his remaining Banjo finger in the back of his jeans before reaching for a jumper and grey canvas jacket covered in flaps and pockets.

"So, what do we do?"

"We'll block the road with Raymond's car," said Jamie.

"Do murderers stop at roadblocks?" asked Tash. "Genuine question."

Tash glanced out at Raymond's tired old Princess. It wasn't handsome. When it first launched in the UK, someone had suggested the designer responsible for the front and the designer responsible for the rear weren't speaking to one another.

It was Jamie's turn to glare now. "Get dressed then!"

Tash looked at him for a moment, then dashed to find the clothes left by Maureen.

Chapter Nine

As Tash ran out of the house to the frosty Princess, Jamie was already at the driver's door. He was visibly shocked to see his sister wearing a thick knitted twinset with a tied bow around the high neck. He couldn't see her woollen skirt from where he was standing but guessed the rest of her looked like Margaret Thatcher too.

"Say one fucking word about this outfit, Jamie, and I'll tell everyone you have a favourite pope."

"Everyone has a favourite pope," said Jamie.

"They really really don't. That's not a thing."

"I don't want to argue, Tash," said Jamie as he twisted the key in the cold lock and forced open the frozen driver's door. He slumped down into the seat and leant over to flip the lock on the passenger door. Tash climbed in.

"But you can't tell me that Jean-Paul eleven didn't have the kindest smile," said Jamie, fumbling with his seat belt.

"It's two. It's pronounced two. Not eleven. It's a two," said Tash struggling to insert her seat belt buckle at the same time as her brother.

"Whatever – he's my favourite pope. You always prefer the

pope who was pope when you were growing up as a kid. Fact, that."

Jamie was now peering around the steering column to insert the key into the ignition.

"Are you confusing the pope with James Bond? Or Doctor Who? Hurry up," said Tash.

"No," Jamie's literal Asperger's kicked in. "The dress bloke, in the Vatican. The pope."

"Start the car, Jamie."

"What?"

"Start the car. Shit!"

Jamie stopped fumbling and looked at his sister. "What?"

"They're coming back. Duck!"

Both chose the same spot by the radio to safely hide their head, and so the all-too-familiar clunk of two skulls colliding resonated around the faux velvet interior of the Princess. Tash moved again, bashing her head again on the glove compartment. But both were now safely out of sight as the milk float slowly hummed past them.

They could just about make out the voice of Maureen through the stacked crates of empty bottles. "Raymond, do something! The Breville's still plugged in."

Jamie turned the ignition, and after only eight or nine attempts, the Princess soon fired into life, and Radio 1 started to play. Jamie had helped Raymond connect the stereo to the ignition, soon to be a feature on many cars as the decade progressed. Jamie had carefully twisted the round rubber dial to select the clearest signal for their usual routes, and this had happened to be Radio 1 (or "the noisy one", as Maureen had called it.) Limahl was singing 'Never Ending Story', ironically not a metaphor for his new solo career. Jamie's eleven-point turn in the slender road had provided Tash sufficient time to rethink the plan.

"Let's just call the police. Give them the newspaper and tell them where they're heading?"

Jamie considered this as he ground the gears one final time before starting their pursuit.

"In fact, that's a brilliant idea," said Tash, turning to him. "Stop the car."

"Show them a newspaper from tomorrow?" asked her brother, ignoring her command.

"Okay," said Tash. "Forget the paper. Just tell them there's a murder about to happen."

Jamie thought as he reached the end of the road, the milk float just in sight up ahead.

"Two reasons we can't do that," said Jamie. "One – they'll think we're involved! How would we know about it?"

"They won't think we're involved – just give them an anonymous tip-off," replied Tash. "Stop the car – let's get back in the house and call the police."

"Well, that's the second reason," said Jamie.

"Go on?"

"There's a lock on the phone."

"A lock on the phone? How is that even a thing?"

"Maureen has the key."

"What? Isn't there one on the keyring?" said Tash – gesturing at the ignition key.

"Oh! Yeah! Good idea!" said Jamie, pulling over and stopping the car. He removed the key and looked at it, hanging from a leather embossed Leyland key ring.

"No. There isn't one."

"There is. What's that?" asked Tash.

"That's for the garage," replied Jamie as a thought struck him. "We could take the C5?"

"No!" said Tash. "The last time we parked that in London, it got nicked. We leave that locked away until I go home."

"We go home," corrected Jamie.

"That's what I said."

Jamie looked at his sister for a moment, then started the engine again. On the tenth attempt.

CHAPTER TEN

Jamie's idea was to cross Kennington Park to avoid the congestion that lay ahead on Brixton Road. Usually, it would have been a great idea, but there was no road running through Kennington Park, so it was actually a bad idea.

A really bad one. A really, really bad idea. Awful.

The sight of the red Princess skidding across the water-logged turf had understandably created quite a bit of a panic amongst park visitors that lunchtime, not least the two five-a-side football teams that had parted like a biblical sea to allow the muddy vehicle through. The manic shaking of the car's suspension was elevated to something profoundly disturbing by the tribal thumping of Duran Duran's 'Wild Boys' that played from Raymond's radio.

"Where are the fucking police when you want them?" said Tash as she nervously gripped the padded door handle with one hand and the dashboard with the other. "We're driving a fucking car through a fucking park! In the daytime!"

"We don't want the police yet," replied Jamie as he

swerved to avoid a Labrador arching its back to take a dump on the faded chalk of the football pitch penalty spot. "They'd just arrest us. We want them to arrest the baddies."

"Baddies?" Tash looked at her brother and observed just how much his head was vibrating as they bounced over the undulating ground, spraying muddy clumps of turf up the sides of the car. "Have you been watching re-runs of *The A-Team*?"

"They're not re-runs yet. They're on for the first time. And no one says 're-runs' yet either. They call them repeats. Series and repeats. Not seasons and re-runs."

"Do you actually have an actual plan to actually get us out of here, actually?" Tash was looking at the perimeter fencing and trees that were rapidly approaching.

"Gate!" shouted Jamie as a pair of painted iron gates came into view. Only one was open, and the other was pinned to the ground with a rusted lift-up pole like so many homes had attached to their driveway gates before getting scrapped so front gardens could become expanses of homogenous concrete to park extra cars,

"Pull up, and I'll open," said Tash, hoping to finish the sentence with "the locked one", but Jamie had opted to smash through it instead. Luckily the pole that held it in place snapped quickly from its rusted housing, and the gate swung open, allowing the Princess to clear the pavement and join the road. It was a miracle that they didn't meet pedestrians or vehicles on their way. Jamie also implemented a hand brake turn to bounce the Princess in the correct direction to continue their journey. Other than the mud-splattered sides, turf-sodden tyres, smashed-off wing mirrors, creased chrome front bumper and smashed driver's headlight, the car looked totally inconspicuous as it completed its rubbery screech onto the tarmac.

"Wait!" said Tash, looking over her shoulder.

The milk float was now stuck in traffic behind them, still on Brixton Road. They had overtaken it, and it was indicating right, most probably on a shortcut through the quieter streets of Walworth. Happily, the Princess hadn't yet passed the turning.

"Take the next turn. We're ahead of them!" said Tash. "They're indicating right."

Jamie did, then parked up just past the red brick tube station on Braganza Street. Then they waited, their heartbeats louder in their ears than Simon Le Bon's warning that 'wild boys never lose it'.

"They're coming," said Tash nervously, looking over her shoulder as the milk float finally crossed a gap in oncoming traffic and joined them on their side street.

"What's the plan?" asked Jamie.

"I have no idea. Maybe we should block the road?"

"What would we do then?"

"I don't know. What are we actually trying to achieve here?" asked Tash.

"Saving Raymond."

"Yes. Yes. That's a good idea. But I can see two immediate problems with that. One – how? And two..."

Jamie stared at Tash. "Go on."

"No. I've thought again, and it's just the one problem. How?"

Suddenly the familiar hum of the milk float was in their ears again, and being creatures of habit, they opted to smash skulls again by the radio knob. Tash's nose was the first to find her brother's skull, then the rest of her face joined it as the two heads cracked together.

"Sake!" said Tash as she checked her nose for blood.

Jamie peered over the speedometer into the road ahead. "They've stopped."

Tash tried to peer around the front of the Express Dairies float that held Jamie's new family, but all she could see was a wall of blue crates sitting above a sign that read: *Fresh Milk's Gotta Lotta Bottle*. The milk marketing board were proud of that one.

The Overcoat didn't get out. Instead, the driver appeared on the pavement and walked towards the first terrace house alongside the Underground station. Credit to the guy, he'd gone full-on with his disguise. To an untrained eye, this was a milkman, not an abductor intent on a vicious and grisly murder.

"Maybe a halfway house?" said Jamie, now trying to peer around the float too.

"Come on..." said Tash, as she opened her creaky door and stepped out. Jamie followed her lead, and together they tiptoed to the stack of crates at the rear of the float.

"What are we..." Jamie started talking considerably too loudly, so was interrupted with Tash shushing.

"Just help me," whispered Tash as she carefully started to unload the crates of mostly returned bottles onto the road. One by one, she passed them to Jamie, who stacked them very badly like a blue plastic Jenga on the edge of the kerb, just out of sight of the whistling 'milkman'.

"Faster," said Jamie, glancing around the float at the open front door of the terrace house.

"Shh," repeated Tash.

The milkman exchanged paperwork with the lady in the doorway, occasionally casting a furtive glance up and down the road. She was giving him quite a telling off. Jamie was simultaneously impressed and distressed to see the head of the mafia gang was a woman.

"We'll get them both off," said Tash, still removing crates, "then you put them on the Tube."

"Tube?" said Jamie, taking another crate from his sister. "Where to?"

"Shhh!" said Tash. Jamie was absolutely shit at whispering. "Anywhere. Don't care. I'll meet you back at their house as soon as I can."

Tash was secretly pleased. She would use this as the perfect time to part company with her brother once and for all and head back to her son in 2020. She suddenly realised how relaxed she felt compared to the last time she was trapped in 1984. Back then, she was unsure if she'd ever get home again, whereas now she knew she could return, and she knew how. She just wanted to make sure it was soon. Raymond and Maureen were buried deeper than she'd realised. She was now emptying the second row of crates.

"Raymond," whispered Tash.

"Maureen," said Jamie.

"Shush," said Tash.

"I *was* being shush! Stop shushing me!"

"Shush!" said Tash, holding her palm out over Jamie's face to silence him. She'd heard something. It was Maureen. A muffled Maureen. But definitely Maureen.

"Stop leaning on me, Raymond! You're leaning on me!" said Maureen.

"Maureen!" shouted Tash, abandoning her own silence rule. "Maureen!"

"Well," said a voice. "This is interesting."

Tash looked around to see the mafia milkman standing at the rear of the float, staring at the mad couple stacking his crates by the pavement. He had a look of pure evil about him, not unlike Dudley before he pulled the trigger on his gun back in October. At that moment, Tash realised she had a talent for spotting psychopaths simply by the sparkle in their eyes.

She had no time to spare before this bastard did the worst, so without thinking, she threw the milk crate in her hands square at his face. Hard. He fell backwards and landed on the pavement. His cap protected his skull from taking the full impact as his head struck the ground, but the split across his nose was clear to see. Empty milk bottles smashed on the floor with leftover sour milk creating sorry grey-white pooling around his shocked, inert body.

"Raymond! Maureen! Come on!" shouted Tash, clawing through the crates in despair.

Jamie started to tug at Tash's sleeve.

"Help me, Jamie! Help me!" said Tash, shrugging off his hand.

"Raymond! This is gold top. It's going to stain!" said Maureen.

"Sorry, Maureen," replied a muffled Raymond.

Jamie tugged again. Tash was becoming irritated by him.

"What?" she asked without taking her eyes off the task in hand.

Jamie pointed at a milk float slowly overtaking them on the road.

The milk float. The actual milk float. The milk float they had been following before the shortcut through the park. Tash glanced down at the milkman on the ground, rubbing his bloody gash and attempting to clamber back to his feet.

"GBH," said Tash. "I've just done a GBH, Jamie."

Tash stepped over to help up the poor sod she'd ruthlessly attacked. He cowered away from her, but she was insistent.

"I'm trying to help you, you prick. It was a mistake," said Tash, grabbing the man's hands and pulling him to his feet.

"Tash, they're getting away," said Jamie, already heading back to the Princess.

Tash registered this thought and let go of the milkman, who fell back onto the pavement into the pile of broken glass and musty milk.

"Sorry," she shouted over her shoulder as she climbed back into her seat.

Jamie took just six attempts to start the engine and then nearly steered around the parked milk float. So very nearly. In fact, he might have believed he'd cleared it if it wasn't for him and Tash smacking their heads on the windscreen as the Princess struck the corner of the Express Dairies' vehicle.

"Sake, Jamie," said Tash as they watched some more crates fall onto the road and onto the milkman. She thought now was a good time to reach for her seatbelt.

"There's a lot happening," said Jamie.

Tash glanced out at the milkman. "Sorry!" she shouted whilst trying to find the button to lower her window. "How do I get the window down, Jamie?"

"Spinny thing," said Jamie as he reversed the car away from their blockage and selected first gear again. A sticker, *Defend Doorstep Delivery of British Milk*, hung limply from the rear of the crumpled milk float.

Tash tried to spin the manual window winder down but was far too rough, and it came off in her hand, so she opted to open the door and shout out of it as Jamie finally moved the car forwards. None of this was helped by frogs croaking along with Paul McCartney's 'We All Stand Together'.

"We said we were sorry!" shouted Tash before slamming her door closed again. "It wasn't my fault."

"Let's just follow them this time," said Jamie.

"And not attack any strangers?" replied Tash.

Jamie looked over to explain his logic but was distracted by the blood beneath Tash's nose. It had run over her lips into her mouth, causing her teeth to stain red around the edges.

"You've got a bit of..." Jamie started to say whilst gesturing at her mouth.

Tash lowered the sun visor expecting a mirror, and when confronted with nothing but more padded vinyl, she pulled the rear-view mirror into a position to see herself. She really shouldn't have done.

"Feel sick," said Tash before turning white.

"Seven eleven breathing, Tash, you'll be fine."

Tash had passed out before Jamie finished speaking.

There were two things Tash didn't like. One was the sight of her own blood, and the other was her life right now.

CHAPTER ELEVEN

Jim Diamond was singing lots of 'I's before admitting he should have known better.

"Okay, here's the new plan," said Tash. "I'll drop you at the warehouse. You go in and make sure no one gets killed. I'll..." but Jamie couldn't move on to the next point with her.

"How do I do that?" he asked.

"There'll be time for questions at the end," said Tash. "I'll contact the police and say that I saw some people with guns or knives or whatever, breaking into the warehouse and that they need to come quickly or else there'll be a murder."

"And they'll come along and arrest the baddies, and then everything will be okay?"

"Yes. That. Exactly that," said Tash.

"I've just thought of another question, actually."

"Do you want to do your first question? Or shall we do this new one?"

"Let's do the new one."

"Shoot," said Tash, happy in the knowledge that right

after calling the police, she would be heading back to Raymond's garage that housed her ride back to 2020.

"Well, all I want to know is, how do I land this?" asked Jamie.

Tash was briefly confused, but as she looked out of the windscreen of the Princess, she too had the same thought. Tower Bridge was bathed in winter sunlight which also deflected off the mighty glazed face of The Shard. The streets of London were easily three or four hundred metres beneath them. The cityscape was magnificent this frosty afternoon, and the Thames twinkled below. Her view reminded her of the insert shots in *The Apprentice* when Lord Sugar has just told twelve or sixteen idiots that he wants them to film an advert for a really shit product that will never go on sale.

And that was the problem.

The car wasn't a flying car. And Jamie wasn't a pilot. And The Shard wasn't built in 1984.

"Sake," said Tash.

Her own words woke her, and she was depressed to see she was still in the car alongside Jamie sitting in queuing 1984 traffic, although Jim was still singing.

"How long was I out?" she whispered.

"What?" said Jamie, oblivious.

"How long have I been unconscious?"

"Erm."

Tash was livid.

"You didn't even fucking see that I fucking fainted? Jamie, I could have died!"

"Sorry. I've been concentrating on a route."

Tash sat up and stared through the windscreen. "Where are they?"

Jamie shrugged.

"Jamie, don't tell me you lost them?"

"That's the thing. We don't need to follow them! We

know where they're going. I thought we could go straight there. I have a key. We can let ourselves in, call the police and then hide. Just in case. Until they come. The police."

"Jamie, that's brilliant!" said Tash before adding. "How about I drop you off so you can get in and hide, and I go and call the police, though? Just a slight tweak to the plan. Then I'll come to find you."

"You keep wanting to leave. Why do you keep wanting to leave? Is there something you're not telling me, Tash?"

"No," lied Tash.

"I say we stay together. The last time we split up, I ended up stuck here for two months."

"That's cos you didn't show up when we agreed," said Tash.

"Neither did you, apparently," said Jamie, who paused as a thought swam to the surface of his brain.

"Oh my God. You're trying to go home without me, again!"

"Rubbish," said Tash.

"Shit!" shouted Jamie as he turned into Bay 3, and his eyes settled on the warehouse shutter door. It was open.

CHAPTER TWELVE

Ever since Jamie missed his rendezvous with Tash back in October, he'd been helping Raymond at work in exchange for bed and board. For almost nine weeks, he'd spent his days in the storage facility that Dudley Hobson had leased for his contract with Sinclair to store their pre-sale C5s ahead of their market launch next month. January 1985 would see the world stop and stare in wonder at the carbon-neutral mini-cars that Clive Sinclair had been developing for an unsuspecting – and ultimately uninterested – public. Over recent weeks, as the C5s had been shipped to satellite storage units and the Hoover main factory (they were in charge of servicing them), Raymond had been frantically trying to fill the massive void with new stocks of storage for any business with a demand for freezing cold, low-quality racking beneath sporadically leaky roofing. Unsurprisingly, few had been forthcoming, but he had succeeded in securing a few short-term contracts with a fabric importer and a modelling clay special-ist. All the while, Jamie had taken his lunch breaks pacing back and forth across Tower Bridge in the hope that Tash would make a further visit to their agreed meeting point to take him home to 2020. And then she'd arrived outside his bedroom window last night, so things were certainly looking up for him.

Jamie led Tash slowly towards the warehouse's main entrance, both leaning against the yellow London stock brick wall that enveloped it. Jamie had seen this method of approach used to great effect many times recently – from Bodie and Doyle in repeats of *The Professionals* to the chief of police in *Scooby-Doo*, and it seemed to serve them well today. He stood alongside the gaping entrance, but his body refused to move one inch further. He knew he had to look inside, but his innate senses declined to send any instructions to his trembling muscles. He may as well have been glued to the wall like the wallpaper paste advert they kept showing on the telly, with the guy in overalls pasted to a board suspended over a snake pit of cobras. Why people needed their wallpaper to be so irreparably bonded to their walls in 1984 was something Jamie would definitely Google when he got home. He'd felt it rude to ask Raymond and Maureen as they loved the advert. They would sit up and lean in when a favourite ad came on. Jamie thought the ad-makers tried harder in the 80s as the poor sods couldn't fast forward through them like more advanced civilisations in the 21st century. The ones that paid gym subscriptions and scrolled through mobile phones for eight hours a day in case they missed something life-affirming. Yes, 2020 had progress written all over it.

Then he had a thought and gestured silence to Tash, then tiptoed back to the Princess. They hadn't slammed their doors fully closed for fear of alerting the baddies of their arrival, so he was able to swing his driver's door open and lean inside. He reached across to the rear-view mirror and wrestled to free it. Unable to do so, he sat in the seat and tried using both hands. When that failed, he slid the seat back as far as possible, lifted his knees to his chest and then kicked with all his might at the mirror. Happily, this freed it, although not entirely how he intended. It came free as the sole of his shoe went right through the windscreen, causing it to smash into thousands of tiny square pieces.

Jamie could just about make out Tash's attempts to shriek 'the fuck?' as quietly as possible.

He carefully extracted his leg from where the windscreen used to be, and then himself from the car, leaning in to grab the mirror before tiptoeing to join his sister.

"I got the mirror," said Jamie at his usual volume.

"I saw," replied Tash before adding her usual pointless reminder to shush.

Jamie stood parallel with the warehouse door opening, clutched the mirror in his hand, and stretched out his arm at full length to gain a stolen view inside Raymond's workplace. They both squinted into the small reflection and could see that it was devoid of any people or movement.

"It's empty," said Jamie, breathing a sigh of relief.

"Right," said Tash, marching past her brother into the vast storage area. "Let's call the police."

It was almost two months since she'd been in here, according to the calendar, but only a matter of hours in her life, so she was quickly able to find her way to the hinged door that accessed the caged office area. She was disappointed to see that Jamie's general lack of good order had somehow passed via osmosis to his new boss.

"This place is a fucking mess, Jamie. You should be ashamed of yourself."

There were clusters of half-opened cardboard boxes and battered crates where Sinclair C5s had nestled side-by-side along countless rows of multi-tiered racking. Fabrics spilled over a few shelves, and piles of modelling clay littered the floor like plastic molehills. The floor of the office was covered in mountains of paperwork, discarded litter, and broken electrical equipment. Any drawer in any rack that could be open, was open.

"Looks like it's been ransacked," was the last thing Tash said before lifting the phone to her ear.

It might have been her choice of words or the silence from the old grey plastic phone that she held to her face, but that was when the penny dropped.

"It's been ransacked," said Tash. "It's been ransacked."

Jamie was spinning around in disbelief at a vision of complete wanton vandalism and destruction. It was sensory overload for anyone, let alone someone on the autistic spectrum, and he handled it well but was unable to stop the tears from filling his eyes.

Tash was hitting the little black pegs that stuck out of the phone cradle. She'd seen that on films and always thought it was absurd, so wasn't sure why she was doing it now, but she continued as she whispered, "The phone's dead."

She looked down and followed the phone line just twelve inches before it ended with a clean cut.

"They cut the phone lines, Jamie. They cut the fucking phone lines."

The sound of an engine outside jolted them both into action.

"Follow me," said Jamie.

"We've totally fucked this up, Jamie! Totally! This wasn't what you told me to do!"

She stopped the moment she'd said it. Hopefully, he hadn't heard. His shoes on concrete were surely enough to have covered her lapse in concentration. She couldn't let him know that an older Jamie had sent her back to save Raymond's life. An older Jamie that had somehow found love in the 80s.

But when the hell had he found it?

And where the hell was Martha?

It was surely her that she'd seen outside Grandma's house on Christmas morning. Jamie had even said it. And besides, Tash recognised her face and pink hair. It was Martha, and Jamie, and their son, and their son's wife, and their grand-daughter. There was a whole family tree.

Whenever it was, Tash knew that her brother had found something he'd failed to in the 21st century – love. So, despite how much it pained her, she needed to let that story play out. And to let that story play out, Tash knew that she needed to fix the Raymond scenario with minimum impact on anything else and go home alone.

But that had to wait. Right now, she just needed to follow Jamie and hide. And not say anything stupid like that again.

Jamie wasn't as scared as he thought he would be for one particular reason: that wasn't a milk float they heard. Milk floats hummed quietly to ensure customers slept soundly in their beds whilst deliveries continued through the early hours of every morning. What they'd heard was a throaty petrol engine. So maybe it was nothing to fear? Perhaps someone had witnessed the break-in and called the police anyway? After passing fifty or sixty yards of shelving, Jamie took a turn and opened a fire door for his sister to run through. He followed.

Inside, Tash continued to the end of the small corridor, stopping only to swear at her brother.

"What the fuck are we doing in here? There's no way out."

She was right. The corridor seemed to exist as an oversized storage room. One barred window above head height allowed daylight in.

"We can wait here and think of a plan before we go back in," said Jamie.

"You want to go back in?" asked Tash. "Are you mental?"

"What else can we do? Raymond's going to get killed!"

Tash took a deep, exasperated breath. "At the risk of repeating myself, what's the actual plan?"

Jamie scanned the floor and reached down to gently pick up a mousetrap that was offering up a smear of what might once have been cheese.

"I've eaten, thanks," said Tash.

"A weapon!"

"Shh!" replied Tash, aware that Jamie wasn't top of her list of quiet people you'd choose to hide in a cupboard with from a murderer.

"You want to attack an assassin with a mousetrap?"

"Could be lethal if you stick it in the right place," said Jamie, as he mimed ramming it in her face.

"It hasn't even caught a fucking mouse, Jamie."

"Fine. I'll take it then," said Jamie keeping it for himself and scanning the sparse corridor again. "You'll need something, though"

"Shh!" repeated Tash, as she too started to peruse her options.

Chapter Thirteen

The squeak on the hinges seemed deafening as Jamie pushed the door open, but the sheer volume of the warehouse on the other side swallowed it easily. Jamie peered around the long rack of shelving closest to them to see if their path was clear. Happy that they had sufficient time, he tiptoed over to a dustbin and dragged it over to his sister, wincing a little at the screech of steel over concrete. Tash watched as Jamie pointed to the lofty towers of storage above, then clambered onto the bin and climbed onto the first tier of shelving. He reached down to help up Tash, which proved a little slower as she was now clutching a fire extinguisher. She figured this could knock some bastard unconscious if they came near her. The storage racks were only the width of one pallet, so the drop on either side kept them both highly alert. In fact, Jamie was experiencing the unpleasant tingle in his groin that he usually saved for hotel balconies and YouTube videos of free climbers clinging to skyscrapers.

"We need to get higher up," whispered Tash unhelpfully, and with that, she clambered up the metal racking supports to reach the tier above. Jamie reluctantly followed, dodging the fire extinguisher that Tash kept swinging behind her as she struggled to get a better footing. They repeated this inelegant manoeuvre twice and then rested – confident they were high enough to remain out of sight but still able to get an eagle-eye view of whatever was about to transpire way down below.

If they were brave enough to peer over the edge, of course.

Jamie opted for a minimum risk strategy of laying completely flat on the shelf board with all his limbs spread out like a starfish – there was no way gravity was taking him with this approach. It was a little bit overkill, but Tash decided to leave him to it. At least this method minimised the risk of injury from the mousetrap he clutched in his left hand.

Jamie inched cautiously forward until his fingertips reached the rack edge and then stopped. He had a better idea. With his free hand, he fumbled in his pocket and pulled out Raymond's rear-view mirror. He slowly held it over the edge of the racking and twisted it until he could perform a detailed recce of the ground below. It was far darker now. The front shutter must have been closed, and the strip lights suspended on chains had been switched off. But it was seemingly empty and devoid of life, so he nodded at Tash and slid further forward to peer safely over the edge. The borrowed light from a few overhead corrugated plastic roof tiles was all he had to help gauge what might be happening down there.

Suddenly loud voices cut the air. Tash joined Jamie at the edge of the racking and peered over, but there was nobody to be seen, just the silhouette of two plastic chairs that had been placed outside the office and positioned to face the long aisle that lay beneath Tash and Jamie.

The rattling sound of the hefty shutter lifting was accompanied by a momentary flood of December afternoon daylight into the bays, before the same sound shut it out again. The Overcoat was back, and he was jostling a silhouette much like Raymond across the cold floor, a journey that could have been considerably quicker had he been generous enough to unbind his legs. Another Overcoat appeared – shorter than the one they'd seen on Gaywood Close – and this one was leading a Maureen-shaped silhouette behind her husband. She, too, was shuffling, but this Overcoat seemed more patient.

"We need to do something," whispered Tash.

Raymond and Maureen were forced into the adjacent chairs, and the Overcoats took one step back before one of them shouted something that Jamie thought might be Spanish.

"Comenzar."

There was a brief pause, but it was time enough for Tash and Jamie to hear Maureen berate her husband as she squinted into the gloom.

"This place is a disgrace, Raymond."

"Sorry, Maureen. It's not how I left it."

Then something peculiar happened. Even more bizarre than what had already happened.

Pop music reverberated about the warehouse atrium like it was Wembley Arena. Jamie and Tash simultaneously spun their heads around to stare into the depths of the aisle. A portable beatbox on maximum volume flashed LED lights in the distance. 'Pánico en El Edén' hadn't troubled the British or American charts over the summer of 1984, but Tino Casal had enjoyed one week at the top of the Spanish Top 40 in the middle of June. It was quite an accolade, given the Spanish had gifted this slot to Frankie Goes To Hollywood, Culture Club, Michael Jackson and Stevie Wonder, over the past twelve months. Despite its unfamiliar melody, Jamie was soon nervously tapping his toes to the euro beat and nodding his head to the hypnotic hook of 'Oh-Wohhh, Oh-Wooah'.

The portable stereo was moving now. Not fast, but definitely moving. As their eyes slowly grew accustomed to the dark, they could see the outline of someone or something propelling themselves slowly forwards on a wheelchair, the red flickering lights resting in their lap. Bizarrely, white flashes lit the path of the chair as it rolled towards Raymond and Maureen. Tash spotted the source of the light show – it was the two Overcoats shaking torches in time with the music. Suddenly one of them briefly illuminated the head of the wheelchair user, and the sight was horrific.

A Dalek head placed atop a white-suited body sitting in the chair. It suddenly twitched in synchronisation with the synth bass as it copied an electronic drum fill into the Spanish verse. The hands moved the wheelchair in jerky movements towards the seated couple, who watched in bewildered terror.

"The fuck?" whispered Tash. Jamie didn't reply. He felt safe in his position, but the random flickering of the torchlight display and the relentless loud music were pressing all his Asperger buttons. Jamie just wanted it to stop. He glanced over at Tash, who gently placed a reassuring hand on the back of his neck.

Tino's vocals continued as this robot-headed, white-suited apparition continued beneath Tash and Jamie towards the torches. It stopped briefly to do a wheelie, followed by a 360 spin before continuing over the final few metres to the chairs.

"Where's my golden buzzer?" whispered Tash.

Suddenly a Spanish radio presenter started to talk over the end of the track. The chatter was the familiar rapid-fire style that Tash recognised from the airport taxis that would take her and Nathan to their rental apartment in Mallorca or Marbella.

"Tino Casal, todavía entre los diez primeros esta semana con '*Pánico en El Edén*', un ex número uno en España, y esto también, pero está subiendo en la lista de nuevo, es Rockwell"

As the DJ said the word Rockwell, the intro to '*Somebody*'s *Watching Me*' started to play, and the figure in the wheelchair looked quite animated, possibly irritated. It seemed they were trying to switch off the cassette that was still playing. This unique spectacle clearly should have ended before the song did, but it was very tricky to find the soft-touch stop button on a Sharp portable stereo whilst wearing a Dalek helmet.

"Maldito DJ!" shouted a man's voice from inside the head. Jamie was in no doubt he'd just shouted 'fucking DJ!' at his cassette and was pleased it wasn't just the British who tried to tape the charts without interruptions from over-excited DJs.

Suddenly Rockwell stopped, and there was silence interrupted by another eruption from the head in the wheelchair.

"Las luces! Las luces!"

One of the Overcoats looked frantically around to find the bank of light switches and flicked them all on, followed by the usual 80s on-off, on-off flickering of the fluorescent tubes that Tash had last seen in the BBC basement on her previous visit to 1984. Eventually, most of the tubes ended the strobe light show with the 'on' setting, and Tash and Jamie could finally see things more clearly. Raymond and Maureen were sitting alongside one another, covered in binding tape and dried up spillages of dairy products. The Overcoat they'd seen earlier was a thirty-something moustachioed man, and the Overcoat returning from the light switch was a similarly aged woman.

Slowly and very purposefully, the white-suited man in the wheelchair ceremoniously raised both hands to his Dalek head and teasingly suggested the impending reveal of his identity. He was enjoying this, and his body language made that perfectly clear. First a clean-shaven chin, then a thin-lipped smile was displaying nicotine-stained teeth. Next, a respectable black moustache, a slender nose, dark brown eyes with impossibly long eyelashes, and finally a head of greased back, receding greying hair, straight and long – up to a clipped, shaved, tanned neck. He waited a moment and then burst into hysterical laughter.

"You think it was Tino Casal. Yes? Tino Casal beneath this erm, this Darth Vader mask? Yes?"

His Spanish accent struggled to say these words without belly laughing again.

"I wear his cloak and sing his song, and you think it's Tino Casal, yes? Here in London town?"

This was too funny. He was almost tearing up with the delight of his little joke at their expense.

Maureen stared at Raymond, who didn't lose eye contact with the mad man. Instead, he returned his manic smile with a terrified one of his own.

"Tino Casal?" repeated the Spaniard before embarking on some acapella 'Oh-Woh, Oh-Wooah'. In case this helped with his question. Surely repeating the song they'd just heard would help the peseta drop?

"I told you. No one knows Tino Casal outside Spain, Papá," said the lady Overcoat before being silenced by the white-suited man placing a finger to his lips.

"And it's a Dalek head. It's not Darth Vader," she said in her British accent.

The man glared at the Doctor Who prop in his hands and discarded it to the floor.

Maureen winced as the Dalek head cracked down onto the concrete, and the telescopic pole that had been its eye snapped clean off.

The BBC had filmed external shots for *Resurrection of the Daleks* at Butler's Wharf the year before. Much as the Dalek scenes had been shot in the studio back in Shepherd's Bush, someone had brought a Dalek head along just in case they needed to shoot a close-up of one entering the warehouse. In the end, they'd lost the prop deep in the back of Bay 3. It was a testament to their thorough ransacking that the Overcoats had uncovered it earlier today, neither Jamie nor Raymond had come across it during their day-to-day routine.

"Allow me to introduce myself," said the man, expertly tossing a business card onto Raymond's lap. Raymond squinted down and read the italicised ink:

Jesus Morón.
   Experto Ejecutivo en Negocios.
   No job too big.

Raymond took a moment and then looked up at Jesus, who indicated that he could share this information with his wife with a charming sweeping gesture. As Raymond could not move his arms, he opted to tell her rather than pass the card over through the medium of magic.

"He's called Jesus, Maureen. His name is Jesus Moron."

"Hey-sus," corrected Jesus. "Hey-sus Mor-rón," heavily accentuating the second syllable of his surname.

It did sound better that way, although these Brits would struggle with that pronunciation.

"Erm, my name is Raymond, and this is my wife –" Raymond was interrupted before he could say Maureen.

"I know your name. I know where you live," replied Jesus.

"Yes, of course, you do. Sorry, Mr Moron," said Raymond.

"Don't talk to him, Raymond," said Maureen.

"What?" he replied.

"Ask him what he wants," demanded Maureen.

"Don't talk to him *and* ask him what he wants?" replied Raymond.

"Just ask what he wants!"

"He can hear you!" said Raymond.

"Where is Dudley Hobson?" asked Jesus.

"Oh!" said Raymond, visibly relieved. "There must be

some kind of mix-up. He's not here. It's just been a mix-up, Maureen!"

Raymond smiled at everyone present as if his answer had cleared up any confusion, and he would soon be back in Gaywood Close watching Desmond Lynam present *Sports Review of the Year*.

"We know this... We look for him," said Jesus gesturing around the ransacked warehouse.

"Well, you've been very thorough," said Raymond as kindly as he thought possible. Yes, a compliment of sorts might just change the mood, he decided.

"We look in his house also," said Jesus.

And he was right. After trashing the warehouse at 9am, they'd headed to Dudley's one-bedroom flat in Holburn, and after gaffer taping his ex-landlord to his own staircase, they set about trashing Dudley's tiny home and then in the interests of leaving no stone unturned they repeated this on the rest of the terraced house whilst the other tenants watched on, also taped to the staircase. The landlord was doubly pissed off as not only was he down two months' rent from his ex-tenant, now the staircase spindles needed repainting. Once he'd peeled himself, his tenants and the tape off them. Then if he had time, he could look for his teeth.

Maybe it was the Dalek head, or the Spanish music, or the white suit, or the wheelchair, but Raymond and Maureen both realised they hadn't quite taken everything in. Something was moving behind Jesus. Something alive. An animal was perched on the back of his wheelchair, peering over his shoulder.

"Don't move! There's a little fluffy animal on your chair!" said Raymond.

"You have seen my friend," said Jesus leaning back and allowing the owl to climb onto his hand. He gently rubbed his other palm down the back of the brown and white plumage.

"Meet El Buho," said Jesus.

"That's a nice name," said Raymond.

"It is Spanish," replied Jesus.

"Lovely. What for?" asked Raymond, hoping this rapport was building.

"Owl," replied Jesus, his smile dropping from his face. He looked at Maureen then looked back at Raymond.

"Buho is hungry. Do you know what Buho eats?" asked Jesus.

"Sausages?" asked Raymond to a non-plussed Jesus.

"Sausages? He's an owl?" asked Maureen.

"There was one on *On Safari* last week. With Biggins. He ate sausages."

"That was a puppet," said Maureen.

"Based on fact, Maureen. They're not allowed to lie to children," said Raymond. He really thought he was onto something.

Jesus pointed to the male Overcoat, who nodded, walked away, and returned with a tube of Primula squeezy cheese spread.

"Oh! Squeezy cheese!" said Raymond. "Lovely!" He turned to Maureen. "He likes squeezy cheese, Maureen!"

"I'm here too, Raymond. I can see," said Maureen.

"You like this?" asked Jesus as he watched the Overcoat remove the screw-top lid from the tube.

"It's not really my cup of – oh," said Raymond. His 'oh' arrived when the Overcoat started to squirt the cheese onto Raymond's face. He then used his fingers to smear it evenly around to completely cover Raymond's forehead, nose, chin, and cheeks. First, he smelt the nicotine on the Spaniard's fingers, then the processed cheese. It was the type with bits of prawn – or prawn flavour – in it, so Raymond now looked like he had measles and was simultaneously melting.

Jesus started to laugh again at the vision in front of him.

"You think he eats the cheese? This is so funny! Cheese owl! A owl that is eating the cheese!"

Raymond's attempts to join in weren't too convincing, and his giggles stopped pretty soon after they started. He sniffed in a bit of prawn, so he followed that with an assertive exhale from his nose to try and flush it out.

"No, no!" said Jesus. "This owl does not eat cheese."

"Thank goodness for that!" said Raymond, now more confused than humiliated as he found himself swallowing the bit of prawn; it had clearly found a way around the back.

"He eats mice," said Jesus nodding at the Overcoat, who promptly upturned a bucket of tiny live mice onto Raymond's head.

Maureen's screams made everyone jump. It was hard to tell, but they might have even stopped the fifteen or twenty mice from nibbling away at Raymond's face buffet for just a moment. The woman Overcoat silenced her with tape over her mouth whilst appealing to Jesus's better nature if he had one.

"Papá, cálmate."

He raised his free hand to silence his daughter once more whilst muttering her name, "Isabel."

Raymond's mouth was tightly shut, and his nostrils flared as he tried to breathe as calmly as humanly possible with a bucket full of mice feeding off his face. Maureen stared at him as tears filled her eyes.

"I ask you one more time, or Buho will visit the restaurant," said Jesus, wheeling a little closer to Raymond.

A metallic clang resonated around the warehouse and everyone looked up to the shelf below Jamie. He lunged backwards out of sight to see that Tash was gone. Christ, they must have heard her climbing down. What was she thinking? Jamie quickly reached into his pocket and extracted Raymond's rearview mirror, and then threw it as far as he could across the warehouse. It bounced along the chain-link roof of the office before landing just inside the doorway behind the Overcoats.

Everyone froze.

Jesus nodded instructions to Isabel to investigate, but she simply shrugged, unable to see what had landed.

"You have one chance to answer," said Jesus to Raymond before slowly asking the question one final time.

"Where - is - Dudley - Hobson?"

"The thing is – I honestly don't know!" mumbled Raymond through cheese and mice, his suddenly high-pitched voice faltering badly. Jesus looked disappointed.

"Dinner time, little bird," said the mad man, and without a second thought, he offered the barn owl over towards Raymond. It was only about a foot tall, but the moment it opened its wings, they easily spanned a yard or more. My word that is one big bird, thought Raymond, simultaneously impressed, and mortified. It covered the distance effortlessly and attacked immediately with no mercy.

CHAPTER FOURTEEN

The owl had swooped forward and landed on Raymond's head, its talons digging into the creases in his cheesy forehead, releasing a single trail of blood that continued down the very centre of his twitching nose. The initial chaos of feathers flapping and wings whooshing had disorientated Raymond. He was now frozen in anticipation of the mighty creature's first peck at its supper somewhere on his face. The tiny mice were cleaning cheese off Raymond's face and preventing themselves from falling off by nipping their little claws into his cheeks. The result was a pretty grim trail of tiny red footprint scratches in random patterns on his skin. Amazingly the owl already had its first mouse in its beak. It must have scooped one up on landing. Maureen's muffled squeals at the freaky spectacle weren't helping Raymond's efforts to stay calm, but they did distract the male Overcoat, who let his concentration momentarily lapse.

So, he didn't spot Margaret Thatcher's ninja sister drop down behind his boss. Within half a second, Tash had twatted Jesus around the head with the large red fire extinguisher and was now emptying its contents straight into Raymond's face, the hose trembling in her quivering hand. It was the carbon dioxide type, so all anyone could see as Jesus slid down from his wheelchair onto the floor was a massive cloud erupting around where Raymond once sat. The noise was like a hurricane.

Tash stopped spraying pretty soon as she wasn't sure how much CO2 might kill a man, so as the fog started to dissolve around Raymond, the vision before them wasn't unlike the chorus part in a Cliff Richard video. That was undoubtedly Maureen's train of thought anyway. Yes, he was gasping for oxygen right now, but Raymond's hair was swept back like Cliff's, and the immense pressure on his face had resulted in a temporary facelift. He looked a good ten or eleven years younger. The cheese was mostly just in his ears now; the mice were magically gone, and the owl was now enjoying the spectacle from the shelf alongside Jamie, who was attempting to clamber down unseen. The pressure had removed most of the bloodstains from Raymond's face, but the cuts were still fresh, so suddenly, the red dots on his cheeks filled again, and the talon wound started to trickle scarlet down his nose. Maureen's heart stopped fluttering and 'Devil Woman' stopped playing in her head.

The momentary freeze frame ended as the male Overcoat leapt forward to disarm Tash. She was cross at herself as she'd missed the opportunity to spray her assailant by just half a second. He grabbed the fire extinguisher handle with one hand and caught her in a neck hold with the other. God, this guy was strong. And what the hell was that smell? She was inches away from his armpit, and it stank. It stank amazingly. Tash wasn't familiar with the Insignia For Men body care range, but this guy was clearly no stranger to it. It was all over town and all over him. Shame he was a twat and wanted to kill Raymond because Tash could instantly picture a promising future together if she lived in 1984, which she didn't. And if she didn't have a baby waiting for her in 2020, which she did. Okay, there were a few hurdles, but it was good to have a starting point, and it was good to have something to aim for. It was then she wondered where's Jamie, and why isn't he helping? She glanced over as far as her headlock would allow and spotted Isabel tending to Jesus and helping him back into his wheelchair, his eyes half-closed as he tried to make sense of how the hell he'd ended up on the floor.

Then Jamie spoke.

"Jesus, let Raymond and Maureen go, or the owl gets it."

Everyone looked around to see Jamie standing behind Jesus's wheelchair. Talon scratches created a three-tier red stripe across his cheek, his thinning hair stood in mad directions, his jumper was ripped, and he had a general look of being covered in owl shit. His appearance told the story of a man who'd admirably struggled to get an owl in a neck hold. No easy task for an animal with no apparent neck, but here it was being pinned to Jamie's chest, firm but fair. It wasn't distressed. Jamie wouldn't have allowed that. But the bird was definitely incapacitated, and its wide eyes glared at Tash as if betraying its evil plans for the moment this prick let him go. Jamie's free hand was holding a loaded mousetrap at arm's length, with the respect you might offer a de-pinned hand grenade.

Jesus glared at Jamie. He'd struck a nerve. "Owls never forget."

Jamie swallowed as this bizarre threat landed.

"Must get one. I'd never miss the dentist again," said Tash.

"But, he wouldn't be able to remind you, would he? Cos he can't speak," replied Jamie.

Tash paused to look at her literal brother. "We'd have some wing signals for dentist."

Jesus spoke again, in fact, he almost snorted. "You think this trap will catch a bird?"

"No," conceded Jamie, his brain frantically searching for something scary to say. "No. But it won't be pleased if I stick its beaky face in it."

Everyone grimaced, even Tash from beneath the armpit.

"Or I could stick one of its toe things in it," said Jamie, clearly running out of ideas.

Everyone grimaced again, and Tash corrected him. "Talons."

"Talons," copied Jamie.

There was a brief silence interrupted by Maureen's tummy rumbling and Raymond chivalrously taking the blame once more. "Pardon me."

Then Jamie had another thought to ramp up the pressure.

"Or I could stick its knob in it," said Jamie confirming he really was out of ideas before looking at Tash. "Do birds have knobs?"

"It's a good question, Jamie. Terrible timing. Great question. Maybe you can ask Terry Nutkin in heaven. In a couple of minutes."

"He's not dead yet. It's 1984."

"Oh yeah," replied Tash. "It's been a long day."

Jesus nodded at the male Overcoat and said, "Antonio."

With this, Antonio reached inside his Overcoat and extracted a handgun.

The hierarchy of threats is ever evolving, thought Jamie as he applied pressure to the small but deep pinhole that the mousetrap had made in his middle fingertip. A purple bruise was slowly revealing itself around the other side of his knuckle too, and he wondered if he had a black fingernail to look forward to in the coming days. Just five minutes ago, a trap would have been enough to trump a mouse. Then it was an owl. Owl trumps mouse, so the owl was the threat. Then a fire extinguisher was holding the cards, as a cosh and a temporary freezing agent. Not the cold type of freezing, the freezing-time type with its unexpected bewildering capacity. And then Antonio had trumped all of that with a gun.

"Gun trumps pretty much everything," said Jamie, not realising he was no longer using his internal voice.

No one answered.

Why hadn't they just pulled the gun at the start? That would have been a good enough threat to get Raymond to spill the beans. Not that he had any beans. Raymond really did have no idea where his former boss was. But no, this Jesus guy had psychopathic tendencies, what with the cheese spread and the mice and the pet owl and all that. So, it wasn't so surprising to see this madman happily gesticulating to what turned out to be his son and daughter in matching overcoats as they set up part two of their siege. The part that made everything else seem tame. So far, they'd been very much living in CBeebies or Nickelodeon world.

Things were about to get very Amazon Prime.

Chapter Fifteen

About twelve feet above the warehouse floor, angle iron was spanning the gap between two sets of racking. Hanging from it was a seriously thick rope noose. Jesus had mercilessly asked Raymond to stand up so his son could measure his height and then used some rudimentary maths to calculate the optimum height for the rope.

Bizarrely, instead of a trap door or step up to the noose, there was a sort of drum wrapped in wax paper, and now standing on it with his head through the knotted rope was a very pale-looking Raymond. He'd had better days.

Jesus clapped his hands to get the attention of his tied and bound audience. Maureen remained strapped to her chair, and Jamie and Tash were bound back-to-back on the floor at her feet. All of them experienced a new low of despair in the pits of their stomachs.

Attempts by each and every one of them to start a dialogue with Jesus had failed, and they were all clutching on to the hope that this little pantomime must surely include an opportunity to extricate themselves from this gruesome ending.

"Raymond," announced Jesus.

"Yes, Mr Moron," replied Raymond breathlessly. His mouth was entirely dry.

"I fix problems."

"You couldn't help me with this one, could you?" replied Raymond.

Jesus laughed again and wheeled a little closer to Raymond.

"People around London town must know that Jesus Morón is not a fool, yes?"

Raymond glanced at this weirdo in a white suit with an owl on his shoulder.

"Well, this is it," said Raymond.

"Papá, no sabe nada. Está aterrorizado, ya es suficiente. Detener," said Isabel to her father, which seemed to irritate him, he spun his wheelchair to glare at her.

"Tiene veinte mil de sobra? Quieres que esta ciudad cree que soy un payaso?" his voice sounded like a bark.

Jamie was taking it all in. His A-Level Spanish hadn't incorporated mafia vocab, but he believed he was getting the gist.

"She's telling him to stop. They're just trying to scare us," he said to the prisoners around him. "I think Dudley owed him money. Twenty grand or something."

"Oh my God, where the hell will we get that kind of money?" whispered Maureen before turning her attention to Tash. "You bring problems every time I see you."

"I came to fix things!" whispered Tash.

"Well, I'm so pleased. This is all working out so well," replied Maureen before tearing up again and nodding at her husband. "That's my whole family up there!"

Jesus turned to the hostages. "OK. Let's go around the room and introduce ourselves one by one, starting with me. Hallo. I am Jesus Morón."

His audience waited. He raised his pa to his shoulder, and the owl hopped onto his hand. As he rubbed its plumage, he continued.

"I am a man of business. I help people. I help people with problems. Dudley Hobson had problems. He come to me and say – Jesus, I am a man of honour. A man you can trust. And he asks for my help. Twenty thousand pounds of help. It's business. He spends my money on this..." he gestured at the shithole they were all trapped in, "and then agrees to repay me my money plus a little of his money in Diciembre. So when I come here, and he is not here, I worry. So, I visit his house. He is not there. He is gone. With my money. And I am now no longer a man of business, but I am el payaso, yes?"

Everyone nodded in earnest agreement.

"Payaso is clown," said Isabel.

Everyone stopped nodding, and all spoke simultaneously with lots of 'not-at-all' and 'absolutely-not' type platitudes.

"But you refuse to tell me where he is?" said Jesus.

"We don't know where he is," said Maureen. "We don't!"

She thought for a moment before nodding at Jamie and Tash. "Well, they might, but I don't think you should believe a word they say. Especially her."

Jamie and Tash opted to keep quiet. How the hell would the truth help right now?

Oh, the thing is Dudley died a few months ago; he'd travelled back to 1920 and lived in Vermont and made millions.

No, even Tash couldn't make that sound right.

"I think if my clients hear that I kill Dudley for stealing from me, then my life will be far simpler from now on, yes?" said Jesus.

"Well, here's an idea Mr Moron... can't you just *tell* them you er, you er, that you killed him?" suggested Raymond. "I mean – I won't tell them the truth?"

Everyone muttered their agreement with lots of 'neither

would I' and 'that's a brilliant idea' and 'I'm glad we got that sorted, actually' type remarks.

"No. I have a new idea," said Jesus before looking straight into Raymond's eyes.

"Te matare," said Jesus. He explained. "Is Spanish. It means 'I kill you'. People will get the same message, yes?"

The room went quiet, then Jamie spoke.

"I have a question."

"Yes?" asked Jesus.

"Seems strange that you would choose the familiar 'tu' variant," said Jamie.

"What?" asked Jesus.

"No, I'm just saying, surely killing someone you don't know should deserve a more formal *Voy?* Something like *Voy a matar usted*?"

"I'm just mentally running through some of the observations you've shared with strangers over the years, Jamie, but this one's a game-changer," said Tash.

"This is nothing personal, you understand. But I must protect my honour," said Jesus, ignoring Jamie.

"Where did you get your hands on twenty K?" asked Tash.

"Excuse me?" asked Jesus.

"You heard. Where do you get all your capital?"

"That's my business." Jesus smiled.

"You're a launderer, aren't you? If you had twenty grand of clean money, why would you risk it on a no-hoper like Dudley?"

"Launderer?" asked Jamie.

"Money launderer. Like in *Ozark*," explained Tash.

"What's *Ozark*?" asked Maureen before turning to look at Raymond. "What's *Ozark*?"

"It's on Netflix," said Jamie.

"Probably won't have time for that, Jamie," replied Tash

before turning to Maureen. "Imagine MTV but with movies instead of songs. And all the movies are the same. And have Adam Sandler in them."

"Who?" said Maureen.

"You see Jamie? See what you've started?"

"Can anyone tell me what's happening?" asked Raymond from behind the group.

"Jesus here, cleans dirty money," said Tash. "Probably stolen or drugs money. He replaces it with legit stuff. He lends it to people like Dudley – people who need cash – desperate people. They take the risk – but they're not spending it all on one go, so chances are they'll go under the radar when they spend it. Then they pay it back plus interest – and it's all clean and untraceable."

"You are very clever," said Jesus.

"Not really. I'm supposed to be setting the table for Christmas dinner," said Tash.

"So, you're down twenty grand?" asked Jamie.

"Thirty," replied Jesus, "if you add the interest."

"Wow. Fifty per cent interest, impressive," said Tash.

"What if we laundered some money for you? Would you let us all go?" asked Jamie.

"Oh, for Christ's sake, Jamie, don't make things worse," said Tash.

"What if we cleaned a shed-load of money for you in twenty-four hours?" said Jamie with alarming confidence.

Everyone was silent – Raymond and Maureen with hope, Tash with despair.

Jesus glared at this strange English man, staring back at him with wide-eyed excitement.

"And how do you do this?"

"That's my business," replied Jamie.

Tash held her breath. Christ, that was brave. Or extremely

stupid. She was already resigned to losing her brother to his new life in the 1980s, but she wasn't ready to see him dead. She leant back and whispered over her shoulder, "What the fuck are you doing?"

But Jamie was playing hardball with Jesus – neither wanting to be the first to blink.

Then Jesus spoke. "Antonio, loosen him."

Antonio untied Jamie from his sister and pulled him up to his feet, then tied Tash to Maureen's chair leg.

"Come with me," said Jesus, and wheeled himself through the doorway of the office. Now was the first time they'd all noticed the squeak on the left wheel. He looked over to signal Jamie to follow, which he did. Antonio guarded the door, and Jamie lowered himself onto the leather Chesterfield sofa as Jesus started to question him, out of earshot of the others. They occasionally glanced over at Raymond before their conflab continued. He was shuffling a lot, almost like he thought there might still be a mouse secreted somewhere about his mostly nylon outfit.

"Hands up, who thinks Jamie's been replaced by an alien?" said Tash, unable to raise her bound arms and aware that the others couldn't either. She stared for a moment.

"Hands up, who can't put their hands up?"

"Is there any chance I might loosen this a little? It's giving me a bit of a friction burn," said Raymond nodding down at his noose beneath his chin, and eyeing Isabel.

Isabel slowly walked over to Raymond before being stopped by Jesus.

"Isabel. Get the money," he demanded, nodding at the shutters.

"What?" she replied.

"You heard me. Get the money."

"How much?"

Jesus turned to Jamie to ensure he heard his slow and slightly threatening reply.

"All of it."

He gestured to his son to help.

CHAPTER SIXTEEN

The orange VW T2 camper van was parked around the corner of the entrance to Bay 3. Tash and Jamie hadn't clocked it on their way in, probably because the left hand drive 1979 model didn't look out of place outside Butler's Wharf in 1984. The location had yet to become gentrified, and the diversity of traffic typically included the lesser marques and models compared to 2020. The painted-out windows were subtle, and the E badge on the rear bumper, and Spanish registration plate suggested it was well travelled. As Antonio finished unloading from the side door, Isabel gently poured water into the mouth of a trembling milkman who was tied and bound to the floor. She then replaced some gaffer tape over his mouth and reassured him he would be home soon. She stepped outside and slammed the door closed, ensuring it was locked before helping her brother carry the baggage over to the warehouse. They both side-stepped past the milk float then Raymond's Princess as they continued to the large door.

The sound of the roller shutter lowering was followed by the sight of Isabel and Antonio returning. Isabel clutched a long holdall in both hands, it was a very dark, dirty shade of red, and the side indicated the remains of a long since peeled off Dunlop logo. Antonio held another with one hand. His was a brown Gola branded one, with Iberia flight labels still stuck around the handle. His other hand pulled a suitcase behind him. This was the first-generation Samsonite roller type, where the classic suitcase design remained, but a large metal bar could be extended from one side as a long dragging handle, and the opposite lower corner housed two tiny wheels. It was an admirable skill to cover more than a metre without the top-heavy design falling over, but he was handling things capably.

Jesus and Jamie exited the office, and Jesus offered his hand to Jamie, who cautiously shook it whilst keeping one eye on the owl.

"Children, let our guests see our stock," smiled Jesus.

Isabel started to unzip the holdalls as Antonio lay his case down and flicked open the lid. He spun it around so his audience could see. At the same time, Isabel opened the holdalls wide.

"One. Million. Pounds," said Jesus.

"Nice," said Tash. "We'd clap, but you tied us up."

"Clean this, and we forget everything," said Jesus.

"What?" said Tash. "Launder a million quid?"

"No problem," said Jamie.

"Have you any idea how much a million quid is worth in 1984?" said Tash to Jamie, causing Jesus to frown in confusion.

"No problem," repeated Jamie.

"Jamie, stop talking to Colonel fucking Sanders! Stop agreeing to crimes!"

"And everyone lives?" said Jamie, ignoring her.

"Of course," said Jesus, who then kindly smiled, showing his stained teeth.

"Wait, you're saying you'll let us walk out of here with a million quid? And you're trusting us to come back with it?" asked Tash.

"There are police from all over Europe looking for this money. You'll be arrested the moment you try to spend any."

"We won't spend any. We'll clean it," said Jamie.

Tash's mouth made various shapes as she attempted to formulate a sentence that fully conveyed her utter bewilderment and despair, but before she was able, Jesus spoke.

"Good," said the Spaniard before gesturing to Raymond and nodding at Antonio. "Release him."

"Thank you, sir," muttered Raymond through dry lips. "Gracias."

"Not at all," said Jesus.

Then he added a tiny caveat.

"You have three hours."

He pointed at Maureen.

"Or I kill her."

Maureen let out her loudest whimper of the day so far.

CHAPTER SEVENTEEN

As the shutter door lowered, Jamie spotted the Princess mirror on the warehouse floor and attempted to reach inside to retrieve it but failed as the concertina steel slammed closed to the ground. It didn't quite make the warehouse as secure as it should, given the damage inflicted on it during the break-in, but it was good enough. One amber globe glowed across the cobbled driveway. They had been inside longer than they realised, and the dim streetlight just about showed their breath in the late afternoon air.

"What the actual fuck, Jamie?" was the first thing Tash said as they walked toward the parked Princess.

"I have a very, very good plan," said Jamie, laden with a holdall on his shoulder. Raymond pulled the suitcase, and Tash carried the remaining holdall.

"What the flipping heck have you done to my car?" said Raymond, as the Princess came into view. Damn, thought Jamie. How the hell had he spotted the damage?

"The bumper's hanging off!"

In fairness, Jamie knew that would have been evident sooner or later.

"Where's the wing mirror?" said Raymond.

"You know Kennington Park?" asked Jamie.

"Yes?"

"There."

Jamie moved around the back of the car and opened the boot. "Bring yours around."

"What is the actual plan, actually?" asked Tash.

"I'll tell you once we're away from here, from them!" replied Jamie.

They all loaded their bags and the suitcase into the boot and then climbed into the car. Tash climbed in the passenger seat, Raymond up front and Jamie in the back, who leant forward between the others and flicked on the internal light.

"See? That still works!" said Jamie.

Raymond reached up without thinking to adjust the rear-view mirror. His hand continued through the gap where the windscreen once was.

"Where's the mirror... Wait, where's the windscreen?"

Jamie shrugged.

"How am I supposed to see what's behind me?" said Raymond. "We can't drive this thing anywhere. We'll get arrested!"

"We need to get moving, he said three hours," said Tash.

"I'm aware of how long my wife has to live, thank you."

"What about your Transit? Where's that?" asked Tash.

"Jermaine took it to Brighton for a trip," replied Raymond.

"Will he be back soon?" asked Tash.

"Doubt it," said Raymond.

"Why?"

"He was due back last Sunday," said Raymond, looking distinctly sad. He twitched again and peered inside his jacket to check he was vermin-free.

"He's nicked your van?"

"Well, we shouldn't judge until we find out what happened, with regard to, you know," but he was interrupted by Tash.

"He's nicked your van!"

"Why don't we take the milk float?" suggested Jamie, climbing out of the car and heading towards the stolen milk carrier. He was keen to change the subject.

"What? We can't drive a stolen vehicle. I don't want to get fingered for a crime I didn't commit."

"I don't think it would come to that, Raymond. They'd probably just arrest you," said Tash.

"I think we've taken too much on," said Raymond.

"You think?" said Tash. "The nicking a milk float part – or the laundering one million pounds of stolen money bit?"

"The keys are in!" shouted a delighted Jamie, immediately followed by the hum of the engine and the headlights lighting up the interior of the Princess.

"My God, there's blood on my radio!" said Raymond.

"Don't worry," said Tash, climbing out of the car. "That's mine."

"Are you alright?" Raymond looked concerned as he clambered to his feet too.

"Oh yes. This is fine. All of it. No problem with my day at all."

Jamie started to empty the boot of the Princess and transfer the holdalls and suitcase to the rear of the milk float. Tash walked over and sat herself upfront on the bench seat, staring into space. How the hell had things escalated so quickly? She was supposed to post a newspaper through a letterbox and then go home to 2020.

Raymond needlessly locked his beloved car, stopping to check the door handle before making his way to the milk float and opting to slide alongside Tash.

"Can you drive, please, Raymond?" said Jamie dragging him back onto the cobbles. "I need to explain the plan."

"You have a plan? I'm so pleased," said Tash.

Jamie nodded and slid alongside his sister to the middle of the seat. Raymond cautiously sat behind the wheel and perused the small bank of switches at his disposal.

"Do we have to deliver some eggs first, or can we hear the plan now?" asked Tash, irritated by Jamie's silence.

"Here's how I see it," said Jamie. "Jesus wants thirty grand off Dudley, but Dudley's dead, so he wants thirty grand off Raymond, but Raymond doesn't have it, so he's going to kill Maureen to let his other clients know that he's not a man to mess with."

"That's very perceptive, Jamie, but I think we're all up to speed already. Particularly with the Maureen death thing."

Raymond was now attempting to reverse the milk float into the main street, and in fairness, he was doing OK other than his muttering of, "We're only third-party fire and theft on the Princess. I'm going to need another bank loan."

"So, I suggested we took his dirty money and launder it for him, instead," said Jamie, ignoring the distractions.

"Yeah, I have a few questions about that one, Jamie," said Tash, turning to Raymond for his permission and asking, "OK, if I go first? With the questions?"

Raymond nodded, so Tash turned to her brother and started shrieking in his face. Really loudly. "WHAT THE ACTUAL FUCK?"

Before thinking and adding, "YOU KNOB!" And then nipping his arm.

Jamie didn't like loud noises, and Tash immediately felt terrible but similarly justified as she'd had to let her frustration out somehow. Yes, he was on the autistic spectrum, but that didn't stop him from being a legitimate tit from time to time. Tash took a deep breath and then spoke more calmly.

"How do we swap that million for another million?" she asked whilst gesturing to money amongst the crates behind them. "Have you even given that any consideration? They're going to kill Maureen, Jamie!"

On being reminded of this yet again, Raymond reversed into the VW camper van parked behind them. They all rocked a little, a muffled shriek from the VW went unheard, and Raymond selected the forward gear. Jamie fumbled in his jeans pocket and then unfurled the front page of tomorrow's *Observer* newspaper, the one that had delivered the news of Raymond's impending death later today. He leaned in to squint at it and then glanced up to see if there was an interior light to help his sight. After fumbling with a few rubber strips, he found a tiny plastic rocker switch that lit a tiny bulb. His fingers followed his gaze to a small box of text on the newspaper's front page, titled *BRIEFLY...* His fingers slid below and over the print to the subheader: *£1m jugglers.* Then he read a story that barely covered an inch of the broadsheet:

"Yesterday, the BBC found its safe was bigger than the TV Centre corridors, so staff were drafted in to secretly move one million pounds in ten-pound notes from the entrance to a studio for Paul Daniels to record a trick for the magician's Christmas show."

Jamie stopped reading and smiled at his sister.

"Oh my God," said Tash burying her head in her hands. "Oh my God."

They drove in silence for a moment before Tash added her next thought.

"Oh my God."

"I don't understand," said Raymond, slowly driving the milk float along the side road, squinting at the glare from the interior light.

"This is tomorrow's newspaper. They'll be filming that tonight. We just swap our money with theirs," Jamie made it sound as simple as posting a letter. Assuming you had the correct address.

"Oh my actual God," said Tash.

"I also have another idea to make a million, but it might take a little longer," said Jamie.

"Let's have it," said Tash.

"OK," said Jamie. "You know when bands or singers release *Best Of* albums? With all their biggest hits on them?"

"Yes," replied Tash impatiently. "Does this entail us releasing an album?"

"Kind of," said Jamie.

"And it sells millions, does it?"

"Yep."

"What's on it?" asked Tash.

Jamie was proud. He sat up straight and took a deep breath before revealing his get-rich plan.

"It's a double album..." he said. "And it's *The Best Of... The Best Ofs*!"

"What?"

"Imagine, it's the best of all the best ofs. Now that's gotta be a good record." Jamie meant it.

"Does this go any faster?" said Tash to Raymond, who responded by shaking his head slowly.

The milk float approached the junction with the main road.

"I think we've taken too much on," said Raymond as he looked for the indicators.

CHAPTER EIGHTEEN

BBC TV Centre in Shepherd's Bush was impressive from the front. The iconic *Television Centre* logo clung high on the outer brick wall of Studio 1 (or TC1 as it was known to staff), the largest and most famous of all the studios. Jamie immediately pictured the shiny pinballs bursting out of the walls on the opening credits of Saturday morning's *Live & Kicking* show when he was a kid. Living in London did nothing to remove that tingle of excitement when seeing this iconic building, especially now – in its former mid-80s glory. By 2020, the building had been repurposed, refurbed, partially demolished before being rebuilt as mostly apartments. Some studios remained, but these were commercially available for all broadcasters. In fact, in 2020, Jamie still felt odd watching Phillip Schofield and Holly Willoughby presenting ITV's *This Morning* from the BBC forecourt. Although right now, that wouldn't be physically possible given that the whole front of the building was a packed car park.

An eight-mile-an-hour journey across the eight miles from Butler's Wharf to Shepherd's Bush wasn't as frustrating as

Tash had suspected, given the slow pace of all the other London traffic. Some drivers had even flashed the milk float to allow it to enter roads ahead of them. Jamie said it felt like being the fourth emergency service. Until they remembered the coast guard. And then Tash remembered that the AA staked a claim to that sort of thing as an advertising campaign some years before, too, so they agreed they were somewhere around the ninth or tenth – as the population did need calcium. Their route had bizarrely taken them past St. Thomas Hospital, where they had collectively spent far longer than they might have hoped back in October. They had even been around the same roundabout in Shepherd's Bush as last time, but on this occasion, Raymond stuck diligently to his lane to avoid being arrested. And this time, they had taken the right turn as they'd opted to approach the main entrance to TV Centre. That was Raymond's idea as he feared the back gate might be locked and unmanned.

Bizarrely, the mere sight of a milk float approaching the gates was enough for them to open to allow the vehicle to trundle straight in.

"I need to get me one of these for home," said Tash, in amazement that nobody had even questioned their identity or intention. They were delivering milk, of course they were.

"Evening," said the commissionaire by the gate, barely glancing up at a very nervous Raymond clutching the wheel. "It's a cold one. I could do without being stuck here!"

"Yes," said Raymond. "Sorry."

As they drove from earshot, Tash started to lose all confidence in the sketchy plan they'd half-formed as they idled across the streets of London.

"This is fucking ridiculous."

"Don't have a wobble, now," said Jamie.

"What if we're too late?" said Tash.

"They record shows in the evenings. We know that."

"What if they've already started?" Tash was glancing around the building for signs of a queueing audience. She'd seen queues before when passing. Audience members were usually held outside for as long as possible, but there was no sign of anyone tonight.

"Tash, you're not helping," said Jamie.

"Maureen will be livid when she sees the car," said Raymond as he slowly parked the milk float under the colonnade by the entrance into the main reception.

"Well, look on the bright side," said Jamie.

"Is there a bright side?" said Raymond.

"Well, if we mess this up, she won't see it at all, will she?"

Raymond's jaw dropped wide open.

"He's kidding," said Tash. "Tell him you're kidding, Jamie."

"I was being honest," said Jamie.

"Can you find out which studio they're recording in, please?" said Tash, momentarily distracted from her despair by that of Raymond, and pushing Jamie away.

Jamie slid off the bench seat and walked through the doors into reception. Well, he walked into a locked glass door to start with, but when he struggled to push it open, he moved along until he found an opening one. A rather stern-looking lady glanced up at him over her enormous horn-rimmed spectacles. She had a look of a severe headmistress who'd just received a rogue snowball in her face from a pupil who had dared to confuse a blizzard with joy.

Happily, Jamie wasn't great at reading expressions, so Tash remained confident that Jamie wouldn't be in the slightest part intimidated and might just get most of the information they needed. She glanced through to the inner courtyard of the circular building and eyed the turned off fountain. She'd seen many TV shows broadcast from here growing up, usually presenters walking through from one place to another with such a casual demeanour betraying how magical it must feel working in a place so exciting.

But her thoughts soon returned to the job in hand – she was about to commit a massive crime. Something she wished she had more time to plan. She'd already decided that she would do the lion's share of the money switch, as she would soon be safely living in 2020. Raymond and her brother would need to continue their lives in 1984, so it wouldn't be wise to have identikit pictures of their faces plastered on next month's *Crimewatch*. Bizarrely, Jamie was now laughing with the lady at reception, and he seemed to be writing something down. She pointed over her shoulder to the stage doors on the far tiled wall, and he listened intently before making more notes.

"We could just call the police and tell them everything," said Tash.

"What?" Raymond wasn't expecting this crisis of faith.

"This is stupid. We're innocent. We should just call the police now."

"No. Jesus said if he heard any police, he'd... he'd..." his voice trailed off, unable to finish the sentence.

"But the police don't need to rock up with sirens and stuff. We'd tell them everything. Maybe they'd send in the SAS or something? You never hear them coming!"

"Maureen wouldn't like that sort of thing," said Raymond. "She hates people sneaking around. Makes her jumpy."

"It's not really about what she likes, Raymond. I'm guessing she quite likes living?"

Raymond considered this. "Well, yes."

Tash nodded.

"I think so," added Raymond, squirming again in his clothes. "She keeps her cards very close to her chest."

CHAPTER NINETEEN

Tash glanced over at reception. What was Jamie doing now? The lady had opened the double doors and was gesturing down the corridor. Jamie was nodding and frantically making even more notes. This was either going well, or he was asking how he might get his next painting on Tony Hart's *Gallery*.

Their plan to switch one million pounds of dirty money for clean was essentially quite simple, but Tash also feared quite naive. They'd had sixty minutes to fine-tune it on their journey over, and despite their limited resources, they'd all agreed that they didn't have further options. So, it had been decided. They would attempt Jamie's really shit idea, or Maureen would die.

"I bet we're too late," repeated Tash, shuffling on the seat.

"You're not really helping actually," said Raymond, rubbing his hands together.

Tash looked over at him.

"Sorry," he added.

"No. I'm sorry, Raymond," said Tash, rubbing his arm.

Jamie was walking towards them now and turning to say

farewell to his new friend. He pushed the glass door open, except he didn't, so he smashed his face into another fixed one. As he finally opened the actual door, his expression was difficult to gauge.

Were they in time?

Would Maureen live?

Did his face hurt?

"She was lovely!" said Jamie. "Did you know they turned that massive fountain off 'cos it was too noisy? The polo shape of the building amplified the noise, and people couldn't hear anything!"

He was pointing to the base of the Helios fountain that Tash had been admiring moments before.

"Tell me you didn't forget why you were in there?" replied Tash.

"Not at all. I told her I was a reporter for the *Daily Mail* and I knew about the money being moved around the building. She was very happy to fill me in. She told me everything! Who decided on the plan, the route to the studio, everything!"

"So, we're too late?" said Tash. "We're too late, aren't we?"

"Only a bit," said Jamie, sliding onto the seat next to his sister.

"How late is a bit?" asked Raymond.

"Six days," said Jamie. "They recorded it last Sunday. That's why she told me everything."

"Sake," said Tash. Why weren't even the most bizarre tasks even slightly straightforward? How hard could it possibly be to infiltrate the BBC and steal a million pounds from a magician in a tuxedo?

"We'll just explain to Jesus that we've had a spot of bother," said Raymond. "He'll understand. Maybe we could come up with another plan?"

"You've got a mouse on your shoulder," said Tash, watching it circle the stitching on his shirt.

Raymond recoiled and knocked it off. It fell on his lap, and he squealed. Tash did too. All three of them leapt out of the milk float and peered into the cabin. The mouse looked back at them. This was a real battle of wills. Who would blink first?

"I knew it! I could feel it!" said Raymond.

"It's just a mouse," said Jamie, trying to calm everyone.

"You got out too," said Tash.

"Maybe we've got some cheese in the back of here?" said Jamie, looking into the crates on the float.

"You want to feed it?" asked Tash.

"I want to set a little trail to coax it out," said Jamie.

"Raymond, just twat it with a milk bottle or something," said Tash.

"What it?" asked Raymond.

"Twat it! Hit it!" said Tash.

"Kill it?" Raymond was horrified. "It's more scared of us, look."

"No, it's not. They carry diseases. Look at its face. It's planning something. You can tell it works for that bastard."

"I've still got my trap!" said Jamie, fiddling in his jeans pocket and holding up the vicious contraption. It snapped on his finger again causing him to shout. "No!"

"We need to get on," said Tash. "Maureen or mouse, Raymond. Maureen or mouse? Who are you gonna save? Maureen? Mouse? Maureen? Mouse?"

Raymond thought and leant in to extract one of the few full bottles of milk. He upturned it and practised using it like a cosh into the palm of his hand.

"Get on with it then," said Tash.

"Really?"

"I'm not getting back in there with a mouse," said Tash.

Raymond leant into the cabin then started flailing madly, thumping the bottle onto the seat, again and again, and again.

An outsider might assume he was unleashing thirty-odd years of repression; others might think he just hated mice.

"Bloody hell," said Raymond.

"What is it?" asked Jamie.

"The top's come off."

"Of the mouse?" said Jamie.

"Eugh!" said Tash.

"The milk," said Raymond.

"Did you kill it?" asked Tash.

"I can't see," said Raymond turning to Tash, his face and hair dripping in milk.

They all peered into the milky seat and agreed that maybe the mouse had made a run for it, as Raymond had spectacularly missed his target.

"Get back in," said Tash perching on the remaining dry part of the bench seat, lifting her legs off the floor in case the mouse remained. Raymond rubbed his face and hair to flick off the milk and then sat alongside her.

"What's the plan?" he asked.

Tash took a deep, exasperated breath and couldn't believe her ears when she heard her own voice.

"We're going back to last bloody Sunday, aren't we? Sake."

CHAPTER TWENTY

"I'm really not sure about this. I'm not a great traveller," said Raymond.

"No one's going anywhere if we can't find a plug," said Tash.

They were standing in Raymond's garage on Abbot's Park. Jamie was rummaging through some painted wooden drawers housed in a cabinet along the back wall. Tash struggled to pull the garage door closed from the inside. She needed to hide their efforts from prying eyes outside. The parked milk float disappeared as the door finally slammed shut with a metallic twang.

"If it's anything like a boat, I can't go," said Raymond, now stuttering in fear as he examined the modified Sinclair C5 that sat on the concrete floor before him.

"Why would it be anything like a boat?" said Tash.

"I'm just saying. I had a bad experience on a pedalo in Salou."

"I don't think there is any other kind of experience on a pedalo in Salou, is there?" said Tash.

"Got one!" said Jamie holding a 13-amp three-pin plug

proudly above his head before dropping it. "No!" he added as he crouched to pick it up from the floor.

Raymond's expression was the perfect picture of a conflicted man. He'd just found out that it might still be possible to save his wife's life, but it meant travelling on a DIY time machine that had only brought outright misery wherever it went.

Jamie had evidently visited the garage before as he managed to find a screwdriver in no time and set about opening up the plastic plug so he could attach it to the main cable that lay stripped bare at the tail of the C5.

"How does this work, actually?" asked Raymond, slowly pacing around the go-kart.

"There's an electric motor," said Jamie, without looking up from his work. "It powers the left rear wheel. It's coupled with a two-stage gear drive."

Raymond waited for more. When nothing came, he spoke.

"I know how the C5 works, Jamie. I want to know how it travels through time."

"Oh!" said Jamie before he started laughing. "I thought you meant the C5!"

Raymond joined in with an awkward laugh. "No! No! I wanted to know how time travel works."

They both laughed a little more before silence returned.

"Well?" said Raymond.

"No idea," said Jamie. "Grandad built it."

"I'm not sure all three of us will fit on there," said Tash, eyeing up the seat that her grandfather had extended to take two riders. "And even if we do, surely it won't shift under the weight?"

"The torque is what makes it shift," said Jamie, choosing not to add any further explanation, which disappointed Tash as she was hoping for a little more.

"We're gonna fall out if you keep talking like a twat off *Top*

Gear," said Tash. "What do those words mean?" She hated engines and hated TV shows with know-it-all knobs talking about engines.

"It needs a downward force to make it go."

"Right," said Tash, looking Raymond up and down. His paunch belly was visible for all to see. "Raymond's packing quite a lot of force, though, isn't he?"

"Me and Maureen quite like Sue Baker. She didn't mince her words on the new Montego," said Raymond, oblivious to the body shaming.

"Say again?" said Tash, a little bemused.

"You said the *Top Gear* hosts were twits," said Raymond.

"She said twats," interrupted Jamie.

Raymond acknowledged this minor correction then continued. "We like watching Sue. And William whatsisname."

"Well, enjoy it now," said Tash. "'Cos the pricks take over sooner or later. One after another after another after another. Awful show."

"I suppose we need to decide the best place to arrive," said Jamie, still busily attaching the coloured wires to the plug pins.

"Best place?" Said Raymond.

"Yeah. When we go back to Sunday, we need to choose the best place to arrive. Maybe around the back of TV Centre or something."

"We're going to arrive here, Jamie. So we can hide this in this garage under lock and key. There is absolutely no way whatsoever that I'm leaving this thing to be stolen, or stripped, or damaged in any way. Not like before. This is my ticket out of here."

If Jamie registered her saying 'my' and not 'our', he didn't let on.

"How will we get to Shepherd's Bush, then?" asked Raymond. "In the milk float?"

"Was the milk float outside the garage on Sunday?" said Tash.

"Oh," replied Raymond, visibly deflated. "No."

"What about taking your car?" asked Tash.

"We'd need to set off quietly, though, so as not to disturb ourselves in the house," said Jamie.

"How do you mean, exactly?" asked Raymond.

"There'll be two lots of you and me," said Jamie. "We're going back in time. And we can't allow ourselves to be seen by our old selves, 'cos our old selves need to continue with what they were doing to allow us to be here now."

Raymond stared at Jamie for what felt like an hour.

"No, you've lost me."

"Just do what we say. You'll soon get the hang of things," said Tash. "What time did they move the money, Jamie?"

"What?"

"The money that we're going to steal. What time did the staff move it to the studio? We need to know that so we can switch the cash."

Jamie pulled the notes from his pocket and squinted at the bullet points he'd made during his spontaneous interview with the BBC receptionist. He flicked the paper over, then back again. He carried on staring at it. Then at the other side again. "Erm."

"What time, Jamie?" asked Tash.

Jamie looked again. "I don't know."

"What? You don't know what time we need to be there to intercept one million quid?"

"Er," said Jamie, reading again. "The money arrived... soon after half four." He looked happy with this news, adding another "half four" with a smile. Well, half a smile.

"Cool. We can be there waiting. It doesn't matter when they originally shifted it, does it, as long as we don't arrive too late?"

"Hang on, we used the Princess to go to the Berni Inn for Maureen's birthday on Sunday night," said Raymond.

"Sake. What time did you set off?" asked Tash.

Raymond looked at Jamie, and together they both muttered a few uncertain times before turning back to Tash and replying in unison, "About six," which Jamie followed with "thirty," causing Raymond to look confused again.

"Right, we need to be there by four and back here by six," said Tash.

Raymond nodded and repeated, "By six." He had his best listening ears on. This reminded him of the time Maureen explained how to use the grill. All was quite clear so far. Oh God, though. What if Maureen died? Maybe Jamie knew how to use the grill.

"How long does it take to drive from here to TV Centre?" asked Tash.

"Well, right now, it might be quite busy," Raymond started to say.

"Not now. We're not going now. We're going last Sunday," said Tash.

"Yes. I see what you mean. Well, it won't be too busy on a Sunday. We'll probably go through Clapham Common, take Battersea Bridge. Then Earl's Court," he continued, with his eyes half-closed as he pictured the route. "Then, erm, what's it called? Erm. Holland Road! That's it. Yes, Holland Road to Shepherd's Bush. And then we just tootle along Wood Lane."

Tash looked at him. He smiled back. She looked again.

"*How long* was the question, Raymond. *How long* will it take?"

"Sorry, yes. Erm. Well, let's see, if you were to walk it," he started to say, but Tash lost her patience.

"We're not going to fucking walk it! We're going to take your car! Last Sunday!"

"Yes. Yes, of course. It's all this past-tense stuff. It's a bit confusing. I've never done a heist in the past."

Tash checked the zips on the holdalls and then stood square in front of Raymond.

"Raymond. It might surprise you to know that we haven't either. But if we take things one step at a time, we might just pull this off. Personally, I have no faith in either one of you, and think we're going to fall at the first hurdle. So, tell me. How long will it take to drive from here, to BBC TV Centre, last Sunday afternoon?"

Raymond swallowed. The scratches on his face were dry now, and the trail of blood beneath his nose had turned almost black. Tash could see remnants of cheese spread, gluing the grey hairs in his nostrils.

"I would say we should allow perhaps an hour," he replied gently.

"Maybe more if we stop off anywhere," said Jamie, tightening the main screw on the plug cover.

"Stop off anywhere? What, like for a scotch egg or a happy meal?" asked Tash.

Jamie thought for a moment, then placed the screwdriver in his pocket.

"And how long to get back do you think, Raymond?" asked Jamie, detecting Tash was getting irritated.

"Is that a serious question?" asked Tash.

"I would say," replied Raymond, half closing his eyes again. "probably go Holland Road, and then...."

"Don't do the fucking route again, Raymond. Don't do the route! It's an hour! It's one hour. It's the same! One hour there, one hour back!" said Tash, before calming down and second-guessing they might know about some roadworks or something. "It is one hour, isn't it?"

"Give or take," said Raymond.

"So, we need to leave here at three, to get there for four.

And we need to leave there by five to get back here for six. And doing the maths, that means we have one hour to do the job. Any questions?"

Jamie raised his hand.

"You don't need to put your hand up, Jamie," said Tash.

"What time does Maureen like to have a play in the bath, Raymond?" asked Jamie.

Tash snorted. "What?"

"It starts at half two, so she likes to be in by then," replied Raymond.

"A play in the bath? What?" asked Tash.

The Afternoon Play on Radio 4," said Raymond.

"With you," said Tash.

"Although I seem to remember she was a little late because she watched the World Chess Final on BBC 2. I reckon she got in the bath around three," said Raymond.

"A real hoot, Sundays in your house, Raymond," said Tash.

"She doesn't really like chess if I'm honest, but she likes to say she's watched it to the rest of her poetry group," said Raymond quietly.

"She likes poetry?" said Tash. "She's a bit wild beneath that faded exterior, isn't she?"

Raymond didn't hear the insult. "No, she doesn't like poetry. It's so she can talk about it with her knitting group."

"Well, we really should draw a line under all this tremendously exciting Maureen stuff," said Tash, clapping her hands together. "Shall we agree on three o'clock, then?"

"Three o'clock is great," said Jamie. "Maureen had her birthday bath, and me and you went up the loft for the Christmas tree." He smiled at Raymond.

"You only put the Christmas tree up on Sunday?" Tash was genuinely surprised.

"Yeah, no one puts them up in November in 1984," said Jamie. "Weird!"

"It's all a bit H. G. Wells, isn't it?" said Raymond, looking at the Sinclair again. Things had suddenly become very real in his head.

"What is?" asked Tash.

"This. This travelling in time. It's like something you see on *Tomorrow's World.*" In 1984 this 'vision of the future' technology show kept viewers engaged for thirty minutes or so, before *Top Of The Pops* began.

"I remember *Tomorrow's World*!" said Jamie. Delighted to have arrived at a mutual TV connection. "Philippa Forester!"

"Maggie Philbin," said Raymond, correcting him. "She's married to Cheggers, you know! She demonstrated a new kind of magic glass the other week. Technology really is amazing, isn't it?"

"How was it magic?" asked Tash.

"I'm not sure. We're still getting to grips with the video timer so it sort of flicked over to *Duty Free* on ITV."

"Sounds good, though," said Tash. It didn't.

"It was," said Raymond. He chuckled at the memory. "A dog stole David's shoe."

"Are we still on *Tomorrow's World*?" asked Tash.

"*Duty Free*. Quite amusing, really."

"It sounds hilarious, Raymond. The more I hear about it," replied Tash. "Anyway..."

Raymond looked morose. "She loved *Duty Free*, did Maureen. Not that she'd admit it, of course. That's why we taped *Tomorrow's World*. So, we could watch *Duty Free*, then watch *Tomorrow's World* later, so to speak."

"She's not dead, Raymond!" said Tash. "You keep past tensing her."

"No. You're right," agreed Raymond, perking up.

"Not yet," said Jamie, kindly but factually. Ever mindful of voicing the truth.

"Probably didn't need to say that bit," said Tash.

"Can we go over the plan? I'm not completely sure I understand it. I'm finding this all a little bit much, to be quite honest," said Raymond.

"Jamie, over to you. Quick as you can," said Tash.

"I don't have a plan," said Jamie.

Tash and Raymond looked at one another.

"Maybe not that quick," said Tash. "Bit slower?"

"I know that we're going to switch this money for Paul Daniel's money," said Raymond, pointing at the dirty cash. "But it can't be that simple. How do we do it? When? Where?"

"The security company pulled up at the main doors, the Beeb staff told them the safe wouldn't fit through the corridors. The boss got staff to shove it in their pockets and walk it from there, all the way to the studio," said Jamie.

"So, where do we come in?" asked Raymond.

"They held it in a lift, until the studio got their own safe," said Jamie. "A smaller one. I thought we could switch it in the lift."

"You make it sound so simple. We don't work there," said Raymond, "how do we get in?"

"Well, I know someone who has a BBC security pass," said Tash.

"Brilliant!" said Jamie, then a thought flashed into his brain. "Wait! I have one! In my bedroom!"

"Kind of what I meant," replied Tash.

CHAPTER TWENTY-ONE

"Get on," said Tash, the moment Jamie lifted the garage door. She had already seated herself upfront, and the glow of the portable TV screen was illuminating the holdall of cash stuffed onto her lap. The C5's power cable stretched from the rear into a surface mounted single socket on the wall. Jamie was clutching the BBC pass, still tied with string to a now heavily twisted and snapped off telescopic TV aerial.

"You tied a good knot, Jamie," said Tash as Jamie handed over the pass and string and bent aerial. "Might be time for you to have another go at shoelaces?"

"Thanks. Have you got another plug?" asked Jamie as he walked towards the C5.

"One step ahead of you," said Tash, holding a spare three-pin plug in the air. One constant of time travel was the need to replace the 13-amp plug that their grandfather hadn't considered would be sacrificed on each departure.

Raymond sat upright behind Tash, causing Jamie to double take at his head.

"Nice hat."

"It's a crash helmet," replied Raymond, from beneath an upturned Russell Hobbs slow cooker that he'd tied under his chin with the power cord.

"Are you sure?" asked Jamie.

"Of course, I'm sure. If I'm going to travel on this thing, I'm taking no chances."

"It's Maureen's Christmas present," explained Tash. "He's hidden it in here, so she doesn't find it. Get in, Jamie."

"Get in where? There's no room," replied Jamie, looking at the other holdall jammed tightly behind Raymond. Grandad had made an impressive job of converting his Sinclair C5 into a two-seater for his young grandchildren. Still, the extended seating arrangement was tight for two adults, let alone a rotund third one wearing a kitchen appliance.

"Get in!" shouted Tash. "And don't let go of that!"

Jamie looked over the other side of the C5 to see the Samsonite suitcase standing to attention with its pull bar awaiting Jamie's grasp. It was clearly Tash's intention that he'd drag this alongside them as they travelled.

Jamie awkwardly lowered himself onto Raymond's beige Farah trousers and was immediately struck by how wet they were.

"You're wet, Raymond."

"I do tend to perspire a little in stressful situations," explained Raymond. "I'm the same when we have the Princess M.O.T.'d."

"Well, at least that's something you don't need to worry about anymore," said Tash. "What with it being fucked and everything. Right, Jamie, suitcase. Hold tight."

Jamie grabbed the suitcase pull bar, Tash struck the ENTER button on the Spectrum keyboard, and the familiar musical routine started to play out as the rear wheels began to turn slowly.

"This is Band Aid!" said Jamie, as he heard the current U.K. number one single play from the speaker.

"Grandad changed the tune," explained Tash as she gripped the handlebars beneath her legs.

"Oh my God! I never asked you about Grandad! How did it feel seeing him? Did you have to explain everything? Did he tell you off? How did it feel?" said Jamie, suddenly quite emotional.

"It was a bit..." Tash stopped speaking as her head flung back and struck Jamie's chin, causing him to billiard into Raymond's slow cooker and protruding nose.

"Ow!" was the last thing they heard before the C5 sped from the garage into the open tarmac of Abbot's Park, straight towards the row of garages opposite. Raymond grimaced as he tried to ignore his amplifying anxiety levels. This was happening. Actually happening.

But then nothing really happened.

Everything went black for the briefest of moments, and then Tash found herself swerving to avoid a head-on collision with a painted purple aluminium up-and-over door that was speeding towards them. The ninety-degree turn would have been easier with a handbrake, so, Tash squeezing the bicycle-style brakes did very little. The three of them, and the C5, spun embarrassingly onto their sides and slid along the tarmac. Which was now wet.

They slowly sat up and examined their scratches and cuts. The C5 rear wheels spun slowly to a halt.

"Well, this won't be covered by the guarantee," muttered Raymond removing his slow cooker and examining a crack down the side.

"Help me!" said Tash, flipping the C5 back onto its three wheels. Jamie dusted the wet grit from his baggy jeans and stepped in to help Tash.

"It was the last one, as well. I'll have to go shopping on

Christmas Eve now," said Raymond. "Maureen won't like that one bit. We were going to listen to *Pride & Prejudice* on Radio 4."

"Oh well, every cloud," said Tash.

She leant down to steer the machine slowly back into its hiding place with Jamie pushing from behind, tiptoeing to avoid the stripped power cord trailing pathetically behind. Raymond slowly stood up, still gazing at his broken slow cooker, the end of the cord loosely wrapped around his neck.

"Get the suitcase!" shouted Tash, pointing over at the battered Samsonite that lay by the purple garage door.

"Maybe I'll get her that electric knife," muttered Raymond as he set off to fetch it. "If I can afford it."

"What?" asked Jamie.

"An electric knife. For Sunday roasts," explained Raymond sadly.

"You are an old romantic, Raymond," said Tash. "What about a new Hoover?"

"There's nothing wrong with her old Hoover," replied Raymond, genuinely perplexed.

"Frugal and romantic. You're such a keeper."

"Where's the milk float gone?" asked Raymond, suddenly aware of his surroundings.

"It's Sunday. Keep up," replied Tash.

Raymond absorbed this development and started to feel his face and limbs to ensure time travel hadn't deformed him like Dr David Bruce Banner in the *Incredible Hulk*. He loved the theme tune but still shuddered a bit when Banner shouted, "go away", as he started to morph into a green giant. But no, other than the damp trousers and a new nosebleed from Jamie's skull, things seemed OK so far.

"Blimey. So that's that then," said Raymond.

"What's what then?" asked Tash reversing the C5 into its final position. Jamie was already loosening the back of the new plug to fix it to the bare wire . The old one had flipped from the plug socket was lying scorched on the floor, minus one of its pins.

"Well, you know. I'm a time traveller," boasted Raymond in the way only a boastless man could.

"Do you want a badge?" asked Tash.

"Is there a badge?" replied Raymond, betraying his child-like joy at the prospect and bending to pick up the Samsonite case that struggled to cover more than a few yards on its wheels without tumbling over.

"No," replied Tash.

"Oh," said Raymond. "Still. Quite something."

Tash bit her lip this time, seeing that this sensitive soul was experiencing a significant life-changing moment.

"I feel a bit like an astronaut," he said.

"Well, you look like one," said Tash as kindly as she could muster.

Raymond blushed a little. "Do I?"

"Yeah," lied Tash.

"If NASA sent sweaty fat men up with chip pans for helmets," said Jamie, without looking up from his plug.

"It's a slow cooker," said Raymond before thinking. "A deep fat fryer's a good idea, though."

CHAPTER TWENTY-TWO

Raymond was crying.

"It's only a car," whispered Tash as she crouched on the road behind the Princess out of view of Raymond and Maureen's front window.

"I know, I'm sorry. It's all just a bit much," said Raymond snuffling snot and blood back up his mangled nose. His fingers caressed his perfectly intact wing mirror. "We've just been through so much together."

Tash nodded as patiently as she could, then spoke. "You're talking about Maureen, aren't you?"

"Yes," said Raymond.

"I just wasn't sure if you meant the car," she replied. "Cos I have a baby waiting for me in 2020, but this little breakdown is fine by me. You cry it out." Then added, "As long as it's definitely not about the car."

"Are we getting in then?" asked Jamie loudly, as ever unable to lower his volume. He was standing bolt upright at the rear door, trying the handle.

"Get down, Jamie!" hissed Tash.

Jamie squatted down with the others but couldn't stop his mouth from sharing his usual accurate logic.

"But Maureen's in the bath, and we're in the loft."

"He's right, Raymond. Give me the keys so I can unlock the boot," said Tash.

Raymond handed over the dull metal key, and Tash shuffled to the rear of the Leyland to open up the boot that had imprisoned her and her brother earlier in this hideously long year.

Jamie and Tash loaded the boot with the holdalls, then lifted the Samsonite case together and placed it on top of the bags. This larger rigid case was now protruding too much, but it didn't stop Jamie from trying to slam the boot lid. His capacity for gauging volume and physics wasn't like his sister's. His dyspraxia was evident as he continued to bash the lid several times, hoping that he would get a different result each time.

"No... No... No... No... No," repeated Tash each time, and each time moving to take over. Eventually, she grabbed the boot lid from him and prised it fully open. "They're in the way, aren't they? Give me a second."

Tash leant fully into the spacious boot and managed to separate the holdalls sufficiently to make a suitcase-sized space, one that she wasn't expecting to be filling with her own body.

But now she was.

"The fuck, Jamie?" said Tash as she felt his hands push her foot firmly down out of sight and slam the lid closed.

"What are you doing, Jamie?" came a female voice that sounded suspiciously like Maureen.

"I thought you were going in the loft with Raymond?" shouted Maureen assertively from the steamy bathroom window, with a peach-coloured shower cap covering her rollers.

"Oh my God, she's seen us," whispered Raymond, lying flat on the road on the other side of the car.

Jamie stared up at Maureen's face, tightly squeezed through the gap in the single-glazed pane. Pressed against the obscured glass of the closed window were her naked breasts. Maureen's ones. Maureen's breasts, thought Jamie. This isn't right. All he could manage was silence. Then some more silence. Luckily Jamie didn't realise how little the silence was helping, but his brain had few other ideas, so more silence it was.

"Say something to her. But don't say anything. Say something. But nothing," said Tash from the darkness of the cramped boot. How the hell had she ended up in here again?

"Would you like a deep fat fryer for Christmas?" asked Jamie with a painted-on smile, his eyes somewhere between her rollers and the sky.

"Not that," whispered Tash.

"What?" shouted Maureen.

"Not that," said Jamie, parrot-fashion.

"What?" She was mightily perplexed.

"Sake," emanated very loudly from the boot.

"Can you get back in here and help Raymond, please. I don't want him falling through the ceiling!" said Maureen.

"Will do," said Jamie. But his feet were glued to the road. Glued and nailed. And screwed. Which was how he felt. Then it was a stalemate as Maureen glared at Jamie, and he beamed stupidly back at her. He even thought that blinking might give the game away, so he let tears stream freely from his blurry eyes. Was she really waiting for him to walk back to the house? Was she going to wait until he did?

"Jamie, stay where you are," whispered Tash, hoping she couldn't hear his heavy footsteps through the steel boot lid.

"S.O.S.," said Raymond as quietly as he could.

There was an eerie silence other than Jamie's rubber soles reluctantly thumping the tarmac.

"Did you just say S.O.S.?" said Tash in a loud whisper.

"He's going in the house!" replied Raymond, peering at Jamie's shoes walking up the path to the front door.

"S.O.S.?" said Tash.

"We're being covert! I needed help. I'm not very good at this sort of thing!" replied Raymond. "We need to do something."

"I'm locked in a fucking boot. You do something!"

Raymond slid to the car's rear and glanced up to see the keys hanging from the boot lid. He extracted them and crawled S.A.S.-style back to the driver's door. He cautiously opened it and slid into the seat – ducking his head as much as his battered spine would allow. He fumbled with the ignition and tried to gently close the door. Tash heard the metallic chunk sound, despite Raymond's efforts to mute it.

"Raymond? Is that you? What's happening?" said Tash from behind the back seat.

Raymond squinted up at the house. The upstairs of these '60s box houses projected a little from the downstairs to create a covered shelter for people underneath to find door keys or fill bins. Jamie was holding himself flush with the house like Spiderman – with arms outstretched and clinging to the peeling white-painted timber cladding.

"Jamie's hiding next to the front door," whispered Raymond, "he's buying his time."

Raymond dropped the ignition key and started to feel around the footwell to retrieve it, but it had slid under his Halfords rubber floor mat, and the steering wheel prevented him from comfortably reaching it.

"Don't you bide time?" asked Tash from the muffled boot.

"What?" replied Raymond breathlessly as his fingers stretched impossibly to reach his leather keyring.

"You bide your time. You said buy."

"You really do say the strangest things sometimes," said Raymond.

"Are you taking a dump?"

"What?"

"You sound like you're taking a dump."

"I'm reaching for my keys."

"Don't set off until Jamie's here!"

"Got them!" said Raymond, happily sitting upright and then blinking madly to erase the millions of grey and brown stars from his field of vision. He really should bend over more, he thought. Maybe this temporary blindness wouldn't happen if he bent over more.

"Don't set off until…" Tash stopped speaking when they both heard a knocking on the passenger door window. Raymond looked over to see a delighted Jamie smiling back at him.

"Get in!" said Raymond. "Get in!"

Jamie slid alongside Raymond. "That was close!"

"Sit tight. I might have to go quite quickly," warned Raymond.

"OK," said Jamie, fastening his seat belt tightly.

Raymond removed the handbrake and rolled the car slowly down the hill so that he could start the ignition out of earshot of the house.

"I've known you go quicker," said Jamie, turning on Radio 1.

Laura Branigan's 'Self Control' played very loudly as the ignition finally fired into life. Sure enough, Raymond then performed a handbrake 180-spin at the bottom of the cul-de-sac, not unlike something he'd seen on *Knight Rider* this week. Other than *Duty Free*, Maureen didn't really like to watch ITV. Especially their American shows. She said they were common, but she'd had an early night with a milky

Maxwell House and a couple of Rennie. She'd blamed the posh food from the Berni Steak Bar on Sunday night. Marie Rose sauce might be alright for Mediterranean people, but it was all the proof she needed that they had no reason to return to Spain. If it was from Spain. It certainly sounded like it. Not that they'd tried it in Salou. They were Full Board, and the hotel only served authentic Spanish meat and two veg. She had no idea how Joan Collins and the Queen could eat stuff like that. Maybe rich folk get used to it after a while.

Jamie giggled a little and straightened himself in his seat.

"What's the plan?" he asked.

"Let's just get this over with," said Raymond, straining to be heard over the *'oh-oh-oh' clang 'oh-oh-oh' clang* of Branigan's cover of the Italian track.

The fact that neither of them thought to let her out of the boot disappointed Tash but didn't surprise her in the slightest.

CHAPTER TWENTY-THREE

As the Princess trundled through Clapham Common, Raymond turned down '99 Red Balloons' to speak to Jamie. He'd been thinking long and hard.

"I'll flash your security badge, and hopefully, they'll let us in again," said Raymond, with one eye on his watch. He was starting to sweat again, and his mouth was dry.

"My what?" asked Jamie.

"Your security pass," said Raymond, turning to look at Jamie.

"Do we have time for this?"

"Beg pardon?" said Raymond, trying to straighten his ruffled hair in the rear-view mirror.

"Aren't we gonna put the Christmas tree up before we go to the Berni?" replied Jamie.

Raymond stared at Jamie for a moment, pausing to look at the black sponge of the Walkman headphones that hung around his neck. When had he put those on? Raymond blinked and blinked again. He often did a blink to think.

After opening his eyes for the third time, he slammed on the brakes and flicked the hazard lights on as the rubber tyres squealed to a stop, blocking the traffic behind. He leapt out of the car, slammed his door shut, ran off, then ran back again and opened his door.

"I'll be ten seconds," stammered Raymond across to Jamie.

Jamie nodded and turned up Radio 1.

Raymond shut the door one more time and ran to the boot, ignoring the beeping car horns around him as he struggled to unlock the lid. His trembling fingers weren't behaving, and the keys fell to the ground. He bent down to pick them up and smashed his face on the back of the car. Wow. That hurt. Raymond straightened up and leant on the car to collect his thoughts and his vision again. The stars soon cleared. He took a deep breath and bent down once more. He was muttering to himself now as he grabbed the keys.

"I think we've taken too much on. We've taken too much on."

The key slid into the boot lock, and the moment he pressed the release, it flung open, and a very sweaty Tash sat bolt upright and gasped for air.

"You twat," whispered Tash. "I've been shouting you. You absolute twat."

"Shhh! We've got a bit of a problem," said Raymond, nervously eyeing around the boot to the passenger seat.

Tash looked around to get her bearings.

"Where are we?" she asked.

"Shhh!" said Raymond silencing her with a gentle palm over her mouth.

She recoiled and berated him. "Don't shush me!"

Raymond was dancing on his tiptoes like he might wet himself at any moment. He reminded her of a young Jamie after he'd drunk too much Sunny D and just discovered someone else was using the loo.

Impatient drivers in queueing cars started to pump their horns.

"It's, it's, it's..."

"Calm down, Raymond. What? What is it?"

"It's, it's, it's..."

"Breathe, Raymond. Seven eleven breathing."

"It's... It's..." Raymond took a deep breath and slowly exhaled, counting in his head.

"That better?" asked Tash.

"Is it count seven in or count seven out?"

"Doesn't matter, we're just trying to trick your brain. Is it working?"

Raymond nodded slowly.

"Good... What is it?"

"It's..."

Tash nodded to encourage him to say more. She watched as he pointed to the front of the car...

"It's the wrong Jamie."

Chapter Twenty-Four

Ten minutes earlier, the right Jamie had been beckoned to the house by Maureen as she leaned from the bathroom window. He looked back and spotted Raymond squatting at the boot of the Princess. What was he to do, though? He knew he couldn't go in the house, as he was already in there with Raymond. Well, the wrong Jamie and wrong Raymond. The ones from last Sunday. Which was also now.

Blimey, this was confusing.

The right Jamie decided to walk out of Maureen's view and press his body flat to the front of the house. Hopefully, Maureen would get in her bath, none the wiser that Jamie and Raymond were already in the loft. The right Jamie just needed to stay here until Maureen closed the window. He held his breath. Come on, Maureen. Close the window. He knew she wouldn't leave it open, not with gas bills being her favourite topic of conversation. He knew he would hear it slam. All the windows slammed. They expanded with the winter moisture and needed a shove to open and a slam to close.

Come on, Maureen.

Slam the window.

Jamie glanced over at Raymond – or the right Raymond, as he needed to think of him now – and watched as he crawled out of sight to the other side of the parked car.

Come on, Maureen. Come on.

Then the window slammed.

Brilliant, thought Jamie, as a smile crossed his face, and he breathed a sigh of relief. It didn't last for long. Something startled him. Something very close. A metallic twang pierced the silence and the unmistakable sound of the front door Yale lock turning. He pressed himself closer to the wall, ensuring every single inch of his body was touching the house. He mustn't be seen by whoever was about to leave the house, which was pretty ridiculous unless you were a chameleon with an affinity for blending into 1960s Brixton architecture.

This was a terrible turn of events. Whoever was leaving was bound to see him.

Unless the person leaving the house was completely and utterly oblivious to their surroundings. Which was lucky, as Sunday Jamie walked out and slammed the door shut behind him. Sony Walkman headphones over his ears leaked Van Halen's 'Jump' as he walked down the path without looking back. He did a double-take at the parked car outside and was surprised to see Raymond – the man he had just left in the loft – sitting in the driving seat. He walked over and knocked on the passenger window as he pulled his headphones around his neck and fumbled for the STOP button in his pocket.

The right Jamie dived behind the corrugated steel rubbish bin at the other side of the front door and peered over in horror. His head suddenly filled with the memory of the loft light bulb going 'pop' on Sunday when he and Raymond fumbled around for the Christmas tree and decorations. Raymond had sent Jamie to get a replacement from the pack of 40-watt Osram's in the garage. Jamie had asked if they were screw or bayonet, and Raymond had asked why British bulbs would be screw? He'd seen spotlights with these twist in fittings but saw no reason for them to replace the reassuring push and twist of a bayonet. Jamie had dropped the old bulb as Raymond handed it over but caught it before it smashed on a joist. It was close.

Damn, thought the right Jamie. Yes, I left the house on Sunday to fetch a light bulb.

He didn't know which was more alarming right now, the fact that he'd changed history and his Sunday-self was climbing into the car with a Raymond from the future, or the fact that he could see a substantial balding spot on the back of his own head. He felt the area of expanding skin on the crown of his skull. As his fingertips attempted to ruffle his hair over the thinning patch he watched in horror as the Princess rolled away down the hill with the wrong him in it.

CHAPTER TWENTY-FIVE

At Clapham Common, Tash let this latest development land in her head. The chilly winter breeze was cooling the sweat on her face, and the sound of car horns was far louder now the boot lid was open, but she was able to force a question from her lips. Surely Raymond was wrong. I mean, look at him. His face looked like he'd wrestled a badger, and his hair looked as if each strand had fallen out with the one next to it. Surely the wrong Jamie would have questioned Raymond's appearance? But then Tash thought again. Jamie had once asked Tash if she'd put weight on. Not a particularly generous thing to say to your sister, but nonetheless probably not so unusual between sparring siblings. She'd been modelling her wedding dress for her mum at the time. Jamie had walked into the living room and didn't register the tears of joy, the metres of lace, the scarlet Jimmy Choos that peeked from the hemline. Asperger's meant that Jamie wasn't the best at gauging facial expressions, so reading the mood of a room was always a challenge. Well, not a challenge for him, more so the others in the room. He could enter

145

a disciplinary hearing and start telling a joke. And on the day Tash had tried on her dream ivory gown, Jamie had walked in to let his mum know that the toilet was blocked, and on seeing his sister, he asked if she had put on weight. In his defence, she had been worrying so much about the wedding preparations that mum Andrea had voiced concerns that Tash was losing weight, so Jamie probably thought he was being kind.

"The wrong...?" said Tash from the car boot, but before she could say 'Jamie?' Raymond absentmindedly forced her back into the boot and slammed the lid shut. He leant down and whispered "sorry" through the catch and then ran back to his driver's door, muttering "sorry" over and over at the collection of traffic accumulating behind him.

"Right," said Raymond, as he climbed back into the car and started the ignition.

"The exhaust pipe seems fine now. Let's get you back to last Sunday. To today. To home. Let's go home."

Many drivers would have continued forwards to the next junction, taken the next right, and joined the road heading south. Some bolder individuals may have braved a three-point turn from where they were. So, even Raymond was surprised as he mounted the kerb onto the grass then executed an extremely wide arc-shaped U-turn over the muddy field to their right, taking in the view of the derelict bandstand before crossing the kerb and re-joining traffic on the opposite side of the road. Madonna's 'Like A Virgin' drowned out the occasional "Sake!" that emanated from the boot as Tash's head struck the rigid Samsonite suitcase in the darkness.

Jamie was utterly indifferent, distracted by the Needlers Fruit Sensation that he was trying to unwrap. It had obviously been in his jeans pocket longer than he'd realised, and the wrapper was refusing to come away from the boiled sweet. Maybe the softer inside had somehow leaked through the outer shell. Not to worry, it would soon be scratching the roof of his mouth, and he was looking forward to getting home to decorate the Christmas tree.

Chapter Twenty-Six

As the Princess drove down Gaywood Close, Raymond's collar itched, and the sweat on his back clung to his C&A polyester shirt. He was kicking himself for forgetting Jamie had left the attic to fetch a light bulb on Sunday afternoon. But all he had to do was swap one Jamie for the other, and he'd had an idea.

"I'm going to park the car, Jamie, and I'd suggest you go straight to the garage to get that bulb, but Maureen has asked if we could both use the back door now as she's shampooed the doormat."

"OK," said Jamie. It came as no surprise to him that Maureen would attempt to shampoo a coir doormat. She hoovered inside the fridge and polished the apples in the fruit bowl. Why would she not squirt Timotei onto the stiff bristle mat?

"Shall I get out here, then?"

Jamie pointed to the row of garages approaching them on the left, including Raymond's, which housed his storage of tools, light bulbs and paint tins.

"Not really, no," said Raymond and continued past then

parked up outside the house. He needed all the time he could buy to resolve the whole 'wrong Jamie' situation.

Jamie climbed out and closed his door, then set off back up the hill towards the garage. He stopped and walked back to the car then knocked on the window. Raymond leaned over and wound it down.

"Are you not getting out?" asked Jamie.

Raymond thought.

"Yes," he said. "Of course, I am! Of course, I'm getting out!"

He leant down to look up to the terrifying house.

"I mean, if I don't get out now – and then walk around to the back door of the house – how would I get up into the loft to see you when you come back with the light bulb?" This timeline had helped clear things up for himself.

"Are you alright?" asked Jamie.

"Off you go, then," said Raymond. "And remember, don't come back this way past the car. Go the back way from the garage. By the stairs of the maisonettes."

"You sure you're OK?" asked Jamie.

"And Jamie. Don't mention the car exhaust to Maureen, cos she's a worrier. In fact, don't mention this little trip at all. Not even to me. In the loft."

Jamie looked confused but nodded and walked up the road, occasionally looking back at Raymond, who watched him depart in his rear-view mirror. Jamie turned and walked back down and knocked on the window again, which Raymond rolled down once more, trying to hide his exasperated sigh.

"What now?" asked Raymond.

"Are you not getting out?"

"Yes, Jamie! Yes! I said I was."

He didn't.

It was stalemate again. Jamie stared at Raymond, who

stared back. Eventually, he rolled up Jamie's window and then climbed out of the car at a snail's pace, slowly closing the door as silently as possible with one eye on the house.

"See you around the back, then," whispered Raymond.

"Pardon?" asked Jamie with his usual volume.

"See you around the back of the house," whispered Raymond, gesturing the route with his hand, clearly concerned that they remain as quiet as possible. "I'm going to go the other way."

Jamie set off again up the hill, glancing back to watch Raymond walking down the hill towards the end of the terraced houses, both checking on the other as they made their progress. The final time Raymond looked over his shoulder, he watched Jamie turn the corner into Abbot's Park. Immediately Raymond turned around and ran as fast as his legs would carry him to the rear of the car, fumbling with keys the whole time. Nervously looking over his shoulder, he unlocked the boot, and the lid flew up again. Tash's sweaty head popped up again.

"Sake, Raymond!" she whispered as quietly as possible whilst gasping for air and attempting to claw herself out of the boot. Raymond's attention was distracted by the unmistakable sound of the front door opening again. Impulsively he placed his palm over Tash's face and once more shoved her back into the boot before slamming the lid down, muting a "What the fuck?" just as the catch clicked shut. Raymond looked up just as the front door squeaked open and watched a very anxious Jamie walk through it. He closed it slowly behind him and rushed down the path whilst pointing at his face.

"It's me! Jamie! The new Jamie!"

They both climbed into the car, and Raymond released the handbrake allowing the car to roll away silently.

"I forgot about getting that lightbulb!" said Jamie.

Raymond was borderline hyperventilating as he twisted the ignition key. "Yes. You did."

"Well, we both did," said Jamie. He was right.

They drove off in silence, soon broken with a noise in the boot.

"Well, luckily, I don't think anyone noticed," shouted Tash from behind the back seat. "You pair of absolute knobs."

CHAPTER TWENTY-SEVEN

"That was a bit risky, don't you think?" asked Raymond, and then thought twice about being quite so assertive. "You know, I mean, in a way."

The Princess was passing through Clapham Common for the second time. Tash looked at a bizarre arc of car tyre tracks to her right making a perfect semi-circle of mud across the turf towards the bandstand.

They had pulled up to let her get out of the boot and swear at them the moment they'd reached Tulse Hill. Raymond and Jamie had agreed that was far enough away to avoid being spotted. Tash had scrambled out of the boot, catching her foot on one of the holdall handles and smacking her face on the road, which hadn't helped her mood one bit.

"You'd both been gone ten minutes, and I could hear the other you shouting at me from the loft," explained Jamie. "I didn't want Maureen to get out of the bath."

"I think we can all agree with that," said Tash.

He'd explained how he'd decided the best plan of action was to go and get two lightbulbs from the garage. A 40-watt one and a 100-watt one. He left the 40-watt bulb at the foot of the stairs – hoping the other Jamie would find it a little later – and then climbed in the loft to offer the 100-watt bulb to Raymond. This would buy time. He knew Raymond wouldn't want a bulb that burnt so much energy up there; that would be fiscal madness. What if Maureen had found out? 100 watts of light? In the loft?

And Jamie was right. So, had been sent back out to the garage once more.

In truth, he'd just slammed the front door loudly and remained in the hall with one eye on the road, fully expecting the Princess to return soon. And his gut instinct was right. (Unlike the night Tash didn't turn up at their Tower Bridge rendezvous back in October. Not that he realised - as he didn't either).

"It's all worked out OK," said Jamie to the silent car. "We're on our way."

"We've lost twenty minutes, though," said Raymond, looking at the plastic fingers of the analogue dashboard clock. "We're going to be arriving just ten minutes before the cash."

"We have a plan," said Jamie, trying to reassure himself as much as the others. "At least we have a plan."

"We have half a plan," said Tash. "One fake ID, and one million pounds of stolen money in the boot."

Somewhere deep inside the radio speakers, Robert De Niro was waiting for Bananarama. So, at least they were having a better day than this trio.

Maybe they could pull this off, thought Raymond. Just maybe.

Maybe they could pull this off, thought Tash. Probably not, though.

Why had that shit card won the Band Aid Christmas Card competition? It didn't even stand up properly, thought Jamie.

Then they heard the siren of a police car.

———

It was a Mark 2 Ford Granada Police car this time, and Jamie was quite impressed with the straight lines in a retro kind of way. He had grown used to the smaller sized vehicles in 1984, compared to the mammoth SUV's that lined the streets of 2020. People hadn't yet started digging up their roses to house their 2nd and 3rd cars, and Jamie quite liked it. He felt sure that he could see more pavements, more leaves, and more birds than his life in 2020. And much as 21st-century cars were undoubtedly safer in the event of a collision; surely, they were more likely to encounter a crash given the higher volume of cars on the road in 2020. It was a catch-22 situation that Jamie struggled to reconcile in his mind. He had no answers, so he turned the radio back on, Raymond had turned it off so he could see better when the police siren had sounded.

Paul Young did his best to placate the passengers of the car by explaining that 'Everything Must Change'.

"Jamie, what are you doing?" asked Tash, nervously perched on the back seat. "Turn it off!"

"Radio's not illegal, Tash!" said Jamie. "We need to behave like we're innocent."

"We are innocent!" said Tash. "We've not stolen anything yet!"

"We've still got a stolen million quid in the boot, though," replied Jamie, exceptionally loudly.

"Shhhh!" said Tash, leaping forward to turn the radio up, despite her own advice.

They both watched Raymond standing at the side of the road, his hands visibly trembling as he spoke to the police officer towering over him. Then, the officer reached out for Raymond's arm, walked him to the back door of the Granada before opening it and gesturing for Raymond to get inside, which he did.

"Oh my God, they're arresting him!" said Jamie. "The policeman put him in the back of the car."

"Do you have keys to drive this?" asked Tash.

"What? We can't leave him!"

"Jamie, we really can. He'll tell them about Maureen, and they'll go and save her."

"Jesus said he'd kill her if the police turned up," said Jamie.

"He was bluffing, probably," said Tash dismissively. She was already working on a damage limitation exercise to bin off Jamie somehow and travel home to her son.

"You didn't say that earlier," said Jamie.

"He wasn't sitting in the back of a police car earlier," said Tash, before adding, "shit!"

Jamie turned to look at his sister. "Shit, what? What shit?"

Tash gestured through the windscreen, and Jamie followed her gaze.

"He's coming over," said Tash, as the police officer walked purposefully over to the parked Princess. Raymond was straining his neck to peer through the rear window of the police car. He looked very pale.

"What the fuck do we say? What shall we do, Jamie?"

Jamie squirmed in his seat and adopted a painted-on smile for the approaching officer, who walked alongside Tash's rear window. He gestured for her to wind it down. She used the roller handle to lower the glass slowly.

"Hello, officer," she said.

"Are you alright, madam?" asked the officer.

Christ, they really did call women "madam" in the 1980s, thought Tash.

"Yes, thank you," she replied.

The officer considered the reply before turning to Jamie's

door, opening it, and offering non-negotiable but straightforward instructions.

"Out you get."

"What?" said Jamie, glancing at his sister.

"You heard, no funny stuff," said the officer, now clutching Jamie's jacket to extract him forcefully.

Within a moment, Jamie found himself standing on the road with his chest pressed against the closed door as the policeman kicked his feet apart and put Jamie's arms above his head.

"Keep them in the air."

"Tash!" said Jamie, in pathetic desperation, but she was out of ideas.

Jamie was frisked from head to toe. And far more thoroughly than when he made the security body scanner beep at Luton airport when he flew to Palma. And Malaga. And Alicante. And anywhere now he came to think about it. It was every time. What was wrong with him? Maybe it was true about all that mercury in fish.

Suddenly he was face-to-face with the police officer. He'd somehow been flipped around 180 degrees and could smell coffee breath through a moustache that was long overdue a trim. Hands continued to fumble around Jamie's body until the officer seemed reassured that he was not in the presence of an armed criminal.

"Say one word more, and I will smash your face in," said the policeman, before placing his hand on Jamie's chest to hold him in position, then turning to Tash and smiling.

"Madam, can you tell me your relationship with this gentleman?"

"He's my brother," said Tash.

"And the short fat guy?"

"Pardon?" replied Tash.

"He's your dad, is he? The one in my car?" He nodded at the squad car.

"More of a family friend, really," she replied.

"Can you explain why a lady matching your description was seen being dragged out of the boot of a car with this registration plate, on Tulse Hill?"

Tash thought for a moment.

"Was that you?" he asked.

Tash thought a little more.

"It was me, but there's a perfectly logical explanation for that," said Tash.

"Go on."

"I was sleeping," said Tash.

"You were sleeping?"

"Yes."

"In the boot?"

"Yes."

"Not the back seat? You chose the boot over the back seat?"

"I need it dark, or else I can't get off," she replied.

"Right. My wife likes the dark," said the man. "She often climbs into the cupboard under the stairs for a kip."

"Does she?" asked Tash, unable to hide her astonishment.

"No, that would be ridiculous, wouldn't it?" he replied. "Can I have the truth, please?"

Tash took a deep breath as her head spun. Then she looked him in the eye and confidently said: "No. Because you wouldn't understand."

He wasn't expecting that response. "Try me."

"OK. I was actually in the boot because I was hiding from him," she said, pointing at Jamie. "But not actually him. I was hiding from him six days ago, which is today. We're currently on our way to switch some props with Paul Daniels at BBC TV Centre so that we can save a life."

He stared back at her. She didn't blink, and she certainly wasn't behaving like a hostage.

"Madam, if you are under any duress or pressure to cooperate because these gentlemen have threatened you, now is the time to tell me."

"I'm not. Not at all. And we're in a bit of a hurry actually," said Tash.

Jamie nodded in agreement. The policeman considered this and released his grip on him, before asking, "Do you have keys for the boot?"

"Pardon?" said Jamie, his mouth suddenly very dry indeed.

CHAPTER TWENTY-EIGHT

Tash and Jamie stood at the rear of the Princess alongside the police officer, and all three watched as Raymond inserted the key into the boot lock, which was quite difficult considering just how much his hands were quivering. Images of Maureen locked in the warehouse flashed in his mind, then memories of the cell at Shepherd's Bush Police Station where they had all spent a night in October. He really had taken too much on.

"It's not turning, actually," he attempted to say. "Maybe it's a little bit cold." He wasn't a great liar.

"Stand back," instructed the officer, and Raymond did.

The police officer stepped forward and easily turned the key before releasing the boot catch.

Jamie looked at Tash and then at Raymond.

Slowly the boot lid raised, and the police officer looked inside. He started to lift one of the holdalls out but struggled with the unexpected weight. He turned to Jamie.

"Give me a hand?"

Jamie looked at Tash, who reluctantly nodded, so he

stepped forward and strained to lift the holdall out and onto the road.

"We have absolutely no idea what is inside," Raymond started to say before being interrupted by the policeman who was now leaning fully into the boot.

"Don't beat yourself up, mate. A lot of people don't," he said as he fiddled with some black carpet that covered the rear of the lighting cluster. He revealed the back of the brake light housing and reattached a loose copper wire to the bulb.

"Try the break light now, please," he said to Raymond, who delightedly rushed to the driver's doorway too fast, causing a Mini Metro to slam on its brakes to avoid killing him.

"Sorry!" he shouted as he climbed into his seat.

"Wanker," came the reply from the Metro driver as they ground their gears to drive off.

Raymond placed his foot firmly on the brake pedal, and Jamie and Tash watched as the police officers face glowed red.

"I'm too busy to book him for this," said the officer to Tash, "but make sure he knows to check his lights more often."

"Yes," replied Tash. "Of course." Her smile was massive.

"Do you not want to look in the bag?" asked Jamie.

Tash turned and stared at her brother, her face turning deeper red than the brake light.

"No, you're alright, mate," replied the officer as he walked away. "I've got work to do."

CHAPTER TWENTY-NINE

Understandably, it's not yet known if dogs can clearly comprehend humans or form their own thoughts and conclusions. But Lulu, the fluffy brown dog of no discernible parentage, would argue her point if only she knew how. Her mum Jill (because she was her mum, Lulu was in no doubt about that), was distracted by the conversation she was enjoying with Peggy on the way out of Wood Lane tube station. Peggy was going with chicken this Christmas, her husband Sheldon would be cooking, and he had finally had his way as they'd agreed turkey was simply too dry. Jill was nodding her agreement, but deep down, she had already concluded it was dry on account of Peggy's electric oven. A flame was the only way to make a juicy Christmas roast. Lulu would take chicken or turkey, dry, moist, or still alive, to be fair, but right now, she was distracted by the ambulance across the road. As a city-wise mongrel, she had no issue with the hustle and bustle of West London, but she had an innate talent for spotting metal machines that might emit high-pitched noises, before they emitted high-pitched noises. She hated high pitched noises. Twisting her snout to see through her shaggy eyebrows, Lulu braced herself for the inevitable siren from the ambulance that was making its way towards them. She even recoiled a little, just be safe, in the hope that the umbrella of mum's pleated tweed skirt might silence some of the hideous noise. But the siren didn't come. And Lulu was even more surprised to see the ambulance stop and watched a young lady leap from the back doors before tapping on them. This alerted the driver to move slowly further along the road. Then, Lulu's heart skipped a beat! This lady wanted to play! First, she ran ahead of the ambulance to the service road next to TV Centre, and then she lay down in the middle of it. Oh, this would be fun! Lulu pulled on her lead, hoping that mum would cross the road and they could join in with the game. But mum was still debating whether fruit juice constituted a starter on Christmas Day, even if you did place the glass on a plate.

The ambulance edged past the service road, stopped and performed a reverse turn towards the lady on the ground. Oh no! It hadn't seen her! It was going to reverse over her! Lulu let out her best bark which only briefly interrupted the fruit juice chat. Happily, from what she could now see, the ambulance had stopped. And two people had leapt out, one speaking into a walkie talkie.

As mum and Peggy continued along Wood Lane, Lulu got a better look at the lady on the ground. Her face was bloody, and people gathered around to watch the ambulance staff tend to her. Lulu hoped – because it turns out dogs can hope – that the lady would be OK.

CHAPTER THIRTY

"*D*o *you not want to look in the bag!?*" said Tash, mimicking Jamie.

"I thought he'd forgotten," explained Jamie.

Raymond was driving with extreme vigilance and caution as the Princess turned into Wood Lane.

"Don't ask anyone else to look in our bags, not now, not later, not ever," said Tash.

"Can I have your security pass now, please, Jamie?" asked Raymond. He was swallowing a hell of a lot now and could feel his clothes sticking to him again. And losing all this fluid was causing him an almighty dehydration headache.

Jamie produced the bent snapped aerial with the BBC pass still swinging from string attached to the top. He handed it to Raymond, who was busy steering the car slowly into the TV Centre main entrance.

"Say 'hello again'," said Tash.

"What?" replied Raymond.

"Say 'hello again' like you know him. It will help," said Tash.

"Will it?" asked Raymond.

"Of course. They didn't even ask for your pass last time," she added. "Not surprising those lesbians were able to sit on Nicholas Witchell, is it?"

Raymond looked over his shoulder at Tash in a perplexed state.

The commissionaire walked out of his tiny office to Raymond's car window, and Tash gestured that he was there. Raymond turned back and wound it down.

"Hello again," said Jamie, leaning to smile across.

"Not you," said Tash.

"Sorry," said Raymond.

"Pardon?" asked the commissionaire.

"Hello again," said Raymond and held up the wrong end of the snapped aerial.

"What's that?"

Raymond looked at the aerial and upturned it, displaying his BBC pass, not remembering to cover the photo. Luckily, he had grey hair like the man on the pass stolen from Elstree back in October.

The guy looking at Raymond had a look of the Elstree guard. Muscles, tall, ex-military.

"Anywhere you can find, sir," said the sixty-something man as he opened the gates.

Raymond nodded as he tried to engage first gear and drive in. As he wound up his window, he stammered one more time: "Hello again."

"Christ, Raymond, you're gonna have to calm down," whispered Tash.

"I think Nicholas Witchell sat on the lesbians, actually," said Jamie.

"What are you both talking about?" asked Raymond as he carefully reversed the Princess between a green Bentley and a golden brown Jaguar XJS

The Princess looked a little bit uncomfortable in such

company. Like it would rather be somewhere else. A bit like Paul Weller in the Band Aid video.

"Section 28," said Tash. "They were protesting about it. Or Clause 28."

"Still lost me," said Raymond.

"Maybe not happened yet, Tash," said Jamie. He turned to Raymond. "A thing that banned schools from teaching kids you can fall in love with whoever the hell you want."

Raymond was happy they'd reached the back of the parking space, so he carefully applied the handbrake.

"Doesn't sound like Nicholas Witchell at all. Maybe it was self-defence?" he suggested. Witchell seemed a very well-rounded and upstanding news anchor to him.

Jamie pulled the door handle catch, and Tash shouted, "Careful!" at the same time that Jamie's door struck the Jaguar.

"It's every time, Raymond," said Tash. "We have to park by the bins at the supermarket – it's just not worth the risk. Dent a Chelsea tractor in Waitrose, and you get a very irate Karen on your tits."

"I'm not sure I understand what you just said," replied Raymond.

"Sorry," said Jamie. "Sorry, Raymond."

"Just be careful," replied Raymond as politely as he could.

"Can I have the pass, please?" asked Jamie as he squeezed himself out of the car.

Tash looked mortified at Jamie taking control. "What? Wait. What?"

"I'll lead this," said Jamie, taking the aerial and BBC pass from Raymond, then slamming his door closed.

"Hang on, we didn't agree to that," said Tash, shuffling along the bench seat out onto the car park, carefully avoiding the gleaming paintwork of the Bentley.

They walked to the rear of the Princess and opened the

boot. The familiar squeak of the lid was interrupted by the piercing squeal of an alarm. It ended as soon as it began.

Tash looked over her shoulder and shrieked.

Oh God.

Surely not?

CHAPTER THIRTY-ONE

"At the rear gates now, Gareth. Over," said Piers, as the lorry came to a standstill.

"Don't use his name!" said Robert, in the driving seat, peering around all quarters of the HGV as best he could. The road was tight, even in 1984 before people started parking two or three of their cars outside their townhouses. His mirrors were close to useless, but he was relatively happy with his current position, blocking the rear gates of the building.

"What do you mean?" asked Piers as he lowered his CB radio.

"People might be on that channel. Use a fake name," said Robert.

Robert pulled a rubber torch from a rucksack by his side and turned down Harriet Cass on Radio 4 discussing Mikhail Gorbachev's visit to Britain today. Mrs Thatcher had said she liked the Soviet politician, and would very much like to –

But the broadcast fell silent as he continued twisting the dial until it clicked off.

He flicked on the torch and spied the inside of the cabin. "This is filthy."

The CB radio crackled. "Is that you, Piers? It's Gareth, over."

"Pack it in!" said Robert, still examining the black plastic dashboard.

"Is that Robert? Over. Hi Robert!" said Gareth, down the radio. "Over."

"Oh my God, why don't we just do a fucking register!" said Robert. "Stop saying names!"

It went quiet. Then Robert turned to Piers at his side.

"Do you know where the hazard lights are?"

Piers shook his head and glared at the selection of switches that faced them. "No."

Robert grabbed the CB from Piers then pressed the button before speaking into the handset.

"Do you know where the hazard lights are?"

Nothing.

"You need to say 'over' at the end," said Piers, rubbing his fingers through his thick black moustache.

"What?" said Robert, still squinting at the dashboard.

"You need to say 'over' so Gareth knows you've stopped talking."

"But I have stopped talking, Piers; that's why it went quiet."

"That's just the rules of CB. It's just the way it is," explained the younger man.

Robert tried again. "Do you know where the hazard lights are?" Then he smiled sarcastically at Piers and added: "Over."

Nothing. Robert tried again. "Do you know where the hazard lights are? Over."

Then the radio crackled into life. "You talking to me, Robert? Over," said Gareth.

"Course I'm bloody talking to you. Over."

"You didn't say my name, so I wasn't sure if you were talking to me or Piers," said Gareth.

"Stop saying everyone's fucking name, Gareth!"

"Now you've done it!" said Piers.

Robert clicked the CB handset again and spoke in his best passive-aggressive tone. "Do. You. Know. Where. The. Hazard. Lights. Are?"

More silence. Robert barked into the CB radio. "Gareth!" Before adding, "Over!"

"Yes! Over!" replied Gareth.

It is inconceivable to most people that more silence could follow this exchange, but it did.

Piers peered through the windscreen to get a better view of the rear of the vast structure ahead.

Robert took a deep breath and patiently spoke into the CB one more time.

"Could you tell me where they are, please?"

"Over," interjected Piers.

"I know! I was about to say it!" shouted Robert before clicking the handset again. "Over."

There was a longer than usual crackle before they heard Gareth's voice again.

"They're on each corner of the vehicle, over."

CHAPTER THIRTY-TWO

The Securicor van was blue with painted out windows. It looked to Jamie like a beefed-up Amazon delivery van; far less imposing than a G4S van from 2020, which is what Securicor was destined to become after a merger with Group 4.

The commissionaire on the gate didn't flinch at the siren. He was expecting it. Understandably, it was against company policy for the driver of the security van to lower his window, so he had actually sounded his siren twice in rapid succession. This alert was documented on the commissionaire's notes to confirm that this van was the one delivering the money, and that it was here on legitimate business (and hadn't been held up).

The commissionaire had struggled to sleep last night, given his pivotal role in today's covert operation. He'd not seen such responsibility since the war and was in no hurry to jump to the sound of anyone's beat. He extracted a propelling pencil and reread the instructions, marking two pencil strokes along-side the notes that indicated this part of the manoeuvre. He then signed the document, with the correct time and date, before sliding it back into a brown envelope, straightening his tie and then leaving his office to stand alongside the Securicor van. The driver watched in disbelief as the ex-soldier saluted and clicked his heels. Christ, this was taking ages.

Jamie carried one holdall, Tash the other, and Raymond attempted to keep the Samsonite upright as he struggled with the pulling handle. They raced into the reception area and were immediately presented with a different receptionist. This lady was younger and quite nervous-looking. Tash was struck by her lack of presence as the first face to welcome visitors to the BBC.

And she was right. In truth, Cynthia was covering for someone else, but the serendipity of this timing was perfect.

"Right, we've lost almost thirty minutes, so let's say we have just half an hour to do this," said Tash, mindful that she should lead today's task.

"Jamie, I know you said that you wanted to," but she trailed off. Tash had hoped to finish her sentence before Jamie marched over to the large reception desk beneath a colossal wall of oak panelling, but he simply wasn't listening.

His assertive tiptoed stomp reminded her of his first day at comprehensive school when the whole family had fretted how his Asperger's and dyspraxia would impact his secondary education experience. After all, kids were brutal, and he was entering the lions' den all over again after primary school. And, sure enough, he'd struggled to maintain close friendships, he'd struggled to fit in, he'd struggled to get picked onto sports teams, he'd struggled to get invites to birthday parties. But he'd attacked every day the same; with pure determination and a compulsion to prove he was just as capable as anyone else, even if he saw life a little differently to his peers.

And here he was again – now in his thirties, and still on his tiptoes – taking charge. If only Tash had the faith to believe this was the right time for this confidence.

Jamie stood up nice and square (as his mum was still reminding him daily until he departed 2020). He scanned the reception, from the modest Christmas tree decked in red and gold tinsel with glistening Pifco glitterlights, past the selection of empty lounge chairs beside ashtray laden tables, to the abstract tiled mural that covered the far wall. Beneath that were the double doors, which were their gateway to success.

He turned to the lady on reception, and as usual, avoided eye contact. Instead, after scanning her name badge, his eyes rested on a rather delicious looking mince pie that sat by her trembling fingers.

"Hi Cynthia, I'm Terry from Light Entertainment. I'm in charge of it, actually. Like, the boss," said Jamie.

His quivering voice rose high and seemed to evaporate into the impressive, honeycombed ceiling. He'd been told a new starter called Cynthia had dealt with the Securicor delivery ahead of the furore that followed. He now stood covering his BBC pass photo with his finger, just like he'd practised countless times in his bedroom when he was thinking of Martha and how she'd effortlessly hoodwinked the authorities last time.

Sure enough, the name on the badge was Terry. Well, Terence Barron, to be precise, but Jamie was pretty sure he would have preferred Terry, and he held it proudly for Cynthia to examine.

The fact that his finger was obscuring only the BBC logo didn't matter, as the receptionist barely looked at it. She was sweating.

"Yes, sir," muttered Cynthia.

"We're working with Paul in Studio 8," said Jamie, occasionally glancing at his notes. "And this is," said Jamie before turning to Tash and Raymond and muttering something completely inaudible in their direction before turning back once more and continuing.

"Listen, they've travelled a long way and could use some freshening up, so we're going to head through to the green room. These two idiots have left their passes in their suitcase. Can you let me have two visitor passes? Please?"

There was a pause of about ninety years. Maybe longer thought Jamie. Tash thought she could hear Raymond's pores working overtime.

"Of course, sir," said Cynthia, frantically pulling out drawers to see where Patricia kept them.

Jamie turned to Tash and Raymond. It was hard to tell which one of their mouths was open the widest. Jamie smiled and attempted a whisper.

"I've told her I work here and blagged some passes," he said too loudly.

"Shhhhh!" shouted Tash, placing a finger on her lips.

Happily, Cynthia was dealing with a ringing phone and way too many drawer options, and eventually, she struck gold. She handed the passes over and then found a clipboard and pen.

"Sorry to ask, but can I take their names and ask them to sign in, please, sir?" she asked.

"No need, I'll do that," said Jamie taking the board and pen. "You need to answer the phone."

"Would you mind if I did?" asked Cynthia. She looked immensely grateful.

"Well, normally I wouldn't have time for forms, 'cos I'm busy with my light entertainment stuff, but I can see that you're busy, too."

Cynthia answered the phone. "Hello, Main Reception." She listened and then looked at the main doors. "Not yet, I'm afraid." She glanced at her Mickey Mouse wristwatch.

Jamie walked over to Tash and Raymond, handed them

visitor passes, and scribbled the names Harry Windsor and Meghan Markle under 'visitor name' in his best handwriting. Happily, his best handwriting was still pretty much illegible to anyone other than Tash and his parents, but this performance was flawless.

Cynthia was ending her phone call as Jamie handed back the clipboard.

"Thanks, Cynthia," said Jamie. "Have a good day."

With that, Jamie shepherded Tash and Raymond behind the reception desk and through the double doors behind, jostling with bags and the suitcase.

CHAPTER THIRTY-THREE

"Y ou are on fire!" said Tash as they stood on the other side of the double doors.

"That was terrifying," said Jamie, as the realisation of his performance sunk in.

"Well done, Jamie," said Raymond. "What do we do now?"

Jamie turned and looked at another set of doors.

"Through here."

Passing through the next doors, they could see a long corridor curving ahead to the left flanked with more doors. Jamie glanced at his scrawled notes and nodded.

"Right. There is a lift just past that door on the right," he said, and set off along the corridor to confirm. He looked back at the others, a massive smile appearing on his face.

"Yep. Here it is. They're gonna get the staff to carry the cash there, in bundles. It took nine minutes, from start to finish, she said. The Securicor guys loaded it onto a catering trolley inside the lift, then guarded the lift doors until they could transfer it safely to a smaller safe in the studio."

"But it's a lift," said Tash. "What if someone calls it on a floor above? Like Terry Wogan or someone?" She turned to Raymond. "Terry Wogan was on telly in '84, wasn't he?"

Raymond nodded. "Yes, but he's on Saturday nights." Then added, "He won't call the lift. Today's Sunday."

"Oh, they should be OK, then. If Terry Wogan doesn't call the lift, I'm sure nobody else will in a building of this size."

"They got the staff to disable it," explained Jamie. "No one can call it once they do that."

"*Wogan,*" said Raymond.

"What?" asked Tash.

"The name of the show. They call it *Wogan*. It's a bit like *Parkinson*, where they just use the last name of the host."

"It is a bit, isn't it?" said Tash. "Have you finished?"

"He got the job when Parkinson went to the other side."

"Oh no, he's not finished. He's got more," said Tash to Jamie.

"*TV-AM,*" explained Raymond. "Maureen says people that watch television whilst eating breakfast will get indigestion."

"So," said Tash, clapping her hands to change the subject politely. Well, not that politely.

"We just need to wait here until the staff start bringing the million through, then Raymond does some kind of hypnotic dirty dance for them, and they slip the cash in his knickers, do they?"

"I'm not much of a dancer, to be honest," said Raymond.

"Follow me," said Jamie, walking past them, pausing only to pick up his holdall.

They did as they were told and walked along a new corridor and then through more double doors before finding themselves at the bottom of a stairwell that reminded Tash of her secondary school. Polished oak handrails sat above black painted iron spindles and concrete steps with worn brass tread plates at each edge.

"Oh wow!" said Jamie as he looked around a corner. Above more doors was a sign:

Studio 8. "The actual studio!"

"Tell me you're not planning on switching the cash in front of two hundred people?" said Tash.

"No," said Jamie. "We switch it there." He pointed behind Tash at two metal doors.

"Another lift?" asked Raymond.

"Wrong," said Jamie. "It's the same lift." He looked giddy with delight at his revelation.

"Well, they'll guard that too, Jamie," said Tash.

"Nope. That's what made everyone laugh," explained Jamie. The security guys insisted that the lift was locked and waited outside. They had no idea there was another entrance around the back."

"But they locked it," said Tash.

"Only the lift. Not the doors. Fire regs. That's why they stood outside," said Jamie, before pressing the button outside the lift, which whirred into life.

"What are you doing?" asked Tash.

"Just showing you," explained Jamie.

"I know how lifts work. What if someone's in it? Why have you pressed it? Sake! We're standing with a million pounds in stolen cash."

"That's not how lifts work, Tash. People don't wait inside for someone to press it so they can get out."

"They call them erm... hang on. No, it's gone now. No, wait, hang on," said Raymond.

Tash and Jamie looked at him as patiently as they could.

"No, it's back, yes. Elevators. They call them elevators in America, you know. Lifts," said Raymond.

"I'm really glad we waited for you to finish that sentence," said Tash.

"Excuse me, coming through, excuse me," came the voice of a very flustered individual.

They looked over to see a man in his late thirties. He was marching so fast that his corduroy trousers were in danger of making sparks. His burgundy tank top covered a sensible shirt, unbuttoned at the top, and the ensemble looked like it was making him extremely hot.

In truth, the temperature in all the studios was increasing because a heat exchanger in the bowels of TV Centre had failed early in the afternoon. Despite their best attempts to repair the twenty-five-year-old equipment, it had been essential to call in outsiders for a fix. Hopefully, very soon. A similarly aged lady followed behind. She, too, looked flustered and was dressed sensibly in a knee-length skirt and creased pink blouse. "Can't they tow it through?" asked the woman.

"No. Something to do with bloody hydraulics" replied the man, visibly irked that she might ask him such a stupid question ninety minutes before the audience was about to fill the studio.

"What about the crescent?" she asked.

"Ambulance or something. Christ knows," he barked as they both walked out of sight towards reception. "I can't believe we're going to have to use the bloody lift. That was meant to be a joke!"

Sure enough, in the planning meeting at the start of the month, every eventuality had to be signed off before the BBC chief execs would agree to the million-pound stunt. When someone queried a contingency for a studio fire, the producer had suggested the goods lift outside TC8 (BBC speak for Studio 8) would be a safe house for the stash. He also agreed that this should be a holding room in the event of any unforeseen hiccups, like a terrorist attack or biblical plague. He'd been taking the piss, of course, but the lady taking notes – a secretary in her first week at the BBC – had written it down, and so it became part of the plan. He'd only found out yesterday and howled with laughter when he read it in the confidential document.

"I think that was the producer in charge of the money!" said Jamie, gleefully piecing together the jigsaw. "Sounded like he wasn't expecting it at the front door, didn't he?"

And he was right. They'd just witnessed two light entertainment producers discovering that the delivery of one million pounds loaned by Barclays Bank for a Paul Daniel's magic trick had been diverted to the front door of BBC TV Centre. Securicor had been unable to access Wood Crescent to deliver the money to the hangar-sized doors at the rear of TC8. It was sod's law that an ambulance was currently blocking the route. The other way around the crescent, clockwise, would have been impossible to pass because two hundred members of the public were queuing for a live broadcast that was due to start in TC1 at 7.15pm. All of them had arrived early and intent on spotting famous faces. The area currently looked as close to a rock festival as it ever would.

Securicor's second option had been to drive along Frithville Gardens – known well to Tash, Jamie and Raymond as they'd accessed the rear of TV Centre from there back in October. But that was another story. An articulated lorry had broken down partway through the Frithville Gate, rendering it completely inaccessible to any other traffic.

Why the emergency heating contractors needed to send an HGV to the job seemed overkill, but as the BBC staff had run out of ideas on how to repair the heat exchanger, they didn't question it. One of the TV Centre engineers said the contractors would bring a brand-new unit if a repair were impossible. And they weren't small pieces of kit.

So, right now, a million quid needed hiding in a lift because an exasperated producer had made a sarcastic quip just three weeks earlier.

Tash suddenly looked scared.

"Really? So, it's all starting now? The million's coming through?"

Jamie nodded.

"Right. Right," said Raymond. "Right."

He started nodding before saying "right" a few more times.

"Excuse me, are the dressing rooms down there? I'm not used to this side of the building," came a befuddled gentleman's voice.

They all turned to see a grey-haired man smiling and holding a John Lewis suit carrier at shoulder height. Another voice, out of sight, replied, "No, this way, Mr Grayson."

And with that, the man disappeared back where he'd come from.

"That was Larry Grayson," said Raymond. Utterly and completely starstruck.

Grayson had indeed broadcast from another studio – TC4 – when he took over *The Generation Game* from Bruce Forsyth in 1978. But as ITV's *Game For A Laugh* started to steal his audience, he had opted to bow out two years ago in the hope of another prime-time show. It never came.

"So, what's the plan? Where do we wait?" asked Tash, ignoring Raymond. "We can't wait here. People are coming and going."

"You mean where should we hide until we can do the switch?" asked Jamie, still smiling.

"Yes," said Tash, seeking some instant reassurance from her brother.

"No idea."

"Excellent, a plan with a flaw already," said Tash.

The lift suddenly clunked and then pinged. The doors opened, and they all peered inside.

It was empty.

"There's a sandwich on the floor," said Raymond, looking at a half-eaten egg and cress sandwich abandoned in one corner.

"You go ahead, Raymond. I'm having Christmas dinner in an hour or so," said Tash. "Unless you want a go on it?" she added, looking at Jamie.

Jamie took this quite literally. "No, thanks."

"Come on, then," said Tash.

"Where shall we go?" asked Raymond.

"How about we take in a movie. Has *Footloose* been released yet?"

"We don't have time for a movie, Tash," replied Jamie.

"That's been and gone. There's something about ghosts on at the moment. They sing a song," said Raymond.

"Ghostbusters?" asked Jamie.

"That's it," said Raymond. "But I couldn't watch that without Maureen. We're going to wait until it comes on normal telly."

Tash glared at him. "Not a cinema fan then, Raymond?"

He took the question at face value. "Erm, well I wanted to see *Splash* over the summer, but Maureen heard that you see the mermaid's bosoms so we changed queue at the ABC and saw something else."

Tash waited.

"I'm so sorry, I thought you were going to finish that story off, not that you should feel you need to. Ever."

"No, it'll come to me," said Raymond. "*Bolero*! That's it, we watched *Bolero*!"

"She loves a bit of Torvill and Dean, doesn't she?" said Jamie. "Our Maureen?"

"Yes, we both thought it would be them, actually. But it

turned out to be a sexual awakening film with Bo Derek. It was tastefully done, but Maureen walked out when she saw what the Arab sheik did with the honey. She abhors food waste."

Tash took a deep breath and looked at her feet. Raymond stole his chance to whisper to Jamie. "You saw the lot!" Jamie looked impressed.

Tash clicked her fingers. "Back in the room, boys. Boys! Back in the room!"

"Sorry," said Raymond.

"Somewhere dark, then. Let's go and hide somewhere dark," said Tash, setting off in a random direction. "I'm gonna miss all this."

Chapter Thirty-Four

When Piers and Robert eventually found Gareth, he looked hot. He didn't hear them enter the BBC basement plant room, so he leapt out of his skin when they said "hello," and tripped on the chair he'd been perspiring on. Gareth was a large man who looked like he bought his clothes by the kilo, and given the excessive heat, it wouldn't be unfair to say that the room had a Garethy aroma about it.

"Good God, I didn't hear you coming!" said Gareth, picking up his BBC staff pass off the floor and reattaching it to his tie with the safety pin. It took a few attempts, and Piers thought to himself that this man's nasal breathing was worthy of a David Attenborough commentary.

"This is the failed unit, is it?" asked Robert, glancing at the vast pipe that stretched across the room, jointed with bolts, and displaying multiple pipes and cables at various stages.

Gareth nodded. "Where's all your gear?"

"Corridor," replied Piers, twitching his nose beneath his prickly moustache..

Gareth walked over to the door and looked outside. He half-laughed in disbelief.

"You kidding me?"

"No, that'll do the job," said Robert dismissively. "Let's get on."

Gareth looked at Robert. He was serious. He walked back to his desk and reached out to the telephone beside the heat exchanger.

He dialled three digits and waited for someone to answer. Then he spoke.

"Any sign yet?"

He listened to the reply.

"Well, call me the moment it's in place."

He hung up the phone and turned to the brothers. They reminded him of Cannon and Ball – ITV's replacements for Little and Large after losing them to the BBC in the late '70s. Not just their Lancashire accents, but the older one looked quite serious, and his brother Piers had a head of thick curly hair and his brown shoes jolted next to his black trousers.

"Shouldn't be long now." He told them.

Robert tried to breathe through his mouth to give his sense of a smell a bit of respite.

Chapter Thirty-Five

"This is dark," said Jamie as they dragged their bags and case into the large room across the corridor. His voice disappeared into the high ceiling.

"Should we be in here?" asked Raymond, pulling the suitcase back upright for the millionth time.

"We shouldn't really be anywhere in here, should we, Raymond?" replied Tash. "On account of the whole stealing a million pounds thing?"

The three of them were silhouettes to one another, and their voices seemed smaller than ever.

"How long do you think we should wait?" asked Raymond.

"They took nine minutes to fill the lift. They had to time themselves in case they needed to empty it in an emergency. And the TV people didn't come to fetch the money for another hour. They needed to get a smaller safe into the studio, and the Securicor guys wouldn't let them take it until they knew the safe was there. They wheeled it all through on the trolley."

"Back out the front of the lift?" checked Tash.

"Yep, they never told them about the back doors. Why would they?" said Jamie.

"But how do we know when they've finished putting it in the lift?" Raymond still needed some clarity.

"We can nip around the front, and once we see some heavies in security outfits blocking the door – we're on," said Tash.

They stood in near silence for a moment as they contemplated their situation, their heartbeats audible in their ears and Raymond's intermitted nasal wheeze returning from time to time.

"So, you never heard from Martha at all?" asked Tash.

"What?" said Jamie.

"Martha. The American. The mad lady. She's not been in touch?"

"Why are you bringing her up?" replied Jamie.

"Just curious. She was a big part of that day, and she offered all that money, and, you know, I thought the two of you got along quite well."

Suddenly a metallic noise tinkled from the floor.

"What was that?" asked Tash.

"It was a noise from the floor," said Jamie, sounding anxious.

"Yep," said Tash. "Any ideas what?"

"I think I might have dropped the keys to the Princess," admitted Raymond.

"You think? Or you have?" said Tash.

"Well, when you put it like that," said Raymond.

Soon they were all on their knees, sweeping the cold concrete floor with their hands.

"Sake, Raymond, how hard is it to not put your hand in your pocket and not take out some keys and then not drop them?" said Tash.

"We can't see them 'cos it's so dark," said Jamie.

"Thanks, Jamie," replied Tash. "And do you think it's dark because there's no light on?"

She heard him mutter and walk away, which wasn't her intention. She didn't mean to upset him.

There was an almighty clunk and dissipating fizz that echoed around their heads like a cathedral. They all squinted their eyes to protect them from thousands of watts of light that filled the room.

Tash stood up and perused the view, using her hand as a visor above her eyes like she might block the midday sun as she took in the majesty of a Mediterranean harbour.

Except she wasn't looking at Palma cathedral.

"It's Saturday bloody Superstore!" said Jamie, the delight in his voice plain for all to hear.

"Sake, Jamie! Shhhh! Turn the lights off!" said Tash as she spun around to examine TC7, which was the home of the children's morning TV show through the autumn and winter months of the year.

Jamie had lit about a quarter of the studio. The set itself remained assembled from yesterday's broadcast, with Mike Reid's desk eerily dark, and the banks of televisions sets switched off on either side. The phone number was emblazoned across the front of the desk. Tash continued to take in the café-style seating area where kids would sit with pop stars and asked them bizarre questions. Others would phone in to call them "a bunch of wankers", like a teenager calling himself Simon managed earlier in the year when he asked to be put through to Matt Bianco. To another side was a winter wonderland backdrop with fake trees and fluffy stools.

Then something caught her eye. Something was moving behind the main presentation desk.

No, not something. Someone. Tash felt her heart in her throat as she instinctively dropped behind the suitcase to hide before realising that she recognised the person.

"Jamie? What the fuck are you doing over there?"

"Nothing," lied Jamie, with his head buried in some Sainsbury's style shopping baskets. He lifted some envelopes and squinted at them. Then, unhappy at what he had seen, he moved on to another basket.

"What are you doing?" asked Tash, marching over to him and tripping on some tinsel.

"I'm just looking," he replied.

"At what?"

"Here they are," said Jamie.

Tash watched as he rifled through a basket full of hand-drawn Christmas cards.

"Tell me you're not trying to find that winning Christmas card?" she said.

"Did he win?" asked Raymond, suddenly quite animated. "Well done, Jamie! It was a smashing card!"

"Firstly, no. He didn't win. Secondly, a girl is going to win – when they decide – which will be on Saturday, and secondly again – a girl wins. A girl! It's a competition for girls and boys!"

"I can't find hers, but these are mostly awful," said Jamie. "They launched the competition at the start of the month – people had ages, look at that!" He held up a knitted card of a robin with a thimble for a beak. "They've just not given it any thought!"

"I found them!" said Raymond, holding up the Princess keys.

"Jamie! Get out of Saturday Superstore NOW!" said Tash.

Jamie reluctantly walked around the desk, and the two of them joined Raymond at their bags.

Raymond pocketed his keys and looked at his watch.

"Do you think they've started moving the cash yet?" asked Jamie.

"I don't know," replied Tash. "We really are placing

Maureen's life in the hands of a lot of hearsay and speculation."

"We just need to know when they've finished, don't we?" asked Raymond. "You know, filling the lift sort of thing?"

"I'll go and look," said Tash moving to the doors.

"Wait. Wait!" said Raymond.

"What?" replied Tash.

"Do we need a code word or something?" he replied.

"What for?" asked Tash.

"I'm not sure," replied Raymond. "But we need to prepare for all eventualities."

"Like a shark attack, or..?" asked Tash.

"Actually, you do see a lot of code words in heist movies," agreed Jamie.

"Oh my word, so this is a heist?" said Raymond.

"What about 'fire'?" suggested Jamie. "It's short. It's snappy."

"I like it," said Raymond. "Although, wait. Might people think there's a fire?"

"What's the word for?" repeated Tash. "When do we need to use it?"

"Crocodile?" said Jamie.

"Might cause panic," said Raymond. "How about 'rabbit'? No one's scared of a rabbit."

"Not sure," said Jamie. "It needs to be something you can sneak into a natural conversation, so nobody else suspects anything. But we'd know!"

"We'd know what? For fuck's sake?" asked Tash.

"Got it!" said Raymond, who turned to face Tash and Jamie. But then he paused and muttered,

"Ghost."

They stared back at Raymond, who looked suddenly paler than he had done before if that was possible.

"Ghost?" asked Jamie.

189

"Ghost," said Raymond. Then pointed over their shoulders. They looked around.

Sitting in Mike Reid's chair, above the Superstore telephone number 01 811 8055, was the ghost of a teenage boy.

He waved.

Jamie waved back.

"Jamie, stop waving at ghosts," whispered Tash, pulling Jamie's hand down.

CHAPTER THIRTY-SIX

"We come in peace," said Raymond across the studio to the ghost.

Tash turned to him. "That's aliens, isn't it? Jamie? Aliens?" She looked at her brother.

"Yeah, that's aliens," said Jamie. "And we need to go there for that to work. Whereas he's come here."

Then the ghost started to change. Emitting strange shadows and sparkles.

"Sake," said Tash, taking a step backwards.

Then the ghost turned into a teenage boy.

All three watched in confusion as he lowered the mirror ball and torch that had been illuminating his face in a ghostly manner.

"Gary!" said a familiar voice.

Standing in the open doorway was Paul Daniels, one of the BBC's biggest names, dressed in his black tuxedo, ready for his dress rehearsal. He was smiling at his teenage son sitting behind the Saturday Superstore desk.

"Come on, son. We're gonna start in a bit."

Gary climbed off his chair and walked over to his dad.

"Martin's saved you a seat at the front. Off you toddle," said Paul, ruffling his son's hair as he scurried past into the corridor.

"Paul Daniels," said Raymond under his breath.

But Paul had heard. He looked over at the three odd-looking people at the rear of the studio.

With his gaze fixed on Jamie, he raised his hand to point at him and then used the same finger to gesture 'come here'. It reminded Jamie of Mr Kapoor, his maths teacher, just before handing out detention to all the kids returning from the fried chicken shop at lunchtime, strictly off-limits to non-sixth formers. Assertive and calm, but entirely non-negotiable.

Jamie pointed at himself to ensure he had read the situation correctly. Daniels nodded.

All three walked towards the magician, who calmly raised his hand.

"Do you do everything together?" he asked.

They stopped and shook their heads like berated teenagers.

"Just him," said Daniels pointing at Jamie.

Jamie looked at the others and then calmly followed Daniels away from the studio.

"Jamie!" shouted Tash.

Jamie looked over his shoulder like a hostage in a *Die Hard* movie.

"Don't worry, sis. I've got this."

With that, Jamie walked into the locked door. He blinked a few times and went through the open one.

Then he was gone, leaving Tash and Raymond. And one million pounds in stolen notes.

Chapter Thirty-Seven

J esus heard footsteps outside the warehouse door and gestured to his lips to keep everyone quiet. Maureen was sitting on a plastic chair, looking extremely nervous. Surely this would be good news? Jamie was an odd person, but his heart was in the right place, and it was he who had been so assertive and confident about cleaning Jesus's money for him. It beggared belief that he or Raymond or Jamie's bossy sister could feasibly replace one million pounds worth of stolen or drugs money with legitimate stuff. Maybe Jamie had friends in high places like bankers or police insiders. However, that would have surprised her, given his penchant for Donkey Kong and *Blockbusters* on ITV. Maybe this whole thing had been part of some kind of top-secret Government mission? Him and Tash arriving so strangely, her going missing, Jamie staying with them.

Maybe his behaviour had all been an act?

Perhaps he could tie shoelaces in under five minutes? Maybe missing his mouth with his fork at mealtimes was a ruse to make everyone believe he was just a bit daft? He sure as hell wasn't getting better at these things, despite her kind interventions. But what would he gain by pretending to be clumsy? And what if all this speculation was wrong too, and she was about to die? She didn't want to die. Would it hurt? And what if Jamie saw, he would be damaged for the rest of his life. And Raymond. She loved Raymond. She had hoped to grow old with him in a far-flung caravan, maybe with mains drains, and views of the shower block. Hopefully, with a Debenhams department store Gold Card in Raymond's Spanish wallet – the one with a matador embossed on the front.

Jesus nodded at Antonio to kill the lights, and he did so quietly.

They waited in silence, Maureen unable to break it because of the parcel tape across her mouth.

Oh God, thought Maureen. What if they'd completely failed? What did she mean 'what if'? Why had she believed they could achieve anything? Raymond had tried and failed at pretty much everything he ever attempted. And with Jamie's help, they'd tripped all the electricity for half of Gaywood Close when they tried to fit a Tudor-style outside light beside the front door.

Then the silence was broken by the screeching crunch of the shutter door opening. Maureen had her back to the door, so was straining to see over her shoulder as a single silhouette forced itself into the warehouse. Within seconds they were on the floor with a bag on their head. The shutter door was closed by Isabel, and the lights flicked back on. Maureen watched Antonio pick up the jostling figure in the sack and force it to the ground alongside her chair. She wasn't sure about this. It could be anyone.

"You make a noise, you die," said Jesus.

The figure froze in compliance.

"Is that clear?" asked Jesus.

The head in the sack nodded.

Maureen watched in horror as Antonio extracted his gun and slowly pulled the bag off the hostage's head. She couldn't believe her eyes.

"Sab?" Maureen tried to say through taped lips.

Sab sat upright on the floor, her hair filled with static and her chest heaving with fear. She tried to force a smile at Maureen as Isabel used parcel tape to tie her hands together around her back.

Maureen was doubly distressed. Firstly, because this poor young lady was now involved in this siege, and secondly, because these Spanish thugs were using Raymond's parcel tape like it was free, and it most certainly was not.

Sab shuffled uncomfortably on the lumpy floor then heard a clink. It was probably good that Raymond wasn't around, as she'd sat on his rear-view mirror from his beloved Princess, causing it to crack again. A double crack. Or, as a mechanic might call it, knackered mate.

CHAPTER THIRTY-EIGHT

Paul Daniels wasn't the tallest of men, but he hovered over Jamie right now. Mainly because Jamie was crouched in the BBC car park whilst the magician pointed to the rear wheel arch on his XJS. He'd been quiet as he marched Jamie past the Securicor staff in reception who were chatting with the producers Jamie had seen earlier. They had yet to start forming any kind of human chain, but the back of the Securicor van was extremely close to the main entrance, with a ramp to the rear doors, which remained locked.

"You're not looking where I'm pointing," said Daniels, quite correctly given that Jamie's senses were bursting given his current situation. He was indeed staring at the orange flashing lights on the top of the armoured van and trying to block out the crowd noise from the gathering members of the audience for the TV show in TC1, right next to this car park.

"Here," said Daniels, gently stroking the bespoke three-tone paint on his car, pausing to circle a contrasting colour. The exact same colour of the Princess door which Jamie had slammed into it when they'd arrived.

"See that? That looks very much like the colour of your car, here," he continued, gesturing at Jamie's door. "And I know that because I was sitting in my car, this car," he gestured again, "when you climbed out of your car. That car," Daniels pointed again. He'd made this very clear.

Jamie nodded. "Sorry."

"Repeat after me," continued Daniels. "There is some of my paint on your car, Mr Daniels."

"There is some of my paint on your car," said Jamie, parrot-fashion.

"Mr Daniels."

"Mr Daniels," repeated Jamie.

"But not a lot!" said Daniels before breaking into his familiar warm smile. He'd just delivered the main part of his TV catchphrase to this young man, and surely a laugh would ensue.

"But not a lot," said Jamie earnestly.

Daniels looked at Jamie. Had he not heard of his catchphrase? He'd been on TV for years. Everyone had heard it. Everyone.

"You're gonna like this... Not a lot!"

It was even sung in his theme tune. People said it to him in department stores and petrol stations. It was his thing. Carpet shops. Newsagents. Everyone.

In truth, Jamie had probably heard it in the '90s as a child, but not that it would have registered with him. As far as he was concerned, he was simply being berated by one of Britain's biggest TV stars in front of a few hundred people who had all spotted the magician and his magnificent Jaguar. None came over as they didn't want to lose their place in the studio queue, but Paul Daniels was unquestionably just metres away from them. What a day!

"I was kidding," said Daniels, helping Jamie up to his feet and licking his finger to wipe the paint off his car. "We can't start rehearsals until they've shifted quite a bit of paper, so I thought I'd stretch me legs. When I saw you it was too much to pass by. No offence meant. I'm Paul," he offered his hand, which Jamie awkwardly shook. "Wasn't it hot in there?"

"Yes, it was a bit," said Jamie. "Sorry about the car, though."

"And you are?" asked Daniels.

"Sorry about the car," repeated Jamie. Introductions weren't his strongest point.

"I meant your name."

Was this a trap? thought Jamie. Which name should I give?

"Terry."

"Pick a card, Terry," said Daniels. Christ knows where he produced those from, thought Jamie as fifty-two cards effortlessly fanned in front of his face with a beaming smile beneath from the man behind. "Quick as you like – I've got to a bit of a show to do. Fifteen million viewers."

Jamie struggled to grasp one but eventually managed to extract the five of clubs before dropping it on the ground.

"Debbie's job's safe," said Daniels watching Jamie bend to pick it up before squaring up the rest of the pack. His wife was also his TV assistant, and she needn't fear being replaced.

CHAPTER THIRTY-NINE

"Where the hell is he?" said Tash peering around the double doors into the corridor. People were coming and going now, in and out of Studio 8. They didn't look like viewers; they usually carried coats and snacks. She'd seen them queuing up here in the 21st century for the handful of studios that remained after the BBC sold the building off. These looked like staff. Was this it? Had they started moving money? It was supposed to be going into the lift. Why were they not going to the lift? And why did everyone in 1984 look so deathly ill and pale in the winter?

"Do you want me to go and look for him?" asked Raymond.

"I'll go," said Tash. Then she stopped. "Don't take your eyes off the money."

Raymond nodded. All Tash wanted to do was climb back into the C5 and go back to her son. All she'd agreed to do was post a newspaper. How the hell had it come to this?

"Sake," was the final word she uttered before disappearing behind the door, which quickly swung closed.

Raymond suddenly felt very alone in the massive studio.

He perched himself down on the standing Samsonite suitcase, which fell over under his weight and his face smashed down onto the painted concrete floor. His nose throbbed immediately, and his lip felt warm as blood started to pour from it again.

CHAPTER FORTY

I t didn't take long for Tash to establish that the handful of staff was indeed coming down the stairs and not from reception. She hoped this was a good indication that bosses hadn't yet sanctioned the movement of cash. She walked along the corridor back to the rear of reception and peered through. The two producers were now talking to a Securicor man who seemed to be nodding. His helmet was moving up and down and reflecting the bright lights that illuminated the tiled atrium. Tank Top Producer was exasperatedly looking at a tape measure and shaking his head. Pink Blouse Producer seemed far more level-headed and had assembled a posse of five staff members beside the vast woodpanelled wall and started to give instructions out of earshot of eavesdroppers. Other than newbie Cynthia, but she was staff too.

Sure enough, Pink Blouse Producer pointed to the armoured van and then gestured towards the double doors that mostly obscured Tash from view. Tash darted out of sight and slowly peered back through the slender glass panel again. More guards were now walking up the ramp to release the armoured van door, and the staff formed a queue behind them, giggling awkwardly amongst themselves.

The rear of the Securicor van opened, and there in all its underwhelming glory was a safe that was just one inch too wide to turn a corner in a BBC corridor.

"We're on," Tash whispered to herself. "We're on! Nine minutes from now."

She scanned the reception area in a vain attempt to find Jamie, still muttering.

"Sake! Where are you, Jamie? Where are you?"

Tash turned back to re-join Raymond and smashed straight into him.

"Fuck!" she shouted as she felt her face to check it was still there. She glared at Raymond's fresh scarlet nose trail and cut.

"Don't worry!" said Raymond. "This isn't you. I smashed my face on the floor!" He smiled kindly, pointing at his nose.

"Where are the bags, Raymond?" said Tash. It was all she could think of.

"Don't worry. I hid them. But I just need to get cleaned up, and I think I might need to be sick if we get a minute."

He looked greyer than she had ever seen him.

"Oh, for God's sake, don't faint now, Raymond. The nine minutes has just started."

Raymond started to topple, and Tash scooped his arm and dragged it around her shoulders to walk him along the corridor. She tried the first door she found, and happily, it opened. Inside she fumbled for a light switch and was immediately struck by the size of the room. It was tiny and housed two black plastic chairs beside a low glass coffee table. A white ceramic washbasin gave the feel of a 1960s hospital. Painted over bolts soundly secured the sink to the wall, which good as in the event of a fire, they would need to stand on it to reach the window that nestled just below ceiling height. To their right was a Formica wall-to-wall desktop beneath a large mirror, flanked by lightbulbs, most of them lit. Makeup and various cosmetic products lined the sides. Anais Anais perfume, Drakkar Noir aftershave, L'Oreal Free Style hair mousse, and an orange can of invisible hold Harmony Hairspray that looked more like a can of car touch-up paint.

Two clothes rails housed a handful of discarded garments, including a ladies Burberry raincoat and a gents cashmere overcoat.

"Sit down, Raymond, sit down."

Tash started to remove Raymond's arm from around her neck so she could lower him slowly down onto a chair.

"I feel a bit sick," said Raymond.

"I know," replied Tash.

"I think we've taken too much on."

Happy that Raymond was now squarely in front of a seat, she slowly let him go. For reasons best known to Raymond or Sir Isaac Newton, he didn't fall back onto the chair. He fell forward onto the glass coffee table, and the whole thing collapsed under his weight, throwing a magic wand and pack of cards onto the floor.

Lying face down on the floor, Raymond shouted, "It's OK, Tash. It's OK. I think it's strengthened glass. It hasn't smashed." Then muttered something about *Tomorrow's World* and something about technology, again.

"It's one little win after another today, isn't it, Raymond?"

"I think this is Paul and Debbie's dressing room," said Raymond trying to fix the white tip back onto the magic wand.

"Still wanna vom?" asked Tash, kicking a waste bin towards him.

"I think it's passed. Maybe the adrenaline has helped."

She dragged him up into a seated position and attempted to reconstruct the chrome and glass table.

"How long since I said nine minutes?" asked Tash.

Raymond looked at his watch. "Three minutes."

"What?"

"No, wait. Two"

"Two minutes, you sure?"

"Seven. Wait. The hands keep moving."

"What?"

Tash looked over and was alarmed to see his eyes pointing in different directions. And then he was sick. Tash winced. He'd missed the bin and had emptied his stomach into a pair of white stilettos. Raymond sat up and looked at his watch.

"That's better. Yes. Yes. Three minutes."

CHAPTER FORTY-ONE

Tash was dabbing cotton wool soaked in nail varnish remover over Raymond's owl cuts, mice bites, and split lip. His nose had stopped bleeding, though, so that didn't look so horrific anymore.

He recoiled with each dab which made Tash doubt whether this was some kind of respectable improvised first aid she was offering or perhaps a slow and painful poisoning of his blood.

Oh well, time would tell.

Tash had done a decent job of making him look presentable again. She couldn't get all of the cheese out of his ears or eyelashes; it had dried quite hard. But he definitely looked better than two minutes ago. And yes, she had administered this make-over in two minutes because she had checked Raymond's watch every fifteen seconds or so. She had even peered out of the door onto the corridor a couple of times to see giggling staff walking to the lift and then reappearing with slightly less bulgy pockets or blouses.

"We'd better get back. Jamie will be waiting for us," said Tash, cautiously easing the door ajar one final time. They took one final look at themselves in the mirror, wished they hadn't, and then walked back out into the corridor.

"Back in, please," came a voice.

A BBC security guard was blocking the corridor as more smiling staff slowly paced in the direction of the lift, only to reappear moments later.

"What?" asked Tash.

"This won't take long, but we need to keep this corridor clear, so you will need to go back inside. I'll knock when you can leave. Might be an hour or so."

"Is everything OK, officer?" asked Raymond. The security guard liked that. I mean, he wasn't an officer, but clearly this funny looking little man respected him. He squared up with pride and nodded back.

"Nothing we can't handle, thank you."

"The thing is, we're needed in a studio urgently," said Tash.

The security guard considered this and then looked behind him.

"You can go this way, but not that," he said, offering them a route they absolutely didn't want.

Tash and Raymond looked at one another and reluctantly set off.

"Close to the wall, please," said the guard. "Until you get past me."

They did as they were told and glanced over at the open lift doors as they passed. Sure enough, a solitary Securicor guard, still wearing his helmet, was taking cash bundles from a handful of BBC staff and loading it onto a metal catering trolley. The guard glanced over so they self-consciously averted their gaze and continued around the curved corridor of TV Centre. In completely the wrong direction from Jamie and their dirty million.

"Studio 7!" said Tash, reading a sign up ahead.

"What's Studio 7?" asked Raymond, struggling to keep up.

"It's the one Jamie is in. We were next to Studio 8, right?"

"Come on then," said Raymond looking over their shoulder. The security guard down the corridor was watching the money chain now.

They passed through several doors before they found themselves looking through a single glazed window. On the other side was the entrance to Studio 8.

"This is it! This is the place," whispered Tash. "We've done a little loop. The lift is there," she said, gesturing around the corner. "So, Jamie is around there." She pointed the other way. "In Studio 7."

"We did it!" said Raymond.

They squared up to the door by the window and waited patiently for two ladies to walk into Studio 8. The moment the corridor was clear, Raymond and Tash made their move.

But the doors didn't.

"They're locked," said Raymond, just in case Tash wondered why her nose was hurting.

She rubbed her aching face. "Don't suppose you have any paracetamol on you?"

Raymond shook his head.

"Ibuprofen?" she asked, with little hope in her voice.

"Say again?"

"Anything? Do you have any tablets? Anything at all?"

Raymond shook his head again, then his eyes lit up. "Maureen usually keeps some in her bag!"

"And do you have her bag?"

"No."

"Right. Well, let's hope she's getting a headache right now," said Tash. "A really big one. Massive."

"She was part of a trial for some new painkillers last year," said Raymond.

"Oh good, we have a story about tablets," said Tash. "Can it wait? Maybe for someone else?"

"They wanted to find out if they had any side effects, you see. They call it a medical trial. We need a bit of top-up cash, so to speak."

"No, it can't wait. OK."

"It turned out that one of the side effects," Raymond paused for maximum impact, "was thinking there are no side effects."

Raymond looked very serious as he delivered this news. Tash waited to see if the story had finished.

"Is that a joke?"

Raymond shook his head in confusion.

"But it is the end of the story?" she asked.

Raymond nodded.

"Good. Does Maureen have anything in black, by the way?" asked Tash, gesturing at her borrowed outfit.

"Probably. Why?" Replied Raymond.

"Just wondering. You know. If I had to attend an awards ceremony. Or funeral or something."

Raymond did one of his nervous squints.

CHAPTER FORTY-TWO

The core of the question-mark-shaped BBC TV Centre was famously built like a doughnut, which was simultaneously ingenious and disorientating at the same time. Tash and Raymond had no choice but to travel all the way around the three hundred and sixty degrees of the building to get back to where they had started. The two of them maintained quite an impressive pace and counted down the studios as they passed them, occasionally stopping to cross a cavernous stairwell before continuing on their journey.

"He looked older in real life," muttered Raymond, starting to feel a trickle of sweat down his back.

"Who did?" replied Tash, doing her best impression of a lady who wanted to continue the conversation.

"Larry Grayson."

They ran again in silence.

"But then, everyone looks older in real life," he added.

They ran again in silence.

"Why do you say that?" asked Tash.

Raymond paused for a breather and Tash pretended to tut at this old man's need for air, but she was delighted to take some too. Blimey, this place was hot. Was it on fire? Or maybe it was her? Christ – was this Covid? Had she just unleashed Covid-84?

"Why did I say what?" asked Raymond.

"Everyone looks older in real life," repeated Tash, trying to disguise her gasps. She really should rejoin Virgin Active. She'd read about Grid Training, but didn't fancy explaining about her marriage break up and new baby to all the nosey sods in their Adidas by Stella McCartney.

"It's a fact. Whenever you see someone, they will always be older than the film or photo you've seen them in. 'Cos they are," explained Raymond, proudly.

"Are what?"

"Older."

Tash thought about this for a moment.

"Everyone is always older than a photo." He was getting his breath back now. "It was Jamie who pointed it out, to be fair."

"Oh, I see. Time, please?" asked Tash.

"Two minutes until they finish."

"Sake."

"We still have one hour, though, don't we?" said Raymond.

"No! We only had half an hour when we arrived. 'Cos, we need to get the Princess home! 'Cos you're taking Maureen out to the Berni!"

"This is all so confusing. I don't know how you do it all the time!" replied Raymond.

"I don't do it all the time! It's not a hobby! I hate it!" said Tash. "I'm only doing it 'cos old Jamie asked me to."

Raymond may have been slow on his feet, but his brain was as fast as ever.

"Old Jamie?" he asked.

Bloody hell, thought Tash, she'd said too much.

"What do you mean by that?" he asked.

Tash had nothing, so set off running again, and Raymond followed.

"We're at the wrong side of the building, you've abandoned the money, and Jamie's gone missing. We're not going to get our own heist movie at this rate, are we?" said Tash.

"I don't want a movie. I just want to save Maureen," said Raymond.

"I know," said Tash, doing another impression. This time of someone who had genuine empathy.

"We all want this to end happily. Then you and Jamie can finally go home. That's what you want, isn't it?" Raymond asked rhetorically, with a kind smile. "Although I can't say we won't miss him."

Something very nearly made it to Tash's lips but didn't. Raymond spoke again.

"We never had children. We couldn't, actually."

"Sorry to hear that," said Tash.

They ran in silence again before Tash tried to say something nice.

"You've probably got nieces or nephews though?"

"My sister never married," said Raymond shaking his head.

"What about Maureen though?"

"She was brought up in care," said Raymond in a matter-of-fact way.

"Oh, I'm sorry Raymond," said Tash.

He looked perplexed. "Why?"

"That she grew up in a children's home."

"Well, her dad died in the war, and her mum and sister died in the Blitz." He sounded like he was remembering a film he'd once seen. He seemed totally at one with it.

"That's horrible. She lost her sister?"

"Twin," said Raymond.

"I'm really sorry."

"Nothing to be sorry about." He really seemed to think this. "She was the lucky one! She lived. She met me!"

Then Tash went over on her ankle and dropped in pain. "Ow!"

"Are you OK?" asked Raymond, crouching down to examine her injury.

"Don't touch it!" said Tash, recoiling in pain.

"Sorry," replied Raymond.

Tash let out a frustrated roar. "Why is nothing straightforward for me?"

"Shall I get you some ice or something?"

Raymond looked consumed by the concern he felt for Tash. She was hit by a wall of shame and guilt that she'd never displayed anything close to this in all the times she'd witnessed Raymond injure himself. She shook her head and lay flat out on the corridor floor, then let out a massive sigh.

"Some days last far longer than twenty-four hours. Isn't that incredible, Raymond?"

"What do you mean?"

"When I figure it out, I'll tell you."

Raymond looked down at Tash. "He's really missed you, you know? He talks about you all the time."

"Does he?" she replied.

"Of course. And tells us stories about, you know, the future." Raymond felt a bit daft saying those words. "Sounds absolutely smashing. Really thin televisions and forty-eight-hour deodorants. You couldn't invent it! Well, someone did invent it, but still!"

Tash smiled, then thought of her failed marriage to Nathan, her never-ending inbox of work emails, her parent's restrained but unmistakable disappointment in her questionable life decisions. And then she remembered social media, the cancel culture, *Love Island* and then Covid-19.

"It's really not all that, Raymond. Sometimes I think we're going backwards."

Raymond laughed awkwardly. Surely, she didn't mean it.

"You'll have a better Christmas than me," she said, remembering his dining table set for Christmas dinner. "I guarantee it."

"Not sure about that," said Raymond. "I had to cancel the Christmas Club. Couldn't afford the payments."

"I don't know what that means?"

"Oh, it's fine," lied Raymond. "Just means we need to tighten our belts a bit, you know, with gifts. And treats. And food. And the heating."

"Is Maureen OK with that?"

"She doesn't know yet, actually," said Raymond. "It's tricky knowing the best time to tell her."

Tash considered this.

"Maybe when she's asleep?"

Raymond pondered this.

"She does, sleep, Raymond? Tell me she sleeps?"

Chapter Forty-Three

"One last one," said Paul Daniels to Jamie. They were still standing between the Princess and the Jaguar.

Jamie watched a Securicor guard give the thumbs up as one last nervous-looking BBC sound editor walked casually down the ramp with a massive wad of cash spoiling the line in his *Smiths Hatful of Hollow* t-shirt. One of his hands was under the thin cotton material, ensuring nothing dropped to the floor. The guard was already closing and locking the van door.

"Oi! Over here, pay attention."

"I don't think I have time for another trick, actually," said Jamie.

"Do you have three five-pence coins?" asked Daniels.

"Yes," replied Jamie.

"May I borrow them for the trick? You'll get them back. Maybe." He seemed to have a smile that belied a joke he was having at Jamie's expense, but it was charming and charismatic.

"They're at home," said Jamie.

"Oh, I should have said, do you have three five-pence coins in your pocket?"

"No," said Jamie.

"Not to worry," said Daniels. "Come with me."

They walked over to the crowds queuing outside Studio 1. Couples and families in grey, brown and black coats huddled underneath snoods and scarves, and one by one, they started to gesture at the celebrity walking over to them.

"Good evening, ladies and gentlemen, girls and boys, my name is Paul, and I would like to request a volunteer for a little trick."

"Oh, brilliant, thank you," said Jamie and started to walk away.

Daniels did a double-take that got him a good laugh, so he went for another, before shouting, "Er, Terry, I still need you."

Jamie stopped and turned. He was pretty flustered to see fifty or sixty faces laughing at him and Daniels' shoulders rocking at the hilarity of the situation too.

"This man's in a hurry. Maybe he's on a parking meter!" said Daniels. "Or doing a robbery!"

The crowd laughed, and Jamie walked back over. "Can we be quick?"

"He *is* doing a robbery!" said Daniels, to more laughter. He turned to a lady who looked like all grandmas did in 1984. A duffle coat, a printed floral scarf, a bouffant grey hairstyle, and thick plastic framed spectacles. "Madam, what is your name?"

This must have been the funniest thing anyone had ever said to her, and she went bright red and fell about laughing as she stammered her reply. "Mary."

"Hello Mary, my name is Paul, say hello Paul,"

She did, and everyone laughed again.

Jamie couldn't help but admire the allure of this celebrity

standing before him. The crowd adored him, and he genuinely seemed to like them. In no time at all, Mary had produced three five-pence pieces from her handbag. Daniels was now holding a card – as selected by Jamie – between two small metal hollow pipes, maybe an inch long. As he held the card and pipes up to the crowd, it had the appearance of one solid tube passing through the card, but he reminded his audience that was not the case. After all, Jamie's chosen card was lying flat between two separate pieces of pipe. In fact, to prove it, he dropped not one, not two, but three-five pence coins into the top of the tube, and sure enough, everyone heard them clink as they landed one on top another onto the playing card.

"So, as I say, there is no way that these two separate tubes could suddenly become one, because if they did," at this, he asked Jamie – aka Terry – to hold out his palm face up. He did, and Daniels gently positioned it beneath the tube...

"Because if they did...." repeated Daniels and everyone watched as three five-pence coins dropped from the lower tube into Jamie's palm.

"...the coins would fall right through!"

The crowd started to applaud. Jamie was pretty amazed too.

"Now, that's magic," said Daniels, chuckling at the crowd's applause.

Jamie was squirming now; he looked over at the Securicor van, which started to drive away from the main entrance and into a parking bay.

"I have to go," said Jamie, turning to leave.

"He is a thief..." said Daniels, grabbing Jamie's cuff, "... give Mary her money back!"

Everyone laughed as Jamie tried to hand over the coins as best he could, his fumbling making a couple drop on the floor.

"Thank you for being a good sport, Terry," said Daniels, placing his cards and tubes in the pocket of Jamie's canvas jacket. "Merry Christmas, give that to your kids," he then leant in and whispered, "but remember, a good magician never spills the beans."

Daniels patted Jamie on the shoulder, winked and turned to walk back to reception. He was overtaken by Jamie hurling himself towards the glass doors.

Once inside, Jamie was surprised to see Cynthia had gone. Another lady was on the reception desk, Patricia, and she had aced her exams at the 'School For Hard Faced Head Teachers With No Redeeming Qualities'. Jamie almost ran past her before she protested.

"Stop right there!"

With that, she gestured at a BBC security guard who stepped between Jamie and the double doors.

"You need to sign in. Who are you here to see?" said the lady over the top of her glasses.

"No. I work here, actually. I work for the BBC," said Jamie, fumbling for his pass, which was now sitting amongst a basket full of entries to win a copy of *Frankie Goes To Hollywood's 'Welcome To The Pleasuredome'* LP on the *Saturday Superstore* desk.

"I need to get through there," said Jamie, still frantically searching all his pockets.

"Evening, Mr Daniels," said the receptionist.

"Good evening, Patricia," said Daniels, stopping to look at an out-of-breath Jamie. He looked over at the receptionist. "Is everything okay?"

"He's lost his pass," replied Patricia, "Apparently."

"Oh, I can vouch for Terry," said Daniels. "He's with me."

Jamie meant to say thank you, but his autistic mind simply leapt forward to the next stage of his plan, he had no time to waste, so after a few tiptoed steps, he was wrestling with the double doors. He was almost back where he needed to be.

Which is a shame as his sister and Raymond weren't. And the clock was ticking.

Minus twenty-two minutes, to be exact. Give or take.

CHAPTER FORTY-FOUR

J esus wasn't a complete animal. Not with a name like that. This guy wasn't about to do clever tricks with bread and fish and stuff. He wasn't that nice. No, but he had decided to remove Maureen's face tape so that they could all converse with their new guest. As the tape left her face, she held her mouth to ease the pain and was immediately struck by how smooth her top lip felt. She may well have had the first body waxing of the twentieth century.

Sab had worked with Maureen at Woolworths back at the end of October. It had only been her second day on the job when she'd met Raymond, Jamie, and Tash.

And Jermaine and Dudley, who threatened her with a gun.

It wasn't that moment alone that prompted her to look for other work. She'd explained to Maureen that working day shifts and studying accountancy in the evening wasn't an easy task in addition to caring for her parents. She'd soon left Woolworths, but had kept her hand in from time to time in an attempt to help Raymond at work. His warehousing business had been gifted to him by his boss Dudley, who was now missing and would soon be presumed dead by the UK government.

Raymond had only ever been a gopher of sorts and happier in the employ of someone who dealt with all things financial. Sab had helped reallocate resources and offload the Sinclair C5 stock as soon as the contract allowed. She flagged that a cash injection the business received at the end of summer was dwindling at an alarming rate but had been pleased to see no record of bank loans or third-party funding. It wasn't an official audit, just her way of helping.

Although now she was finding out the truth.

Dudley had not kept a paper trail when this shark delivered a sudden influx of capital.

How had it come to this? Raymond threatened with death, and now Maureen? How the hell did Raymond and Jamie and Tash believe they could fix this problem? Surely, they weren't part of some criminal underworld? How disappointing if they were. Sab was a pretty good judge of character and was shocked to the core by the developments she'd just learnt.

So, they must wait. Really? Just wait? Surely Raymond would call the police, regardless of whatever charade he'd told this mafia?

Sab knew that Maureen was the love of his life, and he would do anything for her.

Anything.

CHAPTER FORTY-FIVE

"Maybe we should just head back to Butler's and say we can't do it?" said Raymond as he passed Studio 2 and stopped for another breather. "Maureen will understand."

"Understand that a psycho wants to kill her to set an example to his other victims?" asked Tash, bending to rub her ankle. "What do you mean? How will she understand? Understand what?"

"I'm not thinking straight," said Raymond rubbing a stitch on his side.

Tash was looking at a sign on the wall that indicated they were nearly at the main exit by Studio 1. If so, then they were basically at the car park where they'd parked the car. They just needed to walk through the reception again and back through to Jamie. They'd walked a complete three-sixty.

"We're nearly there," said Tash. "Get to the end of this corridor, and we're back where we started."

The final corridor was unlike the others because it was crammed full of people, all looking hot and stressed.

"Graeme's running late," said showrunner Gail, dressed in

a dark blue suit, comprising a padded and pleated shouldered jacket and pencil skirt. "There's an ambulance blocking the crescent, and Wood Lane is at a standstill. I bet he's stuck in that. Christ, is anyone else hot?"

"They're fixing the heat exchanger now," agreed Dale, a red-haired man with his parted fringe sticking to the sweat on his forehead. He, too, was wearing a suit, but his shirt was unbuttoned, and a rolled-up tie hung from his breast pocket. "Reception is sending for back-up. Ray someone or other."

Ray Booth was indeed on his way. He'd been working on the final edit of the Christmas blooper tape when the exec producer had called in a favour. Ray knew the score when it came to live broadcasts. He knew about run-throughs too. He would be a good pair of hands until Graeme arrived to take over. Ray was making his way from the editing suite and quite looking forward to lending a hand. He was even humming Ravel's 'Boléro' as he paced the corridors to Studio 1.

"Excuse me," said Tash, trying to clamber past the blockage. It had been some time since she'd been in an enclosed space with so many people, and for a moment she felt her face to ensure she was wearing her facemask. She soon remembered that Covid-19 was thirty-six years in the future. As was her baby son.

"Don't suppose by any miracle that your name is Ray?" asked Gail as Raymond approached her.

Tash continued ahead, but the ever-polite Raymond couldn't blank a lady, that would be impolite. Nor could he lie.

"Erm, yes, it is actually," he stammered. "I'm in a bit of a hurry. I need to help a friend."

"Music to my ears!" said Gail, grabbing Raymond by the arm and shepherding him through the crowds.

"Er, no, sorry, I need to get to the studio," protested Raymond.

"Shortcut," said Gail.

When Tash finally looked over her shoulder, all she could see was a melee of BBC staff comparing notes and disappearing through doors. Soon the corridor was empty. Not a soul to be seen.

Including Raymond.

CHAPTER FORTY-SIX

J amie edged his way along the familiar corridor towards the lift. Sure enough, standing outside with their arms folded were two helmeted Securicor guards.

"Out of use, sir," explained one of them helpfully.

Jamie nodded and retraced his footsteps. So far, so good.

All he needed to do now was access the money from the rear of the lift. This was too easy. He managed a smile as he sidestepped some studio runners chatting outside the entrance to Studio 8. They blanked him, and he continued forwards to Studio 7, then paused before walking through the inner doors to join Tash and Raymond.

He had been planning an apology for his sister. Her mood wouldn't be good, but what could he do? Paul Daniels had asked to speak to him. He was pretending to work for the BBC, so to decline would have been just odd. Jamie took a deep breath and burst through the doors.

"I know what you're going to say, but I'm here now, and I got a free magic trick too," he said to an empty studio.

He was surprised to see neither Tash nor Raymond. He was even more surprised to see a spotlessly painted floor where the dirty million pounds had once stood, which was a bit of a shame. As he peered around the unlit corners of the vast space, he tried his best to whisper.

"Tash? Tash? Raymond?" his voice echoed around the mighty ceiling and suspended lighting rigs.

"Tash?"

The silence was alarming.

What should he do?

Where was the money?

Hang on – where had the silence gone?

What was that noise?

It was awful.

So, so loud.

———

The fire alarm rarely rang across the whole of BBC TV Centre. It was unusual to hear the bell from inside a studio – they were designed to keep as much sound out as possible.

Jamie walked back into the corridor to see confused faces of staff peering out of doors and scratching heads. He walked around the hall to see if everyone was evacuating. They weren't. The bells were ruthlessly attacking his ears, there seemed to be no safe space. The Securicor guys had taken the bells fully in their stride, and a third guard was walking calmly towards them from reception.

"It's some engineering works on the heating. It's all legit," explained the man. "They tripped a switch. They're gonna reset it."

Jamie nodded his thanks to the guards in his most casual way, which wasn't easy given the stimulus his ears were dealing with. Asperger's plus fire alarms plus million-pound heists equalled despair in Jamie's life, but he knew how to appear calm to strangers. Tash would understand what he was dealing with, wherever she was.

"Jamie!" shouted Tash.

Oh, she was behind him.

"Where've you been?" asked Jamie, with unusual anger in his voice.

"Where've *you* been?" replied Tash. A fair question.

"Where's Raymond?" countered Jamie.

"Where's the money?" shouted Tash above the ringing bells.

"I left it with you!"

"Well, it's in the studio then," said Tash.

"Oh."

"What does 'Oh' mean?"

"It means it's not," replied Jamie. "It's gone."

Chapter Forty-Seven

Raymond was surprised. Raymond had been surprised a lot today, so had someone told him that he was about to be the most surprised he'd ever been, he would probably have reason to doubt them. But there was no mistaking it.

Raymond was surprised.

Elton John's hand was smaller than he'd expected, not that Raymond had ever given the matter much thought, but it was a present consideration now. Softer and smaller than he'd imagined. And warmer. But then, everyone was warm right now. The building was like a sweatbox.

"Elton, this is Ray. Ray, I probably don't need to tell you this is Elton John," said Gail standing by a large rostrum in the middle of Studio 1.

"Hello, Ray," said Elton from beneath his straw boater. His glasses were tinted blue, but his eyes were clear to see. He smiled, displaying the famous gap in his front teeth.

"Sorry if I smell of cheese," said Raymond.

"Pardon?" said Elton.

"I was attacked by an owl."

Understandably, this created a moment's silence. Gail pointed to a small black cross taped onto the white floor. "This is your erm; what would you call it, Ray?"

"I beg your pardon?" asked Raymond.

"Elton's marker," explained Gail, "what do you call it?"

"Right. His marker," repeated Raymond in case he needed this information later.

"Oh! I was right!" said Gail smiling at Elton. He smiled back.

Blimey, Elton smelt lovely, thought Raymond. His cologne was probably some of the stuff behind locked doors in the glass cabinets in Debenhams. Aramis or Kouros or some such rock-star indulgence. He loved Elton's song about sad songs saying so much. He wanted to tell him that he liked it. But what was it called?

"Anything you want Elton to know, Ray?" asked Gail. "Just basics, I mean. I'm sure you've done this sort of thing a hundred times!" she added, smiling at Elton.

"Will these alarms stop soon?" asked Elton, gesturing around the studio at the fire alarms that were audible from the corridor outside.

"Yes, I'm going to get to the bottom of that," she replied.

Elton turned to look at Raymond, who was struggling to keep up. What was happening?

He glanced over Elton's white tuxedo jacket to see hundreds of empty seats in the round. Behind the central section was a large screen with graphics projected onto it:

Sports Review of 1984

Raymond looked around the studio. The same graphics continued on painted coloured boards behind the seating. He didn't realise he was doing it, but his hand had started to point at the large logo on the screen. Maybe it was a subconscious attempt to help his brain reconcile what was happening to him on this strangest of days. Elton followed the direction of Raymond's gesture.

"Enter there? OK," said Elton, gauging the distance from the massive theatre curtains to the rostrum. "Quite a walk! Nothing I can't handle. I've walked before."

Gail laughed. "I'll leave you to it. Nice to meet you, Elton. Ray, the results cards are in order – on the shelf."

Gail pointed at a shelf inside the presentation rostrum and started to walk away.

"Sorry, I think someone else should be doing this," said Raymond as assertively as he could.

"Don't worry, the union is fine with this, Ray, so's Graeme. He'll take over as soon as he arrives. Thanks again."

Unions across the UK were still influential in 1984. Maybe not as impactful or disruptive as the seventies, but the cause for the working man was never more prescient than 1984 after a year of news about the miners' strike. The BBC, too, had unions, from musicians to engineers, and undertaking another person's role without clear and exact instruction and agreement from your union was off-limits.

Gail was disappointed that Ray had played his work-to-rule card in front of tonight's surprise star guest, and she'd be sure to flag that with his boss tomorrow.

"I'm sorry, erm, Elton, but I'm not really the man they think I am," said Raymond.

Elton examined Raymond and his variety of cuts. He'd clearly had a bad few days.

"None of us are, Ray," said Elton kindly. "You've told me all I need to know. Curtains," he said, pointing at his entry point. "Cross." He continued pointing at the floor. "Cards." Then he gestured at the cards, accidentally nudging them off the shelf. Raymond watched as they fell on the floor.

"Sorry," said Elton as they both crouched to pick them up, then Elton thought better of it.

"Actually, you should do that. I don't know the order!" He laughed. "Don't want to fuck up the result!"

Elton smiled, and Raymond heard himself let out an awkward giggle. And a little bit of spit too, which was embarrassing.

"No, absolutely," said Raymond, wiping his chin and then scooping up the cards. Then he realised that his vision was doing that 'thing' again. All the letters seemed utterly illegible. Possibly even moving. What did the words say? They were coming back into focus now.

"Blazes," said Raymond.

"You OK?" asked Elton, patiently waiting and examining what looked to be cheese in the hair of this balding man squatting at his feet.

"Yes, yes," lied Raymond. None of these cards listed who had won, just three different typed results, each listing the highest British achievers that year.

Steve Davies (on VT).

Jayne Torvill and Christopher Dean (in-studio, block C front row)

Sebastian Coe (in-studio, block B).

Beneath each were some facts but no numbers. Nothing.

Then Raymond looked up at Elton, but his face had changed. Standing above him, now looking mightily cross, was Maureen. The tuxedo looked a little tighter, the glasses too large, and the hat reminded him of the lady in the Cadbury's Flake commercial, but it was definitely Maureen.

"Maureen," said Raymond.

"Excuse me?" replied Elton. Rod Stewart and Elton often called one another Sharon and Phyllis, but he'd never been called Maureen. And like that, Elton was back in his suit. Raymond stacked the cards together, thought better of his efforts, and thoughtfully repositioned them before handing them to Elton.

"Sorry," said Raymond before walking away. Elton looked at the cards in his hands.

"You sure you got this right?"

Raymond paused, walked back, examined the three cards one more time and placed the middle one on top. Then thought again and put the bottom one on top.

"What's happening?" asked Elton.

"That's got to be right," said Raymond, nodding and handing the cards back to the pop star before dashing away again. He paused at the exit as a memory landed firmly back in his head. He paused to turn around, deciding it would be impolite not to pay a compliment. "I must say, I really enjoyed your song about sad songs!"

"Sad Songs?" said Elton.

"Yes, something about sad songs," agreed Raymond.

"Sad Songs," said Elton.

"Yes. Something about sad songs. It'll come to me."

"Sad Songs," said Elton.

Raymond closed his eyes and bit his lip as he stared to the ceiling.

"No. It'll come to me later, I know it will. I bought it for my wife!"

"Did you?" Elton understandably had little to work with here.

"It jumps, actually. We thought it was the needle. You know, the stylus? So, we changed that, but it kept jumping. So, it's definitely the record that's defective."

"I'm sorry to hear that," said Elton.

Raymond looked sad. "I don't suppose you could sign it?"

"Have you got it with you?"

"No."

"Probably not, then."

Raymond nodded as he absorbed the news. "How about a photo?"

"Of course. Have you got a camera?"

"No."

"It's not going well, is it?" said Elton.

Raymond looked lost in one hundred thoughts.

"I like that other one, too. The one about the piano!" He said. "'Piano Man'!"

"That's Billy Joel," said Elton.

"I'm gonna get off, see you soon."

And Raymond left.

CHAPTER FORTY-EIGHT

The *Saturday Superstore* set looked like the team behind ITV's *Saturday Starship* had broken in and shat all over it. *Starship* was just one of ITV's many attempts to steal the Saturday morning audience from the BBC. *Tiswas* had done well in the '70s, *Number 73* with Sandi Toksvig captured the imagination too. But *Saturday Starship* with Tommy Boyd and Bonnie Langford would only enjoy its current season before being ditched for another creation - *TX* - which soon made way for *Get Fresh*. And it's fair to say that the producers of all those shows might gain some satisfaction from seeing the *Saturday Superstore* being demolished by two squabbling siblings from 2020.

"He didn't take it with him! He was with me! I only left him for two bastard minutes," said Tash as she kicked a fake tree stump stool which turned out to be a real one.

"Fucking hell, that's a real trunk!" she shouted as she fell to the floor to rub her foot.

"You don't think he's done a runner with it, do you?" said Jamie, with his head just visible through the ten-feet-tall

Christmas tree that shed needles and baubles as he fumbled deep into its tinsel laden branches.

"You think he's taken a million quid in stolen notes? And done a runner knowing that someone will murder his wife? And he'll have to live with that decision for the rest of his life? In his mansion in Surrey, sipping champagne and dipping his toes in his swimming pool, deciding where to take his yacht on holiday next year?"

They both went very quiet.

"What was the question again?" asked Jamie.

"Oh, that was close," came a familiar voice from the other side of the studio, followed by an appalled, "What have you done to the *Swap Shop* set?" All these shows were the same to Raymond, and he was sure Noel Edmonds still had this gig.

"Raymond?" said Tash.

Jamie did a double take at the *Saturday Superstore* logo across the desk and then stepped from behind the tree.

"I've met Elton John," said Raymond, purposefully climbing up a spiral staircase barely visible in the shadows.

"Raymond?" said Jamie.

"We hit it off straight away," said Raymond.

"Are the alarms still ringing?" asked Tash.

"The fire alarm?" said Raymond, now at the top of the stairs and dragging one of the holdalls into sight.

"Oh my God! You hid the money!" Tash was ecstatic.

"Yes," said Raymond pushing the bag towards Tash, who was now climbing the stairs. "I mean, no," he continued. "They stopped ringing. The lady in reception says it was a false alarm. It's off now."

Tash started to drag a holdall down the stairs as Raymond turned for the next one.

"Are there people outside the studio?" she asked.

"No," answered Raymond.

"We need to get on then," said Tash before booting the

holdall down the final few steps. "Are you going to help, Jamie, or maybe you'd like another crack at designing that Christmas card?"

"We're not gonna have time for that," said Jamie. "Are we?"

CHAPTER FORTY-NINE

One by one, Tash, then Raymond, then Jamie's faces appeared around the studio door outside the rear of the lift. The million-pound lift. The all-or-nothing lift. The prison or death lift. Jamie had run out of other names, but his mind was still frantically trying to find another.

Next to them, Studio 8 had a brightly lit REHEARSAL sign above deserted doors.

"This is it," whispered Tash.

"What shall we do?" said Jamie considerably louder than anyone might reasonably expect from a cat thief.

"Shhhh, to start," said Tash.

They all huddled together, and Tash took over.

"We cannot make a sound inside that lift. Not one sound. We can't talk, we can't twat the sides with our clown feet...." Jamie knew she meant him but took it with grace, "and we can't take too long."

"Okay," said Jamie.

"Shhhh!" said Tash.

Jamie put his hand in the air, which made Tash sigh despondently.

"Jamie, if I allow you to ask a question, you must try and whisper."

Jamie nodded.

"Go," said Tash.

"Our cash is bound in two and a half thousand-pound bundles," he managed to whisper.

"That's not a question," said Raymond.

"No," said Jamie. "But what if theirs is different?"

"You're getting louder," interrupted Tash.

Jamie doubled down on his whispering attempt, "What if theirs isn't?"

"A million quid is a million quid, right?" whispered Tash.

"No, he's right. The security guys will expect the money to look the same as they left it," whispered Raymond.

"Right, so we'll make it look the same," said Tash.

"Now you're loud," observed Jamie. Loudly.

"Shhhh!" said Tash.

They thought.

"New plan," whispered Tash. "You said the money is on a trolley."

Jamie nodded. Tash took another deep breath. "We have to take one final risk."

"Another one, are you sure?" asked Raymond.

"We wheel the trolley into *Saturday Superstore* and do the switch there," whispered Tash.

"You know it's not a real superstore, don't you Tash?" said Jamie.

"Yes, Jamie. Yes."

"Right, it's just you said Saturday Superstore, rather than the *Saturday Superstore* studio."

"And do you have a point?"

"I didn't want anyone to get confused and think we were taking it to an actual shop somewhere."

"Like who?" asked Tash.

Jamie shrugged before offering a suggestion. "Raymond?"

"Raymond, are you confused?" asked Tash.

"About the plan?" asked Raymond.

"Yes, about the fucking plan, what else would you be confused about?"

"I thought Elton sang 'Piano Man'. I feel a bit daft now," said Raymond.

Tash took a moment to silence the screams inside her head. Then spoke.

"So. We wheel the trolley into the *Saturday Superstore* STUDIO and do the switch there. Yes?"

They all looked at one another and slowly nodded their agreement.

Tash glanced over at the lift.

"So, the question is," whispered Tash, "who wants to get it? Out of the three of us; who wants to steal a million pounds?"

"Well, as I see it, we need someone calm, reliable, and calm," whispered Raymond.

"You said calm twice," said Jamie.

"Shhh!" whispered Tash.

"I thought I had a third thing to say, but I realised I didn't, so I said calm again," explained Raymond.

"So, we're agreed, then?" whispered Tash.

They all nodded in unison before each saying three completely different names.

CHAPTER FIFTY

"He smelt lovely. Tiny hands, too," whispered Raymond.

"Is he still talking about Elton John?" hissed Tash as she re-joined them crouched in the corridor. She had been in the studio to get some straws, but as the *Saturday Superstore café* has been ransacked – and wasn't really a café – she had to settle on tinsel.

"Right, let's get this done," said Tash, offering her clenched fist to the others. Three pieces of tinsel protruded from the top.

"Who goes first?" asked Raymond.

"Sake Raymond – just take a piece of fucking string!"

"It's tinsel," said Jamie.

"Shhhh!" replied Tash as Jamie removed a piece. He held a balding length of silver tinsel that measured no more than four inches. Tash nodded at Raymond. He leant in to examine both pieces before deciding on the green one. Then changed his mind to the red.

"You touched it. You can't change," whispered Tash.

"Can't I?" Raymond looked perplexed. "Okay."

With that, he reached out and grabbed the green tinsel, which was very threadbare. He continued pulling beyond four inches. Then five, then six. Then ten. Then twelve. Then twenty-four. Then he had to lean back. Then he had to stand up. Then he had to walk backwards. They all stared intently as the tinsel continued to unfurl from Tash's closed hand.

"Is it short or long that has to do it?" whispered Raymond down the corridor to the others.

"Long," said Jamie at the same time that Tash said, "Short".

As the end of Raymond's tinsel finally flipped out of Tash's hand, Raymond took one step further back, and his bum struck the lift button, which slowly opened.

"Well, he's there now," said Tash to Jamie, as Raymond turned slowly to feast his eyes on one million pounds stacked neatly in rows on a large catering trolley.

On the opposite side of the lift, two security guards shared their plans for Christmas Day and enjoyed the prospect of sipping a post-meal liqueur and watching Paul Daniel's make one million pounds disappear.

CHAPTER FIFTY-ONE

For some reasons best known to himself, Raymond had opted to remove his Hush Puppies before entering the lift. Which wouldn't have taken long had he not opted for double bows when he put them on this morning. Maureen had bought him new laces from Brixton market over the summer, confident that this would buy him another twelve months from these versatile shoes, but they had only had extra-long ones, so to avoid tripping himself on a daily basis, he'd settled on a nice thick double bow that negated any pavement overhang.

But right now, Raymond – and his feet – were considerably hotter than usual, and his feet seemed to have expanded in his shoes, forcing the laces into a madly tight knot.

"What the fuck is he doing?" whispered Tash as she peered around the corner.

"Taking his shoes off," answered Jamie quite literally.

Raymond had successfully removed one shoe but was now sitting on the floor outside the lift, tongue between his teeth and shoe firmly welded to his foot. His back was keeping the doors from closing. He absent-mindedly glanced into the lift as he worked. "That sandwich has gone," he observed like he was making bus stop small talk.

"Oh well. You snooze, you lose," whispered Tash to Jamie. "Maybe we'll find a vending machine with some more of those shit sweets you like."

"I'm going to help," said Jamie in an impressive whisper.

Tash watched as Jamie walked over and crouched next to Raymond before trying to undo his lace.

"Really? Laces?" whispered Tash.

Jamie wasn't the best at laces, but as Raymond had helped him with his own from time to time, it felt like the right thing to do.

A draught suddenly wafted past them both, and they looked up to see Tash wheeling the trolley out of the lift and back to Studio 7.

She had done it.

She had stolen one million pounds.

And all they heard was Tash's exasperated muttering.

"Sake."

CHAPTER FIFTY-TWO

J amie sat on the *Superstore* warehouse floor – another part of the set with faded timber-effect shelving and racks of props masquerading as excess stock. A polar bear shared the space with a grandfather clock, a Victorian hat stand with some concertinaed paper Christmas decorations, the type that Tash had last seen in Jim and Barbara Royle's lounge. Howard Jones's *The Twelve Inch* album rested against a pile of Duran Duran *Sing Blue Silver* videos.

Raymond stood next to the stolen trolley, and Tash sat on Mike Read's swivel chair.

Between them, they had created an impressive production line, and credit to Jamie, it had been his idea. Happily – and as per banking practices – the stolen million was also bundled in packs of £250.

Raymond would:

1. Extract a stolen bundle of £250 from the catering trolley.

2. Remove the Barclays Bank branded paper wrap from the middle.

3. Place the cash bundle at his feet to the right.

4. Place the loose Barclays wraps in a pile to his left.

Jamie's jobs:

1. Remove Jesus' dirty bundles from their bags, one at a time.

2. Remove the elastic bands that bound them.

3. Place the dirty cash at Tash's feet

4. Take an elastic band and wrap it around one of Raymond's Barclays bundles.

Tash would then:

1. Take Raymond's Barclays wraps one at a time and slide it over the dirty money that Jamie placed at her feet.

2. Place that into a *Superstore* branded shopping trolley. This was the dirty money, masquerading as legit. They would ultimately load all of this back onto the catering trolley.

Occasionally, Jamie would stop to rub his arse. He'd initially sat on a collection of board games by mistake, and my God, games boxes in the '80s hurt. There was no give in them at all. His buttocks came out considerably worse off than these highly strengthened rigid shapes, and he was nursing a deep red scratch from a *Hangman* box.

It took minutes to complete the switch and Tash realised it was probably the most effective thing that they had ever achieved as a threesome. They were very much Bananarama and not Atomic Kitten on this particular occasion, and that felt like a breath of fresh air. In fact, they were a little disappointed that the process was over so quickly.

Once the catering trolley was empty, Jamie and Raymond replenished it with switched bundles from the *Superstore* trolley. The deceit was complete.

They then loaded the stolen Barclays cash into the holdalls and suitcase, taking care not to shin themselves on the brutal edges of the stacked kids' games boxes, clearly designed to last for generations to come. *Cross-Fire* and *I Vant To Bite Your Finger* – a vampire-themed game – were exceptionally sturdy. Sit on one of them, and you'd end up in A & E.

"Go, go," said Tash. "Go!"

Raymond set off towards the exit pushing the trolley ahead of him. It was heavier than it looked when Tash had manoeuvred it. Tash spotted his tired limp and heard the single clomp of his Hush Puppied foot. He'd still not put his other shoe back on.

"Swap jobs," she shouted and ran over to relieve Raymond, as fast as her ankle would allow.

"I can do it," Raymond protested unconvincingly as Tash took his place.

"Put your geography teacher shoe back on," she said, pointing at the brown nylon sock that covered most of his foot but for the sweaty hole around his big toe.

"If anything goes wrong now, let's agree on a meeting place," said Tash.

"Says the woman who didn't come to the last one," said Jamie.

"Meaning?" replied Tash.

"When you didn't turn up for me at Tower Bridge!"

"You weren't there either, you knob!" said Tash, remembering it was Jamie who failed to make their rendezvous back in October, not her.

"I think we should all try to calm down and remain civil," suggested Raymond. "What would Maureen think if she could hear you squabbling when we're supposed to be helping?"

"I was trying to suggest a place to meet in case things went tits up again!" said Tash.

"I think it's a good idea," said Raymond. "Somewhere we all know."

"What about Trafalgar Square?" said Jamie. "We all know that, right?"

Raymond considered this.

"Well, you know what they say? No idea is a bad idea," said Tash. "Except that one. That is a uniquely shit idea."

"Why?" asked Jamie.

"Cos we're in Shepherd's Bush, Jamie," she replied. "I was thinking maybe somewhere closer."

Jamie looked at her.

"To Shepherd's Bush," she clarified.

"How about the car?" suggested Raymond.

"Bingo," said Tash.

"Our car?" asked Jamie.

"Yes, I think our car would be a good idea," said Tash, patiently. "But whatever happens, *whatever happens,* do *not* let that money out of sight."

Tash left the studio pushing the dirty cash whilst Jamie dragged the holdalls across the floor, and Raymond looked for his shoe.

CHAPTER FIFTY-THREE

The corridor remained empty, and not wanting to take any further risks, Tash sped to the closed lift and pressed the button. As she had hoped, the doors opened immediately. It was bizarrely challenging to push the trolley, compared to pulling it. The weight of all the cash was considerable, and the rubber tyres were refusing to mount the chrome strip that edged the corridor floor into the lift.

She would have to pull it into the lift, from inside. But the prospect of actually climbing inside went against all her better judgement.

Balls.

Tash awkwardly squeezed past the front of the trolley into the lift, then gently tiptoed into position square in front of the money before placing her sweating palms onto the trolley handle. She glanced over her shoulder at the closed doors behind.

Don't open now. For God's sake, don't open now.

Tash took her deepest ever breath and pulled.

The trolley moved slowly at first and then eased over the chrome strip and into the lift, immediately causing the whole floor to lower an inch under the weight of one million pounds in stolen used notes.

The movement caught Tash off guard, and her legs gave way underneath her, her knees smacking onto the trolley and her bum landing on the floor. She spun around and was relieved to see the front doors remained shut.

"Get up Tash! Get up!" she whispered to herself.

The trolley was back in place, and the only thing she needed to do now was stand up and get the hell out of there. So why was this taking so long? She'd stood up millions of times before. It was easy. You just stand up. Why wasn't she standing up? What was happening?

Then she realised. She'd snagged Maureen's two piece and her skirt on the trolley's wheel and was trapped in the brake by five inches of pulled wool. The more she pulled, the more the material unfurled. She glanced up at the rear doors to ensure that no one was witnessing this crap robbery.

She somehow managed to hoist herself so she was sitting on her ankles, and then used an almighty pull and pivot of her knees to stand herself up. The wool snapped moments before garrotting the back of her knees, and the pain was mighty, but she was up!

But she was still moving backwards.

She'd pulled so ferociously that she was about to either fall flat on her arse again, or twat her head on the closed doors – both options harboured elements of audible risk.

She could NOT draw attention to herself now.

She hurled her hands behind her to prevent a fall.

And it was then that her left hand struck the *open door* button behind her. The doors that Securicor were guarding.

CHAPTER FIFTY-FOUR

Anneka Rice was a twenty-six-year-old TV presenter in 1984. She was probably most famous for climbing in and out of a helicopter whilst wearing a jumpsuit and frantically running around sunny locations in the UK trying to solve a treasure hunt on behalf of a contestant in a Channel 4 TV studio. She was funny, enthusiastic, charming and a natural broadcaster. The show was enjoyed across all age groups, and series three was about to start on the 27th of December. So, inviting her to be a guest on Paul Daniel's Christmas Day show was a clever booking. And it would be remiss to ignore the fact that she was also a beautiful object of desire for many viewers of all persuasions, not least the sort of middle-aged man who might work in security in December 1984.

So, it was with a certain amount of good luck and serendipity that Anneka Rice left Dressing Room 207 in TV Centre and walked to Studio 8 to rehearse the trick that would open Paul Daniel's show. It also pleased Sanj and Rod from Securicor that she wore a halterneck sequined top and a matching skirt. Quite a short one, to be precise.

Because of Tash's fall, she was now inside a lift with doors open on both sides. So, had anyone left Studio 8 and looked into the rear doors of the goods lift, they would see a perfectly loaded catering trolley laden with one million pounds in stolen notes. Behind was a red-faced younger sister of Margaret Thatcher, staring in horror through the other side at the back of two security guards fixated on Anneka Rice walking past them.

The guards looked happily at one another and then again in the direction of Anneka's path. Well, Sanj was looking at her arse, if we're all being honest. Rod was looking at the magnificence of the overall ensemble.

Sanj secretly dreamed of being with Anneka.

Rod secretly dreamed of being with Sanj.

Much like a theatre curtain, the lift doors slid closed behind them, helped in no small amount by the Thatcher woman frantically pressing the *close doors* button as silently as possible. And like that, Tash was hidden from them once more.

The guards had seen nothing, Tash had seen her life flash before her, and Maureen had seen the last of her third favourite twinset and skirt. But as the doors closed, they emitted a loud clunk. Far more piercing than the rear doors. These were used far less frequently, and the springs in the closing mechanism needed greasing.

Sanj looked at Rod. Rod looked at Sanj. They both turned around to examine the lift doors behind them. Both firmly shut. Sanj reached out and pressed the lift button. The same springs re-engaged, and the doors whirred before slowly sliding apart.

CHAPTER FIFTY-FIVE

Rod and Sanj peered inside the lift. The trolley was still in place, the money still there, and soon they would be accompanying it to its ultimate destination. Panic off. What a story to tell the team back at work. This and that bird off Treasure Hunt.

As the doors automatically closed, Sanj noticed a single piece of tinsel on the trolley, tied on with wool. Nice touch, he thought.

———

"What's happened to Maureen's skirt?" asked Raymond, closing the suitcase lid shut, as Tash walked back into Studio 7.

"I fell," said Tash, looking down at her skirt, strangely misshapen where the fabric had stretched and snapped.

Raymond looked mortified.

"I'm fine, by the way," said Tash.

Jamie was now tidying up the *Superstore* set. "Look! My pass!" he said and retrieved it from the basket and happily placed it in his pocket, the aerial still attached and hanging loose.

"Well, thanks for asking, and yes, the switch is complete, and yes, It went well," said Tash.

"That's her third favourite skirt," said Raymond.

"Well, the fourth just got bumped up the list," said Tash itching her legs beneath the hideous skirt. "I can only imagine how beautiful that might be. Is it made from hessian, by any chance?"

Raymond lifted the Samsonite upright.

"Right, that's us." He looked at his watch. "I hope Maureen's okay."

"She will be," said Jamie.

"You think?' asked Raymond.

"She'll soon be eating Steak Diane and sipping from a bottle Mateus, Raymond. It's Sunday evening!" said Tash.

"Right. Yes. I forgot."

Tash walked over and strained to lift a holdall, Jamie did the same, and Raymond took about nineteen years to get the handle to pull the suitcase effectively. But eventually, they were ready.

As they walked to exit the studio, Tash looked over at them both.

"Well done, that was the hard bit. This is simply walking out of a building. How hard can that be?"

CHAPTER FIFTY-SIX

"What's in the bags?"

Tash stopped dead in her tracks.

They had left Studio 7, walked around the bend and past the doors to Studio 8. Behind those, Paul Daniels had started rehearsing a trick where he and Debbie McGee magically poured a glass of wine out of a newly opened Christmas card. On Christmas Day, fifteen and a half million people across the UK would watch him toast their health with it.

But now, a curmudgeonly BBC security man was glaring at Tash and her colleagues, blocking their exit.

"What?" Tash asked assertively. Attack was usually the best form of defence. In all circumstances, even when wrong. Especially when wrong.

The three of them could see the reception area through just one more set of doors. It was all so achingly close.

"What's in the bags? They look heavy," said the man.

Tash thought carefully and glanced over her shoulder at Raymond, who looked like he might drown in his own sweat, and Jamie, who was suddenly incredibly interested in the floor tiles. Then she said the first thing that came into her head, at precisely the wrong time.

"We're make-up."

No one had heard the door to Dressing Room 205 open and were surprised to hear a man reply.

"Excellent, I'll have mine in here. I don't need to be wandering all over the place. Haven't got time for all that."

And with that, Tash continued her masquerade. She led Jamie and Raymond, and their bags, past the security guard and into the dressing room of Robert Maxwell. The security guard folded his arms and watched to ensure they closed the door. They did.

In 1984, Robert Maxwell was a media mogul. Born in Czechoslovakia, he'd escaped Nazi occupation and lost many members of his family in Auschwitz. So, his successful adult life in politics and publishing was an extremely positive outcome. But his bizarre death in 1991 would lead to the uncovering of hundreds of millions of pounds of misappropriated pension funds from his staff at the Mirror Group. The result was that these people received about half of what they should in retirement. Tash was seven when Maxwell died, but given her career path, she was more than familiar with the rotund man smiling before her now.

"You're the pensions guy," said Tash, turning down Debussy on Radio 3 that played from a Roberts radio by the mirror. That kind of music just reminded her of being on hold with her bank. Maybe he started all that crap.

"I'm sorry, dear?" replied a gregarious Maxwell, sitting down on a chair in front of an illuminated mirror.

He was there as an independent observer to Daniel's million-pound disappearing trick. Maxwell would join the show alongside Owen Rout, the manager of Barclays. The spectacle would be impressive. A safe would enter the studio on a forklift truck, and Daniels would unlock the safe and extract another from within. Inside was one million pounds in cash, and these bundles were loaded into a clear Perspex case before the studio filled with smoke, which cleared to reveal an empty Perspex case.

The money had magically returned to the safe within a safe.

Maxwell, in particular, would look excited. He was good at making millions disappear himself but had never seen it done so publicly.

Jamie had his hand up, but Maxwell was more interested in his reflection as he straightened his purple bow tie. Tash glanced over at her brother.

"What's happening?" asked Jamie.

"We've not got any make-up," whispered Raymond. He looked very uncomfortable.

Tash looked back at Raymond.

"I probably just need a slap of something on the nose and forehead," came the booming voice of Maxwell. "And a glass of water, too, dear."

He gestured at an empty glass to his side. This was a far nicer dressing room than the one Tash had been in earlier. This had mood lighting, carpets, a television, and an en-suite.

Tash wandered over, picked up the glass and walked through to the bathroom. She ran the tap, scooped a glassful of water from the toilet bowl, then turned off the tap.

Maxwell was indeed thirsty. He emptied the glass without taking a breath. Tash peered through a gap in the main door and glared at the back of the inquisitive security guard. He was now listening intently to Bonnie Langford, another guest on the show, and they were both laughing about something or other. He pointed over her shoulder and walked her to Studio 8.

"We're on," said Tash, and with that, the three of them

grabbed their bags and case and marched purposefully out of the dressing.

"Have you forgotten something?" shouted Maxwell as his room emptied.

"You're quite right," said Tash before turning around and walking back over to him. She leaned very close to his face before saying, "try not to be such a wanker."

CHAPTER FIFTY-SEVEN

Every instinct told them to run through the main reception area and straight through the doors to the car park. But their baggage was cumbersome, and they didn't want to draw any more attention to themselves than they already had. The Samsonite case wheels clicked across every grout line in the tiled floor, and Tash and Jamie breathed heavily under the weight of their holdalls. Jamie reached the doors first, except he tried to push the locked ones for considerably longer than you might expect. Tash effortlessly pushed the opening door for Raymond, then herself to exit.

"Jamie," said Tash, "this way."

They loaded the Princess boot, climbed into their seats, and set off for the gates.

The commissionaire had no interest in people leaving, so happily opened the barrier. They joined Wood Lane, only to slam on the brakes to avoid a head-on collision with an HGV driving considerably faster than Raymond would have it.

The Princess had stalled, and after only nineteen or twenty attempts, the engine sprung into life. As he set off again, Raymond hit the brakes once more to avoid hitting a lady with a Silver Cross brand twin pram. She was strolling across the road and hadn't seen him at all. She'd simply stepped into his path, which was a bit silly, but Raymond hated to judge people. She might have things on her mind. He watched as she struggled to mount the kerb on the other side of the road. She was getting nowhere.

"Go around her!" shouted Tash.

"What?" replied Raymond.

"No!" said Jamie before opening the door and climbing out.

"What are you doing?" asked Tash. "Jamie! No!"

"You know what it's like with the pram," said Jamie as he walked over to help. And Tash did.

Bloody hell, these were well-fed babies, thought Jamie, as he struggled to ease the large, spoked steel wheels up onto the pavement. The thick, white-walled tyres were quite beautiful. Jamie remembered Tash's deliberation over prams when her son was born. Bugaboo or Mamas & Papas? Prams in 2020 looked like 4x4s compared to the '80s versions. But this one was easily vintage already, maybe '50s or '60s? Superb leather and steel suspension, and a sturdy tray beneath, overflowing with Christmas shopping no doubt, it was too dark to tell. The two deeply upholstered hoods faced one another and kept the cold night air from penetrating the mobile crib. Two little siblings were blissfully unaware of the near miss, and Jamie thought of his nephew for a moment. He missed the cuddles. Once two wheels were eventually up onto the kerbstone, the magnificent suspension of the Silver Cross enabled Jamie and the mum to drag the third and fourth, pulling her young family safely off the road. The woman's face was shielded from the icy wind with a wraparound grey snood that she'd pulled up to the very bottom of her eyes. Oh God, maybe she was homeless, thought Jamie, and was dragging all her worldly possessions around Shepherd's Bush. She turned to walk away with no thanks nor eye contact. But then, Jamie didn't really do eye contact, so he wasn't offended as he climbed back into the car. He just felt a slight tinge of emotion about this poor soul and realised how lucky he was.

Tash watched as the pram disappeared into the darkness and thought of her son back in 2020.

"Come on, Raymond, let's speed things up a bit," said Tash.

The Princess ground into gear one more time before continuing south of the river.

CHAPTER FIFTY-EIGHT

The drive back to Gaywood Close was far more relaxed in mood than the journey from it. Almost euphoric. Other than the overly cautious Raymond who was driving at least five miles per hour beneath the speed limit – where traffic would allow, of course. Which was a dangerous strategy, given their deadline for parking the Princess outside the house was rapidly approaching. Maureen would be liberally spraying her favourite scent, Tweed by Lentheric, over her second favourite twinset right now.

"How are we doing for time?" asked Jamie.

"There's a clock there," replied Tash, gesturing at the analogue dial alongside the speedometer.

"Can't read it," said Jamie from the back seat.

"Well, the big hand is pointing to the nine," started Tash.

"I meant I can't see it," said Jamie.

"We have four minutes to park and to empty the boot," said Raymond.

"Terrible idea," said Tash.

"It's not an idea – those are the facts," replied Raymond as he turned the Princess into Christchurch Road.

"I mean the order of things," said Tash. "Stop the car by the garage. We'll empty the boot. Then you park the car and run back up to meet us. Assuming you have your Jimmy Choos back on?"

"Run?" asked Raymond.

"Waddle, roll, moonwalk," said Tash. "I'm not giving any shits."

"You could walk fast?" suggested Jamie.

"What, you mean like a brisk walk?" replied Raymond

"Yeah. A brisk sort of walk."

"That's an idea, I suppose," said Raymond.

"Are we really having this conversation?" said Tash. "Just don't get seen!"

Raymond nodded and indicated left. They might just pull this thing off.

"Oh, and if things go wrong," said Tash.

"Yes?" replied Raymond.

"Don't shout S. O. fucking S."

"We won a war with the Enigma Code!" said Raymond.

"We did, Tash; he's right about that," said Jamie.

"One, we used the dots and the dashes to communicate S.O.S. We didn't shout S.O.S. And two, no, we fucking didn't! You're thinking of Morse Code. The Enigma Code wasn't even ours!"

"Alan Turing. A very clever man," said Raymond.

"He was," agreed Tash.

"Homosexual apparently," added Raymond.

Tash glared at him. "And?"

"Terrible shame what happened. He was persecuted. For loving someone," said Raymond.

"Oh!" said Tash, happily. "I thought you were gonna say something homophobic. You said something beautiful."

She wound down her car window down, and leant her head through it into the cold evening air, then shouted,

"Can everyone in 1984 start being a bit more Raymond, please?"

Jamie laughed. Raymond blushed.

"Except the shoes," said Tash to Raymond. Then she leant out and shouted, "Except the shoes!"

CHAPTER FIFTY-NINE

J amie and Tash were strangely comfortable straddling the holdalls outside Raymond's garage. They reminded themselves of the kids they would see at the airport on top of those pull-along animal-shaped kids' suitcases. Alongside them stood the Samsonite case. A passer-by would be hard stretched to imagine they were guarding one million pounds worth of banknotes stolen from BBC TV Centre.

Tash was laughing. "You're kidding. Tell me you're kidding?"

Jamie was laughing too. "No." He had no problem laughing at himself. If something was funny, it was funny. Simple as that. No matter who was being laughed at, and that included himself.

"How many?" asked Tash.

"Fifty," said Jamie, drying his eyes.

"Was he mad at you?"

"Raymond doesn't get mad," said Jamie. "He's a gentleman."

"But he trusted you to buy stock, and you bought fifty

microwaves...." Tash started to laugh again, so Jamie finished her sentence.

"With inward opening doors."

That was it. They were hysterical.

"What did you do?" asked Tash when she caught her breath.

"Threw them in the river in the middle of the night," said Jamie.

"No!" said Tash.

"Do you know what Raymond said? Whilst we were shoving them off the Wharf side? I think it was his way of telling me off," said Jamie.

"What did he say?"

"He said, Jamie, we're going to have to stop throwing things in the river."

They both howled again. Jamie wiped his eyes and then leant over to give his sister one of his bad cuddles, where neither had space to place their face.

"I've missed you, Tee," said Jamie.

He'd not called her that since they were kids, and the moment wasn't lost on Tash.

"I know you have," she replied.

Christ, was she really going to be able to finish what she'd set out to do? To save Raymond's life – albeit now Maureen's life – and then ruthlessly abandon Jamie? After all, that's what he'd told her to do. Just not this Jamie. But where the fuck was Martha?

"What are you doing out here? We should be out of sight."

They looked around to see a flustered Raymond.

"Is everything OK?" asked Tash, standing up and brushing bits of tarmac off Maureen's ripped skirt.

"No! The moment I climbed out of the car we all came out of the house. I had nowhere to hide!"

Raymond looked very dirty.

"What did you do?" asked Jamie.

"I had to roll under the car until we got in, then roll out again before we drove off." Raymond was marching towards them and glancing nervously over his shoulder. Was his face bleeding again?

"How did that work out for you?" asked Tash as Raymond stepped into clearer view.

"I think my belt caught on the exhaust. They dragged me for the first twenty yards."

His face was indeed bloody and grazed, and his left nipple was showing through his ripped shirt.

"Well, there's a solid argument for braces if I ever heard one," said Tash.

"Why aren't you in the garage – we're about to drive past!" said Raymond, glancing back at the road.

"Someone has the key," replied Tash.

"You do," said Jamie needlessly.

Raymond fumbled for the key and struggled to find the garage keyhole with his trembling hands. Tash took over and pulled open the door. They all dragged themselves and their haul inside and lowered the door seconds before the familiar engine of the Princess filled their ears.

Inside the Princess, yet unfettered with turf, soil and yet to be annihilated by a mercy dash across London, Maureen, Raymond and Jamie happily continued along the road to Tulse Hill. Frankie's 'The Power of Love' filled the unusually warm car, as they dreamed of mixed grills and lemon and sultana cheesecakes. Maureen was also wrestling with the idea of throwing three pounds at half a bottle of Liebfraumilch. After all, it was her birthday, and life was finally looking good. 1985 might just be their year.

CHAPTER SIXTY

Raymond sat beneath the cracked Russell Hobbs slow cooker, with the power cord tied beneath his chin. Jamie climbed onto him once more, and Tash sat upfront pressing the keys of the ZX Spectrum.

"Never as much fun on the way back, is it?" said Jamie. "Just the prospect of lots of dirty washing and going back to work!"

"What?" asked Raymond.

"I was doing a joke about the flight home from holiday," explained Jamie.

"I'm not really in the mood for jokes," said Raymond. "Sorry."

"Look on the bright side, Raymond," said Tash, still typing away. "Maureen will see you with fresh eyes when all this is done and dusted. You'll be a hero, like Daniel Craig."

"Who?"

"Oh yeah. He's our James Bond. Think Sid James on steroids."

"Tash is right," said Jamie. "You might have a second honeymoon."

"We didn't have a first," said Raymond.

"Really?" asked Tash, pausing to look back at him.

"A bit of a problem with the ferry," said Raymond.

"Oh God, I'm sensing an anecdote," replied Tash.

"We missed it. The car broke down, and I didn't have an AA membership. I'd cancelled it to pay for the campsite."

"A risk-taker," said Tash. "I can see what she saw in you, you big flirt."

"We called a number we saw in the phone box by the main road. *24/7 Car Rescue*, but the man who answered said they were shut."

"Not really twenty-four-seven then," said Jamie.

"I asked him about that. But it turned out he'd named the business after his wife's birthday, which was the twenty-fourth of July," explained Raymond. "Twenty-four-seven."

"You do have some bad luck, don't you, Raymond?" said Tash patiently.

"They were shut then too, on account of it being her birthday," he added.

"I've forgotten what we were talking about, actually, but I would like it to stop. Shall we make tracks?" said Tash.

"We were talking about Raymond's honeymoon," said Jamie.

"Do you know, now that I think about it..." Raymond started to say.

"No," said Tash and struck ENTER on the Spectrum keyboard.

It seemed to be like a familiar migraine to Tash now. The same stars in her eyes, the grey metallic feeling of dread, and now with a soundtrack where Phil Collins performed drum infills over Midge Ure's programmed drum track. She'd heard that Midge was too polite to tell Collins he'd already pre-recorded the synth drums. After all, the frontman of Genesis had arrived at this supergroup ensemble – and he'd look great on the Band Aid video. So maybe the microphones to his drum kit were recording, thought Tash. Or perhaps they weren't. Or maybe, it was a combination of –

Darkness.

CHAPTER SIXTY-ONE

I t often happened when Tash travelled through time. Her head filled with either utter despair or the strangest speculative thoughts. So, as she pictured Phil Collins' curious stripy tank top and him biting his lip, her body jolted as Jamie's skull struck her from behind. She found herself steering the C5 through the same – but drier – landscape now. She tried her hardest to slow the Sinclair without tipping over, so found herself performing a figure of eight to avoid smashing into any of the other garage doors. She forgot that a further turn would steer them straight into the side of their parked milk float, but it was too late. The C5 and its passengers lodged themselves beneath the steel skeleton of the rectangular machine.

"Sake," shouted Tash as she peered at a milk crate less than six inches from her nose.

"Everyone OK?" asked Jamie.

Raymond didn't answer.

"Raymond?" asked Tash.

Nothing.

"He's not there," said Jamie.

"What?" asked Tash, unable to turn around to see.

"He's not there, Tash! Raymond's gone!"

———

Jamie had climbed out first. But the weight reduction had caused the C5 to lift a little, jamming Tash further under the milk float.

"Push!" shouted Tash.

"I am pushing!" replied Jamie.

"Not from behind, knobhead. You're forcing me under," said Tash, finally able to twist to see behind. "I meant push *down* to lower my height."

"Well, I didn't know what you meant. You're just shouting a lot!" said Jamie, changing tack.

He put his entire bodyweight on the seat he'd vacated and pressed.

"Now pull!" said Tash.

"How can I push and pull, Tash! That's not even a thing!"

"You push down and pull back, for fuck's sake!" shouted Tash.

She had been trapped for at least three minutes now, and it felt like hours.

"Should I try and drive the milk float off you?" said Jamie.

"Don't touch the fucking float! You'll rip my head off!" replied Tash.

Jamie stopped doing anything because nothing seemed good enough. He was used to this feeling.

"How did you lose Raymond? You were sitting on him!" said Tash.

"I remember bouncing, and when I landed, I felt the seat instead of his sticky trousers."

Jamie walked forwards and looked at the milk float.

"What if I empty this?" he said. "That will make it lighter. You might come loose?"

"It's worth a try," said Tash in a voice that should have sounded far more grateful.

So Jamie set to work. He started with the crates on Tash's side of the milk float to begin with, and after ten or twelve were on the ground, he attempted to push the milk float up and off the C5 bonnet that was nipping down and trapping his sister firmly in place.

"It's moving, Jamie. It's moving," said Tash.

With one more push, Jamie could see the tiniest gap between the metal of the float and the plastic of the C5. Motivated by this, he started to rock the float to get a bigger gap each time. "Can you pedal backwards?" he strained to say, over the sound of milk bottles falling and smashing from all sides.

Tash could, and she did.

Now she and the C5 were free.

Jamie let go of the float and doubled over to catch his breath.

"Well done," he said.

"What a mess," said Tash.

"We can clear this up," said Jamie.

"I meant Raymond. Where the hell is Raymond?"

Jamie paced to the rear of the float to retrieve some broken glass. Then something caught his eye. On the opposite side of the float, faced down, and covered in spilt milk and broken bottles, was a Farahs-wearing ripped-shirted man wearing a slow cooker. And he wasn't moving.

CHAPTER SIXTY-TWO

J amie and Tash had placed Raymond onto the bench seat of the milk float. Tash attempted to remove his slow cooker helmet but realised the more she tugged, the more the cord beneath his chin was digging into his throat. She was alerted to this by his sudden choking, so she stopped and slowly fiddled with the knot instead.

"It's a good knot, Raymond. How are we doing?" she asked as the helmet slowly slid away.

Jamie ran over from the open garage with a bottle of water in his hand.

"Here. Have a drink of this," he said.

Tash nipped Raymond's nose, so his lips opened involuntarily, and Jamie poured the liquid straight into his mouth. The reaction was like a science experiment where you drop a mint into a bottle of Coke. An Instant Raymond Mouth Fountain.

"Bit fast, Jamie," said Tash.

"Turps! Turps!" stammered Raymond as his eyes started to stream with tears.

"What?" asked Jamie, looking at the bottle. "It's a water bottle!"

"It's a turps bottle," said Raymond, now sort of coughing and choking and speaking, which was quite a talent.

"It looks like a water bottle! Doesn't it?" said Jamie to his sister. "Water?"

"What even is a water bottle?" asked Raymond.

"A bottle of water! From the shops!" said Jamie. "A water bottle!"

"Bottled water? Where do you think you are, France?" said Raymond.

"In fairness, Raymond, everyone drinks bottled water in 2020," said Tash.

"You can't drink tap water?" he asked.

"No, you can drink tap water," said Tash.

"So, why do you pay for bottled water?" asked Raymond.

Tash looked at Jamie. Jamie looked at Tash. They both thought really, really hard.

"I've got nothing, Raymond. We'll park that one, yeah?" said Tash.

"Would some milk help?" asked Jamie, reaching to the back of the float. Amongst the empties some bottles were still intact, and some still contained produce.

"I could use some Aspirin and a couple of plasters, to be honest," said Raymond.

"Really? I think you'll be fine," lied Tash. "Just a few scratches." She didn't want to prolong things.

Raymond looked like he'd been fighting a lion. With both hands tied behind his back. And the lion was tooled up. And pissed off.

"Come on, Jamie's right. Let's find you some milk. It's the nectar of the Gods. The bees, the cows, whatever." Tash was desperate now. She took a bottle from Jamie and tried to remove the foil lid but struggled to unpick the edges.

"The fuck does this work?" asked Tash, examining the baffling lid, where foil seemed impossibly sealed around the top of the bottle.

Jamie leant in and firmly pressed his thumb into the centre of the foil, causing the perimeter to loosen. He lifted it off; he'd had two months experience of doorstep milk bottles.

Tash lifted Raymond's head a little, pinched his nose to open his mouth again, and started to pour.

"That's it. Good boy, isn't that nice?"

Liquid that wasn't making it down Raymond's throat was pouring down either side of his face onto the seat.

"That's so good for you, actually; we often overlook how good milk is," said Tash.

"That's cream," said Jamie leaning in to examine the bottle.

"Even nicer," said Tash. "Drop more?"

Raymond covered his face with his hands.

―――――

Jamie glanced up at his sister as she slammed the garage door closed. She was taking no risks again, and the C5 was safely out of sight. He placed the final crates around the million pounds, and happy that the bags and case were out of sight, he climbed alongside Raymond on the bench seat. Tash rushed over to them and shuffled alongside her brother.

"Can you see yet, Raymond?" she asked.

Raymond turned to look in her general direction.

"I can see," he reassured her. "Just not out of both eyes, yet."

"That'll be the turps," said Jamie, giving a confident nod to his sister.

They both looked at the poor man behind the wheel. His

face was scratched, bloody, cheesy, creamy, and now bewildered.

"You'll be fine," said Tash. "Come on, start her up, Raymond. Between us, we have five good eyes. Nothing can go wrong now."

"Yeah!" agreed Jamie. "Let's go and save Maureen!"

"Yeah!" joined in Tash. "Let's do this!"

CHAPTER SIXTY-THREE

"What sort of vehicle uses a fucking battery?" shouted Tash.

"Well, all cars will by 2035," said Jamie.

"Really?" asked Raymond, squinting his bad eye in the hope it might recover a little more focus.

"Electric cars! The future sounds amazing."

"That's the plan. Cut out the carbon emissions. Global warming's terrible," replied Jamie.

"I'd like it a little warmer, to be honest," said Raymond.

"Yeah," said Tash. "It doesn't work like that. We just get shit winters and shit summers."

"Oh," said Raymond. "But still, those toilet seats that close really slowly without sort of slamming down, though. They sound good."

"So, how do we charge it?" asked Tash.

"We have to take it to the dairy, I would imagine," said Jamie. "They might want to know where their milkman is, though."

The stolen white float looked anything but inconspicuous under the forecourt lighting.

"I thought these things drove for miles," said Tash, glancing up at the illuminated *Gulf* petrol station sign. The logo reminded Jamie of the Burger King one, which Tash refused to accept was meant to be a burger, insisting Jamie was wrong and it was actually a fried egg because the yellow was shiny. Or yolk, as she called it. And she had a point.

It had been quite a humiliating twenty minutes for Raymond when all was said and done. The milk float had just suddenly stopped working at the busy crossroads by Camberwell Green. So, he had asked Tash and Jamie to push the vehicle three hundred yards to the *Gulf* garage on Camberwell Road whilst he steered. On arrival, they'd jostled it into position by a pump, and Raymond had walked around the circumference twice, looking for the fuel cap before the penny dropped. So, the lady in the kiosk reminding him that milk floats used batteries was too much to bear. She'd opened a small window and leant out with a battery-powered loud hailer in her hand, which Jamie noticed she seemed to enjoy more than he would if he was imparting bad news.

"It's been driving all day, hasn't it? Then the baddies stole it," said Raymond, rubbing his head.

"The *baddies*? Is this a thing in '84?" asked Tash. But her attempt to humiliate Raymond was lost on him.

"Yes, the *baddies* at Butler's," explained Raymond as his ripped shirt flapped in the freezing breeze. "They would have used a good few battery miles. Then we drove it to the BBC, and then home."

Raymond thought for a moment, and he and Jamie spoke almost in unison, along the lines of ,"It's quite impressive, really!" and, "It's done quite well, hasn't it? All things considered?" followed by a, "Well, this is it," from one of them. Then, "On one battery!"

. . .

"So, what's the plan now?" asked Tash, shifting her weight from one foot to another impatiently.

Jamie raised his hand. Tash took a deep breath and nodded at him.

"I think a new plan would be a good idea at this stage," he said.

They all waited.

"Are there any more words making their way to your mouth, or are we done?" asked Tash.

"No, well, I was just saying, I think a new plan is a good idea."

"I think he's right," said Raymond. "A new plan is the way to go."

Jamie nodded. Raymond nodded and added an assertive "yes," followed by, "so, it's decided then. A new plan."

"Well, pushing seemed to work pretty well. How would you feel about us pushing you the remaining three or four miles, Raymond? Along these dark roads? And hope the stolen money doesn't fall off whilst we stroll behind?"

"I'd be happy to do that," said Raymond.

"Okay," said Jamie.

"I was fucking kidding!" said Tash.

They all stood in silence for a moment, then Raymond felt around inside what remained of his pockets, tentatively at first in case of mice. He then repeated this process with the same outcome.

"Jamie. Do you have any cash?" asked Raymond, looking over his shoulder.

Jamie searched his pockets and pulled out one banana Toffo coated in a lot of fluff, a Lego windscreen, and a crumpled banknote.

"A fiver," he replied. "Why?"

"New plan," said Raymond and pointed across the fore-court. Everyone turned to look at what had caught his eye.

It was a bus stop.

Chapter Sixty-Four

The flickering streetlamp illuminated three figures and a concrete pillar bus stop. The light softened the surfaces it found, which were few, but happily, one of these areas was Raymond's face, so his scratches, swollen nose, cut lip, and creamy coated cheeks weren't apparent until you got within a couple of metres. Which Tash sadly was, so she was enduring the full horror of his injuries plus his unique aroma, which given the events of the past few hours, was not unlike a train's lavatory. She was about to turn downwind as politely as possible when she spotted the warm glare of a brightly lit bus back down the road.

"Here we go," said Tash.

"That's a bus!" said Jamie.

"Which one do we want, Raymond?" asked Tash.

"What?" asked Raymond, fumbling to find the handle on his suitcase.

"What number?" replied Tash.

"I've no idea. Maureen hates buses," replied Raymond.

"But you live south of the river," said Tash.

"You live north, but I bet you couldn't name all the bus routes," replied Raymond.

"Not from the year I was born, no!"

"Forty-two. Tower Hill," read Jamie as he squinted towards the red double-decker down the road.

"Bingo!" said Tash, grabbing the handles to her holdall before stopping to gently rub the swollen blister that had formed on her right palm.

"Excuse me!"

They all ignored the shout from the middle-aged lady behind them.

"I'm talking to you, Worzel Gummidge! And your carers!" This time it was through a loud hailer, and in fairness, Raymond had a look of the TV scarecrow.

They glanced across at the lady from the *Gulf* garage. She looked smaller outside her kiosk but considerably more aggressive.

"You can't leave your ice cream van here. You're blocking my forecourt!"

"It's a milk van," shouted Jamie.

"I know. I was being insulting," replied Deniece, not that they could read her name badge, but that was her name. Her voice bounced off the Georgian townhouses across the road, she cropped her cigarette and stomped on it.

"The thing is, we are in a bit of a hurry, actually," said Raymond, as loudly as he could. He turned to look at the Routemaster bus. It had stopped and was unloading passengers one stop before theirs. A small crowd waited patiently to board.

"Move it. Now. Or I'll call the police!" said Deniece. She was heading towards them.

"Not gonna happen, sorry," said Tash.

Raymond was indescribably self-conscious of his appearance as pedestrians joined in with the queueing drivers who started glaring over at the three of them.

"Tash, we don't want people seeing us," said Raymond.

"Shall we quickly move it?" said Jamie.

Suddenly a white flash illuminated the three of them. Deniece had raised a Polaroid Instant camera to her eye and was commemorating this magical moment. She reached out for the photo as it ejected through the plastic slot and then let the camera rest around her neck on its carrying strap. As she wafted the picture in the air to dry the developing ink, she raised the loud hailer again. Which was overkill given she was now less than ten feet away from them.

"I've got this for the police now," came the amplified threat as she held the mug shot in the air.

"Sake!" shouted Tash as she lifted her heavy holdall and struggled in the direction of the float, attempting to snatch the photo on her way past Deniece but failing as the feisty lady pulled out of grasp.

Jamie and Raymond followed dutifully behind, with one eye each on the stationary bus.

Tash opted for the driving seat this time as she climbed in the float and placed the holdall on the seat next to her. She watched as Jamie and Raymond rammed the other bag and the case next to her and then walked to the front of the float to push it backwards. A car behind started to beep. Tash peered around to see the blocked exit route.

"Balls! We're gonna have to go forwards!" she shouted at Jamie and Raymond, who turned to establish the best route off the congested forecourt.

"I'd go around the red Escort and past the blue Montego," suggested Raymond as he passed Tash on his way to the rear.

"Through the gap, you mean? Good idea!"

"Yeah, through the gap," Jamie confirmed as he joined Raymond.

They both started to push. And then push again.

"What's happening?" asked Tash.

"We're pushing," said Jamie through clenched teeth.

"It's not moving," said Tash.

"Is the handbrake off?" asked Raymond.

"Of course, the fucking hand brake's off!" said Tash, her eyes darting around the minimalist interior.

They pushed again.

"Remind me where the handbrake is?" said Tash.

They stopped pushing and drew almighty breaths. Raymond attempted to speak between his gasps.

"On the right. By the. End of the. Bench."

"Why aren't you pushing?" asked Tash impatiently. She peered out and glanced along the road at the bus indicating to rejoin the traffic. Luckily, the traffic lights at the crossroads in front of it were changing to red.

"Is the handbrake off?" asked Jamie.

"It's off. It's off!" said Tash.

The float started to move gently forwards, and Tash manoeuvred it through the parked cars until it was facing the road, enabling ample clear access for fuel customers.

"Not there!" came the voice of Deniece through the loud hailer again.

"What?" shouted Tash, leaping from her skin.

"You're blocking the pavement."

The hailer was particularly bizarre as Deniece was standing right next to Tash.

"Sake!" shouted Tash.

Jamie and Raymond ran to the front of the float and started to shove it backwards. As they slowly passed Deniece, Tash snatched the photo from her hand and forced a smile. Deniece begrudgingly made her way back to her kiosk.

Jamie and Raymond knew the float could go no further when it struck the brick wall next to the tyre pressure machine. Luckily this was out of sight of Deniece, so they were able to drag their bags and case and stumble across to the bus stop, seconds before the bus arrived. Amazingly, it stopped for them.

It was a 1960s Routemaster, which were still in service during Tash's younger years, so it was quite nostalgic for her to be standing at the open back. A large advert on the side read: *Brilliantly Simple Sharp Videos*. Happily, they were the only passengers waiting to board, so Tash struggled on first with her holdall, declining help from the courteous conductor who stepped to one side to allow her to pass into the smoky interior. Jamie was next, and his Asperger's presented itself in the form of him dragging his holdall whilst also handing the scrunched-up fiver towards the conductor and requesting, "Three adults to Bermondsey, please." He did this whilst looking at the floor, which irritated the conductor even more than trying to pay whilst blocking the path of the curious-looking pensioner behind.

"Sit down, I'll come to you," said the conductor, ignoring the banknote.

The pensioner wasn't a pensioner. He was a good few years shy of a bus pass. Despite his struggle, he was unable to lift his cumbersome suitcase onto the bus floor.

"Hop on mate, I'll take that," offered the conductor, it was all part of the job to him, and he liked to help the oldies.

"No, it's fine, I can manage," said Raymond whilst simultaneously not managing, but mindful that there was about half a million quid in his case, and now wasn't the time to entrust it to a stranger. Despite this, the conductor was now on the pavement, relieving Raymond of the suitcase.

"Let him! Come on!" shouted Tash, shuffling onto one of the bench seats at the rear.

Raymond muttered a few thankyous and sorrys before

climbing onto the bus, unable to go further as Jamie stood blocking the way, still holding out his fiver.

"Move down!" shouted the conductor from outside.

"Move down," said Raymond to Jamie, who complied. His senses were on overload.

Nobody saw what happened next, but they were all surprised to hear a curious dull thud and scream. The bus rocked a little too. Raymond turned to see the milk float resting on the corner of the bus. Happily, it hadn't damaged any paintwork. Having rolled from its resting place, it had struck the conductor – now sandwiched between the windscreen of the milk float and the metal chassis of the rear of the number 42 bus. His squashed face was glaring at Raymond.

"Help," whispered the man, as best anyone could with all the wind knocked from their lungs.

"Pardon?" said Raymond.

"Help."

Raymond's "Did you apply the hand brake, Tash?" was lost in the depths of the bus amongst the many gasps from the other passengers. At the front, the driver turned in his seat and slid open the spilt window that separated him from the main cabin. He peered down the bus.

Jamie walked down to Raymond and was relieved to see that the suitcase was still in the hand of the conductor, soundly wedged between the milk float bumper and the bus.

"Let me take that," said Jamie as he started to jerk the suitcase frantically up and sideways, over and over again.

"Help," said the conductor.

"No, it's okay, I can manage," replied Jamie as it finally came loose. He was able to slide it onto the bus floor.

"Help me," said the conductor.

"We need to help the conductor," said Jamie into the depths of the bus.

The hydraulics of the bus hissed, followed suddenly by the

sound of car horns and screeching tyres. The driver had leapt from his cabin into the road, his intention was clearly to help his colleague, but he hadn't factored in a Ford Fiesta Xr2 boy racer living his best life whilst overtaking the parked bus and attempting the rap at the start of Chaka Khan's 'I Feel For You' at the top of his voice (which wasn't going well at all).

For the boy racer, it was a 'good news, bad news' thing. The used brake pads that his mate had just fitted for twenty quid to get the car through its MOT were functioning well, but now he was parked over a bus driver who had been hoping to clock off work in thirty minutes.

"What's happened?" asked Tash, straining to look over her shoulder.

More gasps from passengers silenced Jamie's reply.

"Who do I pay?" His hand was still holding out the five-pound note.

CHAPTER SIXTY-FIVE

Despite their looming deadline, the three of them were all encouraged to see how speedily and efficiently the London ambulance service operated. The driver was on good form as medics tended to him in the back of the ambulance. The Fiesta had floored him but had stopped short of his torso, trapping only his legs, which both seemed to be working.

Police had arrived too, but not before Jamie and Raymond successfully released the trapped conductor. He was sitting on the kerb drinking a cup of tea provided by a kindly lady who lived in one of the flats across the road. She'd administered a decent amount of whisky into the drink too, which was now announcing itself on his breath. As an employee on a final written warning for visiting pubs on his lunch breaks, this didn't sit well with him; he knew he was next up for police interrogation. Given that he was able to walk and was only expecting some deep purple bruises, he intended to say as little as possible. Tash had agreed this was a good strategy when she'd checked him over. She was a nurse, after all. Well, she'd told him she was. She was surprising herself with her predisposition to deceive.

"Are we gonna be much longer?" asked a teenage boy dressed as a beautiful girl with dreadlocks as he sucked on an Embassy cigarette, before exhaling in Tash's general direction.

"You in a hurry are you?" asked Tash.

"Got a tube to catch," he casually held up a ticket and added, "Culture Club, Wembley. Starts at half seven."

"There'll be a support act, there's always a support act. And they're always shit."

"There is. King. And they're not shit, I want to see them too. This cost me seven fifty." He wafted the Arena ticket, which moved the smoke around even more.

"This delay isn't doing my finny haddock any good, is it?" said Alexandra, an eighty-something passenger squashed alongside Tash. She glanced at her gold watch, which hung loosely around her liver-spotted wrist, and held up her VG stores shopping bag.

"Well, at least that clears up the smell situation," said Tash. "Can't say I'm not relieved."

"I'm not dicking about with any questions from the filth," said Alexandra, peering outside at the flashing blue lights. Tash was taken aback by her choice of vernacular.

All the passengers had waited patiently in their seats in case the authorities needed witness statements, but pretty soon this had become a tedious inconvenience. They'd grown tired of the group singalong of *why are we waiting?* (which Jamie loved, but Tash considered clichéd). Raymond has spent the whole time looking at his watch.

"Ladies and gentlemen, if I could have your attention, please?"

The downstairs passengers all looked over to WPC Gayle,

a calm and friendly lady standing at the foot of the stairs. She spoke with authority and assurance, but most of all with volume. From her position, her words easily resounded around the upper deck too.

"Can everyone hear me upstairs?" she continued.

"No!" came the reply from a cocky teenage girl, followed by laughter. The WPC allowed herself a smile and continued.

"You'll be pleased to know that the driver of the bus is well."

This news was greeted with cheers.

"And is going to be taken to hospital."

This was met with boos, followed by a voice that sounded very much like Tash's saying, "Sake."

"A replacement driver is being allocated to complete the route," she continued.

The cheers arrived again.

"But this may take up to an hour."

The boos were thunderous now, and it was, without doubt, the voice of Alexandra that said, "Fuck that."

"Don't worry!" said Tash.

Everyone turned to look at this curious lady, dressed older than her years. She'd managed to conceal the significant damage to Maureen's clothes.

"There's another driver on the bus," said Tash.

"Really?" asked the WPC.

"Yep, and I can vouch for him. I work for London Transport," she continued, holding up the conductor's pass. She'd swiped it during their brief chat earlier. "You can leave this with me now."

The WPC considered this. She glanced at the pass, which seemed legit from this distance. It only had an initial and surname, so she had no reason to doubt it belonged to Tash. London Transport had yet to introduce photo ID, so that helped Tash tremendously too. The WPC took a step closer to read the badge and copied the name onto her pad. She walked to the back of the bus and passed the note to a colleague, already talking into a walkie talkie.

"Check they work for London Transport , Ali."

Ali nodded and turned away to continue his chat.

Tash held her breath.

Ali turned back and glanced deep into the warmly lit smoky bus before whispering to the WPC, who nodded her thanks before turning back to the passengers.

"Alright," said the WPC. "Looks like you're good to go."

The applause was tumultuous.

"Merry Christmas," she added as she climbed from the back of the bus.

"Who's the driver?" whispered Raymond to Tash.

CHAPTER SIXTY-SIX

"It's not stealing, Raymond, stop saying *stealing*," said Tash through the spilt window to the driver's seat, just before her face hit the closed pane again, as the bus slammed to a stop. "Fuck sake, Raymond!" she added as she rubbed her nose.

"The brakes are different to the Transit!" he replied. "Why is it always me? Why do I have to drive?"

"Cos, you look like a bus driver!" whispered Tash.

"You do look like a bus driver," agreed Jamie, sitting behind his sister. They each had a holdall alongside them on the seat, and the suitcase rested on the floor.

"Left!" shouted the whole of the bus.

"Left," repeated Jamie helpfully.

"Yes, I got the gist of that, thank you," said Raymond, looking frantically for the indicator.

"Where's the indicator?" he asked.

"Anyone know where the indicator is?" asked Jamie to the passengers behind him.

"Shh!" said Tash, thumping her brother on the chest.

"I thought he was a driver?" came a voice from the rear.

"He is a driver!" replied Tash.

"Oh my God, we've got a jumper!" said Jamie in horror.

Tash followed his gaze to an older man standing at the back of the bus, one hand holding a *Presto* supermarket shopping bag filled with library books and the other clutching onto the full height vertical pole at the foot of the stairs. The road whizzed by through the open corner, inches away from him.

"Sit down!" shouted Tash. "Sit down!"

"I want to get off," replied the old man.

Tash thought for a second.

"Oh fuck, I forgot about bloody stops," said Tash to Raymond.

"What?" replied Raymond, taking the broadest left turn the bus had ever seen in its twenty-four years of service.

"Bus stops, you've not been doing bus stops! Call yourself a bus driver!" said Tash.

"No, I don't," replied Raymond.

"Where is his stop?" Jamie asked Tash.

"I'm sorry, Jamie. Much as I'd like to help you, I have no fucking idea where that stranger lives."

"Where do you live?" Jamie shouted to the man.

"Leatherhead," replied the man.

"Leatherhead," repeated Jamie to Raymond.

"Leatherhead?" replied Raymond.

"That's south, isn't it?" said Tash. "We're going north."

"We were north of that when we got on," said Raymond, narrowly avoiding two parents at a crossing with a pram. The whole bus did a sharp intake of breath at the near-miss and then continued in silence.

"This doesn't go to Leatherhead," said Jamie to the old man.

"He's confused," said Tash. "He's just a bit confused." She turned to shout down the bus. "Just sit down,"

"I know it doesn't go to Leatherhead," replied the man.

"Well, why did you say that's where you want to get off?" said Tash.

"I didn't. I said I lived there. I'm going to see my mum," he replied.

The bus passengers replied with lots of *Ohh! ... That makes sense now... He's seeing his mum.*

"Blimey. He's got a mum. She must be like a hundred," said Jamie, a little too loudly.

"And where is your mum's stop?" asked Tash.

"Back there," said the man pointing over his shoulder. "We went past it."

"Well, why didn't you say anything?" asked Tash.

"Right!" shouted the whole of the bus, and Raymond slowed down to join the filter lane to continue the bus route.

"I was enjoying the company," replied the man.

The whole downstairs erupted with lots of *ahhhs* and *enjoying the company* type mutterings.

"And if I'm honest," added the man, "I hate her. I was pleased when the driver got knocked down."

The bus fell silent.

"I supposed that makes me a bad person, does it?" said the man.

The bus responded with a chorus of replies, *Yes* and *Well, it does a bit, really*, punctuated with a voice that sounded very much like Alexandra's.

"What a wanker."

Chapter Sixty-Seven

"Woah!" and other protests filled the inside of the number 42 bus as Raymond steered it badly – and recklessly – across oncoming traffic into Queen Elizabeth Street.

The upstairs expected the bus to continue its usual route along Tower Bridge Road over the bridge itself. But it didn't today.

"Oh, they don't like this," said Tash over Raymond's shoulder.

"Tell them we need to run a little errand," said Raymond as he signalled for the next left. He'd found the indicator stalk now and was following as much of the highway code as he could. Other than hijacking the bus in the first place, which would almost certainly be a fail on a driving test. Certainly in 1984, anyway. In 2020 it might be considered offensive to fail someone for this without a trigger warning in advance.

"We need to do a safety check on the bus," shouted Tash to the passengers. That shut them up for a bit.

"Do we?" Jamie looked concerned. "What's wrong?"

"I made it up," whispered Tash. "I can't tell them we're paying off terrorists, can I?"

"What sort of safety test? Where?" shouted out a suspicious man from beneath a waxed flat cap.

"It's nothing to worry about, but we need to get some terrorists to look at it straight away," said Jamie, trying to join in the deceit. Before adding, "Mechanics. I meant mechanics."

But it was too late. The bus had erupted in chaos.

"Let me off!"

"He said he's a terrorist!"

"Are they IRA?"

"My finny haddock is going to have to go straight in the bin."

Tash thumped her brother again and turned to face the passengers, raising her palms and gesturing to calm down as a headteacher might to an overly rowdy assembly of children.

"If everyone could calm down, please. Calm down!"

People upstairs were still shouting, "Wrong way!"

"Shut the fuck up and calm down up there!" shouted Tash, which did the trick.

"It's only fair that we tell you the truth," said Tash, walking to the foot of the stairs to address the whole bus, just as the WPC had earlier in the journey. The bus was now bouncing along a very slender cobbled road running parallel with the correct route, albeit at a lower level. The passengers downstairs clutched their bags closer to their chests and looked back in fear.

"We are time travellers from 2020. Well, he's not," she added, pointing at Raymond, "the one that looks like he's shat himself."

Raymond performed a bizarre little wave over his shoulder.

"We're paying a ransom to some kidnappers so that Raymond, the driver, can save his wife's life. She's being held in a warehouse. We three are going in, not you. You'll be quite safe, and then you can all go home."

The bus remained silent.

"Seriously, who are you?" asked Alexandra from behind her fish.

"We're filming for *Game For A Laugh*," shouted Raymond over his shoulder. "The whole thing has been a wind-up. Even the driver getting knocked down. And we just need to deliver the bus to a warehouse to wind up the owner."

"Are we gonna be on telly?" said a teenager, hiding a bottle of Taunton's Dry Blackthorn cider, and clutching The Thompson Twins' 'Into The Gap' LP, clearly on his way to a party.

"Yes!" said Jamie.

The bus erupted in applause and lots of chatter like, *Game For A Laugh... TV... I thought I recognised him... wasn't he on Crimewatch?* and stuff like that.

"But we need to act normal," said Jamie. "Everyone up for it?"

"Yes!" shouted the bus.

"Do we get paid?" asked Alexandra.

"No," said Tash. "But we'll give you a fiver for your fish."

Tash gestured at Jamie, who walked down and handed his money to the lady.

"What's *Going For A Laugh?*" asked Alexandra as she extracted her purse from her leatherette handbag to lock her windfall safely away.

"*Game For A Laugh*," said Giles, a rotund man stretching a tracksuit to capacity beneath a leather blouson jacket and eating a Rowntree's Cabana. This was a posh cousin of the Bounty; in addition to coconut, the chocolate coating also boasted cherries. One of which was stuck between Giles' front teeth right now, not that it was about to stop him talking or indeed eating.

"What?" said Alexandra.

"You said *Going For A Laugh*, the show's called *Game For A Laugh*," explained Giles.

"Has that been on this year? We loved that," said Freda, a retired librarian.

Then she attempted to recreate the iconic catchphrase that the four hosts shared at the end of each show.

"Join us again next time, when you'll be watching you, watching... No, I got that wrong."

Giles knew when a pensioner needed help, so he joined in despite a fresh gobful of Cabana.

"You'll be watching us, watching you," he paused to swallow.

"Watching us," said Freda.

"I know, I was swallowing," said Giles, taking another bite before continuing, "you'll be watching us, watching you, watching us...."

"No," said Peggy, interrupting. "They always start with: Join us again next week, when we hope you'll be watching you," She had turned fully around in her seat to join in, squashing her granddaughter against the window.

"Us," corrected Giles.

"What?" asked Peggy.

"You said *you*," replied Giles.

"Did I?" asked Peggy.

"Yes," said Freda. "Yes, you did."

Giles wanted to take it from here. "Join us again next time...."

"Week," interrupted Freda.

"What did I say?" asked Giles.

"You said *time*," said Freda.

Peggy wanted another go. "Join us again next week, when we hope you'll be watching us...."

Giles joined in for the following line. "Watching you..."

Freda joined in next. "Watching us..."

All but one of the lower deck passengers joined in with the conclusion: "Watching you!"

The one that didn't quite nail it was the elderly 'jumper' who'd missed his mum's stop.

"Watching us."

But he was living his best life.

CHAPTER SIXTY-EIGHT

As they turned the bus into Shad Thames, Raymond felt a sudden pang of fear. Along the road, he could see the entrance to the warehouse and the reflection of a streetlamp on the roof of his destroyed Princess.

Would they still be inside the warehouse?

Would Jesus be true to his word and let Maureen live?

Would Argos be open on Christmas Eve so he could buy a deep fat fryer? They wouldn't be open tomorrow, it was Sunday. Maybe he could wrap an IOU, he thought.

"She wouldn't like that," said Raymond out loud. "She says vouchers are for slouchers."

"What?" asked Tash.

"Sorry, I thought I was saying that to myself."

"Don't lose it now, Raymond. We've come this far," said Tash.

"Yes. No. Sorry," said Raymond. "Do you think Argos will be open on Monday, with it being Christmas Eve? And Gateway? And do they take green shield stamps?"

Tash considered the question, then completely ignored it.

"I think we should park here. These pricks could blow the

whole thing," she whispered, gesturing to the patient passengers.

Raymond nodded and applied the brakes. Again, Tash smashed her face on the glass panel behind him, and again, she rubbed her face.

"Nice and smooth, Raymond, lovely. If this doesn't work out, there's a career for you driving hearses, that's for sure," said Tash.

"You think?"

"No," said Tash.

Jamie had his hand in the air.

"Question incoming from Jamie," said Tash. "And cut to the chase, if you could."

"Do you have life insurance for Maureen?" said Jamie. "'Cos if, you know, this doesn't go quite to plan, you'll be quids in."

This was arguably true, and Jamie had assumed that a kind reminder might be quite reassuring right now. It wasn't. Raymond ignored the question as he peered down from his three-quarter height driver's door and pondered the best way to climb onto the cobbled street without losing any more blood.

"What are we doing now?" asked the teenage Boy George.

"This is when we have to pop out for a sec, but you guys will soon be on your way again," said Tash to the passengers downstairs. She turned to Giles. "And you can finish the story about your infected TB jab! I was loving that."

A middle-aged lady made it quite clear that she was checking the time, yet again, on her watch.

"Sorry about your wait," said Tash with as much venom as she felt she could get away with.

"What's wrong with my weight?" The lady was offended. She turned to her husband.

"There's nothing wrong with your weight," replied the husband.

"There's nothing wrong with my weight," said the lady to Tash.

"I meant how long this is taking," said Tash as she stood up from her seat.

The lady pointed to her watch. "Well, it is taking a while, to be honest. I think we...."

Tash silenced her by placing her index finger over the lady's lips.

"Shushy-time, please," said Tash before wiping her finger on her top and addressing the bus. "So, if everyone could be super quiet from now on until we come out again, that would be extremely helpful. Any questions for this man on TB jabs or just generally how to be an interesting person will have to wait," she turned to Giles, "sorry."

He took the news with a philosophical nod and a fresh mouthful of peanut Treets. Tash walked to the exit, passing obediently silent passengers. She leant to shout up the stairs.

"Did you get all that?"

"Yes," came a dutiful choral reply from the upper deck.

"Tash," shouted Jamie, climbing from his seat. She turned to look down the bus. "Did you forget something?" He gestured at her holdall. She walked back down to fetch a few hundred thousand quid.

"Sake."

CHAPTER SIXTY-NINE

S
had Thames is the name given to the ancient road separated from the Thames by Butler's Wharf, a vast old brick shipping warehouse. If you visited the area in December 2020, you would see pristine pavements, shops, cafes, and apartments. Albeit mostly abandoned because of the most recent Covid-19 lockdown, but gentrified none-theless. Had you visited in 1984, you would have seen the same architecture, but unloved, abandoned, repurposed in part for storage, and generally bleak. It featured in countless TV shows and films, not least *Doctor Who*, but also gritty crime productions like *The Sweeney* and *The Professionals*. It was what Tash liked to call 'a bit of a shithole'. Very few of the streetlights were lit, so the darkness was a perfect hiding place for rats, vagrants and probably ghosts of rats and vagrants.

Having walked from the bus, Tash, Jamie, and Raymond were now on the last twenty-yard stretch ahead of Bay 3 and 'the drop'. For some unfathomable reason, this final distance seemed quieter than the Lake District at midnight. They could all hear Raymond's wheezing breath, and Tash was convinced the others must be able to hear her heartbeat because it was deafening her. They stopped to take a breath and assess the final stages of the plan.

"I think I should do the handover. I don't want either of you getting injured," said Raymond.

"OK, cool," said Tash.

"Hang on, wait!" said Jamie.

"Shhh!" said Tash.

Jamie tried to continue as quietly as possible. "We have a bag each. There's no point in you dragging each one in, Raymond. Let's just take one each, hand it over together."

"That's one idea," whispered Tash, "but I quite like the idea of me staying out here."

"No, come on, sis. Maureen's looked after me. We owe her this," said Jamie, in his best whisper.

"Right," said Tash. "Fine." She managed to say the word in a way that left nobody in any doubt that it wasn't.

"OK. Is everyone ready?" whispered Raymond.

Jamie nodded.

Tash nodded.

"Did you nod? It's just that it's quite dark," said Raymond.

"I nodded," whispered Tash.

"I did too," said Jamie.

"Shhh!" said Tash.

"Why are we being quiet?" asked Jamie.

"Always better to arrive unannounced," said Tash. "Gives us the upper hand."

"Does it?" asked Jamie.

"Yes," said Tash before adding a caveat. "Unless you're coming to visit me. Then I always need a text and phone call to check it's OK."

"Got it," replied Jamie. "Except you've moved back in with mum and dad, 'cos your marriage went wrong."

"Meaning?"

"Meaning, we're already there. So, we don't need to text." Jamie was sure of this.

"The marriage didn't go wrong. We just wanted different things."

"Yes," said Jamie, then thought it would help to bring Raymond up to speed. "She wanted to stay married, and he didn't."

"Jamie!" Tash was struggling to whisper anymore.

"Shall we set off after three?" said Raymond, throwing his hat into the ring as UN peacekeeper.

"OK," said Jamie.

"One, two, three," whispered Tash, crouching down to get one final grasp on her holdall.

As they sat off, it was clear that Raymond had opted to drag his suitcase despite the cobbles, and the resultant noise was reminiscent of checkout day at an all-inclusive hotel in Ayia Napa. Except instead of a hen party from Preston, this was just one suitcase and an echo chamber of a road.

"That's loud!" said Jamie in a raised voice to be heard over the loudness.

Naturally, the next thing they heard was the roller shutter doors opening.

"In terms of elements, I think surprise is over-rated," said Tash, waving self-consciously at Isabel, who was now peering out into the darkness.

"Stop there!" she shouted.

They did as they were told.

In no time, the three of them were lying face down on the dirty cobbles being frisked.

"At least I didn't lie in a puddle this time," said Raymond.

"You're very glass half full today, aren't you, Raymond?" said Tash.

"Are there foxes around here?" asked Jamie.

"Foxes?" Replied Raymond. "I doubt it. Cats, maybe."

"Right," said Jamie. "Then, I've got cat shit on my chin."

CHAPTER SEVENTY

In Isabel's defence it was Antonio who enjoyed playing the tough gangster, not her. Unless of course she was planning some kind of good cop/bad cop thing that she'd yet to reveal.

Most of the warehouse lights were out as Tash, Jamie and Raymond dragged their bags and suitcase into the freezing building. Antonio punctuated each step on the concrete floor with a gesture or flick of his gloved hands around their backs and the occasional clipped, "This way."

"I know the fucking way, Sat-Nav!" said Tash, her temper finally pushed too far.

"Where's my wife?" said Raymond. "I demand to see her!"

There was a pause.

"If that's OK?" he added.

"That told them, Raymond," said Tash, slumping down on her holdall, exhausted.

They peered into the darkness as the shutter door slammed down behind them, sending a metallic echo into the heavens above.

Then Antonio spoke.

"Isabel, enciende las luces."

She turned on the lights as instructed, and no one could have prepared them for what they saw.

Isabel was covered in blood. Her hands were coated in deep scarlet red, and her face splattered with it too. Tash screamed. Raymond let out a strange groan as his knees buckled beneath him. Jamie swallowed in fear and, for the first time in his life, spoke in a whisper.

"Blood."

A hysterical, familiar Spanish voice filled the silence with laughter, then a mighty gasp for breath, then more brutal laughter. Neither Tash, Raymond, nor Jamie wanted to be the first to take their eyes off Isabel. Despite the gory apparition, they each felt ill-prepared to witness what hell she had unleashed inside the warehouse.

"Turn around!" demanded Jesus. "Turn around!"

Raymond placed his hands over his eyes. Jamie placed his hands on his ears. Tash placed her hand on Jamie's shoulder.

"Turn around! I have a surprise for you!"

Tash turned first. She gestured for Jamie and Raymond to do the same, and they did.

CHAPTER SEVENTY-ONE

I t seemed beyond all realms of possibility that this could have happened.

Raymond looked at the clock on the wall. They had been gone for two hours and fifteen minutes. They'd decided to arrive back after a respectable amount of time to avoid suspicion from Jesus and his family, but the potential bus delay had heightened their anxiety. Given the luxury of owning a time machine, they could have come back before they set off but had all agreed that might be confusing or even dangerous, especially if they'd bumped into themselves.

But even one hundred and thirty-five minutes seemed an unfeasibly short duration to undertake what lay before them.

The office was transformed. Any evidence of the earlier ransacking had gone. The office area appeared more organised, tidier, cleaner, and more shiny than ever before. The warehouse was unrecognisable too. Despite the fact it held little stock, each shelving rack was either stacked tidily or swept cleaner than the day it was first assembled.

"This area is wet. Please be careful," said Antonio, who was pointing at the red floor paint still glistening a few metres ahead of where they stood. Antonio was liberally coated in the stuff as well as Isabel.

"It's floor paint," said Jamie. "It's red floor paint!"

Jesus sat in his wheelchair outside the chain-link fenced office. His smile was dipping a little in confusion. What the hell did they think it was?

"Your wife likes things just so, yes?" said Jesus, gesturing at the almighty makeover the warehouse had undergone. "She works us hard but fair, I think."

It was then that Raymond realised Maureen was not there.

"Where is she?" said Raymond. "What have you done with my wife?"

The sound of the toilet flushing was followed by Maureen walking out of the loo with wet hands.

"We need a towel in there. I'll mention it to Raymond when he gets back." She shook her hands and turned to see her husband. "Oh, you're back then? You need a towel in there. It's no place for visitors."

With this, she offered her wrists up to Jesus, who bound her hands together once again. Tash watched the tape being wrapped around a complicit Maureen and turned to Jamie.

"This is a weird day, isn't it?"

"It tops Grandad's funeral," said Jamie, remembering how Grandma had requested 'True Colours' at the ceremony, but for reasons still unknown, the celebrant had played *Colour Me Badd* instead. Ernest's final journey behind the automated curtains was accompanied by 'I Wanna Sex You Up.'

Tash didn't remind Jamie that Grandad's life path had changed after their previous visit to 1984, and he was still living in 2020.

"I nearly forget!" said Jesus, gesturing to Isabel and the light switches again.

They looked over at him as Isabel flicked on a bank of

lights to illuminate the aisle behind him. He wheeled to one side and grandly gestured over his shoulder.

"Another friend, I think?"

Standing on the same curious drum of waxed paper where Raymond had once stood, was Sab. Her hands were taped behind her back, and a noose hung around her neck. She attempted a smile.

"Sab?" said Raymond.

"That wasn't part of the agreement," said Jamie.

"We agreed on a little trade so your wife could help tidy this place up," said Jesus.

"She came to do your month-end accounts," explained Maureen to her husband.

"I thought she'd done them?" Raymond was confused and scared.

"You are welcome to swap places whilst I count this money," said Jesus. "You, or your wife?"

Raymond looked at Sab. She seemed strangely calm, and he didn't especially want to stand with his neck in a noose, but he had to do the right thing.

CHAPTER SEVENTY-TWO

As Isabel guided Sab down to the concrete floor, Antonio helped Raymond back onto the round drum, pulled the noose over his head, and taped his hands behind his back again.

Jesus sat in his wheelchair, perusing a large Michelin road map of Europe. It was vast once it was fully unfolded. A single sheet of coloured paper, covering all the continent's motor-ways, toll routes, and main roads. This was 1984's version of a sat-nav. Tash had memories of her father George shouting at their mother Andrea as they smothered themselves in one of these maps whilst traversing the right-hand side of a sun-kissed road outside Arras in France. Easily topping their 'holiday with the most passive-aggressive exchanges in a vehicle' chart.

And that was before George had tossed Jamie's 'Teach Yourself French' tape out of the window into a toll payment bucket on the road to Paris, yelling "teach yourself roads" to no one in particular. Not his best line.

Jesus was tracing a route from Santander in Northern Spain, past Bilbao and across to the east, his intention clearly to reach the Mediterranean coast as inconspicuously as possible.

He muttered something to Isabel, who ran over and leant in to agree with his musings, stopping to pull her long dark fringe back over her ear. She confused Jamie. So pretty. So elegant. So dangerous.

"Jamie, stop perving over murderers," said Tash, she never missed a trick.

"She's pretty," he replied.

"Course she's pretty. She's in her bloom."

"Her what?"

"Her bloom. One foot in youth, one foot in womanhood. No lines but no fucking idea."

They both watched as she offered Sab a pint bottle of fresh orange salvaged from the stolen milk float.

"She's not had kids, look at her," said Tash in a slightly accusatory tone, still glaring at Isabel, "she's in her bloom."

Jamie watched Sab decline the drink.

"When was your bloom?" asked Jamie.

"Not sure. I think I might have been in Thailand at the time. My gap year."

Jamie considered this.

"Does prison count as a gap year?"

"It says gap year on my CV, Jamie. That's all people need to know."

"You've been to prison?" Maureen didn't like this revelation she'd overheard.

"Thai prison, Maureen. It's very different. Almost a hostel, really. Mistaken identity, and no one need ever know. I gave a fake name and everything."

Jamie laughed. Tash joined in.

"What's he laughing at?" asked Maureen.

"Nothing," lied Tash.

"It doesn't sound like nothing," replied Maureen.

"I'm laughing at the name she gave the police," said Jamie.

"What? What name did you give them?" asked Maureen.

"Anita," replied Tash.

"That's a nice name," said Maureen. "I don't understand?"

"Her second name was Fanny," said Jamie.

"Raymond's Grandma's name was Fanny," said Maureen. Then she thought. "Oh. I see."

Tash sighed loudly. "You spend your whole life working for someone else, dreaming of better days. Then one day you get tied up in a warehouse with three psychos and realised you missed your bloom."

"She is pretty," said Jamie, again.

"Did you never hear anything at all from Martha?" asked Tash, irritated about the baffling state of affairs. Jamie shook his head.

Jesus looked up from his map. "Are we ready?"

Tash glared over at him.

"What for? We've got your money. Why are you putting him through this?"

Tash looked over at sweaty Raymond as he shuffled his tired feet on the drum.

"Yes, yes, let us examine your hard work, yes?" said Jesus, clicking his fingers at the holdalls and suitcase. His children set about dragging them to his feet. Isabel unzipped the first holdall and pulled it wide open. Countless bundles of tightly packed tenners revealed themselves. She did the same with holdall number two. The spectacle was no less impressive.

Jesus pointed at the Samsonite suitcase at his feet; his son unclicked the chrome catches on the edge and forced open the rigid sides to reveal the grey fabric-lined inner. Countless more bundles of money fell to the floor. Jesus was unable to contain his delight.

"Beautiful," he said, unable to take his eyes off the cleaned cash. "I suppose I could ask you where you found this? Yes? And we could go into business together?"

"Why would we do that?" asked Tash.

"So, I don't kill one of you," he replied.

They all looked highly uncomfortable.

Raymond was horrified. Had they been duped? How the hell would they repeat this task? Was this maniac for real? Did Jamie know about the grill, surely it was just a case of pushing and twisting?

Jesus erupted in a manic laugh.

"I am a joker! I want to leave this shitty, grey country immediately. It may be cold, but things have been too hot for me for some time, yes?"

This may have been frustration about his ailing money laundering business, or it may have been something more. The word around much of Europe was that the Brinks Mat investigation was closing in, and much as he had no reason to fear his dirty money was from that, the stolen bullion was causing all manner of problems. During the heist, thieves stumbled on millions of pounds worth of gold bars. But the gold was too clean, too authentic. So the precious metal was melted and mixed with copper coins to reduce its traceability. The introduction of this 'new' gold into the European market was harder to identify. But its movement was invariably followed by currency received from highly dubious practices. There were investigations underway all over Europe.

The best Jesus could do would be to go home, and by home he didn't mean Madrid. He intended to visit his parents' house far away. His children could join him if they wished, or they could find another safe place, but the three of them would now be able to quit London for good.

He had arrived today to kill. That was his plan. He needed

to create a sense of fear and urgency amongst his clients. But this bizarre turn of events could change all that.

Killing someone now would be needless; he had no reason to instil fear in small-time businesses across the East End and south of the river. Especially given the risk of life in prison. English food was bad enough, imagine how terrible it must be behind bars?

No. This could be his clean break. But he wasn't about to tell his captives this, as he was having too much fun.

Jamie raised his hand, causing Tash to wince with shame about his respect for this thug.

"What is happening?" said Jesus, looking at Tash.

"He has a question – just ask it, Jamie. He's not your teacher."

"How do you remove the drum?" asked Jamie, pointing at the waxy drum under Raymond's twitchy feet. "Do you just kick it?"

"Don't ask him that, Jamie, for fuck's sake!" said Tash.

"It smells a bit," said Raymond.

Jesus laughed and leaned over to snatch an umbrella from the coat stand. He capably wheeled himself towards a rusty steel bucket and flicked open the hinged lid. Hundreds of squirming mice immediately spilt out over the rim but were magically stopped by the owl swooping down to help itself to an early supper.

"Oy oy oy!" said Jesus, tapping his shoulder, and like a well-trained puppy, the owl flew back onto his keeper. Jesus lowered the lid onto the vermin and smiled at the owl as it swallowed down one unlucky mouse.

"I like to give people a chance. I am a fair man." Jesus smiled and looked at the drum under Raymond. Antonio started to peel away the waxy paper to reveal a truckle of English Cheddar. More ill-gotten gains from one of Jesus' East End clients, it was easily two feet across and the same high.

"The mouses eat the cheeses, but when they get full, they maybe take a siesta, and then they feed again," explained Jesus, gesturing a tightening imaginary rope around his throat.

"How long would that take?" asked Jamie, genuinely interested.

"Jamie!" said Tash.

"This is my first time, shall we see?" asked Jesus, looking over at the mouse bucket.

"No!" shouted everyone except Jamie and the Spaniards.

"A slow death, yes?" said Jesus, surprising himself at how much he was enjoying this murderous exchange.

"I suppose it depends how strong your toes are," said Jamie. "Cos Raymond could probably slow things down on his tiptoes, but I guess after a while, the reducing depth of cheese would mean his downward force just squashed it. What cheese is it?"

Jesus looked at Antonio, who squinted into the drum. "Cheddar," he read.

"You'd get a slower death with Parmesan," said Jamie.

"Are you wanting to join this circus, Jamie? Or shall we get on?" said Tash.

"You said if they returned with the money, you'd let us all go." Maureen's brave speech surprised everyone. "Now, do it!"

"Steady on, Maureen, I'm sure we'll be heading home soon," said Raymond, examine the cheese under his Hush Puppies.

"Let him down," said Jesus, waving his hand in resignation to Antonio. He wasn't beaten. This was his intention anyway. Why perpetuate this? He'd had his moment of fun. Jesus reached into the Samsonite and pulled out a bundle of notes. Then froze.

He went for another, then another.

"Stop!" shouted Jesus, now flicking through the notes in

DID THEY STEAL A MILLION YET?

any bundle he could find. His face was turning very red indeed, and it wasn't unnoticed by Tash and Jamie.

"What? What's up?" asked Tash.

"Hang him!" shouted Jesus, using the umbrella to flick the bucket of mice over. The lid rolled off, and the mice scurried in all directions, with Jesus frantically coercing them towards Raymond with his umbrella. Antonio hadn't yet reached Raymond to release him, so he stepped away from the couple of hundred mice heading his way.

Maureen was screaming, Raymond was muttering nonsense, Jamie covered his ears, Sab struggled with her hands behind her back, and Tash froze to the spot shouting.

"What the hell are you doing? We kept our side of the deal?"

Jesus pulled the elastic band off one of the bundles to reveal two tenners sandwiching perfectly cut bundles of newspaper in between. *News Of The World*, *Sunday People* and a few pink sheets of the *Financial Times*. Someone had a sense of humour. And it wasn't Jesus.

The next bundle was the same. So was the next. Now Isobel was on her knees, fumbling through the holdall, but it was with the same outcome. Lots and lots of yesterday's news.

Which is what these prisoners would be if they all died now.

CHAPTER SEVENTY-THREE

L ulu turned over in her red plastic dog bed and sighed deeply, in her baritone, satisfying way. She loved the winter evenings where the house mainly smelled of her, her mum's cooking, and of pine needles from the three-foot Norway spruce that was rapidly drying out next to the living room radiator. As she blissfully descended into a canine dream, her tiny paws flapped up and down, and her tail bashed the side of her bed. She relived her exciting afternoon walk where mum had stood on Wood Lane debating last night's *Tarby & Friends* on ITV. Peggy's favourite part was the ad break because it featured the Oxo family. The one where they were rude about their mum's attempts at a casserole. Still, Linda Bellingham silenced them with the reassurance that her stew didn't contain garlic, and they would love it, before licking her lips at her TV husband and adding, "Remember Preston?" It was a little bit blue for Jill, but she liked the Oxo mum, so assumed maybe they had once just enjoyed a lovely hotpot at the Tickled Trout Services on the M6. She'd had a delicious piece of gammon there on the way back from Blackpool, so she was prepared to give the Oxo parents the benefit of the doubt.

Lulu remembered the ambulance across the road. She'd watched in fascination as the injured lady leapt to her feet and joined the two ambulance workers in removing 'Ambulance' stickers from what was now simply a white Transit van. As they climbed back inside, the driver stood on his seat to reach the roof and pulled off a magnetic blue light that continued flashing inside the van. It was funny to watch the passenger trying to switch it off. In the end, she simply covered it with her coat as the driver set off at quite a pace underneath the railway bridge before demonstrating an impressive handbrake turn to the left and disappearing. Had Lulu been able to see around the corner, she would have seen their journey ended there. The van's engine and lights were switched off, and it was instantly hidden from view, perching under a railway arch.

Lulu had been distracted again by the sudden sound of applause from across the road. A short man in the car park seemed to be pleasing a big queue of humans, and Lulu wagged along in full support as she remembered it all. She was at her most happy when other people were.

Chapter Seventy-Four

S melly Gareth hung up the phone and reached over to a bank of switches and dials. Amongst them was a substantial pull-down handle, not unlike the throttle you see in aeroplane cockpits. He placed his hand on it and pulled down. Immediately the sound of the fire alarm filled his ears. He turned to Piers and Robert, who nodded before walking into the dimly lit corridor. Gareth followed them to the goods lift. He cautiously reached out his finger and pressed the button. The ringing bells drowned out the hiss of the lift gear mechanism, so he placed his hands on the doors to confirm there was movement. He was happy. They were vibrating, and the lift was on its way.

"I'm starving," shouted Piers, rubbing his fingers through his Bobby Ball hair.

"We won't be long," replied Robert at the top of his voice, walking down the corridor.

They didn't hear the lift door ping, but all stood back as the doors slowly opened to reveal a catering trolley and one million pounds in beautifully bundled ten pound notes. Piers stepped into the lift and walked over to the rear of the trolley.

Robert appeared at the open doors pushing a pram. He was the 'catcher'.

Piers and Robert effortlessly filled the pram in less than one minute. Gareth unleashed a fresh blast of body odour as his arms stretched to unlock a green locker across the corridor. Inside were two hundred and fifty identical bundles of cash which they loaded back into the catering trolley in one minute and forty one seconds. It took longer getting them in than out.

"All done?" shouted Robert.

Gareth double-checked the locker and nodded. Robert stepped back into the lift and pressed G before leaping out.

"Wait!" shouted Piers, running back towards the moving doors, his brown suede shoes squeaking as he moved. Robert looked shocked as he watched his brother leap into the lift and then miraculously stagger back out again, avoiding the closing doors by a matter of milliseconds.

"What was that about?" shouted Robert.

Piers delightedly held up an egg and cress sandwich before taking a hungry bite.

The fire bell continued to ring.

CHAPTER SEVENTY-FIVE

I t was early December, and Hattie hadn't believed him at first. But Gareth was in no doubt that one million pounds in banknotes would be coming to TV Centre on December 16th. He'd even repeated the news as he poured the remnants of his second bag of KP Chutney Outer Spacers crisps into his gaping mouth, before setting to work on his second pint of Worthington E.

Gareth had worked with Hattie before on far smaller jobs, and so together they'd come up with a surprisingly simple plan to intercept the cash somewhere in TV Centre before it was returned to Barclays Bank.

How and where was made easier when Hattie secured a temp job at TV Centre for Christmas. This was no coincidence, as Gareth had shared the BBC's internal job opportunities newsletter with her. They'd agreed on the best role to apply for to secure access to the people she needed, and then it was simply a matter of applying for the job. Gareth had helped where he could. He'd run through some technical TV patter with her and handed over a 1960s textbook called *Shorthand for Secretaries*. In an effort to give her a final boost, he shredded all the other candidates' applications during one of his self-imposed overtime shifts in TVC. He had the run of the building after 5pm.

Hattie's CV read very well. It should do. Her sister had stolen it from the job centre where she worked, and it belonged to a lady called Cynthia Street, who had nine years' experience at London Weekend Television. It was a no brainer to stick with the name Cynthia. The document was riddled with it. Hattie simply added a footnote that she was unexpectedly moving flats, so any correspondence should come to her new address.

So, it was no coincidence that Hattie – or Cynthia as she was temporarily known – found herself taking notes in a fascinating meeting between some super important BBC execs and a very posh sounding man from Barclays Bank on her first day at work. No stone was left unturned, including all potential access routes to deliver the safe containing one million pounds in cash. All agreed that Wood Crescent was the best way, so the upper entrance opposite the tube station was the planned route. The contingency plan in case of emergency was through the rear Frithville Gate.

In any meeting, there is always one tit who raises their hand at the end. That one person who has such a forensic approach to detail that the whole room has to wait for a further half-hour whilst their absurd question is given the respect management like us to think that they think we deserve.

And things were no different in 1984. Just because Powerpoint didn't exist, pedants still found ways to ruin everyone else's day.

And today, it was Cynthia. It was not the place of the minutes taker to get involved, but the suits present wanted to ensure they covered every eventuality so were happy to hear her reservations.

"What if both routes are blocked?" she asked.

"Like that will happen!" said a man with ketchup on his chin.

"No, no. We should have a third plan," said another man with a face that looked like one you might see on a banknote. Maybe that was his life goal.

"We'd have to bring it through the front door," said a producer in a tank top.

"Couldn't fit a bank safe through the internal corridors," said a man who looked grey all over. He was one hundred and fifty shades of it. Hair, skin, clothes and socks. Only his teeth and shoes hadn't seen the dress code, and they were all brown. His tone shouted, "I know all the stuff about this place that no one cares about, but it's about time you did."

"Well, then we'd just unlock the safe in the car park and carry the money to the studio," said the producer. He'd already clicked his Paper-mate biro closed. This meeting was over as far as he was concerned. "We have a safe somewhere in storage, and we can stick it in there."

"Somewhere in storage?" The bank man looked concerned at the vague response.

The grey man was now opening up a large blueprint of the ground floor of TV Centre.

"It's a tricky one," he muttered, rubbing his moustache.

The tank top producer was losing his patience. He leant into the drawing and tapped a spot on it.

"Worst case scenario, we lock it in the goods lift by Studio 8," he said. "Are we done?"

Everyone peered at the blueprint, and the grey man started to nod.

"That would work, actually."

The producer was on his feet now.

"We'd need to check with Graham, though. He installed the new switching for the lifts," said the grey man.

The producer slumped back onto his chair.

Within fifteen minutes, they were opening the windows because smelly Gareth had joined them. He blanked "Cynthia" superbly.

That evening as Hattie and Gareth rode the tube to the pub, Gareth suggested silencing the descent of the BBC goods lift with the fire alarm. His basement may have been dark and the least showbiz area in the whole of TV Centre, but it contained some critical equipment, including the fire alarm, the master lock for all the lifts on that wing, and the building's massive heat exchanger (something he would easily incapacitate by removing one valve at 1.05 pm on Sunday, December 16th).

The Blue Balls was Gareth's local and was a place you'd find Piers and Robert most nights. They were brothers of dubious character (and dress sense) and more than happy to join Gareth and Hattie in the tap room for a discreet business proposal. Robert was rocking the double denim look, but given his age, it was the one pioneered in the previous decade by Kenneth Hutchinson aka Hutch from Starsky and Hutch, as opposed to Wham! Although even George and Andrew had moved on by now. That look was so Club Tropicana, which was so last year.

Piers was sticking with his halcyon days, too, when it came to attire, so he cradled his half of Skol over some flared black nylon trousers. Years of use had made them shiny too, and a regular source of static electric shocks to anyone daring to get close enough. Piers' brother-in-law drove an HGV, so Gareth agreed to secure tickets to the *BBC Sports Review of 1984* to gift to him – attending that would ensure he didn't take a work shift on that day. All Piers had to do was make an imprint of his lorry key, something he managed with a bespoke clay pad when handing over the tickets during a home visit. A friend of a friend going by the name Chucks supplied the clay, and cast a new key in exchange for new tyres for his Transit van. Robert could always get his hands on new tyres, and no one asked questions. In truth, they were re-treads, but who cared? Or stolen. He couldn't remember, but they were tyres, what more did someone want?

The sight of the van had lit a bulb in Robert's head, and Chucks was soon attending the next meeting in the tap room of the Blue Balls to discuss a business arrangement. He was a massive man, with a constant smile and a dubious aroma of herbs. A little hard of hearing and he tended to only get the gist of things on the second or third time, but other than that a very safe pair of hands. He agreed to drive his van for Piers and Robert on Sunday, December 16th, on the understanding it would have fake registration plates taped to both ends of it. Chuck's daughter worked at a printing company just outside Peckham, so the ambulance wrap was something his daughter could supply, along with the fake plates. She would attend the job too and play the role of 'injured lady'. Chuck's son would accompany them as a backup in case anything got out of hand. The locksmith needed a cut, of course, but he'd been told the heist was for a hundred grand so had held out for twenty-five per cent. A very shrewd businessman indeed. If this went to plan, he'd earn twenty-five thousand pounds for an hour of work.

On the day, they all worked to their schedule perfectly. All parties had CB radios or walkie-talkies and the phone number for Gareth in the TV Centre basement. Chucks remembered the raspberry jam for his daughter's face before she lay on the ring road entry point where Securicor had hoped to arrive.

Robert had blocked the rear of TV Centre in their borrowed curtain-sided HGV. Once he'd eventually found the hazard light button, he and Piers had walked through the rear gate after showing fake IDs to the BBC security guard. He was expecting these two gentlemen and knew to lead them to the basement, where they would fix the heating.

Hattie aka Cynthia wasn't due to work on Sunday, December 16th, nor any Sunday. Her job was on weekdays only, in fact she'd already finished her temp contract. So, when she walked into BBC's Main Reception unannounced at 4 pm, Patricia had been pleased to see her (in her inward way). 'Cynthia' had offered Patricia a Harrod's mince pie injected with a high strength laxative mixed with rum to disguise the taste. She opted not to mention the injection part but knew Patricia wouldn't pass the chance to boast that she'd eaten some Harrod's fare. London's legendary department store was aspirational and perfect for name-dropping. Patricia took it, and took a bite, but Hattie soon realised her plan was over-engineered. As the only member of reception working this afternoon, Patricia had immediately asked Hattie to cover her whilst she paid a call.

She was only too pleased to help and wasted no time discreetly following Patricia to the ground floor WC to witness her irritation that it was out of order. (Hattie had been the one to incapacitate it, two minutes earlier). Patricia inevitably climbed the stairs to the first-floor corridor (out of order too), but happily, despite the darkness, she found the ladies available on the second.

Hattie was soon back on reception. She contemplated throwing the spiked mince pie in the bin but was interrupted by three people making their way into the reception from outside. The thirty-something man at the front walked on tiptoes, and his eyes darted around the room.

"Hi Cynthia, I'm Terry from Light Entertainment," he said. "I'm in charge of it, actually. Like, the boss."

———

Ten minutes had passed.

"Hello, I wonder if you could help me, please?"

The gentleman dressed in a three-piece grey suit was told to report to Main Reception at TV Centre. The lady behind reception looked up and smiled. Her name badge read 'Cynthia' and she looked like she was distracted by something behind the double doors at the far end of reception.

He was patient, and waited until she spoke. But she didn't.

"Hello, I wonder if you could help me, please?" he repeated.

"Hang on," she said as she watched a member of staff walk through the doors, back into reception.

"Are you the last one?" she asked the lady, who giggled and smiled in the affirmative.

She stepped out from behind the desk and dashed through the doors towards the goods lift. The gentleman was perplexed. He waited for one minute more and was relieved to see her reappear and reposition herself behind the desk. She picked up the phone and dialled three numbers, then waited.

"It's in place," she said, then hung up and smiled at the gentleman.

"Hello, I wonder if you could help me, please?" He thought it was worth another try.

. . .

She grabbed her overcoat, smiled at the man, and finally addressed him politely but firmly.

"No."

She walked out into the night, pulling a snood from her ample coat pocket.

CHAPTER SEVENTY-SIX

I f the pace of Piers and Robert slowly pushing a Silver Cross pram laden with 90kg of stolen money across the BBC TV Centre ring road wasn't enough to give away their age, the fact that they had both chosen to hum the theme tune to *The Sweeney* was a dead giveaway. Piers had tried to instigate Cannon and Ball's 'Boys In Blue', the theme from their big screen film, but Robert hadn't heard of it. Hattie had agreed to stand by the rear gate to Frithville Gardens whilst the guard on duty, Alan, investigated the almighty smash she'd heard around the back of TC8.

Obviously, she'd heard nothing of the sort.

She'd walked in the shadows of TV Centre around the back of studios and waited until Piers and Robert appeared from the Scenery Block and lit a cigarette. If she was in any doubt that someone else might have lit a cigarette, she was reassured when she heard the siblings quarrel over who would have first dibs on it. That was her cue to divert Alan.

As he disappeared, Piers and Robert strolled the final fifty yards to the large gate and the silhouette of Hattie. The main gates were still open with the lorry partway through, and the hazard lights illuminated everyone's faces as they finally met. No words were spoken as Hattie took the pram from them and pushed it effortlessly through the smaller gates of Hammersmith Park. Robert climbed into the lorry, and with Piers help directing from the rear, they were able to effortlessly reverse it two hundred metres along the residential street and back into Uxbridge Road in a matter of minutes. Six minutes and four parked cars' wing mirrors, to be exact.

Hattie kept to the right in the darkness of the park and found herself suddenly panicking. Not that she might get caught with a stolen million pounds, but that she might get mugged. It was further than she thought and the cold was nipping at her ears and nose. She pulled her snood further up around her face and entered Exhibition Close. She passed underneath the deep-red, boxy architecture and joined Wood Lane, pushing the heavy pram slowly and anonymously in front of BBC TV Centre. The Securicor van was parked up, and the audience queue for *Sports Review* was slowly entering Studio 1. She blanked a giddy Piers who waved frantically at her from the cabin of the HGV that whizzed past. He switched to thumbs up gestures but soon slammed his face on the windscreen as the lorry screeched to a halt to avoid a rogue car.

Oh God, was it the police?

Did it matter? She had the money.

To her relief, she heard the engine rumble again, and the lorry was soon on its way.

Hattie continued towards the bridge and paused to cross Wood Lane, looking right as she stepped into the road. She didn't look left, so she was horrified to see the headlights and hear the screech of brakes from a family saloon just feet from the pram. She was fine. The pram was fine. She took a deep breath and instantly shook as adrenaline pumped around her body. She under-estimated the effort it took to get the fifteen-

and-a-half stones of pram and paper moving again and was faced with a raised kerbstone to re-join the pavement on the other side of the road. She dragged it back a few feet to try and get some distance for a run-up. No. That just hurt. She tried again. Yep, that hurt in the same places. As she went for attempt three, she realised a familiar face was standing beside her. She immediately pulled up her snood to cover more of her face and looked away into the night.

After Jamie had helped her onto the pavement, she scurried beneath the bridge and took a sharp left. The silhouette of the van was heaven sent. Now, all she had to do was convince Chucks that the pram was laden with one pound notes and not tenners.

If the pram hoods remained up, she might stand a chance. He wasn't the sharpest knife in the block. In fact, he probably shouldn't be driving given the smell of herbs from his hand rolled cigarette.

CHAPTER SEVENTY-SEVEN

The warehouse in Butler's Wharf had erupted into
chaos. Mice were covering the floor, and the owl was
majestically sweeping down sporadically to pick
them up with outstretched talons. The flapping of his mighty
wings was disorientating, and Tino Casal was singing once
more after Jesus accidentally knocked his portable stereo onto
the floor. Isabel was cowering under the cover of an empty
storage rack. Antonio was rifling through the remaining
bundles of notes on the off-chance that some might be legitimate spendable cash.

Sab was strangely calm as she watched Raymond on the
drum of cheese, despite the mice bravely tucking in around his
feet. Her hands were still trembling behind her back, but who
wouldn't shake in that situation? She'd only stopped by to
check in on her friends, and now she was bound in tape and
about to witness a murder.

Jesus was shouting in anger. Mostly just noises. Grunts.
He'd arrived today to retrieve his loan or to kill. He'd been
euphoric that the latter wouldn't be needed, but that brief
moment had evaporated. An execution would send fear

through the community and ensure his other bad debtors got their act together.

For a moment, these liars had deceived him into believing they could solve all his problems. To clean his money and remove all traces of criminal activity from him. He'd even allowed himself to daydream about the ferry trip to Santander, maybe with a glass of Tio Pepe sherry as he watched the sun bounce off the majestic Palacio de la Magdalena, a stunning country mansion on the headlands where the Mediterranean lapped into Santander Bay. And the sun on his face. The actual sun. Why didn't this shithole of a country ever see the sun?

Now everything had changed. Not only had these English idiots made a fool of him in front of his children, but they had also stolen his stolen million.

He had no choice now. It was time to commit murder.

Maybe he would kill them all.

"Antonio," shouted Jesus. And with that, he formed the shape of a pistol with his hand.

Antonio reached into his pocket and extracted his handgun, then dutifully walked over to his father and handed it over.

"In a line! In a line!" shouted Jesus.

"We're in a line," said Jamie.

He was right. They were standing in a row with their hands behind their backs. Further down the aisle Raymond danced on his cheese drum.

"What are you going to do?" asked Maureen.

"Don't ask him that, Maureen. He's a busy man. Got a lot to think about," said Raymond.

"A line over here, with him!" shouted Jesus, pointing at Raymond.

"Cálmate, Papá!" shouted Isabel, begging her father to calm down.

"Now!" he shouted.

The four of them did as they were told, helped along the way by Antonio jostling them to the feet of Raymond, his long arms wafting above his head to keep the flapping owl at bay.

"Anyone need the toilet?" asked Jamie.

"Don't go in there; I've just bleached it," said Maureen.

"I'm not sure toilet visits are an option," said Tash. "Are toilet visits an option?" she asked Antonio, who blanked her. "Number ones? Numero uno?"

"You've made a smashing job of tidying up, love," said Raymond to Maureen. His mouth was dry, but credit where credit's due.

"Is he going to shoot us?" asked Maureen. "Why is he so cross?"

"No hagas esto, Papá!" Isabel was appealing to Jesus to change his mind. She climbed from her shelter and stood in front of the hostages.

Jesus gestured at his children to join him. Antonio did.

"Out of the way, Isabel!" said Jesus, using English to ensure the Brits understood what was about to happen.

"Papa!" said Isabel.

"We stole that money fair and square," said Tash.

"Well, it wasn't really fair, was it, Tash?" said Jamie. "It belonged to the bank."

Isabel squared up; she was going nowhere. Her father nodded to Antonio, who walked to his sister and effortlessly picked her up, slung her over his shoulder and walked back to the office, her kicking legs and punching fists barely affecting his pace.

Jesus raised his gun.

"Don't do this!" shouted Tash. "I'm a mother. I have a baby at home!"

Raymond leant over to Maureen.

"Maureen," he said before coughing a little. "You do know I love...." But before he could say 'you', she interrupted him.

"Did you clean your teeth today? Your breath is awful!"

"Sorry, Maureen. I've been sick in Debbie McGee's shoe."

"Put the gun down," came a voice.

Jamie, Tash, Raymond and Maureen looked over their shoulders.

Sab had released her tied hands, and at her feet was Raymond's broken car mirror. She'd used the sharp edges to cut her binding tape. And now, she was holding a gun. Her own gun.

An actual shiny gun.

And she was pointing it very professionally at Jesus. Like Roger Moore did in last year's *Octopussy*. One hand on the trigger and the other sort if clasping it beneath.

"Put the gun down," repeated Sab calmly.

Jesus thought for a moment. This was something he hadn't expected. Why did the accountant have a gun?

He looked over at his children, then back at the English fools.

"For the final time, put the gun down," said Sab.

"Well, don't force the man, Sab. I'm sure we can all chat about things and maybe..." Raymond said but was interrupted by Jesus pulling his trigger.

Almost simultaneously, a loud crack pierced the air, and everyone saw Jesus thrown backwards off his wheelchair.

"Get down!" shouted Sab, and everyone did. Flat on the floor. Except Raymond.

"Might struggle with that, actually," he said, nodding at his noose.

"Papá!" shouted Isabel as she ran over to her father.

Sab lifted the mirror and swiped it behind Raymond. His hands were loose immediately and he was able to remove the noose and hurl himself to the floor. Sab walked purposefully over to Isabel, her gun pointing at her the whole time. She turned briefly to Antonio and gestured for him to join his sister, then shouted over her shoulder to the others.

"Everyone OK back there?"

"Yes, I think he missed," said Raymond, briefly lifting his head off the floor. "The bullet went into the racking; look at that!"

An upright steel support had bowed just below the empty noose. A shelf above had buckled on the impact – happily an empty one. A few days earlier and a Sinclair C5 would have fallen and caused a nasty injury.

"Faster!" shouted Sab, and soon she had Jesus' children lying on the floor of the caged office alongside him, as she frisked them all.

Jesus' eyes were open, and he was wincing in pain from a bullet wound to his shoulder. Sab effortlessly ripped off her sleeve, rolled it into a ball, and pressed it onto the wound, causing Jesus to recoil.

"Press this firmly," she said to Antonio. "Presiona esto firmemente, si?"

Antonio nodded and did as she told him.

Sab walked to the phone then saw the cut line. She reached into her pocket and pulled out a walkie talkie as she walked cautiously from the cage. She closed and locked the gate door, then spoke into her radio.

"Man down. I need back up and medical at Butler's, now."

Everyone was perplexed.

"On its way," came the crackled reply.

"Keep pressing," said Sab to Antonio.

He did. Isabel was crying.

"This isn't the end!" shouted Jesus. "You are finished, Raymond! Terminado!"

Raymond didn't like the sound of that one bit.

"Should we call the police or something?" said Raymond.

"I am the police," said Sab, smiling as kindly as her adrenaline would allow.

"Oh, fuck," said Tash. Her Christmas dinner had just got delayed again. Maybe forever this time.

What kind of trouble were they in now? Why the hell had she come back to 1984?

CHAPTER SEVENTY-EIGHT

They were still lying on the floor. Sab stood above them, with one eye on the office, gun still in hand.

"I've been on the Brinks Mat enquiry since January," whispered Sab. "That's why I got the Woolworths job. To get to Dudley."

"He did the Brinks Mat job?" Maureen was mortified.

"No, we don't think so. We assumed he was working for someone else. But some cash was traced to him. An unwitting pawn. Then he went missing."

"He went back to 1920," explained Tash, still lying on the floor.

"Yeah, that's not the sort of thing you can put in a report," said Sab. "I wasn't about to jeopardise my nine-year career."

"Nine years? How old are you?" asked Raymond.

"Twenty-seven," replied Sab.

"You look so young!" said Raymond.

"Stop flirting Raymond, she's half your age!" said Maureen. She'd chosen badly when she dropped to the floor, so had more cheese in her fringe than any time in her life than she could remember. And she'd helped out at cub camp, so that was quite an accolade.

"Are you like the Met then, or something?" asked Raymond.

"Flying Squad," replied Sab.

"Like *The Sweeney*!" Raymond couldn't contain his joy at this development. Then he looked genuinely confused. "How do you get time to do your accountancy course?"

Sab looked at him.

"She'll wait for the penny to drop, Raymond," said Tash.

"Can we get up off the floor, now?" asked Maureen.

Sab nodded, and they slowly climbed to their feet, Sab reaching down to help Maureen.

"Oh! You're not an accountant!" said Raymond, far louder than he meant.

"There we are," said Tash. Sab smiled.

"Is your name Sab?" asked Raymond.

"No."

"What is it?" asked Maureen.

"It's Maureen."

"Really?" Maureen looked somewhere between delighted and horrified.

"No."

"What is it?" asked Tash.

"It's Tash."

"Is it?"

"No."

"Oh," replied Tash. "Oh! You're not going to tell us, are you?" asked Tash.

"The penny drops again," replied Sab. This was probably the first time the others had seen Tash get owned, so they politely looked at their shoes.

"You can get up, Jamie," said Sab, examining the bullet hole in the steel post. "Good job he was a crap aim."

"Jamie," said Tash. "You heard."

Sab leant into the steel. "This is a ricochet; the bullet bounced."

"Jamie?" Tash was shouting now. "Jamie!"

She fell to her knees to her brother, who was lying face down on the ground. She rolled him over to see a bullet hole in his coat.

"Jamie!" Tears filled her eyes.

She looked at his face. His long eyelashes. His button nose. His lips open over his crooked teeth. Jamie never closed anything. Toilet doors, dishwashers, zips, his mouth.

His face looked the same as when he was five, and he would climb alongside her in bed to escape a nightmare. And six. And seven. In fact, he did it until he was about fourteen. She made him feel safe. But now, he'd been shot by a madman. And it was all her fault.

She heard a wolf howling, and soon realised it was her.

"Jamie!"

CHAPTER SEVENTY-NINE

Raymond was examining the damage to his Princess again, from the discomfort of his driving seat. Maureen sat alongside him, still slightly shell-shocked about her day. Tash was behind her, staring up into the night sky. There were relatively few streetlights to pollute the view, so the sight of stars twinkling became hypnotic. Tash was transported to her childhood Christmases in Sheffield when Grandad assured her the flickering star was Rudolph's nose.

Raymond pulled up what was left of his collar to brace himself from the icy chill that blew through the gap in the smashed windscreen. He placed his key in the ignition before twisting the stereo dial. Ironically, 'Drive' by The Cars filled the car, too loudly.

"Turn it down, Raymond!" said Maureen.

"Sorry, Maureen," he replied and did as told.

"It wasn't his time, you know?" said Tash. "It wasn't Jamie's time."

Raymond turned and smiled at her kindly.

"Where is Martha? Why does no one talk about Martha?" asked Tash.

"The less said about that woman, the better," said Maureen, with the contempt she usually reserved for people that didn't know how to queue correctly at the British Home Stores cheese counter.

"She did have us on a bit of merry ride, didn't she?" said Raymond.

"Surely she was legit. Did no one think to try and find her?" Asked Tash.

"In America?" said Raymond, like someone might say, 'in Space?' What an absurd suggestion!

There was a knock on Raymond's window, and someone's hand gestured for him to unlock the rear door behind him. Raymond leant over and flicked up the lock, and the door opened.

"Just a concussion," said Jamie as he shuffled onto the seat next to his sister.

His forehead displayed an egg-sized red lump where he'd hit the concrete floor after being shot. He held up two pieces of metal tube.

"Now THAT's magic," said Raymond. He loved a catchphrase.

"Can you stop saying that now? It's getting annoying," said Maureen.

Paul Daniels' tubes were both folded in on themselves and held a 5.6mm diameter ball of lead bullet.

"Are you OK?" asked Tash.

Jamie nodded. "Yep." Then fingered the bullet hole in his jacket. "My pocket's a goner."

An ambulance behind jolted them by briefly sounding its siren. Blue lights flashed on, and through the rear doors, they could hear a paramedic reasoning with Jesus.

"Never heard of him, mate."

"Tino Casal, no?" Followed by his best "Woah Woah" singing to help them along.

"No," replied the medic. "Can you sit back, please? And stop talking?"

The door slammed shut, and it set off revealing another ambulance parked alongside the VW camper van tending to the milkman who'd spent his day inside it. Maureen spotted him straight away and whispered in Raymond's ear. Raymond glanced over and back at Maureen. She gestured for him to get out.

"But I didn't think we were wanting to," protested Raymond, but he was interrupted by a shove from his wife.

Raymond climbed from his car and paced slowly over to the distressed milkman. A police officer intercepted him with an assertive outstretched arm.

"Can we help, sir?" she asked.

"It's OK, I know him," said Raymond, wincing at the sight of the milkman's dehydrated shivering face. The milkman looked up.

"Hello, Mr Christmas," said Raymond. He'd long since stopped thinking it was a strange surname. Mr Christmas nodded a pained hello at the familiar customer.

"Sorry about today, Mr Christmas," said Raymond, stepping closer to the poor man.

"It's one of those things, I suppose," said the milkman in a very British way. After all, surely it was common for people to be carjacked and then bound up in the back of a camper van for nine hours or so?

Raymond nodded and they both paused in awkward silence for a moment. Then Raymond spoke.

"I just wanted to say..."

Mr Christmas glanced up again with his blood shot eyes.

"Could we have half a pint of whipping cream on Monday, please? Maureen's doing a trifle," said Raymond.

There was another silence. Quite a long one, so Raymond thought he should take leave. He waved at the milkman and headed back to the Princess, stopping only to share one final word over his shoulder.

"Oh, by the way, Mr Christmas. Your float's on Camberwell Road."

He climbed back in the car.

"You can't drive that. It's not roadworthy," said Sab.

They looked up through the windscreen gap, and she half-smiled as she pointed to the ex-Princess. Now a shadow of its glory days. Another older lady approached Sab and handed her a large brown Manila folder.

"Really?" said Sab to the lady, who nodded. Sab looked exasperated.

"We'll take this from here," said the lady, before pointing to the folder. "That's your priority now."

"But I was hoping to spend Christmas with..." said Sab before being interrupted.

"Christmas is Tuesday. Today's Saturday," replied the lady.

"Yes Ma'am," said Sab, who watched her boss walk away, before turning back to the Princess and its passengers.

"Hop in there," said Sab and nodded to a modest-looking police car parked behind them. "We'll get you home."

Chapter Eighty

Tash was squeezed between Maureen and Jamie on the back seat of the police Ford. The rear of the Fiesta wasn't designed for three adults. Up front, Raymond was squirming in the passenger seat and having difficulty getting comfortable.

"Stop rocking the car, Raymond. You'll make Jamie sick. He's been shot, and he's got a headache!" said Maureen.

"Sorry, Maureen, it's just a bit uncomfortable."

"You want to try it in the back!" said Maureen.

"Can we just get the fuck going, please? Sorry, Maureen, I think I swore," said Tash. She didn't sound like she was sorry.

Tash was straining to look at the melee of police and ambulance workers to see when their driver might appear. She didn't have to wait much longer. An officer climbed into the driving seat, closed the door and clicked his seat belt.

He turned to look at Raymond. Raymond's face was a picture.

"Oh," said Raymond. "Hello again."

He was the same man who had driven Raymond and Maureen to the police station last night.

"Can you get out?" said the officer.

"Pardon me?" asked Raymond.

"Can you get out?"

Raymond did as he was told, revealing the police officer's portable radio on the passenger seat. He lifted it to examine the damage to the aerial. Usually a straight telescopic type, it now had the curve of Raymond's arse shaped into it and a large crack across the dial display.

When Raymond climbed back in, he apologised again and offered a replacement once they arrived home. As they set off along the road, their headlights illuminated the bus ahead. The passengers were still waiting patiently, and a police constable was standing beside it. He flagged down the Fiesta, and it stopped. The officer wound down his window and spoke to the constable outside.

"Everything alright?"

"Are these the people that kidnapped the passengers?"

The mood inside the Ford changed considerably.

"I supposed you could say that," said the officer at the wheel.

"Someone needs to speak to them urgently," replied the constable before disappearing inside the bus.

"What the fuck, now?" said Tash. "Sorry, Maureen."

"You stole a bus?" asked Maureen.

"We didn't steal anything," replied Raymond. "We just had a spot of bother with the milk float."

"We knocked the conductor over," said Jamie.

"Jamie!" said Tash, before explaining through the window, "he's been shot."

They looked over as the constable sauntered back with an elderly lady. She bent over to look inside the car. It was Alexandra.

"Yes, that's them, constable!" she said to the man behind her.

"Are we being ID'd? Should we get a lawyer or something?" asked Jamie.

Alexandra leant into the car. "I've got it! Are you ready?"

They all looked at one another and slowly nodded. Alexandra cleared her throat, spat onto the cobbled road and then spoke.

"You'll be watching us watching you watching us watching you!"

"Oh, very good!" said Raymond.

"I got it over there!" said Alexandra, pointing to the rear of the bus.

"Smashing that," said Raymond.

"What's happening?" asked Maureen.

"They tell me you're heroes!" said Alexandra.

This was a bit of a turn up for the books.

"Did they?" asked Maureen. She liked the sound of this.

"Not you, I don't know who you are," said Alexandra.

Maureen stopped talking.

"So, we have had a whip-round," said Alexandra before turning around and taking a bag off the constable. She lifted her frail arms to pass it through the driver's window, and Raymond leant across the police officer and took it from her.

"Well, that's very kind indeed!" said Raymond. "There was no need!"

Everyone agreed, including Alexandra, then they thanked her before waving as they drove off.

Raymond attempted to turn on the damaged radio, and they all pretended they could hear Cyndi Lauper's 'Time After Time' through the static crackles from the broken aerial. Even with the whizzes and whirrs of VHF interference, it still sounded like it might be the most perfect song ever recorded.

"The fuck's that smell?" asked Tash as the panda car joined Tower Bridge Road to head south to Gaywood Close.

Raymond peered into the bag.
"It's her finny haddock."

CHAPTER EIGHTY-ONE

The officer had refused Raymond's kind offer of a replacement portable radio for his car, he'd even declined the twisted aerial in Jamie's pocket, and the four of them stood and waved him off like an elderly grandparent leaving on Boxing Day. Well, three waved. Maureen was checking the neighbours hadn't spotted her climbing out of a police car again. She was mortified to see Mrs Wong peering around her unlined nylon curtains. Happily, Maureen spied Ted Rodgers introducing Gary Glitter on ITV's massively confusing variety slash game show *3-2-1* behind her on a new 26-inch remote control TV. She'd bank that for when she needed it. Mrs Wong had been adamant that Saturday nights in December were dedicated to culinary genius Ken Hom on BBC2. She soon realised she'd been spotted and the sound of 'Another Rock & Roll Christmas' dipped pretty quickly from her Phillips. Raymond was still clutching his bag of finny haddock as the Fiesta disappeared. Its 1.1-litre engine started to sound louder the further away it went, which confused Jamie in particular.

Tash was distracted by the voices in her head. What should

she do? She'd saved Raymond's life, as old Jamie had asked her to, and now she needed to go home. But Jamie thought he was coming too. Yet, somehow, the 1984 version of him wasn't the one she'd been expecting. He was living as a single man in a pseudo foster home. Then she was distracted by the engine. It was getting louder.

But it wasn't the Fiesta.

Bright white and orange lights filled Gaywood Close like an alien visitation at the brow of the hill. The noise was getting closer, and the lights were blinding them all. They started to cower away as the lights grew brighter. Jamie squinted and finally spoke.

"It's a lorry!"

"You can't get a lorry down here," said Maureen. "It's residential. What's he doing?"

"He's driving down the hill in his lorry," replied Jamie.

In no time, the lorry was adjacent to them but going no further. They'd stood well back to let it pass, but it had stopped. It reminded Jamie of every time he stood in a bar. He'd lean back to let someone pass him, but they'd just stop walking and effectively stand in his space to chat to their mates and drink. He spent his whole life leaning for other people.

"Keep driving, prick!" said Tash in her usual charming manner.

There was that loud hiss that only lorries make, and then the sound of the driver's door opening and closing.

A weary delivery driver in branded anorak and cap walked to them.

"Delivery for Mr Raymond," shouted the man, impatiently waving a clipboard and pen. "I need a signature."

"What am I signing for?" asked Raymond as he slowly took the delivery note. He signed and handed it back. The driver ripped off a carbon copy and passed it to Raymond.

"A delivery," replied the driver and marched to the rear of

the lorry before unlocking one of the heavy doors. He pulled it open to reveal countless boxes and crates inside. There was a freezing mist that continued into the darkness of the refrigerated container.

"You got a fork?" asked the driver.

"What?" replied Raymond.

"A fork?" said the driver.

"In the kitchen, yes."

"You taking the piss?"

"No. That's where we keep them."

"Fork-lift, mate. Have you got a fork-lift truck?"

"Oh. Sorry! I thought you meant fork!" Raymond half-laughed at the faces staring at him.

No one joined in. "Yes, sorry. A fork-lift. Yes. Yes I do. Well, I have use of one."

"Can you get it then?"

"Oh, no. Not here. At the warehouse."

"Where's the warehouse?" asked the driver looking around the road.

"Near Tower Bridge."

The driver sighed, lifted his cap to rub his head and then perused the four people staring back at him. He squinted at his delivery note and leant towards the streetlight to get a better view. "Hundred and twenty-seven kilos," he said to no one in particular.

He sighed again and pulled himself up inside the lorry by climbing on the bumper.

"Come on, then."

CHAPTER EIGHTY-TWO

It took the five of them seven minutes to lift the heavy crate onto the road and then another four to get it onto the pavement outside the house. None of their efforts looked stylish, and every one of them got a splinter except the grumpy driver who was wearing gloves.

"What is it, actually?" asked Raymond as they all stood up straight to catch their breath.

"No idea, mate," said the driver before walking around the lorry to close the door. He reappeared at the front.

"Can I keep going down this road?" he asked pointing down Gaywood Close.

"Yes," replied Jamie.

The man gave a thumbs up.

As the lorry rolled on down the hill, Maureen did one of her little shrieks of despair.

"It's got cheese in it!" She was reading some of the stencils on the side.

"Cheese?" replied Raymond.

"Go nice with your fish, Raymond," said Tash.

"But he was obsessed with cheese, wasn't he?" said Maureen.

"Yes! The baddie! He was!" replied Raymond.

"Are we still going with baddie this far in? We know his name," said Tash.

"I think it's a bomb!" said Maureen.

"You think everything's a bomb," said Jamie.

"You do think everything is a bomb," agreed Raymond in a tone meant to support Jamie yet placate Maureen. "We can't go back to that Brentford Nylons store." They'd only gone in for pillowcases.

"Shall we go inside and talk about this?" said Tash.

Then it started.

Knocking.

They all jumped and immediately looked up at the house. Their instincts told them that somehow someone must be inside wanting their attention. Or maybe a neighbour had good news. Or bad news. But there was no one at any of the windows or doors.

The knocking started again.

It was coming from the crate.

Inside the crate.

They took one step closer to examine it in more detail.

It was constructed from roughly sawn wooden planks covered with stencilled lettering and labels. A bright red and white logo dominated each side and read:

Saputo

Various airway stickers indicated that Montreal Canada, Newark USA and Gatwick UK played a collective part in this intriguing delivery. Refrigeration stickers and frost logos were emblazoned around the ends. The printed destination address was precise, albeit quite unusual given the lack of surname:

Raymond, 538 Gaywood Close, SW2 3QU, London, England.

The knocking began again, and the lid was moving in time with each one, but it had been inadvertently stuck firmly in place by thick glossy paper 'EXPORT' stickers over the edges.

"You don't think it's...?" asked Raymond.

"Who?" asked Jamie.

"Jesus?" said Raymond.

"Jesus?" Tash was astonished. "He just got arrested and driven to hospital."

"He might have escaped," said Raymond.

"The wheelchair guy might have escaped and climbed in a crate and delivered himself to your house?" asked Tash.

Raymond was only half convinced as he delved in his pockets to extract his door key. "Jamie, get a rock."

"OK," said Jamie. "What size?"

"Rock? What the fuck are you talking about?" asked Tash.

"What do you want a rock for?" asked Maureen.

"To hit him with," said Raymond as he ran the sharp metal of his key through the sealed edge of the lid, cutting the paper as it went.

"I've got a brick?" said Jamie.

"That's part of our wall! Put it back, Jamie!" said Maureen.

Raymond's key had become jammed towards the end of the sticker, not quite cut through.

"Use a shoe," said Maureen. "Not part of the wall. This isn't an episode or *Bergerac*!"

"OK," said Jamie and crouched down to undo his trainer. He soon became distracted by something down there and started to smell his fingers.

"I think I've trodden in dog dirt again."

"You're not to come in the house with those on, Jamie. You can leave them on the step. Raymond will clean them in the morning," said Maureen.

"Really?" said Tash.

Raymond managed to drag his key through the final inches of the sticker, and his hand was free.

Immediately the lid flung open, causing Raymond to drop to the ground. Balls of packaged mozzarella flew up into the air, and a head sat up from the box.

But it wasn't Jesus' head. Nor Isabel's or Antonio's.

CHAPTER EIGHTY-THREE

The hair on the head was bright purple.

"Fuck me; I'm freezing! I need the bathroom, my pee bottle's full!" came Martha's breathless American drawl as she handed Raymond a two pint bottle of Mello Yello filled with urine. She glanced down at the opened lid. "They put a fucking sticker over my door! You see that? They put a fucking sticker over my door!"

Jamie stared in disbelief as Martha glared at the EXPORT stickers that had scuppered her attempts to stretch her legs during her strange trans-Atlantic journey. She wore a red and white overall with 'Saputo' embroidered into the lapel. As she climbed out of the crate, balls and wheels of cheese fell at her feet.

"Martha?" Jamie heard himself say. "Martha?"

"Bathroom, Jamie! I need the bathroom!"

Jamie found himself pointing to Raymond and Maureen's front door.

"Martha?" said Raymond still sitting on the tarmac clutching the luke warm soda bottle.

Martha clambered out into the road and Jamie pulled her

safely to the pavement as the HGV was on its way back up the hill and showed no signs of slowing down. The driver sounded his mighty horn relentlessly as he approached.

"You said I could keep going down the road!" shouted the driver as he passed.

"You can!" said Jamie. "You just need to turn around and come back again."

The lorry continued its way. The driver may have shouted "prick", it was hard to tell.

"Come on, open up, I need to pee," said Martha, stomping her feet impatiently as Raymond climbed to his feet and walked to the door.

"Sorry."

"Did you stand up too quick? You look like your face is still lying down," said Martha, glaring at Raymond's face as he slid the key into the lock.

"I had a fight with an owl," he explained.

"You had a fight with an owl?"

"He started it," explained Raymond.

"Why is nothing straightforward anymore?" asked Tash, lining up to enter the tiny house.

Chapter Eighty-Four

"I thought you were in America?" shouted Tash from halfway up the stairs. The shouting was to cover the sound of Martha depositing six hours of Canadian pee into Maureen's freshly Cleen-o-Pine'd loo. She wished she'd brought more empty soda bottles.

"It's a long story," said Martha through the open bathroom door.

"Are you here with the, er, with the money, actually?" shouted Raymond self-consciously from the bottom of the stairs. He was mindful that the last time he'd seen Martha, she had promised to pay him and Maureen £30,000 for helping her secure a mighty inheritance from her grandfather.

"That's a long story, too," said Martha, flushing the loo and rinsing her hands in the sink.

Raymond continued taking cheese from Jamie at the front door and handing it to Maureen in the kitchen. Her Hotpoint Ice Diamond fridge was being seriously tested by this arrival of Canadian imports. Especially a commercial crate full. Raymond had decided to switch off the radiator in the kitchen, to buy some time before they could offload it all. It might even be an income stream to help with the massive December gas bill. Although right now, the room was still very warm from the Breville sandwich maker, despite Raymond unplugging it the moment he got inside the house.

"Nice soap," shouted Martha.

Raymond pelted back to the foot of the stairs. "That's for show! We use the one on the magnet!"

He really hoped Maureen hadn't heard. This might push her over the edge.

"Use the one on the what now?" shouted Martha over the fast flow of water.

"Well, I think we could all use a nice couple of Anadin, don't you? One tablet or two?" asked Maureen walking back from the kitchen with a tea tray full of tablets and a jug of pineapple Quosh.

Martha bounced down the stairs and brushed past Raymond casually drying her hands on his ripped shirt.

"Got any Tylenol?"

"I don't know what that means," replied Raymond, still as intimidated by this confusing American as last time. She clocked him staring at her purple hair.

"You like the new colour? I'm not so sure."

"Very nice," he replied, suddenly interested in his feet.

"Have you changed your hair up, Ray? You look different?" she asked, glaring at his hair trifle.

"We've had a bit of a day, actually. We took a bit too much on."

"It takes years off you. You could be like, sixty now."

"What?"

"Guys! Can I have some privacy, please? Take this to the front room!" shouted Tash from the bathroom upstairs.

They did, and Maureen closed the door to keep the heat in the room. Tash heard some chattering and even some laughter from downstairs. Good, moods were improving.

There followed an almighty scream.

Tash, unable to leap off the loo mid-stream, shouted down.

"What is it? What is it?"

She could hear raised voices downstairs.

"Are you all OK?"

Jamie opened the lounge door and shouted upstairs.

"It's OK. Raymond misread the mood. He just told Maureen he'd quit the Christmas Club."

"Fuck sake! Why now?"

"He thought she was in a good mood," said Jamie.

"I thought she was in a good mood," said Raymond through the crack in the door. "She'd just had a green triangle. You finish your poo. Everything'll be OK."

"No it won't!" shouted Maureen.

"No. Sorry, Maureen."

"Why the scream?" Asked Tash.

"It kind of means no Christmas wrapping paper," said Jamie.

"Nightmare."

"Or gifts."

"Oh."

"Or turkey."

"Really?" replied Tash.

"Or drinks."

"Well, you have cheese," said Tash, shrugging. "Everyone likes cheese."

"They do," agreed Jamie. "They do. Except Maureen."

"Jamie, the heat is escaping," said Maureen from the sofa.

He quickly rejoined them and closed the door.

CHAPTER EIGHTY-FIVE

Tash had dutifully opted for the skanky soap after flushing the loo, and even attempted a proper wash in the hand basin, but drying off on a cold damp towel proved more difficult than she thought so she guiltily found a fresh one in the immaculately tidy airing cupboard. She tiptoed down the stairs and leant her ear to the living room door to hear Martha laughing at Raymond's recollection of driving a bus. She thought she even heard Maureen chuckle too. She'd not heard that noise before, so was surprised to hear it so soon after the Christmas-being-sort-of- cancelled-in-a-way revelation. Maybe Raymond had found another Baby-cham in the wall unit.

But why had Martha come back in a crate of cheese?

Was she a criminal after all? Maybe the crate contained drugs? Surely not, because old Jamie seemed very happily married. They were about to embark on a very happy life together. So, despite her predisposition to intrigue – or sticking her nose in other people's business as her Mum called it – Tash had to let this one go.

She had to be brutal, and it was going to be hard. Probably

the hardest thing she'd ever done, particularly after the events of this very long day.

She tiptoed to the front door, unable to take her eyes off the entrance to the front room. Please don't open. Please keep laughing. Please be happy. She clenched her teeth in the hope it would help her open the front door silently, and as it started to glide open, she turned one last time to the charming, dreary, tiny home and heard herself whisper.

"I love you, Jamie. I love you so much. But all we ever wanted was for you to be happy." She could feel tears falling onto her cheeks, and her nose was running. Her chest juddered with emotion as she struggled to stutter her final words.

"Always be happy, Jamie. I love you."

"I love you too, sis," said Jamie.

He was sitting on the outside doormat, struggling to undo his shoelace on a trainer in his hand.

"Double knot," he said. "Maureen won't let Raymond clean them unless I undo the laces."

"I thought you were inside?" whispered Tash.

"No. I'm here."

She crouched down and undid his shoelace for him, like she had his whole life.

She was going to miss him – even the annoying bits.

"These stink of shit, Jamie."

As she stood up, she looked at his evergreen smile and threw her arms around him, then squeezed tight. As ever, he ducked his head the wrong way, and they clunked skulls. He didn't manage a particularly tight squeeze back, but it was the one she would remember for the rest of her life.

The thing about Asperger's, and so the thing about Jamie, is that it's such a paradox of complex challenges and utter delight.

Jamie could laugh at more things than anyone Tash knew, including her. And at any time. You fancy some fun? OK, Jamie did. You fancy a chat? Jamie did. You fancy a holiday? A nap? A swim? An ice cream? A cry? Jamie did. Yet, his social reading skills were all over the place. So, he stood here being squeezed by his sister and simply enjoyed it.

He didn't think, *Oh no, what's she going to tell me? Or what does she want?*

He just enjoyed it.

"It's cold; we should go in," said Tash.

Jamie nodded and stepped inside in his socks, leaving his stinky trainers on the mat.

"We need to say our goodbyes!" said Jamie, with utter joy in his voice.

"We do," agreed Tash.

Oh great, break my heart again, why don't you, she thought.

"Wait," said Tash, pausing on the door mat. "I need to get something from the crate."

"OK," said Jamie, walking into the living room and closing the door behind him. Again, not even slightly curious as to what the hell she might need that could possibly still be in there.

CHAPTER EIGHTY-SIX

"What are you doing, Raymond?" asked Maureen.

Raymond was crouching by the video recorder beneath their rented 22-inch Ferguson colour television. This sizeable unit was wrapped in teak-effect plastic and fixed to a chrome-effect wheeled stand. Given that it was a piece of furniture and effectively a status symbol, Maureen displayed her treasured Toby Jug on top of it in pride of place. Since the start of the century, Royal Doulton had manufactured countless designs of these colourfully painted, glossy ceramic jugs in the style of human heads. From kings to pirates and milkmaids to soldiers. Maureen's was called The Clown, and Raymond had once joked (quite accurately) that it had a look of Bruce Forsyth, the all-round tap-dancing singing TV presenting legend, with a famously pointed chin.

He wouldn't do that again. He'd had to spend the following night in the shed and had Alphabetti Spaghetti for tea for three nights running. She even took the R's out to spite him. It was one thing to belittle Maureen's art collection; it was another to do it so fragrantly in front of the chap from Radio Rentals.

"You said we could watch the *Sports Review*?" he replied.

"That's not the *Sports Review*."

She was right. When the dark grey screen had finally warmed up, it was showing *Russ Abbot's Christmas Madhouse*. Russ finished a sketch dressed as Cooperman (a Tommy Cooper version of Superman), which then screen-wiped to himself dressed in black and a yellow blazer singing his party song 'Atmosphere', which had just gone straight into the Top 61 singles charts. In fairness to Russ, it did break the Top 40 in January, but right now in December 1984, some mighty songs had blessed the charts. Wham's 'Last Christmas' was about to be flipped to its double A-side 'Everything She Wants' (so it would continue to sell into 1985), Band Aid was number one, Frankie Goes To Hollywood had followed 'Relax' and 'Two Tribes' with 'The Power Of Love', Madonna was finally back with 'Like A Virgin'. Foreigner wanted to know what love is, and of course, Black Lace were doing the conga. It's no surprise that Shakin' Stevens postponed his Christmas single by twelve months. It was an inspired decision. 'Merry Christmas Everyone' was an easy Christmas number one in 1985.

"No, I know it's not the *Sports Review*. But Jamie taped it yesterday. I was going to play it." Raymond wasn't giving up so easily.

"We have company," said Maureen.

"It's just, I was there," said Raymond, with a childlike appeal in his eyes. "It was a bit sort of exciting. In a way."

Maureen glared at him for a moment. "OK then."

Raymond delightedly pressed the clunky play button on the video recorder.

"Sound off, though," said Maureen.

Raymond dutifully dragged the volume slider on the TV fully to the left.

"What the hell is this? Did you use my pee bottle?" said Martha, spitting Quosh back onto her glass.

"You get used to it," said Jamie, glancing over at Maureen.

Jamie had insisted they buy Pineapple Quosh when he spotted it in Fine Fare, and once home, they all agreed it was horrible and felt like it burnt your throat. But Maureen abhorred waste, so they had to finish the bottle, which suited her as it meant it would last longer. She had an armoury of frugal shopping quirks, like buying biscuits no one liked so the tin wouldn't empty itself too soon.

"Yours is on the tray, Jamie," said Maureen, pointing to a glass with ET printed on the side. "Don't spill it."

Jamie stepped over to pick up his glass, spilling it immediately. Happily, the spill was absorbed by the nibbles Maureen had placed in a bowl beneath the drink – Smith's Crispy Tubes.

"You could try and call Margaret in the morning; she might have some groceries to spare?" said Raymond, mindful that Maureen was still consumed by their empty pantry.

"Beg for food *and* hear about her new ceramic hob? I wouldn't give her the pleasure."

Sometimes failure was better than humiliation.

"What's with the crate, then?" asked Jamie, sitting down too close to Martha. Well, on Martha. He apologised and slid to his side of the Draylon sofa. The last time they'd been on this together, they'd fallen asleep spooning, and his heart skipped at the sudden memory.

"It's kind of a long story," she said.

"This is almost over. It needs rewinding," said Raymond, glancing at the TV, having finally sat down on his armchair. He went to stand up again; Maureen didn't allow him to take the remote control to any of the seats. That was common. Her house rule was that if they needed to use the remote control, they would always place it back on top of the TV set after pressing the necessary buttons.

"Leave it," said Maureen, glancing at Raymond. He sat back down and squinted at the TV screen. Elton John was clapping. The screen changed to reveal Torvill & Dean holding up the *Sports Personality of the Year* trophy.

"Oh look! They won!" Maureen allowed herself a smile as she watched the Olympians celebrate their win. Jamie looked over in confusion.

"I thought Sebastian Coe won. I watched the repeat when I taped it for you."

Raymond spilt his Quosh. "Beg your pardon?" Suddenly, he looked extremely red.

CHAPTER EIGHTY-SEVEN

Tash opened the garage door in Abbot's Park and felt a surge of relief that the C5 was still in there. She had no reason to assume otherwise, but the day hadn't gone to plan. All she had to do was post a newspaper through a letter box and then go home.

Home to her baby. To Christmas. To her life.

The pang hit her hard this time. What the hell will I tell the family? Sooner or later, it's going to be impossible to ignore the fact that Jamie was missing. And she didn't want all the inevitable fallout that would cause. It would be unethical to get the police involved. After all, in 2020, Jamie wasn't technically missing. He was just an older man. And he was an older man because he'd re-started his 35-year-old life back in 1984. Because he fell in love. With Martha.

She was an odd one, thought Tash. Imagine shipping yourself across the Atlantic in a crate to save money on a ticket. She found herself laughing out loud at the thought as she delved through Raymond's drawers to find a spare plug.

But she mustn't worry. She had seen Jamie and Martha in

the future. Presumably happily married with a son, a daughter-in-law, and a granddaughter.

She just needed to think. Maybe she would talk with her grandad. After all, he knew that she knew about the C5. And she knew that he knew that she knew.

But more important than all of that – why didn't Raymond have any spare fucking plugs in his drawer? Where else would he keep them? She cast her eyes around the garage. A green Qualcast Concorde lawn mower was hanging from a custom pair of wall-mounted hooks. Raymond had always dreamed of owning a Flymo; they seemed to effortlessly float on air like a Hovercraft. The Flymo was cutting edge technology as far as Raymond was concerned, weightless almost. There were a number of different models to choose from and he'd narrowed it down to the one with the grass collection box. Probably overkill given the modest size of their back garden, but he'd considered all the benefits and risks, and concluded it was the best decision for the household. Then Maureen saw her favourite actress, June Whitfield, advertising the Qualcast Concorde on the television. The ad strapline, 'it was a lot less bovver than a hover', was all the information she needed.

Tash had no idea of the family history of the mower. All she felt was the tiniest twinge of guilt that she was about to hack off its plug so she could get home to her baby. But as she walked over to it, her plans changed in an instant.

She wasn't sure what hurt most; her knees smacking on the cold concrete floor, or the timber shelf unit landing on her neck. She'd reached out to unsuccessfully break her fall and pulled the shelves and two Crown Plus Two paint tins and several packets of linseed oil putty on top of her. Tash didn't have Maureen down as an Autumn Green kind of girl. But then she'd not seen the rear of their house. The front had been smartly redecorated in Pure Brilliant White in 1982, but the back of the property still boasted green window frames. So now Tash had Autumn Green hair, and not the kind that you can rinse out in six washes. This was oil-based, deep green gloss that would need some serious work to remove.

In seconds Tash was pouring turps over her head to start cleaning up. Luckily Raymond hadn't drunk it all. Everything in moderation. As she muttered a plethora of obscenities, she saw what had tripped her: Raymond's battered slow cooker. Despite her throbbing knees, she lifted the end of the cord and beamed at the white plastic plug attached to the end. It's not like Maureen would miss something she never had. Or wanted.

She'd been taught how to wire plugs by her grandad as a child. He told her that girls needed these skills just as much as boys; in fact, more so, in what he called "this changing world". He was only partially correct. In all of Tash's adult life, the UK government had understandably lost faith in the collective common sense of its population and no longer trusted them to wire plugs. Anything electrical must have one ready fitted. Which kind of made sense. In the '80s, there was nothing worse than arriving home with your new Scalextric or Atari game console only to find bare wires at the end of the power cable.

So, Tash was capably tightening the plug onto the C5 with the benefit of Grandad's shared wisdom and Raymond's 'Do-It-All' chisel. She'd struggled to find the screwdriver Jamie used, but other than the sharp steel tip slipping twice and skinning her finger, this was working.

She stood up and straightened her twisted, aching back. It was burning hot with cramp and felt battered and bruised with the events of her absurd trip.

After forcing the C5's plug into the wall socket, she climbed into the seat. The plastic nose at the vehicle's front had a crack through it – a battle scar from the milk float collision. It may look knackered, but she had every faith in Grandad's machine. This would work. This would get her home, she was sure of it. And when she arrived, she was going to ask him why the hell he'd built it.

Right after she'd got his take on the whole Jamie never coming home sitch, which started her crying again, as she typed her return journey into the Spectrum keyboard. Tash hated the fact that she was so adept at this now. She never wanted any of this. It was all Jamie's fault.

And now, she would live her life without him.

She raised her finger over the ENTER button, took a deep breath and stuck it firmly. As the C5 whirred to life and Band Aid started to play from the miniature speaker, she felt a heavy pain in her stomach. A kind of grief. She was mourning her brother already. Through her tears, she was able to spit out her final goodbyes as the Sinclair jolted forwards.

"I love you, Jamie. You selfish bastard!"

CHAPTER EIGHTY-EIGHT

Sab double bolted the front door of her flat and threw her keys onto the small telephone table stacked with unopened letters, mostly bills and Christmas cards. After kicking off her Reebok trainers, she hung her grey leather blouson jacket on the Yale night latch handle. Her pistol handle peeped over the top of the fabric holster strapped around her grey sweatshirt. She removed the weapon, slid it into a small metal sports locker, closed it and removed the key.

She threw the Manila folder onto the post and walked through to the kitchen, throwing the key onto the cracked tiled worktop. The place could use some TLC. Maybe that's why she rarely switched the lights on. In fact the council had saved her a fortune on her electricity bill with the street lamp outside the large sash window ahead. The amber glow cut a clean strip of light through the cold, black shadows of the apartment. The Eurythmics' 'Here Comes the Rain Again' played on the radio. Her Sharp twin-cassette stereo was an early birthday present to herself, but she evidently needed to get better at turning it off when leaving for work. She opened the under-counter fridge casting a yellow light over the amber one on the floor. She peered inside and pulled out a pint bottle of strawberry milk. After removing the foil lid with her thumb, she effortlessly drank half the bottle without a breath. It had been a long day.

Sab screwed her eyes as brain freeze kicked in and then drunk again. Fight ice with ice, she thought. Should work. On opening her eyes, she was face-to-face with a grimacing woman smiling back at her manically.

Sab screamed and dropped the milk. The smashed glass and pink liquid covered the peeling lino. It was a rented flat; these weren't her style decisions.

It took the smiling woman ten minutes to clean the mess up. The blood took the longest.

CHAPTER EIGHTY-NINE

"I didn't mean to scare you," said Hattie. She'd turned on the big light to help with the clean-up operation, not before closing the limp brown curtains.

"How did you get in here?" replied Sab, wrapping a bandage over the plaster she'd stuck on her cut foot and trying to disguise her irritation.

Hattie stood up with the broken glass and damp kitchen towel in a dustpan.

"I told Mrs Schröder you were running late and I wanted to surprise you with dinner."

"She still thinks you're my sister?" said Sab with a smile. Her landlady had questioned them on the shared stairwell three weeks before, as Sab was paying for sole occupancy and guests were strictly by the owner's permission. Their different ethnicities hadn't crossed Mrs Schröder's mind when they explained they were siblings.

Sab perused the flat, and all seemed well.

"You shouldn't really let yourself in here."

Hattie pulled a chastised child's face and leant in to place a kiss on Sab's lips, which she returned.

"Why were you in the dark?" asked Sab.

Hattie pointed into the lounge. "I was about to light candles, you caught me out."

Sab peered over at a selection of green and red candles positioned around the room and then spotted a heavily filled Fine Fare carrier bag on the coffee table

"You're cooking? What's on the menu?"

"I know you like a surprise," said Hattie, emptying the glass and bloody milky mess into a thick black plastic bin liner.

"Do I have time to shower?" asked Sab.

"Go for it."

Sab walked through the open plan lounge to a door at the far end and pushed it open. Inside, a small double bedroom was lit by fairy lights, with a further door off to a small bathroom.

"Christmas lights?"

Hattie smiled over to Sab. "It's our three-week anniversary."

Sab smiled and walked into the bedroom. The moment she closed the door, Hattie silently picked up the keys from the side, turned up The Eurythmics, and walked through to the hallway.

"How long do I have?" shouted Sab.

Hattie inserted the key into the locker and looked at her watch. She watched Mickey's big hand point to the 10 and the little hand point to the 9.

"Twenty minutes," she shouted back, pulling the gun from the locker as quietly as possible. "Take your time."

She slowly removed Sab's coat from the door, placed it carefully on top of her Reeboks, then grabbed the stash of post, including the Manila folder. She stopped for a moment to delve into Sab's jacket pocket and removed a handful of money before taking her own coat and bag. She walked out, leaving the door ajar to avoid any further noise.

———

Hattie took the stairs two at a time. As she ran into the centre of Myddleton Square, her path was lit by the candles in St Mark's Church's windows. 'God Rest Ye Merry Gentlemen' was being exalted by families in good voice, and an organ warmed the hearts of all in earshot of this Saturday night family service, including Mrs Schröder who watched from her ground floor bedsit, distracted only briefly by the lady running towards the church. Hattie slowed down as she reached a potted Christmas tree, its spiky branches wafting twelve primary coloured light bulbs in the breeze. She looked once over her shoulder to check she wasn't being followed and then walked purposefully around the side of the church and out of sight of Sab's flat. Hidden in the shadows, she peered across the road and waited patiently. Within two minutes, the hum of a thirsty engine approached and then stopped as two yellow headlights illuminated the rear of the church. The driver lit a cigarette before squabbling with the passenger. Together they waved it through the window like two bickering kids who both wanted to hold the same balloon.

"I'll do it."

"Get off."

"Shh."

Hattie ran over and climbed into the back seat of the 1976 Citroen DS. The car set off before she had time to close the door.

"Whose is this?" she asked as she pulled herself back upright and perused the quirky interior. This vehicle was very low and very long. The seats were ribbed and leathery and particularly cold.

"No idea, but I bet they wish they'd locked it," said Robert, sounding even more like Tommy Cannon than the last time they spoke.

"Christ, it's freezing in here," said Hattie, rolling her window up to protests from the front of the car.

"Evening H," said Gareth, sweating alongside her. Hattie smiled and then realised why the windows were all open. She lowered hers immediately to clear the toxic fumes from the engineer's overactive sweat glands.

"Did you get it?" asked Piers dragging on the cigarette and looking her up and down. His thick moustache lit up as the cigarette glowed yellow.

"I got it," replied Hattie. "Told you she'd come in handy."

Hattie had met Sab during a moment of pure serendipity in a Soho pub at the start of December. The attraction was genuine, but having a self-serving personality that never switched off, Hattie had soon established how fruitful this relationship might prove, despite Sab's attempts to downplay her status in the police force. Hattie handed the gun to Piers, who stored it safely in the glove compartment. She then turned her attention to her handful of paperwork.

"Bill, bill, bill," she muttered as she leant to the passing streetlights to read the stolen post. She discarded each one through the open window as she continued to rifle through the stash.

"Christmas card, bill, bill." Each one flicked effortlessly into the December night.

"Shall we have some music?" said Piers in his flat Lancashire tones.

"If you want," replied Robert, approaching a junction.

Piers rolled the radio dial, and the radio clicked on, increasing in volume as he turned it further. After scrolling past Depeche Mode's 'Master And Servant' (Robert hated those pervy weirdos – his words) and then past an ad convincing them they *Can't Get Quicker Than A Kwik Fit Fitter*, they settled on Foreigner's 'I Want To Know What Love Is'.

"Ooh, brown folder," said Hattie, pulling it open.

"Money?" asked Piers, looking over his shoulder.

"Why would it be money?" replied Robert.

"She might be bent," said Piers. "Could be some hush money or something. There'd a lot of bent coppers, you know."

"Hope not. We've just burnt our bridges with her," said Gareth.

"Well?" asked Piers, still staring at Hattie behind him.

"No, just papers and photos," she replied, flicking through the contents of the folder before throwing them out of the window too.

As the Citroen turned into Pentonville Road, the paperwork floated onto the frozen tarmac beneath the stop sign. 'Last Christmas' was playing loudly in the pub across the road, accompanied by a few drinkers who were still getting to grips with the lyrics of this new Wham! track.

"Did you get any more on Chucks from the pub?" asked Hattie.

"Full name Jermaine Chuckley, father of two. Worked south of the river until last weekend. It's not even his van, his boss went missing in October," said Piers over his shoulder.

"Watch your back, Chucks, we're coming for you," said Robert as he floored the accelerator pedal.

"Yeah," said Piers. Then added, "You prick."

Robert glanced over. "You calling me a prick?"

"No, I meant Chucks."

"You looked at me when you said it."

"I was agreeing. I looked at you and nodded and said, 'you prick'. I thought you'd realise I meant Chucks."

It turned out Jermaine Chuckley was far more intelligent

than they'd given him credit for. Or Raymond to be fair. He'd inherited him as a driver from Dudley and assumed he just enjoyed keeping himself to himself as he ran errands in the Transit. After helping Hattie load the pram into his van, Chucks had asked for her help as he reversed back onto the main road. As she'd stood behind and watched for a gap in the traffic, he'd simply sped off straight ahead towards Notting Hill.

This morning, six days on, they'd received a tip-off from the underworld that he'd been spotted splashing some serious cash around in Doncaster's Arndale Centre. He'd paid in tenners for an almighty Christmas shopping list: a Casio electronic organ from Fox's Keyboards, all the Top Twenty singles from Bradley's Records, and twenty-nine bottles of Pomagne (a cider drink in a champagne bottle) from Victoria Wine. He couldn't have gotten far away. Not with that organ.

The Citroen DS drove in silence for a while.

"Maybe you should say his name next time, so we're clear," said Robert.

"OK. Sorry, Robert," said Piers.

"Not my name! Don't say my name! What if the car's bugged?"

"Well, it won't be bugged, will it? We just nicked it!" said Piers.

"Yeah, but what if...." Robert stopped himself from saying any more. He flicked a glance nervously in the rear-view mirror. Hattie looked at him for a moment.

"Me? You think I'm bugged?"

"No," said Robert unconvincingly. "No. I'm just saying. Loose lips sink ships."

"I'm not bugged! He stole from me too, you know!" said Hattie, her anger rising in her voice.

"Alright, calm down," said Robert. "I'm just saying, let's not use names or anything that could give stuff away. No names, no routes, no locations, no nothing. From now on. Agreed?"

They all agreed, then drove in silence for a few seconds.

"Kings Cross is next right, Robert," said Piers, pointing through the windscreen. "I've never been to Doncaster, have you Hattie?"

CHAPTER NINETY

Maureen had decided the TV had become a distraction, so Raymond had been instructed to switch it off and play something on their music centre, as she called it. The Hitachi HiFi sat above the cupboard of their wooden veneer wall unit. The stereo was also wrapped in a wooden effect covering and topped with a smoked grey plastic lid. She'd asked for Christmas carols, but Ken Bruce wasn't playing those on his Radio Two show tonight. She'd never heard of the opera on Radio Three, so she'd relented and allowed Radio One. Right now, Dixie Peach was playing some of the finest songs from the year, and Lionel Richie's 'Hello' had passed the Maureen test for this impromptu soiree. She's even pondered opening her last tin of pineapple chunks, but her mood had soured when Martha kept changing the subject.

"You're going to have to tell us sooner or later. We got arrested because of you, and then you abandoned Jamie," said Maureen.

"She didn't abandon me," said Jamie. "She just didn't really come back as quickly as we hoped."

"Why did you come in that crate?" asked Raymond as kindly as he could. "Couldn't be very comfortable."

Martha looked at the eyes, all glaring back at her, some in suspicion, some in curiosity. Eventually, she took a deep breath and spoke.

"I kind of smuggled something out of Canada."

"Your inheritance?" asked Maureen. She wanted her money.

"No. Me," said Martha.

"You smuggled you?" asked Jamie.

"Why?" asked Maureen. Alarm bells were ringing. "Why didn't you just fly out normally?"

"The US government took my passport, so I got a job in a Canadian cheese factory and then hid inside a crate that I sent to Raymond's house."

"Is that a joke? I don't always get American jokes," said Raymond.

"Why did you come back here?" asked Maureen.

"I figured you could help," replied Martha. "Well, I hoped you would," she said, turning to Jamie.

"Why do the US government have your passport?" he asked.

"I have no idea. Honestly. Apparently, they take passports off everyone in prison."

"Prison?" said Raymond nervously, spilling his Quosh again.

"Awaiting trial," said Martha as if this made it better. She looked at the stunned faces and felt the need to explain a little more. "I'm completely innocent!"

"Innocent of what?" asked Maureen.

"Of the charges!" She replied. "And it's only in America! They won't be looking for me here!"

"Innocent of what?" repeated Maureen.

"Erm," said Martha, trying to downplay things, almost as

if she couldn't quite remember. "What was it? What did they call it? Oh yes. Arson."

There was a collective intake of breath and deafening silence.

"Arson?" asked Maureen.

"It means starting a fire," said Martha.

"I know what it means!" replied Maureen.

"And... some other stuff," added Martha quietly, like it was an insignificant detail.

"Worse than arson?" asked Raymond, his voice trembling again.

Martha thought for a moment as if she was pondering if it was worse than arson before answering.

"Murder."

"Murder?" said the other three in unison.

"Well," said Martha. "Double murder if you want to be picky. I didn't do it!"

Raymond farted, spilt his drink again, and the Christmas tree lights flickered. Possibly unconnected.

"No one knows I'm here!" Martha was doing her very best to reassure these kind English folk. "This can be sorted in a New York minute. I have a plan!"

CHAPTER NINETY-ONE

I n the end, Tash chose not to arrive before she left Sheffield. So, as the rear of her grandparents' house suddenly filled her view, she was in an empty garden, but for the tramlined snow she had created when she departed one minute before.

She slid more than last time; maybe the brakes needed some attention. As the stone of the house got closer, she gritted her teeth and closed her eyes. The crack she heard was the nose of the C5 finally snapping off as it struck the rear of the building. Happily, the impact was enough to stop the vehicle from going any further.

"Sake," she muttered as she leapt out of the seat. She was horrified to see a middle-aged lady glaring back at her from the kitchen. She was dressed like a politician and had a weird green-blue rinse in her hair. It was too late to drop from view. She had been spotted.

Who was this woman? What had she messed up this time? Did her grandparents even live here anymore?

These thoughts flickered in her head only as long as it took her to realise that the apparition was her own reflection. She let out an almighty swear, one that embodied relief and horror, then set about dragging the C5 out of sight. Yet again.

It was heavier than ever. Maybe because she felt like she'd completed a decathlon after the events of the past few hours – or days – or whatever it really was. She fell over far more times than she would like and soon broke a sweat, despite the snow soaking into Maureen's woollen suit.

She would burn the suit. She never wanted to see it again. Dry it out, then burn it. She was already sure of that. As she fell over again, she rested in the snow to catch her breath and heard herself giggling.

She'd stolen Maureen's third favourite outfit, poor woman.

And then she stopped and thought. Would I lend some random my clothes?

No, probably not.

Would I take in a strange man and clothe and feed him because he'd been abandoned by his sister?

She shuffled awkwardly at her innate response to her silent questions and sat up. She wasn't particularly proud of herself. She'd just spent hours living in the past helping to save the life of Raymond, but all she'd thought about was herself. The whole time. Raymond and Maureen were good people. Good, kind, weird people.

She had to climb the apple tree to enter the garage loft, which she'd entered via the gaping hole the C5 had smashed through it when she first rode it with Jamie last night. She raced down the timber steps to Grandad's decorating cupboards. She didn't even clock the VW Up! parked behind her. There were more paint tins than last night, but that's what living for a further twenty-one years does. He'd clearly been keeping the house well decorated. Farrow & Ball tins had replaced his

Dulux and Johnstone's paint tins. To one side was a two-litre clear plastic bottle of White Spirit. She grabbed it and set about her clean-up operation before the family came back from their Christmas morning walk.

Once inside the house, she took off Maureen's wool two-piece. As she threw it to the floor, a receipt fell from the jacket pocket.

She picked it up and dropped down onto her bed, exhausted. As the smell of roast turkey filled her nose, she glanced over at Lucan's empty cot, and then over at Jamie's empty bed. At least she'd be seeing one of them soon.

She lifted up the receipt and read it.

It was a £5 raffle ticket, with Dr Barnado's Children's Homes printed on the top.

CHAPTER NINETY-TWO

The loaned million was returned to Barclays as per the original plan. It seamlessly entered circulation into the UK economy and the dirty cash was diluted easily over the month of January. Not that anyone knew it was dirty. A gentleman looking suspiciously like Piers spent two days in Guys Hospital with severe food poisoning, the day after the *BBC Sports Review of the Year*. No one was able to thank engineer Gareth for his efforts with the heat exchanger. He didn't arrive for work on Monday morning. By January, the loner was reported missing, he even featured in a slot on *Crimewatch* five months later; it had the most negligible public response to date. The engineer replacing him was baffled to find so many copies of cut-up newspapers in his office. Maybe his predecessor was really into papier-mâché. Or helped with *Blue Peter* stuff, they were always dicking about with litter and bottle tops.

Pier's brother in law enjoyed the *Sports Review*. He even had photographs taken with Elton John and Desmond Lynham.

Evidently some people did take their camera. When the prints arrived in the post from Truprint in the new year, he was disappointed to see he was blinking alongside Des, and there was a Quality Control Advice Sticker over Elton. Something to do with keeping his hand still when he next attempted a photo in poor light and stand at least two metres away from the subject. He'd remember that if he ever bumped into Reg Dwight again.

He was euphoric when arriving home to tell his kids about the night. He was still buzzing when he awoke, so he didn't notice that his lorry was facing the opposite direction when he climbed in to set off for Calais.

CHAPTER NINETY-THREE

The doorbell rang at Gaywood Close, and the living room fell silent.

"Don't answer that," said Maureen.

"Why?" asked Jamie.

"Because we're all here," said Maureen.

"What does that mean?" replied Jamie, climbing off the sofa and stubbing his toe on the coffee table.

"It means that we're not expecting anybody. The last time we opened the door, Raymond and me got taped up and kidnapped. Sit down, Jamie."

"We did get into a spot of bother, to be fair," said Raymond, shuffling to the front of his armchair.

"Maybe it's carol singers?" said Martha, ignoring the question.

"In Brixton?" said Jamie.

"There's nothing wrong with Brixton," said Maureen. She wasn't about to start a group critique of her homestead.

Jamie tiptoed to the window.

"Jamie. Don't look out," said Maureen.

"But the police arrested everyone. You're panicking too

much!" said Jamie.

"He's right, Maureen, they did get the baddies," said Raymond.

Martha laughed. Then realised she'd misread the room. "Oh, sorry. You meant to say that."

Jamie slowly pulled the curtain away from the window to see a silhouette at the door.

"They're in darkness. The light's out again."

"I knew we should have paid someone to wire that light, Raymond," said Maureen. "And now we're going to get arrested or kidnapped. Or stabbed. Or worse!"

"Worse?" said Martha. "What's worse than arrested or kidnapped or stabbed?"

"Drowning can't be very nice," said Jamie.

"Can't disagree with that," said Martha.

"I'd hate to be attacked by a shark, actually," said Raymond. "They have this thing in their throats, so you can't get back out."

"They have what?" asked Martha.

"If, say, your arm was in its mouth, they can take a breather to get their strength back, but you aren't able to pull out. So, it's just a case of waiting to be pulled all the way in."

"A breather? Sharks breathe?" asked Martha.

"Or maybe that's a crocodile," said Raymond, reaching over to his Encyclopaedia Britannica books.

"I hope so. We only bought A to F," he muttered, reaching for the volume marked C.

"Can we change the subject, please?" said Maureen.

And then the doorbell rang again. Followed by knocking on the glass in the door.

"This is silly," said Jamie before walking into the hall.

He walked to the front door and reached out his hand to open it before pausing for a moment to shout over his shoulder.

"Stay upstairs, Tash."

"Actually, I might be thinking of the Moray Eel," said Raymond from the living room. "I hope that's under E." He wandered back to his encyclopaedias.

As Jamie opened the door, he heard Maureen's voice behind. She had followed him into the hall.

"Who is it? Shall I call the police?" She had one trembling hand resting on the Trimphone.

On the doorstep stood a solitary figure with their back to Jamie. They were dressed in an oversized coat with the hood up. Jeans were tucked into sheepskin boots, and a very full, very large red holdall rested on the step.

The thoughts that flashed through Jamie's head came fast and thick.

Holdall.
  Million Pounds.
  Mafia.
  Police.
  Guns.
  Brinks Mat.
  Prison.
  Death.
  Is that Banjo bar still in my back pocket? It's bound to have melted.
  Maureen will be livid.

The coat turned around.

"About fucking time," said Tash. "It's freezing out here."

She stepped inside, then nodded at Jamie. "Could you grab the bag, Jamie?"

Jamie was confused, he thought she was still in the bathroom, but did as he was told. The moment he stepped outside an almighty flapping noise filled the sky and as he looked up a massive bird shit landed on his forehead. He wiped it away as best he could and watched an owl land on the crumbling brick wall at the foot of the path.

Maureen watched Jamie struggle inside with the massive red holdall.

"Don't bring that in here. Is it stolen? What is it?"

Tash smiled patiently as Jamie unzipped the bag.

"It's just a few bits," replied Tash, as Jamie and Maureen spied a frozen turkey, bags of food, wine, fruit and the suggestion of some wrapped gifts deep within.

"What?" Replied Maureen. She couldn't process what she was seeing.

"I thought the three of us might stay for Christmas?" said Tash.

Maureen glanced at Tash and her brother, then leant to see if anyone else was in the doorway.

"The three of you?"

Tash unzipped her coat. Strapped to her chest in a papoose was her baby son.

Maureen gasped. Jamie smiled.

"Meet Raymond," said Tash.

There was a curious silence.

"Really?" said Maureen. "You can't call a baby Raymond,"

"What?" Said Tash.

"No. No. You can't call a baby Raymond," said Maureen. "Surely not?"

"She's probably right, Tash," said Jamie, reaching out to lift his nephew from his carrier.

"Sake. Don't you start."

EPILOGUE

At the junction of Pentonville Road and Claremont Square, a couple had spilled out from the Belvidere Pub. They were singing along with Prince on the jukebox but found themselves Acapella after the doors slammed closed. They held one another close to keep out the cold. They hadn't dressed for the weather, as Saturday nights were about dressing up, not being sensible. Her C&A Clockhouse brand ensemble of fake leather skirt and animal print top and his Concept Man and Burton's combo was only really fit for a video shoot.

Had they been famous.

Which they weren't.

But everyone was dressing like Bananarama or Duran Duran these days. Anyone could be anyone. He stopped to itch his legs as the material of his thick pleated trousers was impossibly scratchy, and it was then he noticed his shoelace was undone. As he crouched to tie it, he realised his white leather shoes were treading on some unusual litter. He finished tying and lifted the papers as he stood up, squinting at them under the light from the stop sign. Under some bills, a manila folder and unopened Christmas cards was a photograph with an ink stamp on the corner. It read:

Classified. Federal Bureau of Investigation, USA.

WANTED.

"Check her out!" said the man. "Is that Madonna?"

His girlfriend leant in to look. It was a colour photograph of Martha, her purple hair glowing in the light.

"Put it down, you dirty sod," laughed the woman. "It's litter!"

He did, and they scurried on their way home, singing, "It's such a shame our friendship had to end. Purple Rain, Purple Rain."

If you have a moment...

I hope that you enjoyed "Did They Steal A Million Yet?"

As an independent author, I rely on word of mouth recommendations and referrals to new readers, and most importantly, reviews on Amazon and Audible. I would be extremely grateful if you could find the time to leave a review for this novel.

The story continues in "Wish You Were Here Yet?" (And I hope you will follow Tash and Jamie as their story continues further. You can sign up to be the first to know about my new books on my website jamescrookes.com)

Thank you!

PS:

The story incorporated many truths from 1984...

The Brinks Mat robbery left a trail of further crimes in its wake, for many many years.

The Observer did indeed have the story of the million pounds secreted around BBC TV Centre for the Paul Daniels Christmas Show. You can watch the million pound trick on YouTube, along with the Barclays manager and Maxwell as witnesses (although the original 1984 version of events didn't include a heist, unless you know otherwise). If you have the time or inclination, you can see the whole show including the celebrity guests, some mentioned in these pages. The show was filmed on the same day that the *Sports Review of 1984* took place in another studio. The *Saturday Superstore* studio was next door to Daniels' studio. And Mike Reid's chat with Bob Geldof played out just as it did in the book, on that Saturday morning in December.

If you manage to find footage of the *Sports Review of 1984,* I'll leave it to your own timeline to establish who won!

Warm wishes.

James Crookes

Acknowledgments

Thank you to each and every one of you who read and enjoyed my first book, "Do They Know It's Christmas, Yet?" I believe we are all in a club that celebrates the eighties with great affection, and it's a privilege to be a member with you.

Thanks to Gary Daniels for the generous insights into your father, Paul. And to Steve White for connecting us.

Thank you again to David Hitchcock for your memories of TV Centre, including its maze of corridors and lifts with sandwiches.

Thanks to Duncan Newmarch (the warm voice you may hear introducing Strictly Come Dancing and many other iconic BBC One shows). Your wealth of information helped with factual authenticity more than you can imagine.

Thanks to Sinead Fitzgibbon for your patience and superb editing skills.

Thanks to Scott Readman for all your skills at the start, you are amazing.

Thanks to Christian Mitchell, it was lovely catching up with you and stealing your knowledge of the police force.

Thanks to Kim Marks for a friendship that started long before 1984 and remains despite thousands of miles. Your guidance in these pages was perfect.

Thanks to Dominique and Julian for your keen eyes and unfaltering support.

Thanks to Nikki for making this happen at all.

Printed in Great Britain
by Amazon